WAITING
FOR
THE LADY

Also by Christopher G. Moore

Fiction

His Lordship's Arsenal
Tokyo Joe
A Killing Smile
A Bewitching Smile
Spirit House
Asia Hand
A Haunting Smile
Cut Out
Saint Anne
Comfort Zone
The Big Weird
God of Darkness
Cold Hit
Chairs
Minor Wife
Waiting For The Lady
Pattaya 24/7

Non-Fiction

Heart Talk

WAITING FOR THE LADY

A NOVEL BY
CHRISTOPHER G. MOORE

Heaven Lake Press

Distributed in Thailand by:
Asia Document Bureau Ltd.
P.O. Box 1209
Bangkok 10110, Thailand
Fax: (662) 665-2587
Web site: www.heavenlakepress.com
E-mail: editorial@heavenlakepress.com

First edition 2003 by Heaven Lake Press
Trade paperback edition: copyright © 2005 Christopher G. Moore
Printed in Thailand

Editor: Rhea Tregebov, Merrill Fearson, Busakorn Suriyasarn
Jacket design: Jae Song
Jacket photograph (Daw Aung San Suu Kyi): John Hail
Jacket photograph (landscape): Richard Diran
Author's photograph: Pamela Hongskul

Author's web site: www.cgmoore.com
Author's e-mail: chris@cgmoore.com

ISBN 974-92186-1-2

*For my lady
Busakorn*

A WITNESS TO HISTORY

1

I phoned Hart and told him to pack his bags for Rangoon. In the background I heard the clack of pool balls mingled with the laughter of whores gossiping and singing; playful in that breathless serious way around a pool table where nothing was important but everything was at stake on every shot. I said, "Hey, buddy, did you hear me? We're going to Rangoon." Again Hart said nothing. I knew he was on the line because I heard him breathing, waiting for his next shot, clocking his opponent, figuring the odds. Chances were he wasn't focusing on Rangoon. He took life as one shot at time. One of the bargirls would have her arms wrapped around his waist. How did I know this? Hart wore them like accessories: a belt, rings, or, come to think of it, more like an amulet on a gold chain.

"It's Sloan. Sloan Walcott. I've booked two tickets for this Friday. That gives us enough time to get our visas."

Finally he said, "Sloan, have you been drinking *and* smoking?"

In the ten years I had known Hart, I felt that each year he lost a bit more faith in himself and lost even more faith in the motives and desires of others. That was another way saying that Hart had lost his youth like a bloated giant star that had lost its nuclear fusion just before collapsing in on itself.

"I had two Tigers for breakfast," I said.

The quantity reassured him. He put down the phone. I heard a ball fall into a pocket with a sound as clean and smooth as a painted fingernail flicked against a mirrored headboard. Then I heard another ball hit the mark with the certainty of a double orgasm. The next shot missed and Hart came back on line. "What's the angle? Let me guess. It's the photo of the girl. Am I right?" The English had this annoying tendency to begin and end a conversation with a question.

"Sure I am curious," I said, looking at the photograph of the long-legged girl who couldn't have been more than twenty; she sat on a sofa, wearing a dressing gown, legs exposed, crossed seductively, leaning slightly to the side as she whispered to someone outside the frame. Her face turned to the side, long black hair draped over her cheekbone, giving a hint of beauty in the perfect line of the nose. Only a professional could capture the sensual possibilities of a woman in the tilt of the head, the angle of the legs, the careful way the gown folded back to thigh level revealing a small tattoo.

"Obsessed is more to the point," said Hart.

I couldn't deny a compelling, overwhelming curiosity about the girl in the photograph. Haunted by her beauty and troubled by the mystery of how she came to be on a roll of film that contained images of the Lady. There hadn't been a day go past when I hadn't taken the photograph out of my drawer, stared at it, running my finger over the tattoo on the leg, creating a fantasy world where she became my lover.

Two years away from turning the corner onto forty, Hart was aware of the pointlessness of curiosity and the dangers of exploring every mystery that jerked a man's head around. Hart lived day to day to avoid the larger misery that stood in the shadows of most expat lives, making them irritable, suspicious, and greedy. Hart loved his life. We both loved our lives for different reasons; nonetheless, it was something we had in common. Our friendship had started with a book we had produced together about the Chin in the early 1990s. Writing a book together created a flood of feeling, positive and negative, stretching each other's tolerance, forcing compromise, making a strange, twisted intimacy far more enduring and damaging than casual sex. We neither deserved nor asked for any sympathy from each other or from others around us. Our lives had been tailored to fit exactly what we wanted and what we needed, a compass that allowed us to distinguish between want and need. Neither of us had a boss (unless you think of a wife as surrogate boss). No schedule, assignment, quota to reach, sales report to file, annual performance review. We were, in other words, absolutely, totally free in a world populated by people living in various stages of slavery. All one had to do was look around to see a world of men and women constrained by someone in authority saying *do this, do that, go here, bring this there, come back with one of those, sit up straight, eat this, think that, don't say fuck or throw trash in the street.* We had escaped the worst of the human condition. We should have been not just happy but jumping up and down every day, doing one of those high-five things that football players do in the end zone after they score. Hart was English. He didn't know anything about high-fives, and if he did, he would die in the dirt face down rather than submit to that piece of tribal bullshit. While we loved our lives, we suffered from the easy, carefree mindlessness of tacking back and forth over a small bay without ever getting anywhere. We simply had no idea what to do next. Hart hung out shooting pool in a bar on Sukhumvit Road. In Bangkok there were hundreds if not thousands of outdoor and indoor pool bars where it cost twenty baht a game to shoot pool. For a few thousand dollars you could move around the pool tables until you pitched forward clutching your chest with a heart attack as the cue ball rolled into the side pocket. End of game. Hart knew many of the pool halls. He understood the danger, especially with forty staring him in the eye. Some kind of decision was required before he burnt out. A trip to Rangoon would, if nothing else, pull him off the pool tables.

"You're hustling a tourist," I said.

"That's an unkind way to refer to my work."

Hart hustled tourists for pocket money—that was the only money Hart ever had. He was a writer. Obscure, unread, poor, his career pockmarked by failure—actually his writing career had the topography of the Plain of Jars, a desolate, cratered beauty. The fact was, Hart had the talent and vision, all the makings of a great writer. Instead of writing, he freelanced. Copy editing and proofreading brochures, pamphlets, instruction manuals, speeches, books, stories. I once sent him a twenty page menu to proofread. The Japanese restaurant owner—a friend of my wife—offered to pay top rate. Hart turned him down. He chose to play pool.

I asked him why he turned down the work, and he said, "I am waiting for the right assignment."

4

"And what is the right assignment?"

"One that inspires me. No more menus. No more brochures about holiday resorts in Krabi."

"One that pays money is inspiration enough."

"I get by," he said.

Yeah, sure.

Once I counted his wardrobe. He owned three shirts, three pair of pants, and two pair of shoes. I didn't count his socks and underwear. Except for one pair of shoes given to him by a girlfriend, everything he wore was bought second-hand. Several guesthouses around the Malaysia Hotel, where Hart was friendly with the staff, sold him clothes. It was funny how many tourists checked out of their rooms and forgot items of clothing, underwear, cameras, pens, vibrators, rubber dolls. Sometimes a drug overdose victim produced a full wardrobe and suitcases. Everything Hart owned was a product of carelessness, forgetfulness, a drug problem, or whoring. I admired how he discovered a way to recycle the articles of human frailty and weakness, giving them a new and better life.

An old woman from Isan with coarse graying hair and big eyes that looked as if they had been shorted out rolling around in deep black sockets worked at a sewing machine on the street near a short-time hotel. Next to her a greengrocer with missing teeth and a blue hair pin holding back her hair sold oranges and durian. Behind them was a pet hospital where middle-class women with anxious faces, clutching their poodles, climbed out of BMWs. The woman at the sewing machine mended Hart's second-hand clothes, stitching on patches and sewing on buttons. She never charged him much. He was still young enough and spoke fluent Thai and looked as poor as the Thais and this all added up to a discounted price. Once she sewed an angel over a bullet hole. It had a halo and wings. She refused any money for her work. Hart bought her a bag of oranges from the greengrocer. A woman with a Saint Bernard on a leash came out of the pet clinic next to the VD clinic (it was rumored the doctor went back and forth between the two) and this woman thought Hart was a beggar and gave him twenty baht. So even the oranges from the greengrocer ended up free. Hart had that kind of luck at being in the right place at the right time. That was one reason I wanted him to go along on the trip to Rangoon.

2

To pass the time I raise exotic birds on the rooftop of the building where I keep a room. From the roof I can look down on the street where the lady at the sewing machine, and the lady selling the fruit, and the ladies with their expensive over-bred dogs converge. Birds are more clever than people; give them credit. I taught several birds to say in a tiny drowning voice, "Help me, help me." Four or five birds saying this in a choir has a powerful impact. Sometimes when someone phoned and I wasn't in the mood to talk, I placed my mobile phone inside the birdcage and the birds were coached upon seeing the mobile phone to cry out, "Help me, help me." Not two times but over and over again. Birds never get tired of talking. Once someone asked me why I went to all the trouble to teach the birds to say, "Help me, help me."

I have an explanation that shuts them up. An asteroid is headed towards the earth. This object is about two kilometers of solid rock. Scientists say this giant snowball of rock will smash into the face of earth on February 1, 2019. I've marked that down on my perpetual calendar. That fact is hanging not only over my head, but Hart's head, the old woman who sewed his bullet-riddled clothes and over everyone else on planet earth. Why not teach a bird to say, "help me, help me" when we are doomed? We are waiting for it to happen, and I'm ticking off the days and I said to Hart, "Man, I can understand why you don't want to write. What's the point? No one's going to be reading you on February 2, 2019. So while we are waiting for that monster to take us out like the dinosaurs, why not go back to Burma?"

We had fond memories of the place. At the end, that is all anyone has. One can never have too many such memories. The time was ripe to add to the reservoir. And, as Hart rightly pointed out, I couldn't get the girl in the photograph out of my mind. I had an idea that if I tried hard enough, I might be able to find her, and once I found her, I had no idea what would come next, and I didn't care. In most things in life, it is the search and not the capture that matters.

3

I could have gone to Burma for the last several months. I had wanted to go and find the girl in the photograph. But I needed some cover for the trip; a reasonable excuse. I couldn't tell my wife, "You know the girl in the photo I can't get out of my head? Well, baby, I am going to Burma to find her and I may never come back if I do." What sparked the plan for a journey to Burma was a phone call. During that call, Zaw Min revealed a secret that I promised not to reveal to anyone. Zaw Min phoned from his small three-floor walkup apartment in Rangoon. I had known him for as long as I had known Hart. Almost ten years. This was the first time he had ever phoned me. A long-distance phone call in Burma equaled a week's worth of rent, food, booze and women. Burma was a poor country. Making a phone call overseas was not something the government encouraged. They monitored most calls, so Zaw Min talked in a roundabout code. His phone call to Bangkok lasted one minute. "Phone me back, it is important. It is about big money." Twe Twe, his wife, was counting down the seconds to sixty behind him. She did this in Burmese. Her voice became frantic at the forty-five second mark. I expected her to break into a chorus of "help me, help me" as she hit fifty-three seconds. Zaw Min and Twe Twe were newlyweds. At fifty-nine seconds the line went dead.

I immediately phoned Zaw Min back and we talked for thirty minutes. "Hey man, aren't you and Twe Twe still on your honeymoon?"

Zaw Min's voice was more relaxed talking on my nickel. "Marriage is good. We are very happy. I need your help."

One of Zaw Min's code words for money.

There it was in his voice, that tiny, drowning sound, only Zaw Min wasn't one of my birds singing, "Help me, help me." Zaw Min wouldn't give out the details on the phone—he said that was too dangerous—so he talked in circles, saying he had seen some big money and needed my advice on what to do next.

"How big?"

"I am thinking the number seven."

And I was thinking Zaw Min never had more than a thousand dollars at one time in his life.

"No way you got a million dollars, Zaw Min. Go make love to your wife."

He told me that she often stroked his penis when he was talking long-distance. This seemed to shorten his calls. From the casual, relaxed sound of his voice, I doubted she had her hand down his underpants. This call could go on forever as far as she was concerned.

"I am serious. I have."

"Where is it?"

"In my hand."

Twe Twe came on the line. "He has maybe."

I liked his wife. Her English was better than Zaw Min and she understood the wisdom of throwing in the "maybe" just in case Zaw Min's claim to a million might not pan out. She was hedging their bets.

"Put your husband back on."

I asked him what was this "maybe" that he had, which meant maybe he didn't have.

"Sure. Have. I need you to come to Rangoon."

His voice grew rubbery and thick. Twe Twe was giving him a hand job. They were newlyweds and never stopped putting their fingers on each other. My only question was whether they were giving me a long-distance hand job as well. A million dollars and Zaw Min didn't fit comfortably in the same sentence.

Twe Twe came back on the line. "The Lady's going to be released," she said. "Everything will change."

The line suddenly went dead. In Burma, the phrase "the Lady" triggered a level four reaction like "anthrax" or "rocket launcher with chemical warhead" or "smallpox attacks." In Burma someone cut the line.

4

The noodle stand had three small tables. I sat at the one nearest to the cook, who worked under the shade of a large umbrella covered with Singha beer logos. She wore an apron decorated with tiny red turtles. She wore her long black hair up, held by invisible pins buried deep inside the folds of her hair. She had a large plastic sign installed over her stainless steel cart with bicycle wheels. The sign was in Thai. Hart once told me it translated as the "Floating Balls" noodle stand. He ate noodles at the stall almost every day. She gave him credit. I told her I was waiting for my friend. "You wait, Mr. Hart?" I nodded. She went back to cooking, no longer worried that I was freeloading at one of her tables. I smiled and offered her a cigarette.

"Hart a good man. Poor man but good. Not drink or gamble or beat his *ying* like Thai man." She rolled her eyes, pulled up the sleeve of her shirt and showed a set of five green bruises in the shape of blunt, chubby fingers.

"Bring me a beer, darling. And hold the noodles."

She slipped two cigarettes from the pack, putting one behind her ear and the other between her lips. She leaned forward and I lit the cigarette. She inhaled deeply, looked sadly at the marks on her arm. "No good, Thai man." A few minutes later, Hart appeared in the distance. Bobbing up and down next to him was a dwarf in a broad-brimmed bamboo hat crunched along one side who was dressed in rags and old sandals; the midget was trying to sell him a clock radio. The cord trailed behind her like a thin black snake. The midget's head came up to Hart's armpit. She talked without stopping to catch her breath, sweat rolling down her face from under the bamboo hat. Hart tried to ignore her, pretending she was talking to someone else. The midget had a hunched back and very kind, delicate face, her eyes large and bright and hopeful. Hart stopped on the pavement, dug a twenty-baht note out of his dead man's trousers and gave it to the midget. He wasn't buying the radio. He was buying his freedom. Twenty baht might not seem like a lot, but to Hart, twenty baht meant one less game of pool, going without a bowl of noodles. By the time he sat down at the table, he was down to his last one hundred baht. How do I know this? He told me on the phone that he had exactly 120 baht, and how could he go to Burma when he was broke? Hart was lanky with long arms and tall; his eyes were a deep blue color and girls were forever poking their fingers in his eyes to try and peel off what they thought were colored contact lenses. In Bangkok where most of the long-term resident *farang* had passed the tollgate to the other side of middle age, Hart could still pass for a man in his late twenties. He had one of those trademark public school smiles they taught students held as virtual hostages inside cold dorm rooms in England, and it earned him credit with the *yings*. Too much credit in fact; so much that he was burnt out on women. Few places existed on the planet where someone like Hart had to plot and plan periodic escapes over demands of sex, the overwhelming, constant, never-ending demand to perform, mornings, afternoons, evenings. The *yings* showed up unannounced at his room at all hours. Hart never turned them away.

"No problem. Zaw Min has a million dollars that he wants us to help him spend."

"In his dreams."

"Maybe. But we should check it out. Besides . . ."

The cook brought us over one steaming bowl of chicken noodle soup and set it in front of Hart. Two chicken balls shaped like testicles floated on top. You had to be really hungry to look at the half-submerged balls and the bruises on the cook's arms and still want to eat. My cigarette with a long ash balanced on the end hung from the corner of her mouth. She gave him a spoon and a fork. While I sipped my beer, Hart cleaned both with the edge of his shirt, the one with the patch over the bullet hole. He ate like a man who hadn't eaten for a day or two. When he came up for air, he said, "Besides . . . besides what?"

"You can do a story on the Lady. Man, they are releasing her. It's going to be a big story." He had used up all his material. A writer without material was a sad human being, like someone caught in an elevator in an abandoned building with no choice but to ride up and down the same seven floors forever.

Hart looked up from his noodles. "What have you got up your sleeve?"

"Okay, so I have a little business. Ming bowls."

He stopped chewing, tilted his head to the side, and lowered his spoon.

"Ming bowls, Ming bowls," I repeated. "It's rainy season; we can find them. I know where to look. I phoned Aye Thit. He knows the place. And he's got a pipeline to the Shan tattoo books. And I am not denying it, if there is spare time, I will see if I can track down the girl in the picture. I mean, who wouldn't?"

I had him against the ropes with the possibility of the Lady stepping back into the ring, the Ming bowl was my left hook, and the Shan tattoo books the right hook to the chin, and Hart was down, down hard and for the count. My honesty about hunting for the girl was the final smack alongside the head while he was already on his knees. I had decked him and he stayed down for the long count. Another remarkable feature about Hart, given his meager resources and the source of his wardrobe: he had a passion for historical objects. He was a collector of ancient artifacts—an avocation picked up from his grandfather—and he loved Burmese history, a love inspired by his grandfather who had worked as a shipping clerk in Rangoon before the war and who had written a small book about his experience. The grandfather had once dined with George Orwell in London—the two Englishmen spoke Burmese to one another throughout the evening. After his father's death, his grandfather raised him. Hart's father died in a drowning accident. Under the wing of his grandfather, he grew up listening to stories about long marches through the jungles, ambushes, and dead soldiers floating like logs behind the Sittang

Bridge. Hart would always go back to Burma. It was in his blood. After he finished his noodles, he handed over his British passport and signed the visa application. It was a done deal.

"I will need a five thousand baht advance. It's to clear my rent."

I lit another cigarette and shook my head. "Man, how can you possibly not have rent money?"

That wasn't exactly the question I had foremost in mind. What I was really asking was a question to myself: why did I need Hart to accompany me to Burma, not to mention the five thousand baht advance and the out-of-pocket cost of getting him to Burma, housing and feeding him?

"I've sent people your way. But you turn them down. Forget freelancing, get a job."

"I have one."

"Pool hustling isn't a job."

"I didn't say anything about pool. The *Bangkok Post* has employed me. And I'll pay you back the five thousand baht out of my first pay check."

I didn't know whether to take him seriously. He sounded like he meant business. But what con-man didn't come across as completely earnest and honest? Even if it were true (and I hadn't conceded the point), he'd be lucky to clear five thousand working in the news business.

Among his other non-pool shooting skills, he had studied Ming porcelain. And he knew every fake, phony piece. No one could fool him with a reproduction or a piece from another dynasty. He was good, real good, and bankrolling him on the trip was worth the investment. I slowly took out my wallet and fingered through five one-thousand-baht notes, taking long enough for the owner of Floating Balls to see Hart had friends with some dough in their pocket. He put the notes in his shirt pocket without counting them.

"Aren't you going to count it?"

He flashed his winning smile. "Sloan, I hope you find the girl of your dreams."

"It will be an adventure."

"Don't tell me—one that will change my life."

"You finished my sentence."

He fingered the patch over the bullet hole in his shirt. "Do me a favor."

"What?"

I thought he wanted more money.

"Don't mention my grandfather. And we aren't going to the Chin Hills."

I held up two fingers. "Scout's honor."

5

In this part of the world, experience teaches: never trust anybody. This was the lesson that sex tourists never learned and it was what made economic and social mobility possible for the peasant class of *yings*. I had earned Hart's trust years ago. I promised him that I would change his life and all he had to do was go to Rangoon with me. I told Hart that by searching for the Chin, we would learn profound insights and that would change us. Not so much change but give meaning to our lives, which had grown predictable and weary in Bangkok. That was the first time he told me about his grandfather, an Englishman, an author, someone who had worked in pre-war in Burma and spoke fluent Burmese. This was ten years ago, and experience, like a letter on thermal fax paper, starts to fade after months, and after years whatever was written has disappeared. I could no longer read my own life. It had become a blank. I had dragged him to a remote part of Burma because I needed a writer for *The Art of Chin Ways*. It was a book that would bring into the world the first glimpse of some of the last primitive people living in a state of nature, the last breed of noble savages. The plan was for me to take the photographs; photography was one of my specialties, along with cooking and sculpture. Mastering three superior arts once would have defined a man as a genius. Now everyone was a genius, an expert, while a true Renaissance man was another devalued relic lost to another era. Yesterday, when I checked, our book ranked 352,172 on Amazon. So much for changing the world or preserving the Chin for the next generation. In the marathon race for immortality, the Chin were falling way behind, struggling and staggering to just stay in the race.

I had delivered to Hart once before. I had shown him just briefly a way out of his flatline existence. No more noodles at the Floating Balls stand, no more *yings* pounding at his door day and night, grabbing him by the balls, tearing off his clothes and dragging him to bed.

"You need to rest your prostate, Hart. You are going to wear it out before you hit forty."

"That isn't your strongest argument."

"It will blow out like a tire on the expressway."

"And I will crash and burn."

"Definitely."

This time, though, if I were to be perfectly honest, I would admit that I had left out one or two of the finer details about the trip. When you ask someone to go to Burma, you leave out the trivial annoyances that might cause the kind of problem that might get you killed. Hart's grandfather, who had survived the war, knew this about life. Hart accepted the possibility. That's why I understood Zaw Min so well on the phone, and why his wife, Twe Twe, had showed the possible cross-hairs on the laser scope attached to the barrel of the million dollars her husband claimed to hold in his hand. Ten years earlier I hadn't told Hart how cold it would get in the Chin Hills. He almost died of the freezing cold and nearly found himself starting a family tradition of dying in distant lands. A tradition his father started by dying in Africa. Hart's skin turned blue; he coughed up buckets of shit. He developed a high fever and sweated until the blankets were soaked, but in the end, being young and strong, he survived. But that was another story.

6

The morning before our departure, I took a motorcycle taxi to the five-story concrete bunker that housed Hart's room. It was almost eleven in the morning as I paid the motorcycle driver and walked down a narrow, squalid alleyway littered with bamboo baskets overflowing with trash. I scrambled around kids' toys, circled past dying plants in cracked pots, and climbed the three floors of stairs to his room. I was out of breath, holding my guts by the time I pounded his door. Five minutes later Hart opened the door wearing a bath towel he or one of his whores had stolen from a hotel. I handed him his passport and ticket.

"Hey buddy, it's nearly noon and you're still in bed?"

A *ying* with baby fat cheeks who was sucking on a straw stuck into a can of Sprite darted in on his left with rat-like speed, and a moment later, another *ying's* head with purple lipstick smeared around her face, sucking on ice cream, peeked around his right side, her arms wrapped around his waist. The combined ages of this tag-team might have added up to Hart's. The one with baby fat cheeks had a certain possessive, desperate look; getting rid of her would be about as easy as quietly sliding a cat over the side of a rowboat.

"You didn't pay the rent," I said. I had no doubt the five thousand baht advance had gone to the hookers, who both had the same oral fixation.

Hart yawned, looked at the visa in his passport. "I had a good night shooting pool," he said. "Indeed, I would go so far as to say that my luck has turned."

He raised his foot and pushed the door closed, leaving me standing in a hallway that smelled of cat piss and garlic, without a glass of water, sweat running down my neck. I knocked on the door again. Hart opened the door, holding out an ice cold Singha beer. "I had a feeling you might want this." That was Hart.

I pushed him aside and walked in, drinking from the can.

Another reason I liked Hart was that he was flexible. I looked around his room. Balled-up pieces of white tissue were scattered everywhere as if someone had zapped a fleet of moths with a can of poison spray. The room smelled of sex, ripe, musty, fresh, nauseating like the difference between the smell of your own farts and those exploding out of the bowels of someone else. The two girls sat side by side, legs touching, on the edge of the bed. One wore Hart's long sleeved shirt, the other had on his Bugle Boy striped polo shirt. Every shirt he owned was being worn in the room. Hart smiled, bumming a cigarette from the handbag of one of the *yings*, telling me, as he lit up from the lighter held out by one of the *yings*, that I shouldn't worry, that he had paid the five grand for rent. I held my guts, which were exploding, as I laughed. The *yings* started laughing, one of those barking, ha, ha laughs that makes you want to reach for medication. Only Hart blinked a couple of times, trying to figure it out what was the cause of this mirth.

"What's so funny, Sloan?"

"Do these chicks know that you are dead broke? You have no money, daddy. They sucked the big one and you have no way to pay them off except with a can of Sprite and some ice cubes. You aren't gonna live long enough to have a prostate problem. Man, after they get finished with you, these *yings* will make certain you will never look at the bowl of noodle soup at Mr. Floating Balls Restaurant in the same way. What I am saying, daddy-oh, is that you is truly in big trouble. And I ain't bailing you out of this one. No way."

I opened the door of his wardrobe. I was half-expecting to find another *ying* hiding inside; a spare, in case one of the starting lineup developed lockjaw. Inside were a bunch of empty hangers and two pair of pants. He was the only person I knew who had such freedom from owning things. If he defaulted on a loan, he didn't even have clothes to foreclose on. He was free of the fear of losing anything because he had nothing to lose. I pulled up a chair and sat at his writing desk, glancing at a neatly stacked manuscript.

"Finally decided to do some work. What kind of inspiration do we have here?"

He was off the bed, shoving the manuscript into a box and putting it in the wardrobe. "Sorry if I don't have top secret clearance," I said.

Hart grinned, wiping a hand across his mouth as if wiping off the grin, but when his hand came away, his grin was even bigger. Lucifer, a Siamese cat with eyes as blue as Hart's, rubbed against the inner leg of a *ying*, making her giggle.

"You know Jessie, the manager of Side Pocket Bar?" He closed the wardrobe doors and lit a cigarette.

"The Aussie, yeah, I know him. He die or what?"

"He challenged me to a game."

The *yings* had the cat on the bed, and played with it. One had firm small breasts outlined against the sheets. The cat rubbed its fur against the brown nipple, making it hard.

"You beat Jessie at pool? Get out of here."

"I won. And won again. I took all of his money, and when the money ran out, he bet two bar fines, and when that ran out he bet the service fee for the *yings* as well. These are my winnings. Meet Khun Oy and Khun Kung."

I didn't know which was which not that it mattered. He walked

out of the Side Pocket with Sugarcane and Shrimp, who were in a deeply disturbing game with Lucifer. Actually it was a cat that mooched off everyone on Hart's floor and came around when it thought Hart had fish. It sort of smelled like tuna in his room.

"You hustled Jessie in his own bar?"

"It cost him nothing. The bar fines and money for the girls he'll make up by deducting them against the salary of a non-existent bar girl who appears in the book as 'Pin'—the owner is in Sydney and doesn't know that Jessie is stealing him blind. Plus he's a lousy pool player. He deserved to lose."

It didn't sound like anyone lost except the guy in Sydney who, as Hart said, deserved to lose. He'd broken the rule: don't trust anyone who handles cash. Another good reason to trust Hart about those Ming bowls that I wanted was the man knew a scam a mile away. He smelled a scam; his radar for fakes picked up the smallest give-away in an object, which he would point out to the scumbag trying to hawk as something four hundred years old when in fact the object in question had been manufactured four months ago and buried in the ground, dipped in lime, rinsed, left in the sun, buried again, and then dug up and put in a shop. Hart knew the process.

7

Hart had one more condition before he left Bangkok. I had to cover for his absence from his new job. Just in case the Ming bowls venture didn't pan out with the riches I had planned, he wanted to keep hold of his fall-back position. I thought he had been hired as a journalist. I told him it would be good for the new job if he filed a story about the Lady, especially if the government ended up releasing her from house arrest. In the back of my mind was the idea that *The Bangkok Post* might pay his expenses to Burma. He warmed to the idea. The prospect of writing a news story excited him. He didn't say why it excited him; he smiled and kept silent. I went along with him to *The Bangkok Post* in the late afternoon. The main building was located in an industrial zone. An adjacent area was some kind of major oil tank farm, with dozens of huge white tanks with spiral staircases anchored to the side, and fleets of large trucks crossing the railway tracks at high speed, and beyond the oil tanks were slums with squatter shacks. It was a pretty good neighborhood to conduct the news business. No tour coaches were hauling Chinese or French tourists in search of handicrafts or massage parlors down this road. They didn't come to Thailand looking for crude oil, slum housing, or to dodge cargo trucks barreling to the Port.

"Exactly why are we going to *The Bangkok Post?*" I asked.

Hart explained he needed me to verify that he was going to Burma and needed a week or so extension before starting his new job. In other words, I was his beard, his alibi.

"It's like getting a note from your mother," I said.

"Or a wife," he said, winking, knowing that he had nailed me where it hurt most.

I figured he had some angle for cash. Hart had, off and on, over the years, played the freelance game with newspapers and magazines, but always returned to the pool tables when he ran out of stories. We signed in at the reception and wore little badges saying we were visitors. An uniformed guard opened the security door. We passed the canteen and a row of vending machines. Then I followed Hart up a staircase and down a long corridor with loads of framed photos of horror and misery: buildings and warehouses on fire, wrecked planes and trains.

On the main floor were row upon row of desks adorned with computers, all interconnected. Everyone was witness to what everyone else was doing, who they were talking to. The floor plan matched the basic no-frills inner-city shopping mall or had been ripped out of Lenin's favorite factory design handbook, minimizing rank and position. Or it might have been what one of those oil tanks across the road might have looked like when it was empty. Everyone was a soldier on the front line, on point, in the news gathering business. Hart said the floor plan made perfect sense to him. Editors sat divided into zones with no visible boundaries; they worked at monitors on cluttered desks, sometimes moving out of their own space, but mostly guarding the perimeter like pitbulls. Careful eyes watched from Outlook, Business, Sports, and International as we made our way across the open floor. Three tiers with each floor looking down on the main floor ringed the main newsroom. One bad fart and the entire place would have to be evacuated was my personal evaluation.

We had come to see Alan Dawson, a Canadian who Hart said had news ink in his blood. His grandfather and father had been newsmen in Ontario. Alan did the news round-up page, which always began with, "Good morning, Thailand . . . ." One could hear Robin Williams screaming this out all over Bangkok as readers opened the round-up page to read what should have been on the front page. Hart walked straight towards the computer terminal where Alan sat, glasses on the end of his nose, working on his column. He looked up as Hart came along side and cleared his throat.

"You're early. I thought you were starting tomorrow. Don't tell me, you need more time to you finish your freelance copy edit. Because that isn't a reason I want to hear." Alan kept on typing as he talked.

"Sloan has something of a family emergency in Rangoon and has asked me to fly in with him tomorrow." Hart took out his passport and flipped to the page with the visa.

"We are having some kind of emergency here. So you're gonna have to choose your emergencies carefully."

"While I am in Rangoon, I will cover the Aung San Suu Kyi story. And I can cover the story at no cost to *The Post*. Sloan is picking up the full tab." None of this was making any impression on Dawson but it was making a large impression on me. "It is my chance to cover a big news story."

Hart sat on the edge of the desk, and finally Alan looked up from his computer terminal, his hands wrapped behind his head.

"Alan, if you had been ordered to start as a sub-editor in Toronto the day before the fall of Saigon, what would you have done? Gone on a plane to Canada, walked into your office and proofread copy or would you have stayed in Saigon and gone into the street?"

Hart looked up at me, and the true purpose of my presence became apparent. He needed someone to hear a recount of Dawson in the streets of Saigon on the day Saigon fell. Alan had worked on the movie *Good Morning Vietnam*. He had hung out with Robin Williams. Alan had worked on a lot of films shot in Thailand. He had a knack for local detail that made him invaluable to the producers. During the Vietnam War, Alan had also been the Bureau Chief for UPI. On the day the North Vietnamese drove their tanks into Saigon, he had been waiting on the street with a tape recorder and a microphone, waiting for the North Vietnamese troops to come into Saigon, march on government house, and raise their flag. The war was already over but the symbolism of raising the flag was important. He had stood in the middle of the street when a young North Vietnamese soldier had pointed his AK-47 at him, "What's that?"

The boy soldier had marched into Saigon straight from the jungle. He had never seen a tape recorder or a microphone before. The soldier had been briefed by his superiors not to shoot foreigners. The North Vietnamese were smart. They had won. When you win it is much easier to give orders not to shoot people. Still, if there were a foreigner with a gun, then a soldier had permission to put a bullet between the round-eyed foreigner's ears. The question in the soldier's mind as he pointed the AK-47 at Alan's head was one of technology, or simply the true nature and purpose of the microphone—weapon or not.

It was a moment of truth. Trying to explain in broken Vietnamese to this boy that the microphone was not a weapon. It didn't have bullets. It would not harm him. He left out all the metaphysical crap about how a microphone could inflict more damage on an army than an arsenal of weapons. With an AK-47 pointing at his chest, it wasn't the time for philosophy. Finally Alan got through to the soldier and a tank rumbled past and the soldier fell in behind the tank.

Alan had told Hart that what he remembered most about that day was that he had been a witness to history. The end for the South Vietnamese was the beginning for the North regulars who rode on tanks into a city that would demote Saigon to the second rank of names after Ho Chi Minh. This was a defining moment for a young reporter. Most of the reporters had taken the helicopters out. They were taking no chances. They would live the rest of their lives with the knowledge that they blew it; knowing that they had ran away from a defining moment of history. You were either a witness or you were an escape artist.

"Alan was a witness," Hart said.

I nodded. "That was something." I meant Hart's performance.

Hart told Dawson that he wanted his chance to be a witness to history, to be on the streets, to find that defining moment. He wanted to have a microphone ready when the Lady was released. Alan Dawson thought about Hart's pitch, instinctively knowing that Hart was backed into a corner and trying to find a way out. "This isn't exactly the fall of Saigon," Dawson said.

"When you stayed in Saigon, you weren't sure what would happen," said Hart.

Dawson weakened. But he had one last argument. *The Bangkok Post* had its stringers on the ground to cover the Lady's release.

Maybe if Hart had a background story, just maybe, they might be able to use it. No promises. And of course, Hart would have to foot his own expenses (meaning I had to pay). In the news business, in an open area where everyone could hear, it wasn't a good idea to make promises. The sub-edit job would be open for another week. If Hart wasn't back in Bangkok, in this room, at a terminal working, defining moment of history or not, Hart should think of another line of journalism.

On the way out, I asked Hart, "This job you're so worried about doesn't sound like journalism. More like proofreading. Putting in and taking out commas, semi-colons for a living, that's not being a reporter. That's not reporting. That's punctuation duty."

"It's like looking for Ming bowls in a junk shop. Finding one makes certain people very happy."

8

I was grateful that Hart had long ago stopped inquiring about the royalties from *The Art of Chin Ways*. The publisher never acknowledged our emails or letters. All that Hart ever said on the matter was that publishing had always been a kind of gentlemen's theft. We had found the publisher through one of Hart's old-boy network ties and this may have explained both his sense of resignation that no royalties would be paid and his failure to ever raise the subject with me. Besides, our joint effort belonged to the past, occupying a place which no longer mattered or affected our lives, much like the distant memory of a long dead relative one can only vaguely remember. Like one of my birds, I repeated back what I heard Hart telling Dawson: once inside Burma, we would become a witness to the unfolding of history. The month we had spent researching *The Art of Chin Ways* would seem small, insignificant, and uneventful by comparison. We had recorded a journey that had been to the past; we had mined that quarry for what it was worth. And given that the book had been largely forgotten, we shared more with the average coal miner—the product of whose efforts had already gone up the chimney—than a literary star that continued to shine bright in the heavens. The big tidal events of History with a capital "H" towered over the past; such events were different from chasing after hill tribe people in isolated mountain villages. Most people remembered only a handful of images and emotions, what happened to them, what they saw happen with their own eyes to their family, friends, or country. Hart said his grandfather had taught him that in understanding the events of history, a way was found for redemption: you lived your life by charting your course into the future by following the coastline of the past.

Hart believed in his grandfather's vision because he thought that his grandfather had got it right.

Hart was only thirty-eight years old and had covered wars, revolutions, coups, political assassinations. With each new experience under his belt, Hart once believed that he would live forever so long as he continued to push forward a couple of days ahead of history. When we were deep into Chin state terrain, I learned that Hart was the kind of man who had the knack for fashioning a lapidary phrase for each event, as if to leave his mark on the granite tomb of history saying Hart had been here, well that was cool, really cool. Then he had lost himself in the pool tables and whores and floating balls noodle soup. At the same time, he wanted to go back to the man he had been ten years ago, but, then, what man didn't?

"Twenty percent," he said. "And don't mention the word 'history.'"

"Twelve percent. That could be a big number," I said, thinking of all the Ming bowls we would find. "Not to mention the million dollars that Zaw Min has burning a hole in his safari shorts. I'll give you 20 percent of Zaw Min's million."

"You can keep Zaw Min's million. I want 20 percent of the value of all the Ming porcelain we find."

"God damn, Hart. That's highway robbery."

"Fine. Then keep everything and go alone."

"Okay, okay. Twenty percent."

Hart looked at his ticket and passport. He held out his hand. "Deal."

That's not the story or the history lesson that I am here to tell
. . .

KAZUO'S LOST CAMERA

9

Almost a year had passed since the day I found Kazuo's camera. I had gone to Rangoon airport. I walked up to the check-in counter. The stress factor was off the scale, the needle accelerated into the red zone by too many things to keep track of: carry-on bags, check-in bags, laptops, ticket, passport and duty-free. Returning to Bangkok alone, my hands worked double duty trying to keep everything from slipping, falling, and getting left behind. Sometimes, however, even in the worst of circumstances, one could get lucky. At the check-in counter, a Thai Airways agent, a plump woman in her late twenties, bored, hot, and frustrated, slumped forward in her chair, wishing she had been born into an air-conditioned job. Her official uniform was wrinkled, the armpits damp. Loose hair matted in curly strands covered her forehead. She didn't bother looking up as she held her hand out for my ticket and passport. As I said, my hands were full, and she wasn't the only one at the airport who was hot and bothered. Whether it was the unbearable heat, the rush to get through Immigration and Customs and find a cold beer, or being clumsy and off-balanced, I fumbled with my ticket and passport. The eight o'clock beer had taken the edge off and drilled a small-bore hole straight through the part of my frontal cortex that deals with sequential activity and spatial problem-solving.

In other words, I dropped the ticket.

I gasped as it fell. It floated in the dead, hot air, hanging like a glider. The woman looked up from her computer. I grabbed at it as it fell but missed. She grabbed and missed. The ticket sailed down and landed on her lap. This was dumb luck. But that luck didn't hold with my passport, which fell like a rock. I've never believed that if you dropped a feather and rock from the Tower of Pisa they would hit the bottom at precisely the same moment. It wasn't common sense. American passports don't float even for a second. A flash of blue was the last thing I saw as my passport, fat with extra pages all filled with visa stamps, disappeared like an Indian fakir performing the disappearing rope trick. My passport was in my hand one moment and in the next it was gone. It happened so fast that the ticket agent didn't even see the passport. Over the top of my glasses, I looked at her and she stared back, holding my ticket in one hand, waiting to receive my passport in the other.

"Hey, man, did you see that? My passport was just here. Where could that motherfucker have gone?"

In a dead-of-night voice she said, "Passport."

I leaned over the counter with the childlike hope that it might have fallen into her lap with the ticket. "You sure it ain't on your lap, baby? Have a look."

"Please give me your passport." I once had a teacher who used such a demanding, threatening voice. It gave me a chill, remembering the ruler against my knuckles.

"You must have seen I had a passport."

She stared at me like I was crazy. "It's a small blue book with an embossed gold eagle on the front."

Just as she was about to say something, I lost my balance and one of my elbows rammed hard into the gap between two counters. This was a surprise. Because at first it had looked like one solid counter. Instead the counter was some kind of David Copperfield illusion. In fact, two counters had been shoved together. Over time the two separate pieces of furniture had started to creep apart like the continental drift. I pulled my elbow out of the crack and rubbed it. If this were America, I would have had a million-dollar lawsuit and a small army of lawyers crawling over this organization like killer bees driving north from Mexico.

"Jesus, man, this counter is defective." This was the first line I would instruct my lawyer to use in his opening argument to the jury.

"You should be more careful," she said. She thrust the responsibility back like a clever defense counsel.

"I think that my passport fell inside."

"Inside where?" Only this wasn't the female voice of the agent. A tall Indian in dark trousers, white shirt and striped tie stood beside me. He wore one of those English regimental ties. My guess was he had bought it on the black market to make him look more official. He had short salt-and-pepper hair and heavy stubble as if he hadn't shaved for a couple of days. He had a sweet, slightly off smell like spoiled oranges.

"My passport fell inside, sir," I said. He looked at the gap. "Can you help me move this counter?"

Addressing him as "sir" worked. He told the agent to push her chair back—that took a huge effort to lift her fat ass. Then the Indian helped me pull the two counters apart. There was just enough room for me to stick my head inside and have a look at the mountain of lost, forgotten, abandoned loot inside. Debris had accumulated in layers like one of those excavated ancient cities built upon another ancient city generation after generation without any collective memory of what had gone before. Years had passed since anyone had cleaned the space. Most of the stuff one would have expected from hot, tired travelers trying to check in and balance all of the things needed for travel: eye-glasses, sunglasses, glass cases, keys, pencils, a hotel ashtray, tickets, several coin purses and wallets. On top rested my passport. Sticking out of the side was a camera in an expensive case. I pushed my passport over the camera so that it completely covered it and pulled them out as if they were one object that belonged to me. I could see the agent and the Indian had figured out that I was some kind of Moses, having parted the equivalent of the Red Sea. They were licking their chops already. Think for moment that you were in my position, what would you do? The choices were limited: hand over the camera to the Indian wearing an English regimental tie or the overweight agent with the bad attitude. I had a pretty good idea what would happen to the camera. Booty like this was as good as gold. Men marched to war to acquire such spoils. The camera was as good as cash. No one could blame them for selling loot found from a hidden vault that had been right under their nose. I did what anyone would have done. I slipped the camera into my coat pocket. They never saw the camera. They were too busy sifting through the rat's nest of spoils, already fighting over who got first dibs on what, kicking up clouds of dust, their hands and hair thick with cobwebs; they didn't notice my act of larceny, or if they did notice, they figured this was my cut for opening the vault. I would have placed odds that the woman would have kicked the butt of the skinny Indian smelling of rotting oranges if he started taking more than his fair share.

I checked through Immigration, and then walked through Customs, where I loaded my bags onto the conveyor belt to be thoroughly radiated by a third-world x-raying. No one at Customs bothered to ask me to open a bag, or to ask me how long I had been in the country, why I had helped myself to a motherlode of lost valuables harvested from the check-in counter vault, or how many historical relics I was smuggling out of the country. Heat made them languid. Shoulders drooped forward; their eyes were barely open. I paid one of the guards who worked the x-ray machine to get me a cold beer. I told him if the can wasn't ice cold not to bother. He was happy to do this errand for a dollar. I love airports where Customs officials work as freelance waiters. I walked into the nearly empty departure lounge. On the tarmac, the ground crew loaded cargo into the belly of silver airplanes. In the corner of the departure lounge, rows of plastic seats donated by Philips promised in large letters a "Better Tomorrow." Someone in the advertising department had hit the right message for Burma. Everyone looked to tomorrow, thinking it simply had to be better. You wanted to sit in one of those chairs. I made my way to an empty section, sat down, looked around (no one was watching me) and immediately took the camera out of the case. The guard came in with my beer and admired the camera. I said that I was a photographer and showed him a copy of *The Art of Chin Ways* and my photograph on the inside back flap. I told him last time that I checked, *The Art of Chin Ways* was 278,329 on amazon.co.uk and while that didn't exactly make me famous, people would start looking for me if I disappeared. His eyes narrowed in a threatening way. I had made my case for being in possession of a camera. I liked the power of showing the book and letting the camera assume a natural position as something that ought to be attached to my hands. I popped the Tiger and took a long drink. He poked his finger at Hart's photo, which appeared directly below my photo. "Handsome man," he said. Even when

Hart was traveling to Burma, he managed to appear every time I showed someone the book and they said approximately the same thing that the Customs official had uttered. I was used to it. I bore him no grudge and gave him another dollar. He returned to his post to continue his own personal exposure to radiation from the x-ray machine.

It was important to place in context what I had found in the airport. I am a photographer. My photographs appeared in a well-received coffee table book about the Chin. Hundreds of brilliant photographs. Reviewers from London, New York, and Berlin raved about my use of shadow and light and the mystical quality of the settings and the nobility of the people who lived in the Chin Hills. The images were that good. I would like to say that I know something about photography and cameras. What I had found turned out to be a Nikon Zoom 310 with a Panorama zoom lens, and other bells and whistles. The digital read-out date was: 3/10/96. The camera had been inside the crevice for almost five years—how the battery functioned after all those years was a miracle. The person who had lost the Nikon had taken nineteen exposures before he and his camera went their separate ways at the check-in counter. As a professional photographer, I felt how bummed out I would be if that had been my camera, say with nineteen perfect shots of a tattooed Chin woman's face. This would have been a terrible loss. The world would have been a lesser place for the loss of such beauty. That kind of loss almost made me weep. I recovered quickly, drinking a beer, and thinking where I should start in finding the owner. It had already been five years. A hundred things could have happened and had. Would the owner even remember what shots he had taken? Even if he had (somehow I couldn't imagine a woman losing such a camera), he would have come to terms with the fact the shots were lost, would have found replacement photos and put the incident behind him. Maybe he never thought about the camera now. If it had been me, I would never have stopped thinking about where I might have left the camera. Going over every single movement of the day I lost it, I would have tried to reconstruct each possible point where it might have been left or stolen.

This sadness and dull, dead feeling of dread soon turned to paranoia. What if the camera hadn't been lost? The owner might have dumped it at the last moment. His last chance was at the check-in counter. He saw the gap and pushed it inside. He could have been worried someone at Customs had been alerted and rather than chasing up a cold beer for a dollar, he would have inquired about the nineteen exposures. He might have been followed by intelligence agents, taken out of the line, questioned in a small room with several rough-looking men with large shoulders and big cheek bones circling him, punching him, demanding to know what he had done with the camera. One of those men could have been the man at the x-ray machine who had brought me a cold beer. The camera owner couldn't show them a world-renowned book gracing coffee tables in the fashionable penthouses of the world's capital cities with his name on it and photograph on the flap. He would have had no cover. It occurred to me that they might be playing with me, waiting until the last moment to bundle me into that airless room and ask what was my real connection to the owner. Maybe they had a photo of the owner and had been waiting all these years for the pick-up. They would try and strong-arm me into making a confession of treason. Why was I helping a spy harm the security interests of the country? Treason was a capital offense. The content of the camera would be my death warrant. I stared at the plastic seats that Philips had printed "A Better Tomorrow" on and wondered if I would ever see tomorrow.

I didn't stop shaking until the plane finally was in the air. Only when we landed in Bangkok did I feel that I was beyond their grasp. As I stood in the line at Immigration, I wondered if one of their people could have been on the plane, watching me, planning to follow me. It would be too easy to torture me in Rangoon. They knew they would get nothing out of me. No, it would be better to learn where I lived, who my friends and contacts were, what our true intentions were, and the details of our plan. I leaked sweat at Immigration. I thought the officer was going to send me for a health check before stamping me in. I told him that I had the flu and coughed. He let me through. No one seemed to follow me after I got my luggage and climbed into a taxi. I told the driver to take me to Washington Square. If I were being followed, that would be the place to lose the Burmese security agents. I knew the Square. I had many friends in the Square and they would hide me for days if it came to that.

But it never came to that. No one had followed me. No one had cared that I had the camera. I had a couple of beers at the Silver Dollar Bar and then went home. Saya waited at the door. The dogs had barked as the taxi pulled into the drive.

"Did you see anyone following me?"

She said she hadn't.

I showed her the Nikon. She silently examined the lens a couple of minutes. "It must have been very expensive."

"I found it at the airport in Rangoon," I said.

"How much did it cost?"

"You're not listening. I found it. Really." I held my hand up to show I was taking the oath of truth telling. She had seen me take that oath thousands of times. Some of those times I had been lying through my teeth. "It was inside a crack in a counter at the airport. A skinny Indian and a fat woman helped me move back the counter. You see, I had lost my passport and I found the camera and my passport." The explanation didn't sound remotely plausible even to me. That was the problem with truth and why lying was often such a seductive alternative.

"I like the camera," Saya said. "The rest doesn't matter."

That's why I love my wife.

We went into my study and I turned on my computer. She brought me a double shot of Johnnie Walker Black with one ice cube. I rolled a fat one, waiting for all those millions of bytes to load and make useful software applications. I connected to the Internet, and did a Google search on the Nikon model. Only fifteen hits came onto the screen and except for one they were all in Japanese, Korean, or Chinese. Saya read the script on the Japanese site. It listed the Nikon's specifications. We surfed to a crime reporters' site. I clicked on a reported theft. In 1998 someone had reported that a thief had broken into their house and among the items stolen was a Nikon Zoom 310 valued at $7,500.

"You see that? Man, how could this camera be worth so much money?"

Saya leaned forward in the chair next to me, reading the police report, if it really was a police report. "You can't believe anything on the Internet. People tell lies. They write and post lies," she said.

It was her tone that made it clear that I might be one of those people.

"I want to return it."

"Where do you start looking?"

I leaned over and kissed her. "I don't know. It's a long shot. I may never find him but I am going to try. Think of the search as another part-time project."

She looked at the camera closely. "It has film inside."

"Nineteen exposures on that film."

"We will have to develop the film. Only problem is . . ."

Saya never played on my fears—in Japanese, "Saya" translated as cocoon and within her presence I felt safe and secure no matter how grim things appeared—like any good wife she anticipated them even before she could put the problem into words.

"What kind of problem?" I asked.

"I don't know; really, I don't. What if there are nineteen dead mutilated bodies on that film, and the film developer guy calls the Thai police, and the police in those tight-fitting brown uniforms are waiting at the shop when you arrive?" It hadn't taken her long to find the words to express my fears. "The cops ask you why you killed those people, and you say the film isn't yours, that you took it from a camera that you found in a crack between some old counters in Burma. How does that sound as an alibi?"

"You're saying I shouldn't develop the film?"

"I am not saying that. The film is probably just some snapshots of the market or the zoo. Harmless pictures taken by a tourist to show his family and friends some scenes of Burma. That's what I think. Take the film in and get it developed."

"How do you know it was a he?"

"Women would never spend $7,500 for a camera. Only men are that stupid."

"We don't know it cost that much. The crime report could have been false for insurance purposes or maybe there was a typo. Seven hundred and fifty dollars is more like it."

"It's up to you," she said, leaving my study. "I know you, Sloan. You won't sleep until you know what is on that film."

"Meaning you won't sleep because I'll toss and turn."

Later Saya told me that she had gone out and bought a lottery ticket with the number nineteen. And later still, she dropped in the middle of a conversation that she had won a thousand baht with that ticket. I delivered the film to a mom-and-pop film developing shop on Sukhumvit Road. I avoided another shop a dozen sois away that I usually frequented. The shop I chose was way outside my neighborhood. It was less likely that anyone in that area would be connected to the bamboo telegraph of maids, drivers, street louts, bargirls, and pimps. I felt safe enough to return the next day to pick up the jumbo sized photographs. Each of the nineteen shots had turned out. I flipped through the plastic folder as I walked down the street. There were over a dozen shots of Aung San Suu Kyi, the Lady. A photograph of her in a room with a huge poster of her father behind her, then another shot of her in a driveway with trees and a garden in the background, and a sequence of shots of her inside a car. In those shots, it appeared that the car was in a Rangoon street. Tough young men with menacing faces stood with their sling-shots pulled back, aimed at the person taking the photo. Then a shot of Aung San Suu Kyi in the backseat of the car. Behind her the window had been shattered and in the center was a hole the size of a walnut. The Lady's head was slightly turned to the side, her face placid, expressionless. Then the first clue to the photographer: in the background of one photo was an Asian man in his late twenties with thick black hair and bright, confident eyes, his lips curled into a half-grin. The last photo was of a girl with long, slender legs wearing a robe curled up on a sofa. She sat with one foot tucked underneath her other thigh. I was drawn to her long fingers and delicate hands; one was positioned on her exposed leg and the other she used as a pillow under her face. Under the robe there was a hint of large and firm breasts, the erect nipples causing the robe to tent out. She might have been sleeping or resting. From the angle of the shot, only one eye was partially visible and it was closed. I went into the nearest bar, ordered a beer, and sat alone, studying the photographs. The positioning of the girl had been done by someone who was a pro: a classic after-sex composition, not smutty or overtly sexual, but carefully nuanced with every part of her body in perfect harmony. The girl was so relaxed that any anxiety or tension had evaporated from her body, giving the impression of sensual contentment. When I returned home, I went up to my study, and slipped the photo of the girl in an envelope, licked it, and carefully hid it under a stack of papers in the bottom drawer of my filing cabinet. That night I showed Saya the other eighteen photographs. The first thing she said was, "I thought there were nineteen exposures."

"One didn't come out."

She looked up from the Lady who sat in the back of a Toyota with the bullet-like hole in the rear window a couple of inches away from her head. Saya looked at me in that way she had that let me know that she knew that I was lying. She didn't have to say a word. I got up from the sofa, went to my study, removed the envelope from the filing cabinet drawer, drew in a long breath, then thought for a moment, deciding it was the right thing to do. After Saya opened the envelope, she studied the photograph, and after a long pause, said, "The girl is sleeping. She's not dead. That's good."

"That's what I thought."

She carefully examined the other photographs. Putting them down one at a time on the table, keeping them in order. She said nothing, turning to each one until she was finished. "The man in the photograph looks Japanese," she said.

"How can I find him? I'd like to return his photos and camera."

She fingered the photograph of what we later always referred to as the "sleeping girl" and looked around the room, thinking about this odd request. After all the years we had been married, Saya never could quite predict what strange, novel thing I would drag home or what insane request I might next ask of her. My furtive behavior and fumbling attempts at secrecy for some reason never upset her. It gave her some comfort to know that despite my infidelities no other woman could begin to cope let alone survive in the presence of my personal habits.

Finally she said, "I would start by contacting one of the reporters working for a Japanese TV station or one of the newspaper correspondents stationed in Bangkok. If the photographer was a correspondent, someone was bound to know him. The Japanese news mafia are a tight little group and everyone knows everyone else."

One of the reasons I love Saya is that she is smarter than me, but then she is smarter than just about anyone I have ever met.

Two days later I tracked down a Japanese journalist at one of the news bureaus on the penthouse floor of the Maneeya Building. He looked at the photograph of the Asian guy for three seconds before grunting. "That's Kazuo Takeda. He's dead."

Just my luck, I thought to myself. I asked the correspondent how I might contact Kazuo's family, and this seemed at first to surprise and then to annoy him. Was I going to cause some kind of trouble? I assured him that my cause was noble. That I had come across an item that had belonged to Kazuo and I wanted to find a way to return the item. He repeated the word "item" a couple of times as if it were a trapdoor leading to someplace he didn't want to go. "It's his camera," I said. After that disclosure, everything became much easier with the journalist, who offered me a cup of coffee and a chair.

I learned that Kazuo Takeda had worked as a correspondent for one of the large daily Tokyo newspapers. In August 1996 he had been killed in a road accident near Kyoto. He had stopped to help out a motorist whose car was parked on the side of the road with a flat tire. Kazuo had been working the tire jack when a truck carrying livestock struck him. Not a truck loaded with computers or fancy TV sets on the way to port and destined for Detroit or Miami. But a large truck with a busted headlight loaded with cattle destined to become Kobe beef. The correspondent gave me the name of Kazuo's old editor and his phone number. That night, I phoned him and confirmed that Kazuo had indeed been a correspondent on assignment in Burma. I asked him—actually I handed Saya the phone and she asked him in Japanese—for a way to contact Kazuo's family. I doubt that I would ever have received that information myself, but he was forthcoming in giving out the family phone number. Mr. Akira Takeda, the father, answered the phone after it rang three times, and through Saya we told him the story about how I accidentally had found his son's lost camera wedged between two counters at Rangoon airport, and how I thought a father would be proud to have his son's historic and valuable pictures. Saya explained to Akira Takeda that the photos included the Lady and were not just standard shots, either, but photographic evidence that the government had thugs firing missiles at her car, coming within inches of killing her. Saya explained to him that there was a photo of the Lady and his son. If I had a son, and he had died, this was the way I would like to remember him—as someone who had tweaked the nose of the devil. She didn't translate that part over the phone. She did say, however, that I thought his son had been something of a hero, and we would immediately send him or Kazuo's family the photographs and the camera. Saya left out any mention of the beautiful girl sleeping on the velvet red chaise longue sofa or that the robe that she was wearing was a traditional Japanese kimono. Akira Takeda's son was dead and such a picture would hardly bring comfort to the father. He gave me an address and the next day I sent him the camera and all but one of the photos. I included a note saying that the negatives had been lost to cover the deception. I thought that this would be the end of a strange and terrible story. I had done what I had set out to do. The owner was dead, but I had found his surviving father much in the same way that I had found the camera: by a fluke of circumstances. I had the means now to return his son's camera. It was like closing a circle. One that Akira Takeda, whom Saya thought sounded like an old tired man, in Tokyo had thought would have remained broken and incomplete forever.

A week later, Akira Takeda arrived in Bangkok. Saya received a call from the Japanese Embassy. The third secretary invited me and my wife to the embassy for tea around 4.00 p.m. I thought only the English had the habit of afternoon tea. Saya never drank tea in the afternoon and neither did anyone in her family. "Strange," I said to her.

"The officials want to make you feel like an important guest," she said. Once we entered the embassy compound, straight away we were shown into a room to meet Kazuo's father. It was very efficient and without fanfare. A fifty-something Japanese man—chronologically he was a few years older than me but he appeared to be of another generation, one still connected to a time of bound feet and samurai swords. Akira Takeda also had the seriousness of a man touched by sadness and disappointment, a man whose life had been lived in a narrow trench of familial obligation. He sat waiting at a table inside a brightly lit, sparsely furnished room. A tea pot and cups were on the table. As an embassy official introduced Saya and me, Akira Takeda bowed and held his head in that bowed position for almost a minute, and when he raised his head, I swear to God, their were tears in his eyes, tears flowing without shame down his cheeks. I stepped forward and embraced him. "Jesus, I am sorry about what happened to your son."

Kazuo's father didn't have a lot of English, and again, as on the telephone, Saya acted as my translator. He said that in Japan, in the old days, people would show such sense of honor and dignity, moving heaven and earth to track down the owner of a lost object, and the Japanese had long prided themselves on these most important of human qualities that they believed had set them apart from other races. But that sadly such people were dying out, and with their death these values were slowly but surely vanishing from the Japanese culture. The driver of the cattle truck that killed his son only gave a grudging show of sorrow for what he had done, blaming Kazuo for being so foolish as to have stopped to help someone with a flat tire, and that if he had minded his own business he would still be alive. The owner of the firm employing the driver hadn't acted with much more sympathy. Some flowers were delivered to the house as well as a card that was carefully written not to admit any liability or fault.

Before we left the room, he handed me an envelope and told me not to open it until after we returned home. It was the Asian way, he said. Someone gives you an envelope but you never open it in front of them. There was no dignity in ripping open the envelope and sifting through the contents, making everyone feel uncomfortable and exposed. Saya translated his request. "When you are alone and then you see what it is." I accepted the envelope and bowed in the way Saya had taught me many years ago to bow to her male relatives. That evening, back at the house, I poured a large Johnnie Walker Black, dropped in one extra fat ice cube, and watched it dissolve in the crystal glass. Saya sat on the sofa in her favorite kimono reading a book about Tibet. The envelope, unopened, rested against the bottle of whisky. "It's time," said my wife, laying her book down.

"I know, I know."

It had been a long drawn out, emotional day. Hugging the silver-haired father of Kazuo. Seeing so much grief and regret on anyone's face was a terrible sight. Akira Takeda had repeated over and over how incredible it was that an American had gone to all of this trouble for a complete stranger; that this act of kindness had moved him deeply, and, a moment later, he had returned to his questioning of what had happened to the Japanese. Everyone had said the Japanese had become too much like the Americans, no longer placing value on civic responsibility. Now how could anyone say the Japanese were superior to the Americans in terms of honor? His son had so much regretted the loss of the camera—the Nikon had been a gift from his father—and the photos, well, that was far more than anyone could ever have hoped to retrieve. Akira Takeda had shown the photos to Kazuo's old boss. It wasn't clear whether the boss had believed Kazuo's story of losing the camera, but the photographs had cleared Kazuo's name.

Saya handed me the envelope. I did a drum roll on the side of the crystal glass, and took a long swallow of Mr. Johnnie Walker Black. I put down the glass and tore open the envelope. Inside was a bank draft in the amount of $10,000. My name was on the check. I looked at the check, turned it over and over until I couldn't catch my breath. Saya said that I had nearly passed out. I don't remember. But I did remember waking up in our bedroom; the curtains were pulled open and the sunlight flooded the room which had been filled with flowers—orchids and roses and bird of paradise—spilling out of pots and vases, hundreds and hundreds of flowers that my wife had bought, and she was whispering in my ear how sorry she was to have accused me of lying about the camera. She said how Akira had told her in Japanese that I was a good man, and that she was lucky to have married such a good man. It had been the first time any Japanese male had ever said that to her. When he had told her that over the phone that night, it had made her cry. And, being Saya, it had also made her happy at the same time, lifting from her soul, she said, a stone she had carried for almost thirty years that had suddenly floated away.

10

A couple of days later, Akira Takeda invited Saya and me to a Japanese restaurant in the Landmark hotel on Sukhumvit Road. Saya said he sounded tense. There were, he told her, some unresolved questions about the photographs. All of this was ambiguous in the way of the Japanese. I saw no other choice than to find out what new mystery he would reveal. He arrived before us and a Thai dressed in a kimono showed us to the booth where he waited. We removed our shoes and slid over the mats to sit opposite him. Another waitress knelt down and placed bowls of green tea before us. After a couple of minutes of small talk, his intentions became clear; he wanted to tell us a story about Kazuo and the Lady. Kazuo had remembered every one of the shots inside the lost camera, and had discussed in detail each of the images as if the act of talking would somehow cause those pictures to magically appear. Most of all, Kazuo had been proud of the photos of the Lady the day she had been attacked and nearly killed. Of the lost photographs taken that day, he regretted losing those most. I asked Akira Takeda what his son had told him, and he bowed his head, his hands clasped around the tea bowl. Now that he had the photographs, there was no question in his mind that what Kazuo had told him about that day was the truth. Saya translated as Akira Takeda told us what his son had witnessed and photographed that day.

"On the 9th of November 1996, the day of the attack, the Lady was traveling in a convoy of cars. Four cars left the house of Kyi Maung, who was a member of the Lady's shadow cabinet. Ten minutes later, the lead car slowed and then the other three cars following behind shifted gears, crawling along the road as a large mob gathered. The mob spilled out in the road until the cars could no longer move. Young men, members of a Hitler-like youth group organized by an outfit calling themselves the Union of Solidarity Development Association, clenched fists, shouting at those inside the cars. The USDA acted as shills for SLORC—the junta of governing generals—doing their dirty work on the street. Military intelligence agents with walkie-talkies and short hair who were bristling with sweat milled with the mob. How did Kazuo know these men were military intelligence? It was illegal for anyone other than the military and police to have walkie-talkies. The mob pushed against the front of the cars. They shouted slogans and pounded on the cars with their fists. The Lady sat in the back of the Toyota. Everyone was afraid. Kazuo and his friend had been in a car some distance behind. They got out and walked through the crowd. He was uncertain if the mob would ignite into violence. If that happened, the car drivers and occupants were powerless. They had no choice but to stop and wait. My son thought sending a mob into the street was a campaign to expand the boundary of force to where the Lady would feel their power and authority. They would teach her not only the meaning of fear, but demonstrate she could not rely on the *status quo*. She could never be sure how far they would go. But they were playing with fire; it was an extremely dangerous game with so many people in a crowd whipped up into a fevered frenzy of hatred and anger. Agents circulated rumors among the mob that the people inside the four cars had conspired to destroy the state, and the security of the Burmese people, and that these people threatened the foundation of Burmese culture and history. They said the people in the cars were in league with foreigners, and their intention was to bring the country under the boot and heel of foreigners. The rhetoric was one thing. But how can you control such a mob? Until that day on the 9th of November, both sides knew the rules and the limits of engagement. Such rules weren't written down. They were informal limits on what either side would do or say. On this day, the acts of violence exceeded those rules. Two of the youths pulled away from the others. They aimed slingshots armed with steel ball bearings. Glass shattered. Somehow the mob broke for long enough for the cars to pass.

"The day after the attack my son and another journalist for his newspaper tracked down the Lady. First they had gone to her house on University Avenue. As soon as they noticed the absence of military intelligence they knew she wasn't home. Even SLORC wasn't so stupid as to have their men guard an empty house. After an hour they found her at the house of Kyi Maung, the senior NLD official. Outside military intelligence officers in *longyis* patrolled the perimeter. They allowed Kazuo and his friend inside. This was a miracle. Perhaps it was because they were Japanese; that might have had something to do with the intelligence officers' leniency. Once they were inside Kyi Maung's house, a minor official said that the Lady was meeting with her cabinet. They were assured that once the meeting ended she would see them. True to her word, as soon as the meeting adjourned, Kazuo and his friend were allowed inside the meeting room. The entire cabinet was present. The Lady remained seated at table with her cabinet. Kazuo and his friend were allowed to ask all the questions they wished. My son took pictures of her seated with her cabinet. His friend walked around the room, shooting the Lady, taking shots of her from many different angles. Kazuo was a journalist, you see. His friend's duty was to take the photographs for the newspaper. But Kazuo loved photography and couldn't resist taking photographs, too. No one interfered with their movements inside the meeting room. After the photography session ended, Kazuo was granted an exclusive interview. The Lady said that her father had always had a special feeling for Japan. Most of the members of her cabinet had known her father. Her father had been assassinated at thirty-four. His colleagues were now all older men in their seventies. They spoke a proper British English, the kind of English that no one has heard since the war.

"After the interview ended—and it only ended when my son and his friend could think of no more questions to ask—the Lady rose from her chair and invited them outside. They followed her and several members of her cabinet. Outside the house they assembled near a white Japanese car. I recall Kazuo saying it was a Toyota. My memory fades on such details. But I see from the photographs he took that it was a Toyota, a four-door sedan. They went outside and the Lady opened the rear door and climbed inside. All the time she talked about the attack the day before. The shock of that assault was still fresh in her mind; my son could sense a strong resolve in her to show the damage inflicted. She sat in the back, taking the position she had when the attack occurred.

"'I was sitting here when it happened,' she said.

"His friend's camera malfunctioned. Kazuo said not to worry because he had his camera. Kazuo snapped three shots of the Lady, her face in a dark, slightly obscured profile, but he assured me that if I saw the photograph, I would have no doubt that the person in the photograph was Aung San Suu Kyi. He stood a couple of feet away, kneeling down, shooting inside through the open car door. She wore a brown-colored *longyi*; he remembered the white dots or stars on her *longyi*. On her feet were sandals. Her blouse was also a copper color as if heated in a hot fire. Her face—a slight smile on her lips—was only slightly turned towards the camera. Directly behind her, in the rearview window, a clean hole appeared. A hard metal ball had gone straight through the glass leaving a spider web of cracks along the edges. The thugs had used steel ball bearings. You have seen the photographs. The Lady had been only a fingernail's length away from the hole. A little bit more to the side and she would have been killed. Kazuo had the evidence that the generals were prepared to have a mob kill her. Of all the journalists in the world, Kazuo, my son, was the one person who had taken that photograph. You see in Kazuo's photograph how Aung San Suu Kyi sat inside the car, turning and looking at the hole, the empty space that had opened at the very moment her destiny had forced her to move to the side. If she hadn't moved, well, as I've already said, she would have surely died. There would have been no house arrest. Kazuo talked about those photographs each time we met. He felt such sadness that the camera and film had been lost in Burma. He felt that he had let down his colleague and his newspaper. He hadn't intended to lose the camera. People lose things all of the time, I said to him. He said he hadn't exactly lost the camera. At the time, he had many things on his mind. From the day of the attack, the military intelligence people had followed him. They watched him at the airport, and set a trap once he had checked in. He had no choice but to dump the camera. Only two days before he died, Kazuo had booked a trip to Burma to retrieve his camera. He died before that happened.

"Kazuo said that what he had photographed was historical. That he had a duty to preserve that incident because it was part of a much larger story. Many times the criminal reenacts his crime. But this was the first time where the *victim* had reenacted the crime committed against her. Criminal reenactments are common in many countries. You are an American and you may not understand a culture that brings the press, police, and suspect to the spot of the crime. And the suspect is encouraged to show exactly how he committed the murder, rape, beating, or whatever the crime he was suspected of having committed was. That reenactment is then photographed for the newspapers, it is filmed for TV and showed so that everyone can witness how the crime was carried out. The generals in Burma would not authorize such a thing. For them it wasn't a crime, Kazuo said. Their attitude was understandable, as the criminals who caused this were untouchable. If those who committed violence couldn't be brought to account, then the victims must show the world evidence of the crime, my son said. The Lady wanted the world to be aware that the line had been crossed. She had chosen my son to be her witness.

"I told Kazuo to let go of the past. That it wasn't safe to return for the camera. They would be watching his every move. All he would accomplish would be his own arrest and imprisonment. I reminded him that in Japan we have too much of our own past that people hold tightly to their chest. I said this was our mistake. I pleaded for him as his father to get on with his life. He said, 'Father, you know how I respect you. In this case, I must disagree. Burma is a huge, dark back room. There is no front room. There is no light going into that house. Everything that is done is done off-stage. The men who organized the mob attack were never arrested. That was impossible. Even though inside that locked, dark, secret room where plots are hatched, their names were known. What they have done was done in secret, without names, without accountability. They can do what they want to whom they want and no one can touch them. Our mistake is not to shine a light on such men. Put the torch close to their faces, expose them for what they are. If we don't, who will?'

"I had no answer for this question. I only worried that acting upon these feelings would place him in great danger. He had dumped the camera because he had been followed. He knew the photographs would cause an incident and he wished to spare his father and family the anguish of such publicity."

But now the photographs had been recovered everything had changed. It was agreed that I would find a way to deliver one set of the photographs to the Lady. He said he could arrange such a delivery himself—he hinted vaguely about a backdoor channel. I didn't press him on the point, because in his opinion whatever destiny had caused me to find his son's camera was still in play and I had been chosen as the instrument of his dead son. I found out that Akira Takeda was made of strong, unshakeable opinions. The Lady, of course, was under house arrest but Akira Takeda had full confidence that a resourceful man like myself couldn't be stopped from accomplishing any mission I had set my mind to do.

11

The thing with green tea is that, like good sex, once you start you just keep going on and on until your bladder is about to explode. I squirmed on the bamboo mat and finally had to excuse myself. When I returned, I saw that Akira Takeda and Saya had gone into a rapid-fire exchange of Japanese. His face flushed red as I eased back in and Saya sat with the stoic look that she had mastered.

"So what's up?" I asked Saya.

"Akira Takeda asked if you had heard of the Chindits," she said.

I looked at him, wondering what this was all about, and nodded.

He was testing the waters, trying to determine the depth of my understanding of the history of Burma. I had basic information about the Chindits. They were a legend. You could call them a British special operations group. Dropped behind the Japanese lines in southern Burma, their mission was to disrupt Japanese communication and supply lines.

"I knew a guy named Clarke. He was a World War II glider pilot who flew mules, guns and men into the jungles of Burma. Clarke told his stories in a Patpong dive called Lucy's Tiger Bar. With the passing years, his stories about the number of missions he flew increased along with near misses with Japanese Zeros. Towards the end of his life, Clarke talked mainly to himself. That happened many years ago. Clarke, who smoked forty Lucky Strikes a day, died of lung cancer. He was cremated in Bangkok. A dozen people showed up at the *sala* to pay their respects. I was one of them. Beside his coffin was an old photo of Clarke in a uniform and behind him was a large, ugly wooden-like box with wings on it. He hadn't been bullshitting all those years. He had to die before the photograph surfaced to show that he was the genuine thing. I knelt beside that photo and cried. This was the glider he had talked about all those years to a bunch of guys who thought he was another whacked-out *farang*. But Lucy's Tiger Bar vanished a long time ago, and except for a few old hands it was as if Clarke, the Chindits, and Lucy's Tiger Bar had never existed. They are off the radar screen. Not only do people die, history dies. Killed by MTV, George W. Bush, terrorist bombings, snipers, earthquakes, and a thousand other threats and ways to die. That's what I've got to say, Saya. Translate that to him. And tell him that Clarke held court at Lucy's Tiger Bar and, before lung cancer killed him, told hair-raising stories about the fighting in southern Burma. So I know that the Chindits were named after the half-lion, half-griffin statues outside pagodas," I said.

Akira Takeda understood far more English than either Saya or I had guessed. He didn't wait for her translation. Simultaneous translation exhausted her. She picked at her fingers, removing layers of skin. Nothing that came out of Akira Takeda's mouth was anything like what she expected. She suffered and finally stopped altogether. That didn't deter Akira Takeda; he was like a runaway freight train. He suddenly learned an entire English vocabulary. "My father's elder brother was a naval officer in World War II," he said, sipping his tea. "He was stationed in Moulmein."

He couldn't just say, "my uncle." We had to hear the entire genealogy of the Takeda family. But I let that pass, and said, "I know Moulmein, it's the capital of the Mon state."

"You've been there?" His mouth gaped open, showing two rows of capped teeth.

I had his attention. Akira Takeda's cup hovered between the table and his mouth, waiting for my answer. "No, I've never been to Moulmein. But I've driven as far as the Sittang Bridge."

"Yes, that's the road to Moulmein," said Akira Takeda.

"I wanted to go to Moulmein but the road was closed. Foreigners couldn't go there," I said.

In the late shadows of the afternoon an erect, slender man's silhouette moved against the wall. I thought, I would like to paint

51

his silhouette, capture its mystery and movement, a blur of black and white against a white silk screen. But what did Moulmein and Akira Takeda's uncle have to do with the price of rice I asked myself, and more importantly, what was the connection with Kazuo and the photographs?

"My father's brother's name is Ichiro. He was a naval officer stationed in Moulmein during the war," he said after sipping his tea. As he spoke, Akira Takeda seemed to stare right past me as if he were looking at someone else. I turned and looked over my shoulder. No one was standing there. "The war was very hard on him. He suffered a great deal and nearly died. Fortunately, after the American and British offensive, Ichiro found his way to Chiang Mai, and from Siam to Japan. Many men died during the retreat. Ichiro was one of the lucky ones. After the war ended, he was repatriated. Fortunate, very fortunate for him. It could have ended very badly but he had good karma."

Akira Takeda must have sensed that his vague explanation about his uncle being in the war in Burma was an attempt to guide me to a state of enlightenment. But he had only managed to confuse me. Saya squeezed my hand under the table. This was a signal—the husband and wife thing—that meant caution, yellow light, something is moving into our lane and I can't tell what it is. Akira Takeda's technique was to go the roundabout roads before disclosing his true destination. I had met men like him before. Saya's father was not all that different.

"I am grateful for the photographs you returned. But one of Kazuo's photographs has gone missing. And I wonder if you might know where I could find that lost photograph. Unless, of course, it is with the lost negatives."

The hair stood up on the back of my neck. To protect his son's reputation, I had not sent the photograph of the girl. There was no good to come out of sending a vaguely pornographic photograph to the father of a young man who had been killed. I wanted Akira Takeda to remember Kazuo for the invaluable photos of the attack on the Lady's car by the mob that had been instigated by the government. I wasn't going to be the one who said, "Oh, by the way, after incredible courage under fire, Kazuo decided to get laid and wanted a snapshot of his honey." It hadn't seemed right to include the photo. Or so I thought. But somehow, Akira Takeda had managed to acquire information about the existence of that photo.

"What photograph is missing?" I decided to put him to the test.

"Kazuo told me about every shot he took. He left nothing out. Before my son was killed, we spent many hours together and he described the photographs he had taken. He described all of them. When I received eighteen photographs from you, I knew one hadn't been sent. And I can fully understand your decision not to send it to me. No doubt you felt this photograph would be a stain on the honor of my son. You withheld it from me out of pure motives and a good heart. I am very grateful that you would wish to spare my feelings."

"He described the girl in the photo?" I lit a cigarette.

"Every detail."

Akira Takeda watched me take a long drag on the cigarette before he spoke. Whatever his son had told him, the father shared with Saya a vivid, clear recall of every feature of the girl, what she wore, the setting. I listened to her translation. His son's description had left nothing out. Having seen the photo, I was convinced that if a gun had been held to my head I couldn't have teased out every last, fine detail that Akira Takeda had at his fingertips.

"I will give you the photo."

Akira Takeda's face remained expressionless, "Most people don't know that we Japanese lost twice as many men in Burma as you Americans lost in Vietnam. And like you, our loss continues to haunt us. Or should I say, the old generation is haunted by the hundred thousand ghosts of our soldiers killed in Burma."

Just as I thought we were sailing in the same direction, Akira Takeda sailed off in another, unexpected direction. *The war, the war,* I repeated to myself. He couldn't stop talking about the Japanese army in Burma and his Uncle Ichiro's brush with death in the final days of the war. He was a prematurely old man who continued to grieve for the loss of his son. Any man entering that state of despair you could forgive for becoming morbid and tapping into his memories of pain, suffering and death. I was surprised about the numbers. Putting the Japanese losses in Burma at double the number of Americans killed in Vietnam wasn't something I had thought about. He had a point. Both countries had been losers in war and losses weighed more heavily on losers than winners. Victory or defeat, for the dead, it mattered not. For the living, it mattered a great deal whether the dead had yielded some benefit for the living.

"Inside my mind, I have already seen the photograph," Akira Takeda said. "I want you to destroy it and forget that it ever existed."

I had expected many things, but this came out of left field. This was the first time I thought the girl in the photograph might be connected to his son's accident. Kazuo had witnessed more than one crime. There had been more than one lady. The mystery woman might shed light on whether it was true the camera had been dumped to avoid military intelligence; or there may have been another motive that only she would know to explain how the camera ended up stuffed in crack between the counters at the airport check-in. Kazuo had a reason to end his photo-taking with this beautiful girl. She came last in a sequence of shots that bore witness to a crime against the Lady. Could there have been a connection between the assault on the Lady's car and the girl in the photograph? I understood why Akira Takeda, who had shown no emotion, was red faced, flushed with blood when I came back to the table. One thing was for certain, I could never forget that such a photograph existed.

"Can I ask you *why* you want me to forget about the photo? It could be important evidence. If I destroy it, I might be charged with destroying evidence. I want to know what this photograph is about. If Kazuo told you everything about *all* of the pictures, he must have told you the background of the girl in the shot."

"I make this request in the name of my son and my family. Please tell yourself that it never existed. Cut it out of your memory as if you have a very sharp knife and throw away this image," Akira Takeda said, looking at his watch. "Now I must go. I have another appointment. I would appreciate it if your wife might accompany me."

I looked at Saya who smiled. "Hey, baby do what you've got to do."

"Tomorrow I will return to Japan," he said.

He slid out from the table, bowed, put on his shoes, turned and bowed again. A moment later he had left the room as quickly and silently as rain clouds bending the light of dusk on the journey across snow-capped mountains. I am not an intellectual. What I know and what I think comes from experience, what I can see with my own eyes. But in my commune days in California, there was a guy named Basso who had dropped out of Princeton. Basso had been a third year physics major. One night after we were loaded, someone asked him why he dropped out of school, and he said that he had learned enough to know when it was wise to stop. What had he learned? Basso said, "Nothing is fixed in the past or the present. What we call actual emerges from a fog of many potentialities. Until we observe an event, the forces are fluid, everywhere at once, neither here nor there, diffused and open-ended. It is only afterwards that the witness gathers evidence and only then can anyone say that the event ever happened in precisely that way."

And I said, "Like if a tree falls in a forest and there is no one to hear it fall, does it make a noise?"

Basso answered, "More like measuring light hitting the forest floor. First light is distorted by the trees, the leaves, branches, bark, and trunks. That's why you don't see the forest for the trees. The sequence of possibilities shapes or forms into one outcome because you observed it. By witnessing it, you make it real, you bring it from a potential form into an actual form. And once it is given birth, it can never go back. You can't unwitness something."

The photograph of the girl on the chaise longue—a Victorian kind of bed—her long hair tossed and a blue scorpion tattoo observed upon very fine inspection on her thigh. What were those possibilities? Kazuo had taken the photo. Perhaps the fate of the girl was like that of Kazuo. Was she alive or dead? Ichiro, Kazuo's great uncle, had some hand to the photograph. Kazuo had described the photo to his father, and the old man had come all the way from Tokyo to thank me for returning Kazuo's camera and photographs—or had he come to Bangkok to warn me? By pure chance I had been the witness to something that I shouldn't have seen. And by seeing this photo I had changed some outcome. Short of blowing one's brains out, how was it possible to rewind and undo that sequence of reality? And what was the outcome that I had changed? Not even Basso would have had an answer to that question. I took a taxi to Washington Square and drank and smoked and thought until I decided I had to find out about that girl. I had opened the closed box and looked inside. Was she alive or dead? Like Clarke and his gliders, I, too, couldn't forget. I knew I wouldn't stop until I found her, and only then she would reveal everything or nothing.

THE MILLION DOLLAR BILL

12

The wet tarmac reflected the headlights of an old truck pulled alongside our plane. The rain swept the dimly lit runway, keeping the crews inside their trucks. Stormy and overcast, the airport matched the politics of the country. Nighttime arrival at most third-world airports was a journey into early aviation history. The airport where we landed in Rangoon wasn't all that different from the one used by Hart's grandfather during the war with its broken-down vehicles skirting the runway, a shamble of buildings, and atmosphere of dark conspiracy turning the arrival into a bad remake of a Bogart movie, with a cloaked figure disappearing into the shadows after a murder, or an agent on his way for an appointment with smugglers, drug dealers or gunrunners. We bought our three hundred dollars of funny-money script from an official who stared long and hard at both Hart and me, asking us our business. We said that we were tourists. The official gave the impression he had heard that lie before. We cleared our luggage from the central carousel and worked our way through a line of touts and relatives. Outside the main terminal young beggars in *longyis* stood in the rain smoking cigarettes, their feet wet in flip-flops, looking like bone-tired refugees. A couple of the more predatory ones grabbed at our bags but Hart pushed them back. I looked older, weaker, so they came alongside me, cub lions trying to take down the limping deer falling behind the main herd. I did what any gimpy deer would have done; I handed out cigarettes in the dark, confusing them, satisfying and shocking them at the same time. We walked close to the wall, keeping out of the rain until we reached the far end of the terminal.

The road in front of the terminal was jammed with mini-buses, taxis, pickups, and cars. Windscreen wipers slapping and drivers hitting their horns. We looked for Zaw Min through the fogged-over windows. The drivers stopped long enough to pick up passengers. No one looked familiar. For a guy with a million bucks, it crossed my mind that he might just have blown us off. I leaned against the wall and lit a cigarette.

"He's probably got nothing. But who cares?" I said, but without much conviction.

"There is no million dollars," said Hart.

"Strange things happen in Burma."

"Strange things happen on the moon, too. But the rules of common sense still prevail."

"The money is in the Ming bowls. Remember that."

"As for the girl in the photo, do you really think you can find her?"

"I just might get lucky."

The terminal looked like an old faded provincial bus station. Half of the outside lights were burned out or broken. A fluorescent light, yellowish at both ends, spluttered in the rain. The lights were not much bigger than those found on Bangkok food vendor stands illuminating signs like "Floating Balls" and the small, empty area alongside. Hart took one of my cigarettes. He looked at the fluorescent light on the wall. "Rangoon makes me homesick," he said.

"That's okay. Prison makes some people homesick," I said. Not far beyond the shabby walls with peeling paint loomed a black forest of huge trees. Every time I flew into Rangoon, I had the feeling the forest had inched forward, and that one night I would walk into the airport to find the forest had reclaimed everything up to the baggage carousel and, hopefully, the evil smelling official who forced us to pay three hundred dollars for Monopoly money. If you glanced at your watch under that fluorescent in the rain, rather than the time it would read out: 1948.

Five minutes later, Zaw Min and his wife, who were on foot, had worked their way through the crowd and found us. Twe Twe ran straight up and hugged me. I kissed her on both cheeks. "Darling, you look beautiful in the rain," I said. Hart was a step behind, and she was happy to see him, giving him a big hug. The beggars looked on, waiting for a second chance to lay claim to our bags, which were mainly my bags. Hart's earthly possessions fit into a gym bag.

I hugged Zaw Min, who couldn't stop grinning. The rain glistened on his full head of black hair. "Man, it's good to see you."

"Sloan, I knew you would come," said Zaw Min. "I say to Twe Twe, Sloan will come to Rangoon. He's my friend." No one who hasn't inhaled a lungful on a fat one or had a near-mystical experience in a threesome should ever look as happy as Zaw Min. Unnaturally happy, bouncy, drunk with expectation and hope. In his early thirties, Zaw Min had a fireplug body, broad shoulders, and a perfectly round face. His thick jet-black hair was recently cut. In the rain, his hair had the kind of sheen found on a raven's wing.

"Zaw Min, how very good to see you," said Hart.

"I'm glad you come back, Hart."

Those two could fight the war of the smiles to the death. And I wouldn't lay odds on who would come out on top.

"You know, I love Burma." They shook hands.

"Like your grandfather," Zaw Min said. The Burmese were always impressed that Hart's grandfather had worked in Burma, had spoken their language and had managed to leave before the war. That was good karma.

"He died in London two years ago. Cancer," said Hart. "He was very old and had had a long, happy life. So there was nothing to be sad about."

After his grandfather's death, Hart had taken up pool as a full-time occupation.

Zaw Min nodded, no longer smiling, and then slipped away to get the van, holding an umbrella over Twe Twe's head. The two of them disappeared into the chaos of cars and buses. A few minutes later, a van pulled alongside the curb, the front wheel climbing over and onto the pavement, scattering the baggage touts. Zaw Min's van looked like he had lent it to a successful suicide bomber. Zaw Min had to kick the door on the driver's side before he could edge out, leaving Twe Twe perched up front on the passenger's side. He used both hands to slide open the door and we tossed in our bags and climbed inside. Coils of springs were exposed on the backseats, causing my rectum to involuntarily contract. Old, smelly, torn carpets were stacked in the back obscuring the rear window. All the interior panels had been stripped away, leaving the bare gun-gray metal exposed underneath; the metal, twisted and gnarled, had sharp edges that poked at your legs in the dark. Hart sat straight down on a seat with a gaping hole. Think of a toilet bowl that someone had dumped a butchered grandfather clock into. That was where Hart sat.

Zaw Min had climbed back in front, popped open a can of Tiger and handed it back to me. "Thought you would need this."

His smile had returned.

"Need this? Are you joking?" The cold beer was Zaw Min's way of showing his appreciation and respect. We had gone back a number of years, trekking and boating through the tough, largely inaccessible lands to the north and west; places under the control of ethnic minorities. The Chin state had been such a venture, and Hart and I had turned that trip into a book.

"What is this about you getting your hands on a million dollars?" I asked.

"It's true, Sloan."

"Yeah, Zaw Min—you really have a million dollars?"

"Sure," he said.

"What do you think, Twe Twe?"

She looked over her seat and smiled. "Maybe." She was sticking to the script that she had recited over the phone. It didn't matter we were face-to-face in the van. Twe Twe would only allow her feelings for her husband to color her opinion to a shade of gray. Black and white might have been Zaw Min's colors, but she was true to herself. One of the things I liked about Zaw Min was that he had found himself a really good wife.

13

On the road to the hotel, I rolled down the window and tossed the empty can into the rainy street. It bounced like a flat stone across a lake before being submerged into the darkness. I watched the can until there was nothing but black road behind us. Hart said nothing as I straightened around in my seat. He thought that I chucked the empties into the street as some kind of test of his generation's environmental correctness. But Hart had it wrong. It wasn't a test; throwing empties into the street was one of the great, last freedoms on the planet. And in Burma, where exercising freedom was as likely as dead men dancing the tango in the bottom of shallow graves, you had to steal every small liberty just to remember what liberty felt like. Zaw Min hit the brakes hard, stopping with enough force to scatter our bags and the old carpets forward. Zaw Min was a good man but a lousy, dangerous driver.

"Zaw Min, I am going to need a neck brace if you don't learn how to drive."

"I know how to drive," he said.

"But you don't know how to stop."

In front of the hotel, two bellboys ran around to the side of the van for our bags. Another bellboy held an umbrella and waited until Twe Twe could push open her door and climb out of the van. As we walked into the hotel lobby, it occurred to me that during the drive from the airport to the hotel, Zaw Min had avoided the million-dollar questions.

"Sloan, I have a surprise waiting for you," he said, looking over his shoulder as he walked ahead under the umbrella with Twe Twe.

While Hart and I checked in, Zaw Min and Twe Twe went to the lounge area, collapsing into overstuffed chairs. It must have been going through Zaw Min's mind: "If only I could put a couple of these chairs in the van, then I would really have something."

When we joined them, Hart sat down in the chair beside Twe Twe and I sat on the sofa opposite Zaw Min who was talking to an old Burmese woman in a cotton *longyi* and sunglasses. "Sloan, this is Madam Ni Ni," he said.

Because of her sunglasses, I couldn't tell if the old woman was looking at me, Hart, or the ceiling. A waitress arrived with a beer and I looked the old woman over as I drank. The beer was cold, just the way I like it, and I was starting to feel better. "Does she have the million dollars?"

"She's going to tell your fortune."

I shivered and rolled my eyes. "Man, you phone me and tell me you have some kind of an emergency over money. That you need me in Rangoon like now. And now I am here, before the show even begins we are taking a station break to have my fortune read."

"She's very good," he said.

I caught the old woman looking at me over the top of her sunglasses. I turned both hands palms up and presented them to Madam Ni Ni. "Jesus, Zaw Min. Let's get this over. And then you can show me your million dollars. Okay?"

Zaw Min flashed a noncommittal grin.

The fortuneteller asked me what day my birthday fell on.

"Monday," I told her.

She smiled, her lips parting to reveal betel-red gums. Madam Ni Ni had one of those Hollywood special effects smiles found on B-actors in low-budget war movies. Close-up on a soldier who had been shot in the guts by a sniper and the soldier's mouth all grinning teeth rinsed in a foamy blood-red film. That wasn't Madam Ni Ni's smile; no, she had the sniper's smile, having the satisfaction of knowing his bullet had found its mark. She studied my palm. "You will have success this year. If you work for the government, you will get a pay raise."

"Does he get to become a big cheese?" asked Hart.

Her gloomy smiled vanished as she clenched her jaw, grinding her false teeth the way a child (if a child had false teeth) will sometimes do when scolded. "You will have more friends."

"Fat friends or skinny friends?" I asked. "Blondes, redheads, brunets, old, young, rich or poor?" Zaw Min flinched at the rich or poor part of the question.

The fortuneteller didn't bother to look up this time.

"Be careful of your eyes. It is a bad year for Monday person's eyes."

Great, I am going blind. "But I will still be able to tell the color of money?"

She stared into my right palm, feeling the lines with her long forefinger. "Look after those in need. Give them money."

This sounded suspiciously like self-pleading. I finished the beer and called for the waitress to bring another can.

"When you go to a spirit house, take one apple, two apricots, and a bunch of bananas, and lotus flowers. White is good for Monday people."

"Having another Tiger is better for Monday people."

The old woman dropped my hand and sat back in her chair. It wasn't clear whether she was still smiling or whether that was just her ordinary face. I leaned forward, putting a hand on Zaw Min's knee. "Hey, man, I come all the way to Rangoon because you phone me and say come and help me. I hear that bird voice—'help me, help me'—and I am programmed to respond. Why? Because you and your wife are my friends. Understand what I am saying? I come to the hotel, thinking you have these million bucks, and I am told by a fortuneteller that as a Monday child I probably am going blind. That I should stock up on white and that the government is going to increase my pay. Now if she had said I might hit a brick wall or go insane looking for Ming bowls or a mystery girl in a photograph, then I would have agreed she's a genius. So maybe you can tell me what this is about."

"It's okay, Sloan. I have the money."

"The million dollars."

"Sure. But . . ."

"I don't want to hear any words like 'maybe' or 'but.' Those are weasel words. You know what a weasel is? An animal that knows how to slip away into the nearest hole, fast, with no fuss, and sneaks up on his prey, takes the chance, and if he fails, wham, down the hole, safe and sound. So no weasel words."

"It's just that I am . . ."

Twe Twe filled in the blank. "He's nervous. All he can think about is how he wants his friend Sloan to help and how he doesn't want to bother his friend Sloan."

"Since when is a million dollars a bother?"

There was a long silence.

"You did bring the money?"

"It's dangerous at night. You never know if you will get pulled over."

"For littering for example," said Hart out of the blue. I just knew it bothered the hell out of him and he had been waiting for his opening. He was a weasel. I sat on a sofa facing a herd of weasels. I know weasels don't come in herds. But in Rangoon anything is possible.

"Tomorrow, you come to my apartment."

This was getting complicated even for a Monday person.

"I'll make certain that I wear white."

The fortuneteller adjusted her sunglasses. "Good, very good," she said, one eye narrowing slightly as if she had once again leaned into the sniper's telescopic sight and had me in the cross-hairs.

Inside my head all I could hear was a tiny voice saying, "Help me, help me."

14

As Hart and I walked along the street to Zaw Min's we passed an antique shop. Inside the window was a plaster statue of Elvis. We went inside and I asked the owner the price. He quoted an amount slightly more than I had last paid for a four hundred year old Chinese Ming bowl. I wished the owner luck and we left. "Did you see the layer of dust on Elvis?" asked Hart.

"Someone will buy it," I said. The people had been cut off for so long that they had lost the connection with time; the past no longer had meaning and had lost any value, being replaced by junk and kitsch. Modern icons were hip and cool, acting as a one-way road to blast out of the year 1948.

"They have a highly evolved system," said Hart. "First, they loot old Chinese burial sites, sell the Ming to foreigners, then use the proceeds to buy plaster Elvis busts for their living rooms."

"The Indians sold Manhattan for twenty-four dollars' worth of beads," I said.

"Fashion changes," said Hart. "It's better to own real estate."

We reached Zaw Min's apartment, a three-floor walkup which had a balcony overlooking a street of decaying colonial buildings, the facades crumbling. "Would you want to own this dump?" I asked Hart as we stood outside Zaw Min's building. Draped over the balcony, a rope dangled from the end of a rusty metal pulley. Affixed to the end of the rope was a large clip. Bills, circulars, newspapers, mail, demands, ransom threats were clipped tight, only requiring a jerk on the rope, which rang a bell perched on the balcony. I pulled the rope twice. The bell rang. Zaw Min looked down from the balcony. Then Twe Twe's head appeared; she was buttoning her blouse. They fucked day and night. "Come up," said Zaw Min.

"Give them a couple of minutes to dress," said Hart.

National flags flew from Zaw Min's balcony. That was a change, I thought. He hated the government. I stepped back and looked down the road. Every balcony on the street as far as the eye could see had the same system of pulleys and ropes and fluttering flags. The street had the feel of a neighborhood lynch party, with everyone's head in a collective noose. On the ride from the hotel to his apartment, Zaw Min had sworn that he had a million dollars. That is what he said. I reminded him, "Zaw Min, you don't have a million dollars; that's impossible."

He said. "I have it, and I want you to come to Rangoon and tell me what to do next."

"Hey, buddy, you gotta a million bucks, then why do you need me to come all this way to Rangoon? And why the pit stop with the old fortuneteller in sunglasses? I got a lot of questions, and now I'd like to make one request. Show me the fucking money."

He sat on the sofa holding Twe Twe's hands, both of her hands, rocking a little from side to side like he was nervous or had to take a monster piss. Zaw Min sat hugging his wife, as if delaying to the last moment the act of showing his newly acquired wealth.

"Give me the paper, Zaw Min."

He unwound himself from his wife, walked over to a chest, knelt down, took a key from a chain around his neck, unlocked it, lifted the lid, removed an envelope, and handed to me. I looked at the envelope. This wasn't a good sign. A suitcase or a large carton, that was a good sign. An envelope meant something was very wrong. I opened it and looked inside, finding a sheet of paper; I held up a photocopy of a million-dollar bill. Not a negotiable instrument or a key to a safety deposit box. I looked again inside the envelope, thinking I had missed something. There was nothing inside but the one sheet. I showed it to Hart. He hadn't looked so pleased since Sugarcane and Shrimp were rolling around on his bed with Lucifer. I had one thought: in the history of printed money, when had any government ever printed a million-dollar bill? Hart examined the sheet of paper the way he examined a possible Ming bowl. Slowly and with great deliberation, studying the design detail. The front and back had been copied onto an A4 sized page.

"This is the million dollars?" he asked.

Hart handed the paper back to Zaw Min.

"The one you phoned and said I had to get my ass to Burma pronto for?" I asked.

Zaw Min nodded, the smile still wide and glowing.

"What do you think?" Zaw Min asked. He might have been auditioning for a part. He was so earnest and sincere. In his mind, the million-dollar note was part of some vague transaction he had yet to fully explain; in his mind, there was no question, it was a done deal.

"Have you seen American money before?" asked Hart. He knew very well that Zaw Min had been paid in US dollars.

"Many times."

"Did you ever notice there was a theme in the picture on the front?"

Zaw Min shrugged. "What do you mean, theme?"

"A goddamn dead president of the United States. That theme."

The front of the photocopied million-dollar bill had a not-too-accurate replica of the Statue of Liberty. Whoever had forged the million-dollar bill had no idea of American money and only a passing knowledge of the Statue of Liberty.

"President," said Zaw Min.

"There is a fucking president on every bill. There is no exception, even for the Statue of Liberty, and besides, even if there was, what engraver would not be condemned to stoning by an angry American mob for the crime of lopping off the arms of the Statue of Liberty? She is our national Lady. She is the Lady waiting in the harbor of New York City to welcome all those immigrants from Italy and Russia and Ireland and Poland. Millions of faces have waited on ships going into the harbor to see the Lady. But these assholes have cut off her arms."

Zaw Min stared hard at the photocopy. He was looking at a pre-Adobe Photoshop forgery. You had to be living in a place totally cut off from reality to think this was a million dollars. But that was exactly the environment where Zaw Min and his wife lived. I had

had a bad feeling ever since we stopped to look at that plastic bust of Elvis in the window of the antique shop. Things had gotten much worse in Rangoon.

Zaw Min's wife leaned forward, both of her hands squeezing the leg of her husband, kneading his thigh, waiting for my verdict. Whatever I said would settle the matter.

"Is it real?" she asked.

Neither of them had been listening, or if they'd been listening they hadn't understood a single thing that I said. A new direction was called for.

"Where did you get the million-dollar bill?"

"Not from a friend. But from someone who knows one of my friends." Zaw Min said, thinking his explanation had settled the issue. What it came down to was that the summons to Rangoon was from some guy who knew one of his friends had passed him a photocopy of Miss armless Liberty.

"Is the guy involved in this rich?"

"No, he is quite poor."

I sat back and smiled at Hart, who maintained a totally blank expression. "Think about it, Zaw Min. You don't know the guy. All you know is that he's dirt poor. But somehow he gets his grubby hands onto a million-dollar bill. Not a million dollars. But a bill that has a million dollars written on it. So why does this guy who you don't know need you? You aren't his family or even his friend. He is, as they say in the con business, a friend of a friend. If you had a million dollars, would you ask a friend to put you in touch with this slum dweller because you needed his help in spending a million bucks?"

"That's why I phoned you."

"Where did he get the million-dollar bill, Zaw Min?"

"He saw a foreigner leaving a bank and it fell out onto the street."

"Fell out of what? A Brinks truck?"

"A big black briefcase."

"Zaw Min, there ain't any million-dollar bill. There has never been such a bill in the history of America. Not in the history of the world. Not even Bill Gates would walk around with a million-dollar bill. How do you get change? And even if there were such a thing, it wouldn't have the fucking Statue of Liberty on it. Presidents are put on money. Not Elvis or Brad Pitt or Madonna."

One thing I liked about Min was his ability to recover just at the last moment, when it appeared all was lost. His ability to pull back into his lane a split second before a head-on collision with a fully loaded oil tanker or to fold up a phony million-dollar bill and stuff it back into the envelope once the overwhelming evidence penetrated his skull. "We never thought it was real," said Zaw Min, looking at his wife.

"I thought it looked strange," she said.

"Strange isn't the word," I said.

"Zaw Min, do you remember the phony 1804 silver dollar?" Hart asked him.

Zaw Min would remember the 1804 silver dollar and photocopied one million-dollar bill on his deathbed. That silver dollar had been another time when he had phoned and urgently asked me to meet him in Rangoon. That had been years ago and Hart had witnessed the same situation in the same rundown apartment. There was a special coin; one of only thirteen such known coins in the world. The seller needed cash. He was willing to sell cheap. I knew because Hart told me that there were a lot of fake 1804s in circulation. Most of the time it was easy to spot a phony 1804 silver dollar. The work was flawed, sometimes in a minor way, mostly in a ham-handed fashion like the phony million-dollar bill. An occasional "altered" 1801 was converted into an 1804; one that could fool an expert. The technique was to painstakingly etch the "1" into a "4" and unless you had a microscope and knew what to look for, the "4" appeared real. With 1804 Silver dollars, you couldn't be sure. The only thing that warranted that 100 percent certainty was human greed and despair.

"I thought about the 1804," said Zaw Min. "I really did."

"You didn't mention it on the phone," I said.

He looked sheepish. "I thought you wouldn't come if I said something about the 1804. I hoped that you forgot."

"We didn't buy the 1804," I said.

"And we aren't buying the million-dollar bill," said his wife.

She had hedged her bets on the phone and at the airport. Twe Twe was a master of the "maybe" and that left a hole big enough to drive a freight train loaded with phony million-dollar bills and 1804 silver dollars through. This was just another lousy offer from a friend of a friend trying to break out of a slum, surrounded by a fat wife, a half dozen dirty faced, shoeless children with skinny arms and legs calling "daddy I am hungry." Some guy more damaged and hopeless than Zaw Min. Twe Twe had put the idea in his head that the million-dollar bill might not be what it seemed. But he didn't want to believe her. He didn't want to accept that his chance to escape the rope-and-pulley existence had been a false plan from the start, and he was doomed to be locked up in his cell. They had only been married ten months. He told me that his perpetual state of happiness had begun the evenings before they had been married and they sat on the balcony when she masturbated him as the sun went down. The small apartment crawled with either his relatives or hers who shared the same small place. Privacy was impossible. The only place they could fool around was on the balcony. She refused to have sex until they were married, or to put it another way, screwing on the balcony staring at the bell ready to ring at the end of the rope wasn't exactly romance. They sat close together, holding hands, and she fed him slices of fruit and touched his cheek with the back of her hand. It was hard to be angry with Zaw Min. His future was clear. Twe Twe would have children and they would have even less space and privacy, and what would be left for them? He would be an old man squatting on the balcony with his wife whacking him off, thinking back to the days when they almost had a million bucks and almost had an 1804 silver dollar. With such a heavy degree of inevitability hanging over their heads, it was difficult to maintain any hard feelings. Who wouldn't have a zealot's belief in a photocopied million-dollar bill given the grim alternative?

Zaw Min looked somehow diminished, defeated as he slipped the envelope into the chest and locked it. When he looked up from the chest he held a jar of imported coffee.

"Sloan, I have some very good coffee. I buy for you. You want?"

The million dollars was already consigned to the trashcan of history. Vanished, out of sight, never happened. A jar of coffee was his way of making up for the trouble, a way to forget about the envelope.

"Yeah, I'll have some coffee. Now tell me about the Ming bowls you have been scouting for me."

"I make an appointment with a man who is the number one expert in all of Burma."

"He's not the one who gave you the photocopied funny-money."

"Don't be angry, Sloan. This is a very good man. He's a very educated man. He knows everything."

I wanted to ask why Zaw Min hadn't showed him the million-dollar bill.

"What does he know about Ming bowls?"

"He's a doctor."

"That explains everything."

"I tell him you are a lucky man. Maybe the luckiest man on earth," said Zaw Min.

Hart half-snorted, half-laughed. He knew what was coming. Most of the time, you can live down failure; it is success that never lets you rest, even if the success was the product of pure accident, a fluke that happened once and marked you forever as someone with a direct pipeline to lady luck. I was definitely looking for a lady, but I had a strong feeling she didn't have any luck attached to her, and finding her wasn't necessarily going to be my lucky day.

15

I let Hart into my room and without any greeting he walked past me and flopped down on the edge of my bed. He looked out the window at the lake and trees and a pagoda in the distance. A couple of squirrels hovered on the roof just outside the window. I laid pieces of banana and orange in a dish for them. Hart watched them eating, then he turned to the television set. A BBC reporter stood in the middle of the screen on the TV talking about the possible timing and conditions for the Lady's release. He might have been talking about the handicap of a favorite in a horse race. His racetrack voice-over continued as a montage of photographs of the Lady flashed across the screen. She stood tall above the gate of her house on University Avenue, garlands of flowers tucked in her hair, smiling and talking to a large group of supporters outside. The reporter said that everyone in Rangoon and around the world anxiously awaited her release from house arrest. The newsreader asked the reporter if the Lady had reached agreement with the generals and what the terms of any such agreement might be. The reporter said that there was speculation of a deal but no one could confirm the terms. This didn't stop him from bravely offering his own theory that someone somewhere in the junta was against her release. Perhaps the hold-out vote was a man with a precise memory of the Lady with orchids in her hair moving so easily among the adoring crowds. To be so clearly adored by those who so passionately hated the regime may have caused some last-minute teething problems. Teething problems? It wasn't dentistry as much as the fear that the adoring crowd might easily transform itself into an angry, raging mob and the streets, as they had in 1988, would again flow red with blood.

"What time are we going to University Avenue?" Hart asked.

"Aye Thit is coming with a car. We meet him downstairs in twenty minutes."

While Zaw Min and I had a friendship for a number of years, it was Aye Thit who had been my main man in Burma for more than a dozen years. We had a long history and he was the only man in Burma I could fully trust. He would never phone and say he had a million dollars and produce a photocopy of a bill with the Statue of Liberty. He never stole or cheated even though his personal circumstances were even grimmer than Zaw Min's.

"I have a feeling this isn't the Lady's day."

Hart turned back from watching the squirrels eating the pieces of fruit outside the window. His mind seemed far away. I kept up some small talk but it was clear that I was talking to myself.

"You remember your grandfather's friend who was executed in the war?"

That snapped Hart out of his funk. "Wilkenson, James Alexander Wilkenson," he said.

Before the war, Hart's grandfather had worked in a shipping company. He made friends with an Englishman named Wilkenson. James Alexander Wilkenson had set up an intelligence network in Rangoon. He was detained by the Japanese who assumed he was a spy. He should have been shot on the spot. But wars in Burma had been waged to capture slaves. The Japanese army treated Wilkenson like a slave. They forced him to work on a road crew. And when he tried to escape, the Japanese shot Wilkenson in front of the others as a lesson. Wilkenson was buried in Kyandaw cemetery. We had gone to visit the gravesite years ago. Hart's grandfather had still been alive then and Hart had written him a letter about the grave. His grandfather, like his friend Wilkenson, had been an intelligence operative who had fought in the war deep behind enemy lines and survived but poor James was shot like a dog on the road, and buried in Kyandaw cemetery. Weeks later Hart's grandfather was called back to London to assist in organizing a Burmese exile force.

Hart said his grandfather always felt that it should have been him ended up in Kyandaw cemetery.

"Do you remember the weird string of events of 1996?"

"Every year is nothing but weirdness and then you die," said Hart.

"I know, I know. Nineteen ninety-six was even weirder. Some generals struck a deal to *sell* the Kyandaw cemetery. That was the same year that the camera with the nineteen photos was lost at Rangoon Airport. Kazuo the Japanese correspondent who took the photos died in a freak road accident. The Lady was attacked in Rangoon and she was nearly killed."

"A garden-variety year of murder and torture," said Hart. "Everything is always in motion, flying and smashing apart. Why should 1996 have been any different?" he asked.

Hart was toying with me, waiting for the right moment to pounce; I knew that he remembered 1996. In that year, he had come screaming into my front door, waving a piece of paper. The generals had ordered that all the graves should be dug up and the unearthed remains reburied at a new site outside of the city. The paper Hart waved around my living room was a bill. The descendants of the dead had been given the bill for the digging, transportation and reburial. Wilkenson's next-of-kin had received the bill and sought out Hart's grandfather for advice, who, in turn, contacted his grandson. The generals demanded money to rebury his grandfather's friend. It had all the elegance of a final demand from the electric company before they threw the switch condemning you to darkness and a fridge of rotting food. Two years later, in June 1998, Aye Thit sent me reports of a poltergeist at Myinegone Junction near the cemetery. The whole neighborhood was in turmoil. The ghost or ghosts played havoc with the locals. Spoons and knives levitated off their tables along with teacups and plates. TV sets floated across a coffee shop as the patrons gazed, mouths wide open, watching as the sets smashed into each other, sending sharp gray shards of glass across the room. Women and children hid under the tables clutching each other, crying, confused and afraid. Blood poured out of another TV set. One woman had a seizure and shook uncontrollably, another patron—I wasn't certain whether this was a man, woman or child—started to babble in tongues, his or her eyes rolled to the top of the head, showing pure white.

Hart hoped Wilkenson's freezing hand rose from the grave to protest being shot through the heart—or was it the head—and being excavated like coal and reburied in some other mass pit; no doubt mixed with the skulls and bones of missionaries, murderers, merchants and high-class whores. The next day, Hart received word that his grandfather had died in hospital in London. I believe in coincidences, and subterranean connections that string them together like beads on an invisible string. My secret feeling was the generals had unexpectedly violated the seam separating time and space, where many different worlds folded together, and Wilkenson finding himself on the other side, kicked down a door and the vibrations spread through the neighborhood.

Aye Thit reminded me that it was precisely at this junction near the cemetery that in 1988 about seventy students had been killed. Most of the students had been shot in the back as they fled the advancing soldiers. For days and nights these disturbances from the dark world made normal life impossible. People were afraid to stay inside their antiquated houses. They were bombarded with ordinary objects flying around and crashing into walls, with glass breaking and flying shards drawing blood from howling cats and shivering dogs. One child lost an eye as a sliver of a water glass pierced the retina. Were these the angry spirits of the murdered students? Were they the angry souls of those who had been buried years before and dislodged from their plot? The ghost of Wilkenson seeking vengeance? No one knew the cause but that didn't stop most people, their faces sallow in candlelight, meeting together and blaming the generals for their greed. The generals soon got wind of the public unrest. The usual knee-jerk reaction of sending in the guns and tanks was ruled out. The ghosts couldn't be killed. The soldiers would be too scared to aim a rifle. Killing more people would only add to the drama. They dispatched a military commander to the site and he stood at the intersection as clouds of ceramics, spoons, and nails lay low over the cemetery and read a long incantation, asking the spirits to leave the place, pleading for the clouds to leave the city. His reading was an ancient Burmese custom at funerals.

He read until he was exhausted and then climbed into the back of a large black car, leaving the people in the street to judge whether his words had soothed the spirits. People slept on the pavement in fear, waiting for another attack. The night passed with only minor disturbances. This gave encouragement and soon the whole neighborhood organized exorcism rites. Day and night, monks and citizens and soldiers prayed and chanted and pleaded. They chanted for the Lady to come out of her house and come to the junction; she could reason with the dead. She could ask them to explain what had been done to offend them and what they wanted in order to return to the other side. Two days after the commander had tried his best, the glass and bottles levitated on tables and counters and flung themselves against walls, windows and doors. Several people suffered ugly, lacerating wounds from the flying glass. One old lady had a nipple cut clean off her breast by a flying knife. She came out of the hospital wearing black. Upon her return to the neighborhood, she alarmed the neighbors, who took her to be a witch, and the blame shifted from the generals who had tried to sell the land of the dead to an old woman with the haunted look of someone more dead than alive. No one believed her when she said a soldier had inflicted the wound, a soldier under orders from a clever general who wanted to shift the blame. She said the knife hadn't been flying through the air; it had a hand attached. People debated about whether to believe her or burn her at the stake. That night some men egged on by military intelligence officers into gathering wood for the burning noticed that a man had wandered into the junction around one in the morning. He carried an armload of wood. It was the dead of night and a half-moon light provided only enough illumination to see the outline of the thin figure with silver hair. A soldier reported seeing a man in his early thirties dressed in a khaki uniform with epaulets walking slowly but with resolve to the junction. Under one arm he had a green *longyi* and a white shirt. In his hand he carried burning incense sticks that left a jet-like vapor trail as he entered the junction. He placed the clothing items on the pavement, lowered himself onto his knees, and coupled his hands in prayer, the incense sticks firmly held between his palms. The next day the disturbances abruptly stopped. No one recognized the man. The generals ordered a search but he was never found. Some say it was a soldier sent by the commanding officer who had failed in his own mission. Another rumor circulated that General Aung San had been the mystery man and he had come to lead the angry souls back to the other world. Some said that it was a sign to the generals that the Lady's father had returned to show she was being watched over, and their actions would be held in account. Others said the mystery man was not Burmese but in fact was a British man, a soldier who had been killed during the war. The old woman who had lost a nipple wasn't burned on the pyre.

Hart said, "The man they described fits Wilkenson."

"I thought he worked in intelligence," I said.

Hart smiled. "If you are dead long enough you automatically get an army commission."

"Kyandaw cemetery was a beautiful place once. I remember when it was filled with solid marble headstones. They cancelled the sale of the cemetery but removed the headstones and sold them."

"They negotiated the best deal they could get with the other side," said Hart.

16

The room phone on the nightstand beside the bed rang. I answered it.

"Aye Thit's waiting downstairs," I said.

Hart edged off the bed, giving a last glance out the window. A man rowed a small boat on the lake. We took the elevator to the lobby.

Aye Thit—tall and frail, bony shoulders, deep laugh lines dancing around the eyes—ran up and we hugged. "Hey, man, you are looking good for a granddad, pappy," I said.

He blushed at the word "granddad."

He shook Hart's hand and we walked over to the lobby bar.

"I was raised by my grandfather," said Hart.

Aye Thit knew that Hart's grandfather, a clerk in a pre-war shipping firm, had briefly assisted the Chindits, who were special operational forces, and had been dropped behind the Japanese lines in order to disrupt their supplies and communication. A Burmese-speaking grandfather, half-spy, half-soldier was cause for Aye Thit to hold a healthy respect for Hart. Aye Thit knew the basic outline of the grandfather's connection with Burma. His wartime spying career—which began a month after the London dinner with George Orwell—had ended when a man named Wilkenson was shot in Rangoon. His respect, though, had little to do with the Chindits helping Burma drive out the Japanese—the Burmese were allies with the Japanese during the war—but it was that Hart's grandfather had *experienced* the jungle, long enough to know the rivers and mountains and animals and flowers. It was that kind of knowledge that Aye Thit admired; it was a mirror of his own deep relationship with Burma.

We sat in the hotel lobby and I ordered a cold beer for Hart and myself. Aye Thit ordered an orange juice. He never drank alcohol. His *longyi* was as tightly wrapped as the dark brown outer leaves of a hand-rolled cigar. His wife had ironed his one-dollar Chinese-made shirt—bounty from his last smuggling expedition across the border to China. From a short distance he could have easily passed for a man in his forties; closer up the crow's feet around the eyes, the lines around his mouth, tipped the age needle to register early fifties. Aye Thit hated the idea of being a grandfather or being called granddad. His love and devotion to his grandchild softened this position. He joked that his son was his brother and his grandson was his nephew.

"We go to University Avenue. I have a car," he said. "The driver is from my township. We can trust him."

"If I light up a fat one, he's cool?"

Aye Thit nodded. "Afterwards we go to the museum."

For months, Aye Thit had been telling me about this new museum that had opened in Rangoon. He had been raised in a family of intellectuals. His father was the editor of a newspaper. When Ne Win—the generals' general—came to power, Aye Thit's father lost his newspaper job and the newspaper was closed down. He was anxious for us to go to the new Drug Elimination Museum—one of those structures that only a George Orwell could have predicted—because on the ground floor inside a display case were old newspaper clippings reporting on the army's success in their mountain warfare against the KMT. One of the clippings had been taken from the newspaper run by Aye Thit's father. The father's byline was on the story. His father's name was preserved in a glass case in the museum. And Aye Thit insisted that I see the report his father had written and take into my memory forever his father's byline. I was reasonably certain there was no mention that the government had closed down the newspaper and that Aye Thit's father had been thrown into the street with little means to support a wife and family. But I understood Aye Thit: if the windowpane is covered with grime, one wipes off an area to see inside, because a small, dirty view is better than no view at all. Ask any blind person.

The previous year, I had lent Aye Thit enough money to buy a second-hand pickup truck that had a knockdown price, as the owner had gone to prison and his wife was without any other means of support. Our plan was to start (on a modest scale) a transportation company. In other words, I had given my friend a hand in establishing a family smuggling operation. Not smuggling as in drugs or guns but smuggling as in car batteries, electrical appliances, and clothing. "Any problem with the new business?" I asked.

Aye Thit sighed, and hung his head, staring down at his untouched orange juice.

"Oh, man don't tell me the pickup's been wrecked or stolen?"

"It's in China. My brother-in-law's stuck there."

"What do you mean *stuck*?"

"The army has closed the border on the Burmese side."

"What's in the truck?"

"Peaches."

"What's he doing with peaches?"

"Smuggling them over the border."

Nothing was ever predictable or straightforward in the smuggling business. His brother-in-law was stuck across the border in China with a pickup truck full of perishable contraband. Already the price had dropped on the cargo, and the brother-in-law was eating up further capital paying for a guesthouse, surviving by eating peaches.

"It is terrible for me. Every night my sister cries for her husband. When will he come back?" She waited everyday for her husband to return with the pickup. In Burma it seemed as if everyone was waiting for someone to be released from a border crossing, house arrest or a prison cell.

"When will they open the border?" Hart asked.

"No one knows."

"He could be in China a long time," I said.

"That's why my sister never stops crying. She thinks the pickup is cursed. The last owner went to prison for fifteen years." The owner had tailgated a military vehicle which slammed on the brakes, causing him to hit the rear end. Then he lost his temper and ended up in a fistfight with the driver. A general had been riding in front. The owner had been lucky to get only fifteen years.

I could see where this was going: nowhere. I brought down Kazuo's photographs from my room and laid them on the table in front of Aye Thit. "These are the photos I told you about. The ones the Japanese guy named Kazuo took in 1996."

Aye Thit stared at the table but made no move to pick them up. It was the same year the generals wanted to dig up bodies from Kyandaw cemetery. The year the Lady was ambushed. The year Aye Thit almost left his wife for another woman. "My plan is to give them to the Lady," I said.

Hart looked through the photos and held them out to Aye Thit. "What about the nineteenth photograph?" asked Hart. "Show him the one with the girl."

Aye Thit glanced through the photos. His mind was elsewhere, along the Chinese border, inside the pickup, the smell of peaches wafting through the air.

"I promised someone that I would give the first eighteen photos to the Lady," I said to Hart.

"Why not give her the whole set?" asked Hart.

Aye Thit drifted away as we fought over which photographs I should give to the Lady. Compared to his brother-in-law's plight, the eighteen photographs seemed unimportant and trivial. Handing over the photos would close the circle. As a photographer, it was what I would have hoped someone would have done for me.

"You won't get close to her until she's released," Aye Thit said.

"Hey, man, I hope your brother-in-law gets over the border soon," I said.

"She never stops crying," he said.

17

We set up camp on University Avenue, leaving our car, driver and Aye Thit out of sight on a side street. The first order of business was ordering beer at a roadside lean-to about twenty meters away from the barricades and checkpoint down University Avenue. Aye Thit stayed behind because he didn't want to risk being photographed by the police who were crawling over the place like red fire ants, and having his wife join his sister in twenty-four-hour crying jags. From our table we watched as military intelligence agents questioned every driver who stopped at the barricades. The agents wore pressed white shirts and dark trousers rather than *longyis* and stylish sunglasses, and they were circling with either a walkie-talkie glued to their ear or snapping photographs of the motorists and the journalists circling nearby. Most cars were ordered to turn back and those drivers who *were* waved through just happened to reside in houses located in the Lady's neighborhood.

The half dozen tables were occupied by international TV news crews and mainly foreign stringers who waited in the shade, eyes peeled from the opposite side of the barricade for the Lady's car. It wasn't possible to watch the mindlessness of the barricade routine without nodding off. The problem was there wasn't much else to see or do except watch, drink beer, and strike up a conversation with the journalists at the other tables. Waiting has to be one of the worst ways to kill time except when you are a child: then you look at time differently, thinking that it will go on forever and will carry you along forever as if you were riding an endless wave. All I had to do was feel Kazuo's photos inside my pocket to know better than waste a minute. Hart stretched out, his hands behind his head, as if settling in for a three-day county cricket match.

"You're thinking about Sugarcane and what was the other one?"

"Shrimp," he said without missing a beat.

"Do you ever *not* think about sex?"

He smiled like a cat smelling a piece of fresh raw liver.

A television crew from Japan sat at the next table. The three of them wore matching Banana Republic photojournalists' vests that made them look like a bowling team from Yokohama. They leaned forward on their elbows, in a kind of quasi-huddle, making it clear they wished to keep to themselves. That body language only encouraged Hart. He asked one of the Japanese—the one the others appeared to defer to, acknowledging him as the alpha dog of the pack—if he had heard anything about the Lady's release. I pegged him as the TV anchor. He shrugged off Hart's question and grinned, showing all of his teeth, and said, "It's very hot. In Tokyo it gets very hot." Sweat ringed his armpits. More sweat dripped from the end of his chin. I couldn't help think what Akira Takeda had said about how much Japanese culture and people had changed. We were a couple of white guys to be ignored and that was cool with me.

It wasn't just the Japanese—no one at any of the other tables seemed willing to share any information. News was a competitive business and everyone under the lean-to wanted to have the edge on being first on the air or in print with the story. Some of the journalists had been waiting days for the story to break. Once that happened, they could stop watching their life pass before their eyes at the barricades, feeling the heat and breathing in the dust. I ordered another round of beer. Drinking was how others passed the time. Hart was convinced the generals would order her release in the morning so there would be time for a press conference and the generals could expect the press to broadcast to the world how co-operative the generals had become just in time for the nightly news.

As a couple of the military intelligence officers waved a car from the Lady's side of the barricade through, everyone craned their necks, leaning over their tables, trying to glimpse the occupants of the car. As the car passed, it was clear that the people inside didn't include the Lady; it was one more false alarm. A moment later the photographers slouched back over the tables, putting down their camera gear and clutching their beer.

"It's customary to execute prisoners in the morning," I said. "That way you have the rest of the day for shopping."

"In another hour these blokes will be too drunk to file their stories."

I liked the idea of CNN and BBC reporters, black bags under their eyes, yellowish, washed out complexions, slurring their vowels on air, giggling uncontrollably as the anchor in Atlanta or London asked about the details of the Lady's release, what it meant for the democracy movement and regional stability and, before the entire monologue was finished, their man on the scene was vomiting beer on the shoes of the cameraman.

Hart sat back in his chair. "We may need to go next to Plan B and there is always Plan C," he muttered to himself.

Plan B was finding women and Plan C was finding Ming bowls—after all that was the reason I had brought him along. Deliver the photographs as I had promised, and then get down to the serious business of making some money. It's never too early for Plan B is Hart's family motto, or so he says.

"Think of a weapon system that shoots 350 bullets at one target and only has an 8 percent chance of hitting it," I said.

"What are you talking about?" asked Hart after a minute of reflection.

"Reproduction. Sex. You remember sex, don't you? Remember your family motto that it's never too early for sex."

"What's your point?"

"Sex is inefficient. Every time I get my rocks off, I shoot the equivalent of one third of the population of China. But girlfriend and wife remain unfertilized."

"The planet has six billion fucking people. That's not what I'd call inefficient. If we were any more efficient, the entire planet would have died out thousands of years ago. We wouldn't have been born. We wouldn't be waiting here."

"I asked my girlfriend how many sperm a man shot in one load."

"What did she come up with?"

"Twenty sperm per load. She also thought the human body only had twelve bones." Although she was no intellectual giant, I missed her beauty, supple body and, most of all, her blissful ignorance in the basic facts concerning the human body, science, and art.

One of the journalists, a guy with a definite New York accent, called over to us. He sat at a table behind us. He wore shorts and his knees poked up until they nearly touched his beard. He squatted on a low wooden stool looking like a hired hand off a whaling boat. At the Floating Balls noodle stand, the stools were made from cheap plastic. In this lean-to dump, we sat on solid teak. A mangy dog sprawled under the bearded one's table, sleeping. The lean-to owner walked between our tables, kicking up a small cloud of dust.

"You look familiar," said the journalist, who waited until the owner passed and then pulled his stool over to our table. "Do you work for *Newsweek*?" Up close, I noticed that he kept his beard neatly trimmed, his shorts appeared freshly laundered, but he wore no socks and a pair of old tennis shoes. And he had perfect teeth, as if to announce that his parents had sunk a fortune into making certain that he would always have a winning smile.

"No," said Hart. "We're not journalists."

His smile went sideways, then crooked, tilting into a kind of studied hostility. "You're not journalists? Then what the fuck are you doing here?"

"We're tourists," I said. At first meeting, I never told a stranger that I was an artist and photographer or that my name along with Hart's was on *The Art of Chin Ways*. If he knew about the photographs in my pocket, with usual journalistic ethics, he would have stabbed me in the back with a plastic knife and looted my corpse for them. A huge amount of power lay in non-disclosure of vital information.

"We are civilians," said Hart. He winked at me. Wilkenson had worked undercover and look what happened to him. Hart never divulged that he was a writer. Especially around journalists, as most hacks despised any writer who was spared the daily horror of filing stories against a tight deadline. Writers had the luxury of waiting for inspiration to strike in dusty places.

"And you found this great little dining place in the *Lonely Planet?*"

Hart shook his head and raised his beer to his lips. He refused to acknowledge that an American was capable of irony, treating the question as a genuine inquiry. "As a matter of fact we didn't. My friend and I came to catch a glimpse of the Lady."

The journalist rolled his eyes and broke out into a mad laugh that exposed all of these perfect teeth. "You came to see the Lady? But she's under house arrest. You might have to wait for days, maybe weeks, who knows, it could be years. No one knows."

"We know that. But the generals will let her out. And when they do, we want to see her."

"Why?"

"For the same reason I would have waited to witness the Battle of Little Bighorn. Just to see the expression on Custer's face when the Indians ambushed him and closed in for the kill. He was surrounded; it was just a matter of time before the arrow with his name on it found its mark."

The connection jolted the journalist, who scribbled this quote down on a notepad. "What expression do you think Custer had on his face?"

"It wasn't a Budweiser-moment smile," I said.

"Surprise," said Hart. "Ethnic cleansing was designed by the Americans to kill Indians. They were thought to be primitive, disorganized, and militarily inferior. Army generals were thought to be safe on the field of battle."

"We were inferior to the Australians in Tasmania," I said. "Have you ever heard of a native Tasmanian? No. Because not one survived. That was real cleansing. In America, we played around the edges—more dusting that cleansing."

More notes were scribbled into the notebook. Hart liked giving quotes. It was part of being on the spot. The journalist finally told us that his name was Conley and he lived in Queens. He asked Hart why he thought releasing the Lady would be the Burmese generals' Battle of Little Bighorn.

"I am a non-combatant. I don't take sides. Like the Red Cross, one must maintain neutrality to do one's job properly."

Conley stared at me, his eyes narrowing. "And are you an NGO? Is that your job in Burma?"

I took a sip from the can. I liked his instincts; anyone who had a healthy suspicion about a white man sitting around drinking beer in the morning and labelled that person an NGO had picked up some important knowledge along the way. "I had a fight with my wife."

"Something about cheeseburgers," said Hart. "I wouldn't push him on the matter. He becomes very emotional about cooking."

Conley repeated the word "cooking" several times as if he were learning a new foreign word. As the journalist opened his mouth, Hart put his finger to his lips and shook his head. "It's better to wait and see what happens."

Conley nodded. "If you ask me, I don't think she will be released today. They may wait until tomorrow. Some people likely know. Maybe I know. Maybe you know. It is like a shell game. Under one shell is a coin. But you have to guess and you will probably lose."

"Are you saying we are losers?" I said.

"The word was on the tip of my tongue."

I was grateful to Hart that he knew the boundaries and warned strangers before they tangled with me. Because I could become mean and violent and Hart knew what it took to set me off. And once that happened, what had happened to Custer was nothing. If I punched Conley in the face and the military intelligence came running over to see what was going on, they might search me. They might find the pictures. I clenched, then slowly unclenched my hands, letting the blood slowly drain out of my fingertips.

"My friend is one cheeseburger short of flipping out," said Hart.

Conley looked at his watch. "Gotta run."

Rangoon was filled with rumors about the Lady's release and everyone had a theory about why there had been a delay. The other journalists had begun to drift away into cars and taxis. As the crowd thinned, the guy who had joined our table without invitation picked up his camera bag, scratched his beard, shook his head, smiled with his expensive set of teeth and walked away. Hart knew about the horror story of the three cheeseburger foul-up. He also suspected that if it hadn't been for those three cheeseburgers I wouldn't have likely paid his way to Burma.

18

"Make three cheeseburgers," Saya said, putting her head around the corner.

In our house, I do the cooking and the food shopping. In the morning before I leave the house I ask my wife, "Darling, what would you like to eat tonight?"

As long as it isn't Thai food, I never complain about what she wants me to cook. It had been our mutual choice to live in Thailand. But I had one condition: we don't eat Thai food. It doesn't look or taste like real food, something you happily put in your mouth. Most of it was messy wet noodles or rice swimming in a rich gravy of palm oil, yellowish sauces, green and red peppers, vinegar, and white sugar. The stuff that floats, ball-shaped, soft, or worse, shot through with tiny bones or insect wings. Hamburgers. That was food. You picked up a hamburger with both hands—food that did not remotely look like a severed body part or dog vomit—and when the bread and meat and pickles and mustard and onions and ketchup fell down that long, narrow chute beyond your tongue and finally hit your stomach, you felt full. My wife was twenty-eight years removed from Japan. Enough time to hunger for cheeseburgers rather than dream of eating steaming bowls of rice.

She had given me an order for the three cheeseburgers. Like a good soldier I never questioned an order. When you are married, you understand that whatever you thought your rank was when you were a single civilian, once you enlisted, the first thing you found was that you had been demoted; or, to put it another way, the woman you marry lets you know that whatever the rank you thought that you had, she has exactly two more stars on her uniform. I distinctly remember asking her one last time as I stood in the door putting on my shoes, "Three cheeseburgers, right?" She gave me the thumbs-up and winked. I opened the door and left for the frontlines with two missions to accomplish: sleep with my girlfriend and shop for groceries to make hamburgers.

The key to a world-class cheeseburger is the cheese. You must get the cheese absolutely right. Thailand isn't exactly in the same league as Wisconsin when it comes to finding cheese. But you learn to make do. There was a small cooler with imported cheese in Villa market; I made a special trip for the cheese, crossing Sukhumvit Road and nearly getting knocked down by a bus, then a pickup followed by a motorcycle with a rider whose face was completely obscured by a shiny black tinted Plexiglas helmet. I was dancing in the kitchen. Girlfriend and me indulged in two hours of sex, I hadn't died on Sukhumvit Road and had found the right cheese.

I nursed a big Johnny Black, threw in a couple more ice cubes, topped up the drink, and then flipped the burgers. There's nothing that quite matches the smell of a lean-meat patty grilling as you have the Johnny Black on the back of your tongue. I piled the large serving plate with slices of onion—finely sliced—and thick wedges of tomatoes and crisp pieces of lettuce. I toasted the buns and spread a thin layer of mayo on the inside. Then I flipped the burgers onto the buns. I lined them up on the serving plate and admired my work. There was almost nothing like a perfectly cooked cheeseburger to inspire a raging pride and hunger. This cheeseburger pride was also shared with Saya.

Nui, my girlfriend, would rather have eaten fried grasshoppers than a burger. My wife knows about Nui. She gives me an allowance for Nui every month, which makes it sometimes confusing as to whether Nui is on my payroll or my wife's. We have no secrets: Saya and me made a pact not to lie to each other. Most of the time the agreement works. Like all treaties and alliances, it is human nature for one side to test the outer frontiers of truth. I set the serving plate on a tray, taking care to see that napkins were properly folded—white cloth napkins and not the paper kind—and walked into the dining room wearing a big shit-eating grin. I had a towel draped over my shoulder. Saya's brown eyes grew large as she saw the cheeseburgers. Eyes dilate for sex, drugs and cheeseburgers. I got off on making her eyes dilate, the salvia rising in the back of her mouth. She was like a female wolf waiting at the lair for the alpha male to bring home the kill. I set the plate in front of her and watched the steam drift up from the burgers. I walked around to my seat and sat down. I was so happy and I thought if I was going to die it would be in about five minutes, the amount of time it would take me to eat my cheeseburger.

She helped herself to one of the cheeseburgers and put another on a plate, which she handed to the houseboy. That left my cheeseburger, right? No, wrong. She lifted the last cheeseburger onto another plate and our new assistant houseboy took it out of her hand faster than a magician doing a card trick. At that instant, a sense of panic registered. She had lifted the final cheeseburger—my cheeseburger—and given it away. It all happened so fast, as if while I had been in the kitchen the entire distribution had been pre-planned. She picked up her cheeseburger and just as she sunk her teeth into it I stood up from the table and clapped my hands. I had everyone's attention. The houseboy and assistant houseboy, sensing their food was at risk, immediately stuffed their mouths. This was the point of no return.

"Where's my cheeseburger?" I asked.

Saya chewed what was in her mouth and then said, "Why didn't you make one for yourself?"

"But you said 'make three cheeseburgers.' I thought that when you said three, you meant only three, including my cheeseburger."

She took another bite. Nothing was getting between her and the burger.

"What do you mean, it included yours?" She stopped chewing long enough to see my face growing a shade of red that suggested the situation was spinning out of control. She knew how emotional I could become over food.

"I did what you told me. You said 'make three cheeseburgers.' I made *three* cheeseburgers." I held up three fingers as if that made any difference.

Didn't she know my purpose in the marriage was to take orders without ever questioning my superior? What kind of commanding officer had I married? Three decades into the marriage the command and control structure still required fine-tuning. Where did the operational manual say that an enlisted man had the authority to convert the ordered number of three into the new number of four? Saya said she just assumed that I could figure that much out. Her assumption had cost me my dinner. "You should have thought to make another one."

"I only bought enough stuff to make three. If you had said four, I would have bought more stuff."

"It's not my fault."

The next thing my hand made this involuntarily swift, graceful, awful movement, removing the towel from my shoulder and flinging it across the room. It hit her jaw high and she started crying. Tears spilling down her cheeks, burger juice running out of her mouth. The houseboy and assistant houseboy watched as they ate their cheeseburgers, watching the mistress of the house dissolve into tears. It was like early evening Thai TV.

"You hit me," she sobbed. "You hit me."

I ran over and knelt beside her. "I threw a towel at you."

"It hit me."

"I was angry. I didn't get my cheeseburger. Baby, you know how much I was looking forward to that cheeseburger? You have no idea."

In *The Art of Chin Ways* there is a passage describing how in Chin villages either slaves or wives did the cooking. The Chin—the men that is—couldn't stop laughing when I stormed into what they called a kitchen (which was really nothing but a lean-to and open pit to throw scraps of garbage) and started cutting up a chicken. I grilled the chicken with some onions and garlic. The Chin had never eaten grilled chicken. They boiled chicken until it was tough enough to upholster furniture. Did my wife have any idea how lucky she was not to be a Chin wife? The question couldn't erase the guilt I felt. This was, after all, my wife, and what I had done was wrong. In a split second I had done something I regretted. A few months earlier a university lecturer had been given community service after an argument between him and his wife escalated to violence; he hit her, and she died in hospital. I ran across the room and hugged my wife but her body was rigid, unmoving. When she pushed me away I made no attempt to resist. I tipped over on my side, and lay there for what seemed like a very long time. By the time I opened my eyes, the room was empty and dark. I dragged myself off to bed. Saya lay on her side with her back turned towards me. I could tell that she wasn't asleep, and I knew she didn't want to talk. She had been waiting, wondering when I would come to bed. I quietly undressed, slipped under the sheet, and lay my head on the pillow.

"I'm going back to Burma," I said.

There was no reply but I hadn't expected one.

"I am sorry," I said. "It is a good time to pick up some Ming pieces. And I could always deliver Kazuo's pictures like I promised his father."

I thought if I could gently lead her back to see that I could do the right thing at least sometimes, she might forgive me. From her breathing I could tell she had already drifted into sleep. I was left lying in the dark unforgiven. She would have another one of her nightmares. Two days from now she would sit across the dining room table and tell me how she dreamt about Kazuo coming back from the grave with a Samurai sword and hacking off my left hand, then my right arm, blood spurting everywhere, but I didn't die. And Kazuo, crazed in the way of zombies, couldn't stop himself from cutting off other pieces. She had had this dream before. Saya built upon this dream and she knew how terrified I was of nightmares. I begged her not to tell me about them.

By going to Burma, I wouldn't have to listen to Saya's nightmare and, besides, it seemed the possibility of the Lady being released was real. If I returned Kazuo's photographs like I promised, he would have no reason to come back from the dead with a Samurai sword and rearrange my limbs. There were other benefits. If I got out of town, then I could forget about domestic chores, cooking, girlfriend, and the house full of servants who ate grasshoppers, and water bugs, and about when three cheeseburgers were sometimes four. Also, I wanted to buy Ming bowls. There was profit in antiques. I knew this. So did Aye Thit, and I wanted to help his family. But I had another reason and it had to with finding Kazuo's camera and developing the film. Everyone said that I had already done more than anyone would have expected. Perhaps tracking down the owner was an act beyond what I expected of myself. I couldn't get out of my mind that these weren't just any photos. I suffered the delusion that the photographs deserved a final resting place in Burma. I thought a set of photographs might mean something to the Lady. And I suffered from the vanity that the Lady would welcome my mission in the same powerful way that Akira Takeda had done. I felt a sense of duty as I lay in the dark with an empty stomach next to my wife. Akira Takeda had given me all that money. This was a sign that my mission wasn't over, that it had just started.

Someone said that after too many beers and too many excuses, the real reason always comes last. I intended to do whatever I had to in order to find the girl in the photograph. I lay in the darkness, listening to Saya breathe through her mouth; she was no more than a few inches away, but she could just as well have been in another universe. Half an hour later, I rolled out of bed, switched on the computer, logged-on to Amazon, and typed in Sloan Walcott, then checked the Amazon ranking for *The Art of Chin Ways*, needing a little reassurance after the ordeal over the cheeseburgers—only to find that the ranking had slumped to 312,784. The ranking, like my karma, was in a freefall. It wasn't the book but Sloan Walcott who was standing 312,784th from the head of the line. I knew that until I found the girl I would keep on falling and falling, passport down cracks, book rankings in the void, cheeseburgers in the bellies of servants.

19

I kept all of Kazuo's photos in the sequence in which he had shot them. Maintaining the precise order was the only way I knew to preserve a sense of order and stability in his record. Like a movie storyboard, the ordering of the shots was as important as any single shot standing alone. You learned a great deal studying the images as they unfolded to the photographer, what he chose to record. Akira Takeda had all but ordered me to destroy the photo of the girl. He couldn't provide a good reason why this photo was to be erased from the record. I tried to make him understand my mania for keeping the record straight. I'd told him that my intention had been to preserve and evaluate Kazuo's timing, and to puzzle out of the shots whether prologue and denouement ran from front to back, or back to front. The linear time line was the way of teasing out the answer. But there were many other possibilities. His eyes grew cold and his face stern. "You must not think too much about this. It is best that photo is never seen." This only made me more determined to unlock the mystery. I pored over the photos for days. There appeared to be a lack of continuity in the shots. In the first picture, the Lady was outside. There was a garden behind her. She stood next to officials dressed in *longyis*. There were photographs of the Lady in the car with the bullet-like hole through the rearview window. Photos of the young thugs on the road, slingshots pulled back. All of these photographs ended with the shot of the seductively dressed girl on the old-fashioned Victorian chaise longue. I labeled each photograph with a number, and wrote a short description of the content. I lined them up in rows of four that made four complete rows and a fifth row with only three photographs. I rearranged the photos in rows of three, and then five, and six, but there was always an odd row at the end that destroyed the symmetry. I memorized each photograph. I dreamt about those photos. I closed my eyes and tried to imagine as a photographer what was in Kazuo's head when he snapped each one. It wasn't difficult to calculate his angle or distance but it was impossible to decide why he had made the choices he had. For example, it bothered me that he hadn't taken more photos of the attack on the Lady's car. He had all the film he needed to do so. I would have gone through five rolls of film. I wouldn't have stopped until I had two dozen reaction shots of the Lady, a dozen different angles of the hole in the rearview window, dozens more of the thugs in the street. I would have run around, snapping shot after shot, chasing down bystanders to get their photograph, as well as those of the cops who stood idly by doing nothing, watching, pretending not to see. I would have nailed it all on film.

Aye Thit had no answer when I fired off all these questions. Why had he stopped shooting the evidence of the violence, of the people involved in committing the acts of violence? I had a good idea why he had stopped. Kazuo's photographs disturbed Aye Thit greatly as well. They were evidence that he didn't want found on his person. Especially upsetting to him were the two shots of the thugs with the slingshots. Possessing such a photograph would mean a prison term if you were Burmese and a ticket out of the country if you were a foreigner. From the time I first showed him the photo, Aye Thit had time to form an opinion about the girl in the kimono. He had seen many such girls. Taking a photograph of a prostitute wasn't something he thought was a wise thing to do. "How do you know she's a prostitute?" I asked. Aye Thit shrugged his shoulders, "Girls who sell their bodies dress like this," he said. "And she has a tattoo."

I looked at the photo, trying to see what Aye Thit saw, and disagreed. "That girl's an angel, an angel, I am telling you, an angel." I laughed and put an arm around his shoulder. "I know a hooker. This girl ain't for sale."

Aye Thit understood what set me off, and once that happened, I had this tendency—from childhood—of repeating myself, repeating myself, somehow repeating myself even though I knew I was doing it and wanted to stop but couldn't. What would happen if you lost the camera, and got killed in a freak road accident, leaving behind such an image for your relatives to ponder? What had happened in the gap between shot number eighteen of the hole in the rearview window of the Lady's car and that of the girl? What had Kazuo done in the interval, where had he gone, did he go alone or had a wolf pack of other Japanese journalists trailed along with him? Questions and more questions. Had the girl in the photograph finished a session of sexual intercourse, and if so, was it with Kazuo or had he gone into a room, found her in that position and taken the photo? Why just one photograph? A woman with that kind of beauty you would use three, four rolls of film. It might have been some sexual role-playing fantasy. Or had he taken the photograph because he had some special feeling for the girl? Why was it on the same roll of film that had recorded an important political act of violence? I had all these unanswered questions in my head. Opening another beer, lighting another fat one—nothing brought me any closer to enlightenment.

After Aye Thit looked at the girl he was convinced was a whore, Hart said that he knew a doctor who specialized in examining tattoos of people and that he might be able to tell me something about the girl from her tattoo.

I said, "I want to meet this man."

THE CHIN, TATTOOS
AND
THE DRUG ELIMINATION MUSEUM

20

Since we'd given up waiting for the Lady until the next day, Hart suggested that we visit what I insisted on calling the anti-drug museum (the official name was the Drug Elimination Museum) and find the glass case with the clipping of the article Aye Thit's father had written years ago when his newspaper was still being published, read, and admired; a time when a man could write what was in his mind and heart. The timing was right. I had finished my third beer and Hart had finished describing General Custer as a thirty-something looking man with wild, scruffy dishwater-brown hair, his eyes too close together, thin, cruel lips, a narrow mouth, and a crooked potato nose. That was before he took an arrow or two and died in the Badlands of South Dakota.

Hart pulled a thick wad of kyat from his pocket—my money advanced for his expenses—and paid for the beers. "Time to study the bad effects of drugs."

Aye Thit had his heart set on going to the museum. The idea seemed like a colossal waste of time or even worse a trap or sting operation. No one I knew had ever gone to a museum in Rangoon. The government didn't have enough money for schools, roads, buses, airports, and hospitals—which was the short list. Spending a chunk of dough on a museum about drugs seemed totally off-the-wall. The Burmese had electricity for two hours a day and hardly enough money for food—these people needed a museum like a hole in the head.

"Man, why do you want to go to a museum? Do you really want to see the article that Aye Thit's father wrote?"

"I want to see the social realism of the murals," said Hart.

That had my attention—being an artist, I wouldn't mind seeing some murals to break up the day. "What kind of murals?"

"The way Aye Thit explained them, think of revolutionary art funded by reactionaries like Stalin and Mao."

"The kind of art that looks best when you're loaded."

In the back of the car, I lit a fat one, took a long drag, passed it to Hart, who sucked hard on the end.

"Aye Thit, we decided to have a look at that article your father wrote," I said.

Aye Thit turned around in his seat. I had never seen a bigger smile. He gave the driver directions to the museum in Burmese. We sat in the back and enjoyed our smoke.

The driver wore a shirt with the name of an upcountry law school printed on the front. A lawyer behind the wheel terrified me. He shifted the old car into gear and the engine groaned as we headed up the hill. Hart relit the fat one and inhaled as the driver swung into the narrow winding road, forcing one car, then a second one off the road. Near the crest of the steep hill, four people in flip-flop sandals and *longyis* pushed a pickup filled with packs of ice up the incline. Water splashed on the pushers' legs and feet as they struggled to keep the pickup from rolling back down the hill. The driver swung past the pickup without looking, gunning his car. Cars and trucks were always running out of gas on hills and passengers would climb out and put their shoulder to the tailgate, keeping the vehicle moving. Being a passenger in a car on the streets of Rangoon was nearly as dangerous as smuggling car batteries and shirts from China.

The steering wheel was on the right-hand side; people drove on the right hand-side of the road, so that overtaking inevitably risked a fatal collision as the driver pulled into the on-coming lane to see if anyone was on-coming or else delegated the duty to the person riding shotgun, who would scream and wave to pull back. Head-on collision or a clear road ahead were the main alternatives. And the generals had authorized building an entire museum dedicated to the dangers of drugs when just driving across Rangoon to the museum was five times more likely to get you killed. How had this paradox happened? No one knew for sure. Some said Ne Win had a dream in which an angel whispered that for him to remain safe, he should move to the right. The next morning he gave an order, and with no warning all the cars in Burma shifted from driving on the left to driving on the right. None of this squared with how Freud might have interpreted the angel and the message. Switch from using your left hand to your right hand when cutting into a piece of steak—that would have made as much sense—and would have been far less dangerous. Others said it wasn't an angel in a dream but a fortuneteller who had warned Ne Win to beware of those moving on the left. He interpreted that to mean everyone should drive on the right; walk, think, drink, and God knows what else on the right. Or he may have flipped a coin, deciding heads was left and tails was right. Or a monkey fart blew in through the bedroom window on the left side of the room. Why he issued this order—or even if it was his order—was the cause of endless debates in cafes and markets.

The driver knew exactly the road to take and suddenly he turned into a wide, newly poured driveway with a guardhouse on the side. Two young uniformed security guards in spit-polished combat boots stopped us. The driver rolled down the window. Hart leaned forward and spoke to the guard, "We want to see your museum. My friend is an artist. He has come all the way from Florida to study your murals." We left out the part about Aye Thit's father being an editor of a defunct newspaper and the article written by his father which apparently was a prime feature of the museum.

"I don't think they understand," said Aye Thit, who spoke to them in Burmese. A moment later the guards waved us through. The guards stared at Hart and me, looking over the condition of the car. In their training, there must have been some exercise drilled into them about going to code ten red, full-scale military alert, in the event that Europeans showed up at the guardhouse. What, exactly did we want? Who were we with? Who had sent us? This was to get into a museum. A moment later, they were all smiles.

"Hey, man, what did you tell them?" I asked.

"I said you pay cash in American dollars," said Aye Thit.

This was another explanation of how Moses parted the Red Sea. Later, Aye Thit told us that we were the first foreigners to arrive at the Drug Elimination Museum. What a privilege to be part of history.

The Drug Elimination Museum had a gabled apple-green roof and a canopy that extended over an archway, giving a sense of grandeur to the front entrance. It was as if the designer had blended the basic plan of the average five-star hotel in Asia with Lenin's mausoleum. The grills on the rows of tiny windows was a nice touch, reminding the visitor that a museum could with very little effort be made to look like a high-security prison. The three-story structure, immense in size, nestled inside a vast garden of green grass. A fountain shot water high in the air. Hart thought it looked like a cheesy clubhouse of an upcountry private members' golf club house. As an artist, I can testify that, in my experience, dictators love Greek columns and Roman baths and arches. But in this case, they had broken with tradition and decided they wanted something more modern for the grounds. Some consultant sold them on a design that was more like a theme park but had eliminated the usual rides, popcorn, and gift shops with stuffed animals, T-shirts, and logos stamped on ashtrays and umbrellas. Inside, we paid American dollars for admission. The sign said three dollars for foreigners and five dollars if you wanted to take pictures. Hart paid in the funny-money script denominated in dollars which we had bought at the airport.

The big fat one had put us in the right state of mind. There was no way anyone could have walked down the first hallway straight and sober.

"It says that there will be no more drugs in Burma after 2014," said Hart, reading from the brochure. A schedule of elimination region by region followed.

"So stock up while supplies last," I said. "It should say that, it should say that. What I am saying is it should say that."

"And the Chin state is in the third five-year plan," said Hart, looking up from the brochure.

"Ain't no way the Chin are going to go along with that plan."

"That's what the brochure says," said Hart.

I read in the brochure—it was in English, Thai and Burmese—that the Chin had until 2010 before someone showed up and told them to grow corn and beans and pull out their poppy plants. Fat chance,

I thought. No one in Rangoon would get that message to the Chin and if they did, the Chin would smile and keep on hoeing the soil around their poppy plants.

We didn't have to go far before we found the first twenty-foot wall mural. Local artists had been pressed into painting twenty-foot murals of generals and politicians looking just like Hart said: Soviet-style art of the 1930s. The vanguard always had big muscles, thick necks, trimmed hair, friendly smiles and a pistol strapped to their belts. Aye Thit said that these murals covered every wall on all three floors of the museum, a kind of third-world unpaid-for political advertisement of honor, good deeds, and loyalty to the people.

"Where did they get the money to build this place?"

No one really knew. The rumor I liked best came from Aye Thit. He had heard that a legendary drug dealer had funded the anti-drug museum, a half-Chinese, half-Shan man who had started off holding the reigns of the horse ridden by the mother of all warlords whose name was Olive. A young, ambitious man, he looked after the horse and Olive's cigarettes and lighter, and made certain she had a smoke whenever the fancy struck her. From Olive's servant to the patron of the huge shopping mall-like edifice. Having established his wealth, he had decided to erect this building to prove to the world (read America) his commitment to eliminating drugs—meaning if you are pro-elimination of drugs, how could you be a drug dealer? He had come a long way from lighting Olive's cigarettes in the Shan hills. Whether the funding story was true was like trying to find out why one morning the Burmese were ordered to switch to driving on the right side of the road. There was no way of confirming by whom or how the museum was financed.

Murals were only part of the grand visual experience. Walking down the long corridors, we passed exhibits erected on raised platforms like a stage in a theatre. Each exhibit displayed a part of the story, a variation on the theme of why drugs were evil and harmful, leading to the road to hell. Hart leaned up against the first exhibit; it was life-sized with the action frozen in space and time. The curator must have got a deal on the mannequins. In front center, three mannequins sat on a sofa. One was a foreigner who had a foul, long, ratty brownish wig that sat crooked on his head.

He sat with unfocused marble eyes between two overweight man-nequin waitresses in cocktail dresses. The women didn't look like nightclub girls; these were thick hipped, with bloated wrists and ankles that made them candidates for big-girl fashion departments. Around their necks hung matching pearl necklaces, each pearl the size of a walnut. Their nationality was indeterminate. They might have been Asian, they might have been from Panama or Iceland or Poland. Maybe that was the message of what drugs were supposed to do; strip away your identity and replace it with grotesque jewelry and heavy legs and arms and a fat ass.

"You ever see a fat mannequin before?" I asked Hart.

"In big-women clothing stores. What I want to know is what horror house sold them the wigs." he said.

"I am glad we smoked a fat one," I said.

Hart continued to stare at the mannequin who played the role of the dissolute, ferret-faced foreigner. I could tell when Hart was happy. I snapped a photo of Hart smiling in front of the three mannequins frozen snapshot-like on the sofa. We both had large questions about the lifestyle depicted in the scene but the brochure offered no explanations. They didn't look desperate or crazed or about to go into a drug-induced seizure. Given the life on the street, the models didn't look like they had it all that bad.

Near the sofa, another mannequin held an empty plate—pills, poppers, weed, powder had vanished without a trace—smiling into middle distance at this mystery of invisible drugs. A band played in the background—except they were mannequins and there was no music—and each mannequin wore a matching brown longhaired wig. So you had to imagine invisible drugs and loud testosterone driven rock 'n roll rolling out of the guitar and drums. It wasn't clear if it was drugs or a low-fat diet that accounted for the thin arms and necks on the band-member mannequins. People off the street would have guessed illness or starvation. They would stay with the stuff they knew. The exhibit demonstrated the flawless connection between the evilness of skinny boy bands juiced on massive doses of green and red pills, empty plates, and a single foreigner customer with a pinched face and bad hair. The women were as sexy as cadavers who needed drugs to cure whatever gland problem had caused them to bloat out.

"A handful of amphetamines would do the band a world of good," said Hart.

"I want to go to that bar, man. I want to go to that bar," I said.

"You're repeating yourself."

"I know I repeat myself. I know I . . ."

The empty plate caught my attention. Had it been piled with magic mushrooms and the greedy foreigner had eaten them all?

The next exhibit was a village. The scale was slightly off. Dark clouds and vultures and hills painted on the walls brought home the hard-times message. All of the villager mannequins had emaciated, polished, plastic stress-free faces. They were from the same batch of mannequins that had been used for the boy band, only these mannequins wore farmer clothes—not so much the style found on a Salvation Army clothes rack but more like something pulled out of a house cleaner's rag bag. Shadows had been painted on the faces to give the hint that their metabolism wasn't working well. They were life-sized skeletal figures with bony, shiny hands and wretched mouths opened as if crying out in great pain. In the far corner of the exhibit lay a bunch of rags with a decapitated mannequin's head above what were supposed to be the shoulders.

"Great corpse," said Hart.

It was like Halloween with the painted vultures circling above and wild dogs with fake bloody snouts nuzzling the corpse.

"The dogs are eating the body," I said.

"Sniffer dogs," said Hart.

"Do you see any drugs? I don't see any drugs. Dogs. I see the dogs."

"You're supposed to imagine the drugs."

"That's why people take drugs, to imagine."

"They don't look like sniffer dogs. Sniffer dogs don't eat dead people."

"That only proves they are badly trained."

Aye Thit followed patiently behind, making no attempt to guide us to his father's exhibit. No doubt he wanted us to experience the full impact of the exhibits before we could put this piece of journalism into perspective.

Down another hallway we found the replica of a mountain-top tea plantation. This vast exhibit took up a quarter of an acre of floor space. A great deal of effort had gone into positioning a mannequin dressed as farmer who was walking behind a water buffalo which was hooked to a plow. The anatomically correct farmer had an office worker's hands and fingernails. Being a drug farmer didn't look like it was taking much of a toll. Water buffalo and farmer stood suspended in the middle of a half-dozen furrows of rocky soil. Nothing known to man could have grown in the dry, hard soil. Except maybe poppies, driving home the point: if you have worthless soil and can't grow anything and want to keep your nails in perfect condition, why not try your luck with poppy plants?

Hart said, "There must be four tons of dirt on the floor."

Behind the mannequin farmer caught in suspended animation a half-foot from the farting end of a water buffalo, a scaled down mountain rose from the floor.

"Where are the drugs?" I asked. "I don't see any drugs. I want to see the drugs."

I looked at the base of the mountain and along the four tons of dirt for signs explaining about drugs. Not one arrow pointing to the drugs. Hart found a small pathway cut along the side of the mountain. The exhibit could have been a mock-up real estate site the Thais used during the boom days of the early 1990s. This exhibit wasn't for urban condos but looked more like someone was pitching deals to warlords who wanted a safe rural hideaway.

"Over here," said Hart. He had walked ahead.

Hart read a small sign.

"How high is that mountain?" Hart asked.

As an artist, I have a good sense of distance, height and shape. "Twenty feet max," I said.

"The sign says that mountain is 7,575 feet."

"Get out of here," I said. Then I read the sign.

"At least we've got the scale now. One equals about 380."

"In that case, the stuff is grown by giants." I looked back and forth from the tea plantation to the farmer and the water buffalo.

"The exhibit proves that drugs alter your perception of scale," said Hart.

"You could be a tour guide."

Hart, among other things, was a math genius. He had worked this out in his head after smoking a fat one. He was a complete genius.

On the side of the mountain were tiny poppy flowers. Another sign planted at the base of the mountain read: poppy plants.

Only there was one flaw in Hart's conclusion. Every exhibit had its own scale. We discovered this at the clandestine drug lab exhibit. The Tamadaws had seized the lab. Even the mannequins were one-fourth scale so they looked like tiny mythical figures. Hobbits from the Lord of the Rings doing chemical wash down in tiny tubs on the outskirts of Hobbitville. On the grounds of the exhibit were miniature barrels, chemical troughs, and trucks. There wasn't a kid alive who, after crawling inside that exhibit, wouldn't have been moving those trucks around and making engine noises with their tongues pressing against the roof of their mouths.

"Drugs make you small," said Hart. "That's the message. Smoke weed or pop a benny and you shrink."

"In the bar everyone was big and fat," I said.

"That's up the chain. The consumption level is different from the scale of disaster that happens to farmers and processors. Besides if all you can get are Russian-made mannequins, there are bound to be some gaps. What this exhibit tells me is that at the production level, it is the little people who are producing the shit," said Hart. "That's why they are so hard to find and why the Americans shouldn't be leaning on the Burmese about drug production. Look at them, they can hide in a crack in the wall. You can never find them."

Hart had just finished when we stopped at the exhibit of the clandestine field lab, which still looked to be under construction. A sign announced: Myanmar US Co-operation on Opium Suppression. On the platform Burmese soldier and civilian mannequins looked like scarecrows in the field. The civilians in freshly pressed trousers were taking notes.

"Hart, we are back to life size."

"That's because they are government officials. If you work for the government, then you can never be confused with the little people who process the drugs. The producers are smaller than midgets. You need special equipment to find them."

"What's with him?" I asked, pointing at a mannequin who had his arms folded back and the fingers of each hand curved to form a matching set of "O"s as if the ski poles had been removed. The mannequins' legs were slightly bent at the knee. The exhibit curator had found a batch of mannequins manufactured to simulate skiing rough terrain and planted them into open upcountry opium fields.

"What's this supposed to mean?"

"The reason Burma can't stop the drug production is that the Americans keep sending ski instructors without any equipment to find the little people who are hiding in the mountains where it never snows."

"Or corruption on the acquisition side," I said.

"Or maybe there was a one-time grant from a Canadian agency, and they could only use it to buy mannequins from Vancouver," said Hart. He had a sister who lived on English Bay. The exhibit, for a split second, made him miss her.

Painted on the wall behind the field were more mountains, valleys, and fields. Dreamy paintings like a landscape from *Lost Horizon*. The story according to Hart was this. A crop substitution program run by foreign ski instructors and the Burmese army had about as much chance of succeeding as the Burmese in a downhill skiing Olympic competition. The sign on the wall said Lonh Tanareas, Kokant region.

No sooner had we climbed up to the second floor, than Aye Thit motioned for us to follow him. He had been patient as Hart had explained to him the deeper meaning of many of the first floor exhibits. Now it was his turn to do some explaining. He hurried ahead to a wall display. His face beamed with pride as he stood in front of the article his father had written. Hart and I read the article. It was about the seizure of a shipment of drugs from Chinese warlords. There was part of a longer story about a brave battle and glory in victory against the Chinese. Hart nodded as he read and gave Aye Thit the thumbs up. "A very good article," Hart said.

"You think so?" Aye Thit asked.

"When was his newspaper closed down?" I asked.

"One month later." There was heaviness in his voice, the gloom brought on by an old memory. The pride of authorship unravelled as Aye Thit came back to the reality that his father had been forced out of the newspaper business. And yet that did not stop the authorities from shamelessly using his father's article. There had been nothing in the article that would have hinted that the father was a radical or critical of the government. Instead the article celebrated the success of the army on the battlefield. Nothing in the article gave a hint as to what had caused his downfall or, if the offending article had come first, the description of the glories of the army hadn't been enough to rescue him or his newspaper from oblivion. All that remained on public display showing that his father and his newspaper had ever existed was this single article.

Aye Thit wiped a tear from his eye. His family had nothing but a history of tears. I put an arm around his shoulder and gave him a hug, "It was a wonderful article, Aye Thit. You have every right to be proud of your dad."

With my arm around Aye Thit, I looked up to find the corridor filled with an entire village of Chin. In the absence of drugs, their surprise appearance was the next best thing to lift the feeling of despair. Aye Thit started to laugh as one of the Chin ran over and shook his hand. Seeing the Chin was a homecoming.

21

A small, distant masculine voice echoed down the marble corridor. The voice was familiar, like a song in a half-remembered dream; a chord struck but with no memory of the instrument striking it. "Popcorn," the voice called from the next exhibit. Then the voice grew much louder: "Popcorn." I looked at Hart, his head turned like a hunter trying to decide which direction the geese are flying in.

"Hey, I know that guy, I know him," I said.

"Salai Lian Uk." Hart had a knack for languages. "That's his name."

Getting the name right with the Chin was a major accomplishment for a foreigner. When they were drunk even they could fumble with the right form of address. *Pa, Ku, Khwe, Ko*—but my tongue slipped like a worn-out fan belt, spitting out weird words that were sometimes English and sometimes of an unknown language—*moo, Jew, helicopter blades*. The Chin would stare with the eyes of an amazed child, wondering how the world had ever produced such strange people. They gave me a break with all these complicated rules about names, and I never learned when or where or with whom to plug in the right word. I would just say *you*, "*you* know who *you* are. No need for me to tell *you*." Hart had mastered the structure and rules of their language and this made him even more freakish than an outsider who was clueless.

"Salai Lian Uk," I said, as if I had also remembered his name. At first, I had called him *Ako* or older brother. Salai Lian Uk had smiled. He must have seen right through me as if I was simply repeating parrot-like what Hart had said.

"I thought he was dead," said Hart under his breath. "Wasn't he killed in a boating accident?"

"That was his mother's younger brother. The one I called *Oolay*." I had a knack for Chin words describing relationship. Elder brother, elder sister, uncle, aunt, words in the Chin language somehow stayed with me. I took comfort in knowing who was related and how the families had a pecking order that depended on whether you were senior or junior, male or female. Like in Thailand, everyone came under the tent of one big extended family.

Almost ten years had passed since Salai Lian Uk had eaten the popcorn I had made, washing it down with a gourd and a half of *kongye*. His hands were small and his fingers long and delicate like the farmer mannequin on the first floor. He had used his fingers to hold a single popcorn kernel, bringing it close to his face, rotating it in the light. I told him to eat it. I showed him by throwing a white lotus-shaped piece of popcorn in my mouth, sucking it until it stuck to the roof of my mouth. I opened my mouth to show him and before I could close it, he reached in and pulled it out on the end of his finger. No surprise reaction passed his face as he examined it once again, squatting in the dirt, then put the wet, sucked-on piece of popcorn in his mouth, chewed and swallowed. He put his hand in the bowl and ate until he finished it all. That was his first experience with popcorn. After eating the huge bowl of popcorn, he drank great quantities of rice whisky, what the Chin called *kongye*. He let out a loud belch and smiled.

Then something strange happened. He ate a handful of dirt. A rich heavy loam of earth. He dropped down on his knees, scratched in the ground and scooping up a handful of dirt, put it in his mouth before taking another hit from the gourd. I stared at him and he returned a smile with bits of dirt clinging to his lips. I hadn't ever seen anyone so drunk that they ate dirt. In the Chin state there were many unusual customs and eating dirt was just one of them. Salai Lian Uk assured me that he didn't usually eat dirt along with popcorn. He had never eaten popcorn until that day. He had never heard of or seen popcorn. I had challenged him, saying no one was so remote that they had never heard of popcorn. This was impossible. He ate the dirt because he wanted to demonstrate that he wasn't lying. It helped that he had access to large amounts of *kongye.* I had paid for a half dozen gourds. He drank the whisky through a bamboo straw that had been used to carefully puncture through the skin and flesh of the gourd. Salai Lian Uk explained how the Chin chomped down on a clod of damp earth to swear an oath. His breath smelled of fresh loam. He rinsed his mouth in the whisky and swallowed hard two or three times before the grit from his teeth washed away.

During the time Hart and I lived with the Chin, studying them, photographing them, I showed Salai Lian Uk how to make popcorn and he taught me how to make gunpowder from pig shit and beans. Not just any kind of gunpowder but a charge that when loaded into a musket had enough velocity to blast a slug four hundred yards straight through the eye of an enemy. Salai Lian Uk's gunpowder was far better than anything one could buy in the shops. As he worked, I noticed that on the back of his left hand was a large purple birthmark shaped like a childlike drawing of Italy. The shaman said he had been born outside the world and had come back into this life to make amends for a wrong committed in his last life. The usual upcountry excuse to get a woman into bed. He had committed a crime serious enough to be born with such a mark. He told me this story as he made gunpowder.

The last time I had seen Salai Lian Uk, we were at 2,500 feet above sea level in an alluvial valley west of Tipperah, and around us the forest spread out to the coast of Chittagong. The Chin lived in the region between the Chindwin and the Indian border. A few scattered villages spread along the plains between the Chindwin and Irrawaddy rivers. To the north was Assam and Manipur and to the south Arakan. Aye Thit was from Arakan. Hart had written this description in our book. I memorized it and used it whenever I wanted to get a woman into bed. To be perfectly honest (and I would eat dirt and swear an oath), I am directionally challenged. When someone tells me go north for a block then turn east and look for the small brick shop on the west side of the street, I am lost. I have no clue about how to use the stars to find north. I had an uncle in Ukiah who had a compass in his head. He was never lost. He instinctively knew directions like a flock of migratory birds. I didn't inherit this trait. I developed my own system: north was always the direction I was walking. Don't talk to me about walking west or east—put a gun to my head and tell me to point west. It would be better, more humane, just to pull the trigger and have done with blowing out my brains. Salai Lian Uk was more like my uncle who lived in Ukiah and grew weed and more like Hart. Salai Lian Uk knew directions. He didn't need stars or the moon to tell him if he walking north or south. It was one of those things that he just knew. The first time I met Salai Lian Uk, he was drunk and squatting in front of a tub where he was filtering nitrates from a thick crust of pig shit. He was unsteady on his feet and plopped down just as we came around the corner and there was a sound like the air had gone out of him. He had been working more than six hours picking nitrate crystals out of a sieve. It was a slow, time-consuming process. And to pass the time he drank as his slender fingers patiently removed the nitrate crystals like dwarf pieces of popcorn from the sieve. Like the piece he had removed from the roof of my mouth.

Coming across Salai Lian Uk drunk was no surprise; but finding him smashed inside the anti-drug museum in Rangoon was not something I would have laid odds on happening. It was that totally unexpected, random event like a black swan swimming across a still pond. When he saw me his mouth dropped open. He blinked, rubbed his eyes. Then he ran straight toward me, wrapped his arms around my waist and hugged me.

"I love you," he said in English with real feeling.

"Man, and I love you, too, Pa Lian pa," I said. "But if I may ask, what the fuck are you doing in Rangoon, man? And how did you get here? Walk? Or did someone sign you up for one of those forced labor projects?" Then I remembered the only words of English he understood other than "popcorn" were "I love you." He stared at me with a puzzled expression until Hart translated. The smile came back on his face.

"Bus," said Hart, translating Salai Lian Uk's reply.

"I love popcorn," Salai Lian Uk said, beaming. He loved me for my cooking much like my wife did. But, then, he loved pig shit, too.

"He says he can never make popcorn like you," Hart translated.

I had sprinkled barbiturates over the popcorn. That was a trade secret.

114

I remembered that Salai Lian Uk wasn't called Salai Lian Uk; I called him Pa Lian pa. In theory, if you called a Chin by the wrong name it was better you put lots of barbiturates in his popcorn. When Hart and I camped with the Chin, I had cooked gourmet meals including chicken lasagna for Salai Lian Uk's family, using my last fourteen sheets of lasagna and a bottle of chamel sauce. On another occasion I made his family five magic mushroom and mozzarella pizzas topped with thin strips of wild gaur, dried basil, crushed tomatoes and olive oil. The pizzas exhausted my supply of mozzarella. Half of the village wandered around in a hypnotic state for forty-eight hours. Even the shaman admitted that pizza magic ranked with the best of his own powers. I became a pizza legend in the Chin hills. It was the gaur penis, they said. I had unleashed the mystic powers, allowing them to see visions of eternity.

"I told him that Pizza Hut was still considering your wild gaur dick pizza for their menu," said Hart.

What had stuck in Hart's memory was the massive gaur dick severed by the villagers after they had speared the guar. What had stayed in Salai Lian Uk's mind was the high he got from the popcorn laced with barbiturates. Gaur dick was, in a matter of speaking, old hat to the Chin.

"Very good, very good. I am happy about that, man. How did you get here? I can't believe it is you. Can you believe this, Hart?"

Hart spoke to Salai Lian Uk in one of the Chin dialects and Salai Lian Uk nodded and backed away.

"What did you say to him?"

"I asked him if he remembered our last feast together. The Chin had killed a wild gaur. It must have been six foot high at the shoulder. You showed them how to make sausages. And then I told him that you had come to Rangoon to teach the Lady how to make sausages and popcorn. And he said it would be better to teach her how to make gunpowder."

That was Salai Lian Uk's attitude. Like his ancestors, he had no use for the Burmese except as slaves and kidnap targets for ransom.

Years before, around a fire at night, Salai Lian Uk had rambled about all kinds of things—dreams, omens, old-slights, raiding parties, hunting parties, kidnappings, marriages, sackings, divorces, ransoms, murders—as the gourd was passed around and everyone drank *kongye*. Times had changed since Hart and me had lived with them in the hills, he explained. Ending up in the museum had started with an advance contingent of the Burmese Army which had arrived in the village just after dawn about a week before. They had come by the river, docked their boats, climbed up the bank, and come looking for supplies. At first, it appeared the soldiers were lost. The officer in charge made it clear they knew exactly where they were. They had come on a mission. Their duty was to assess the allegiance of the villagers. The commander made Salai Lian Uk swear an oath promising never to take up arms against the government. But he didn't eat dirt when he made the oath. As far as he was concerned the oath was worthless. And he was drunk when he made the oath. Salai Lian Uk had committed himself under duress—the soldiers had been heavily armed. The commander believed Salai Lian Uk's village was a threat and as the headman, Salai Lian Uk had one choice. It was to go on an expense-paid trip to visit the Drug Elimination Museum in Rangoon or die. Salai Lian Uk thought about this for about two seconds before deciding that a trip to Rangoon was a better idea.

Soldiers delivered the villagers to government officials, who marched them single file into a half dozen old green buses. No one in the village had any idea what a museum was. They figured it was likely another name for a forced labor program to build roads or dams. Whatever a museum turned out to be, Salai Lian Uk was certain that the Burmese would never stop causing him and his village an endless amount of trouble. All those doubts changed, the perpetually puzzled looks vanished, when the villagers saw Hart and me. Salai Lian Uk no longer dreaded that by the time they reached the third floor, an official would open a door to an execution chamber. A light flashed inside his skull just like it had done after eating that fresh batch of popcorn. Suddenly it became clear why the entire village had been forced over impassable trails, down rivers that had dropped to dangerously low levels, and then loaded like livestock on a bus to Rangoon. He knew why they had been chosen. Hart and me had summoned them. This was neither the right time nor place to set Salai Lian Uk right.

Most of his village—seventy men, women and children—formed a semicircle around an exhibit. Until Salai Lian Uk had broken away from the others, a government official had been lecturing the Chin about birth defects and drug use but the Chin looked like children with a chronic attention deficiency. They pressed up against the exhibits, peering inside large jars with yellowish liquid holding deformed fetuses: pig-eyed babies with snouts rather than noses, a half dozen other large bottles filled with what smelled like cleaning fluid containing abscessed brains, lungs ravaged by TB, and mushy cerebral meningitis brains.

Hart edged closer. "How big is that bottle?"

"They could be a Balthazar or a Nebuchadnezzar," he said. "Definitely some non-standard size of bottle."

"In English, please."

"The bottle holds somewhere between twelve to fifteen liters."

"Why didn't you say so?"

"It's an old family tradition," said Hart. "My grandfather always judged every bottle according to how much wine it held. The Greeks had amphorae that held forty liters. Good vintage wine was laid down in either a magnum, double magnum, jeroboam, methuselah, salmanazar, balthazar, or nebuchadnezzar. Depending, of course, on whether it was Burgundy or Bordeaux."

"That's a lot of vintage dead babies."

"A nebuchadnezzar holds fifteen liters of Bordeaux," said Hart.

"Or three deformed fetuses."

"Something like that."

"I can understand how someone puts a model of a sailing ship in a bottle. But a fetus?"

"Special tools," said Hart. "You wouldn't want to watch."

The exhibit could have been on a fairground; at every turn, the Chin were eyeball-to-eyeball with weird mutations of humanlike creatures with deformed, squashed heads, and twisted, wrecked blown-up internal organs looking like the long abandoned contents of a bachelor's fridge spilling out of long forgotten cartons of Chinese take-out, festering and turning into some other substance no longer recognizable as food, or in this case, faces, brains, lungs, arms, legs—you name any part of the anatomy and any thirteenth century disease engineered by nature to dissolve it—somewhere you could find it floating inside a bottle. What all this human carnage had to do with planting, harvesting, processing and taking poppy plants was left a little on the vague side. The Chin villagers were intrigued, not really perplexed, as they had relatives who had died from some of these diseases. It was simply that they didn't see the point; they looked to Salai Lian Uk for guidance, but he didn't know. When Hart and I appeared, we materialized out of nowhere like saviors, someone they knew and someone who might have some idea what all this meant. Salai Lian Uk, hugging me, saying he loved me, spoke loudly in Chin to anyone who would listen about how I made him popcorn and how he taught me the Chin way to make gunpowder. Except for the contents of a couple of the bottles, nothing in the museum had any connection with the reality of their lives in the hills.

We hadn't seen these people in many years. I wasn't certain whether many of the villagers would remember us. I suspected the Chin women who remembered Hart had lost their bloom, having delivered four or five children. He had been young, handsome, robust and had walked along the river with his shirt tied around his waist, his bare chest with curly blond hair creating whispers and giggles. Hart still looked pretty much like his photograph in *The Art of Chin Ways*. I looked nothing like mine.

The Chin moved like a single force of nature steering a path away from the Burmese uniformed official standing erect in his pressed khaki shirt and trousers. The officer lectured them in front of an exhibit of a couple of large bottles that were supposed to give the appearance of the womb of a drug-addled mother, and inside were terribly deformed fetuses—the full horror of cracked frontal lobes, flippers for hands and feet, and empty black eye sockets. The village girls circled around the bottles, noses pressed against the glass. They spotted us. Salai Lian Uk let out a loud war cry and ran doubled forward like the halfback running ahead in a quarterback sweep. His whooping made the other Chin turn away from the bottles. The government official never looked up and kept on reading from a set script. He had not noticed his audience was no longer listening or if he noticed, their fleeing the scene didn't matter. He was like a robot programmed to deliver a lecture; the delivery itself was his job and it made absolutely no difference to his career prospects, his pension, or his commanding officer, whether the audience bused in from the Chin hills had any interest whatsoever in what he said.

The Chin bolted from the vicinity of the jars full of dead babies, lungs and brains. All at once they organized themselves into small groups, lining up like office workers at noon in front of a Sukhumvit Road ATM machine. Then the Chin villagers slowly walked past each of us, shaking our hands. They smiled. Some of the younger villagers looked shyly away. Most of the women remembered Hart. Up close, I remembered many more of the villagers than I thought was possible. They put me to shame by remembering our names. The glazed, confused, glum villagers had been saved from staring at dead babies and trying to figure out if this was the reason they had been in a bus for two long, dusty days to Rangoon. None of that mattered once they discovered Hart and me. They were happy. Making an unexpected connection with an old friend in a strange place registered with the villagers as an omen.

The Chin were big on omens. If you saw two snakes fucking, that meant you were in for a bad day. The conventional Chin wisdom was, if you saw fornicating snakes, then—don't go back home that night. Don't talk to anyone. Chin men sometimes used this excuse with their wives for staying out all night. Like most omens, there was a practical side to it. Inside the anti-drug museum, for a moment, an entire village of Chin stared at us with the same awe and fear as if they had stumbled upon two snakes fucking. It wasn't all that clear whether they should return to Chin land that evening.

Hart interrogated a few of the village women who were studying their own reflections in a nebuchadnezzar. One combed her hair, another admired her jewelry, while yet another examined her teeth as the lifeless babies with dead eyes stared back. He pieced together that some official in some ministry had the brilliant idea to bus an entire village of Chin to Rangoon for a half-day tour of the museum and a lecture on the glory of and medical urgency for drug suppression. It took two days each way for the Chin to attend a half-day lecture. Not one of the Chin carried a brochure. Not that this mattered very much. The Chin had never learned to read or write. In the hills, the skills needed to survive didn't include reading and writing. It was safe to say none of the villagers had any idea what had been written in the official museum brochure printed on cheap paper with dull colors, making the faces of the general the same shade of gray as the dead babies in the jars. If the Chin had been able to read the brochure, then they would have known that the government had given them until 2014 to wind down their dope-growing business.

"I like these people, Hart. Tell them about 2014. And then tell them that in 2019 planet earth's got a meeting with an asteroid."

"That might spoil their holiday, old boy," Hart said. "Why not let them have a little fun in the big city? Look at them. They are happy. This is a party. By 2014 most of their livers will have clapped out and been preserved in Jeroboams of formaldehyde." said Hart.

He had a point. I couldn't deny his logic. Hart had a writer's mind that allowed him to see things, to make connections using words that no one else would have thought of making. Hart had a knack for revealing the song and dance of death; the tune that reminded us that our hope rested on an imperfect knowledge of the world, and that celebrated innocence and ignorance as the essence for happiness. The more we understood the true nature of the human condition, the more we wanted the drugs they didn't want us to have. Besides, it was probably the only fucking holiday those villagers would ever have. They would be telling their grandchildren about their exciting all expenses paid to Rangoon trip. Man, I wasn't going to ruin that for them. So neither Hart nor I was going to piss on their parade by bringing up the 2014 deadline. None of the villagers—and I knew many of them—were the kind of people who wanted to know what terrible reality inexorably, irrevocably lay ahead for them. Who wanted tell the village that their days were numbered?

"No one," said Hart. It was as simple as that. And that included the official in the tan uniform lecturing about drugs causing birth defects. The Chin wouldn't take well to this death sentence; I could see Salai Lian Uk making more gunpowder and waiting out the troops, while others would give up, becoming blue, really going down deep inside themselves, pulling over the lid. The way out of that deep dark pit was lots of whisky and narcotics.

"Do you think they will ever tell them or just send a letter in January 2013 telling everyone to start preparing their patches to plant corn and potatoes? No more poppies. Read our guns. No more poppies."

"That's why they have the museum," Hart said. "They don't need a letter. They have all of this." And Hart stretched his arms above his head and executed a slow turn. "We will put your babies in bottles if you keep growing poppies."

Suddenly the museum made sense. The government was bringing in the Shan, Karen, and others for what seemed like a lecture tour. Softening them up, letting them know what a bad thing all this drug business was so that when the time was right they would already be re-wired to accept growing potatoes rather than poppies. Actually it was a veiled threat about what would happen if they didn't co-operate.

Forget about 2014—that was a zillion years away, and in the meantime, the Chin had won the lottery for hill tribe people; their one chance to see the big city at the expense of the government. The Chin were special among the hill tribes and I am not saying that simply because I co-authored the book about them. The villagers in the hills lived on another planet; they never came to Rangoon. Their clans spoke more than thirty dialects, and without a common language, hadn't ever been able to muster a unified rebellion, let along figure out who should go to represent them on national unity day, the day all the Burmese celebrated their unity. On the day all the hill tribes were bused in for a parade, the authorities always came up empty-handed when it came to the Chin. How could the grand parade start without any Chin to march? That was impossible. How could there be unity without the Chin united, despite their mutually unintelligible dialects? Who said dictators weren't creative when organizing a parade? These guys used magic markers to paint dots on the face of locals to make them look like Chin so everyone could believe unity had been achieved and the Chin were participating, like everyone else, and part of the whole. And from a distance, the actor Chin looked impressively Chin-like.

After some reflection, Hart said, "They have decided the whole point of the exercise was to reunite us with them." It made about as much sense as any of the other reasons. The exhibits with the wildly screwy scales and lavish paintings, freak-show babies, and badly dressed mannequins only made them hungry, thirsty, annoyed and confused. They had been bused into Rangoon because Mr.

Hart and Mr. Sloan had arranged for and paid the government to organize this reunion. It all made perfect sense for the Chin.

Salai Lian Uk had said, according to Hart, "As much as I like you two blokes, there's no fucking way we are going to march in that parade."

The government had never given them anything but a headache. This was the first time I understood how much the Chin hated parades. I promised him he didn't have to march and I'd make some of my special popcorn and for the Chin, next to learning how to make fire, the knowledge of cooking as revealed in my secret recipes was about the best gift anyone had ever given them.

22

We occupy an accidental universe. We bump into a village full of Chin we haven't seen in ten years, and moments later, our paths cross with a *luk-krueng* woman, her features a perfect blend of Asian and *farang*. She appeared around a corner and stepped into our life. Taller than the Chin—she was nearly as tall as me—she stood out. At her throat hung a gold lotus-shaped pendant and the top two buttons of her white silk blouse were undone. The hem of her dress, a deep blue color, stopped above her knee. The polished black high heels didn't have a single scuff mark. On her left wrist she wore silver bangles that jingled like a wind chime as she focused a digital camera, watching the window at the back of the camera, framing her subjects with a quiet resolve. She snapped shot after shot of the Chin women with tattooed faces. The bright flash appeared to temporarily blind one of the old Chin women.

I remembered that woman. She was Salai Lian Uk's eldest sister. Her husband had died the year before we arrived in the hills ten years ago. She had been old then. Now she looked ancient. The old woman had cataracts. Her eyes had a milky white film and although she was nearly blind, the light from the flash startled her. She closed her eyes tight, then slowly opened them. She was seeing stars inside the anti-drug museum.

"Hey, sweetheart, you are photographing an old friend of mine," I said.

"Don't mind him," said Hart.

Those were our two opening lines with Sarah. Women never forget the very first thing a new man who will become part of their lives says to them. Men rarely remember the last thing they said to any woman. It was one of those strange ways that men and women were fundamentally different. Saya remembers to this day what I first said to her—"Green hair, black lipstick, I love your war paint, baby." I have no memory of ever having said this. And she says that she said in answer—"It's not even peace paint. It's love paint." No memory whatsoever of it ever having been said. What I said and what Hart said to the beautiful mystery woman—that I remember even though it is totally forgettable. Perhaps it was Hart's three-word message, "Don't mind him," and hooking his thumb at me.

I half-turned and saw Hart had zoomed in on the woman taking the photos. I looked at her again. Call me a *soi* dog, but I noticed her breasts were large under the white blouse, and the sense of roundness and fullness hinted at by the exposure of skin from the undone top two buttons, as well as her small waist that tapered to reveal well-rounded hips. The genetic package was about as good as you could get from a random combination of DNA.

"Who are you?" she asked, lowering her camera. Her eyes, a deep blue, matched her skirt but they somehow didn't match the face, which screamed for a pair of brown eyes. I couldn't stop staring at such eyes in an Asian face.

"Hey, baby, don't take that attitude," I said. "I was just trying to help. We know these people. If you want to take pictures, they don't care. We've been there, done that. This woman doesn't see all that well. I am trying to tell her not to worry, that you are just taking some pictures and that's cool. If I am out of place, then excuse me."

She smiled and tiny lines appeared at the corners of those blue eyes. And it was abundantly clear that the radiant smile was focused on Hart. I was thinking, if she only knew he had won two hookers named Sugarcane and Shrimp from a corrupt manager in a Bangkok bar, his prize for cleaning the pool table. That tack, however, might have failed. The fact that she had appeared out of nowhere in the anti-drug museum, with an interest in Chin tattoo art, strongly suggested that she was a free thinker, someone who wouldn't take a moral offence because a handsome guy had enjoyed winning hookers. I could come off looking like a total fool. So I decided it might be better to forget about morality, and go straight to the heart of the issue: his poverty. If she only knew he was about to become a newspaper *proofreader*. That search-engine-inside head running the full scan on Hart would have come to a screeching halt. What kind of prospects did a proofreader have to offer a woman? What woman, no matter how free thinking she was, wanted to sleep with a proofreader, his head full of missing commas, semi-colons, and dangling participles, and shooting his load between her legs? Had there ever been a woman who hadn't run for the hills after she found out that a man lacked both moral principles and any reasonable economic prospects of success? One reason would be enough for a man to be jettisoned by a woman. To throw out both morals and money meant she had to look in the mirror and ask herself what in the hell she was doing wasting her time with a whore-mongering down and definitely out man. Hart is no Henry Miller, I was about to say, but she spoke first.

"I am researching for a book on tattooed people," she said.

"I collect Shan tattoo books," said Hart. "It is my passion."

I looked at him but he didn't blink. He had told me that he'd sold his collection. But that didn't stop Hart from passing himself off as a collector.

"I knew you had passion but this is the first I heard it was about Shan tattoo books," I said.

"I have a collection of over two hundred books," she said.

With this woman there was none of the usual *where are you from, where are you going,* or *are you hungry for rice*? The first thing she mentioned was her large collection of handmade tattoo books from the Shan state. The Shan books were legendary in their quality; the binding was teakwood or a fine lacquer. Inside all of the demons, snakes, elephants and dragons were carefully hand painted and the Pali script written around the perimeter of the painted creature. These weren't just ordinary storybooks. The painted images had been passed down the generations as templates that were used by Shan tattoo artists. She pulled one out of her backpack and handed it to Hart, who opened it to a faded golden tiger-like creature. "Lovely quality," he said, handing it back but not before a couple of the Chin with blue tattooed faces grabbed the book and flipped through it.

I saw something familiar in this young woman's face. I easily forgot people and places. Once I spent a week in Athens with Saya. Five years later we went back and she remembered every street, park, and fountain. I didn't recognize anything. Not a single building, bridge, road, shop or restaurant looked familiar. Saya said, "Do you remember that coffee shop on the east side of the road?" I had no idea which side of the road was the east side. Neither side looked like any place I had ever been. So I thought I might be having one of those Athens-like moments when I saw Sarah.

"Aren't those pangolin boots you are wearing?" she asked in a perfect American accent, one I couldn't place. It wasn't New York, or Southern, or Midwestern. Her lips were tight and her eyes narrowed.

I looked down at my boots, pulled up my pant legs and then looked up and nodded. "Look, baby, at how the scales are big at the top, and then how they get smaller as you slide down to the toe. My boot maker on Silom is a genius. I've used him for years. He can make shoes out of any creature."

"Pangolins are on the endangered list," she said. There was a cold wind in her voice.

What can you say to that reply? She had all but declared that she was some kind of animal rights freak or an environmentalist, a save-the-rain-forest nut. I took the neutral path. "I only wear natural fabrics," I said. "The other stuff just doesn't wear well."

"Don't ask him about his leopard hat," said Hart, who had been eyeing the young woman like a cold-blooded reptile, tongue reading the air, tasting a mating opportunity in his path.

I didn't give her a chance to ask. "No shit. I have a leopard hat. It is pillbox shaped. It is so beautiful. So beautiful, beautiful, beautiful. Like a lovely woman, just looking at it makes me want to weep. I had the hat made in Tokyo. And I had a pair of leopard loafers made at the same time. When I have that hat and shoes on, people notice, I mean they notice me."

"He owns the only pair of leopard loafers on the planet."

"Man, I don't think, I *know* I do."

I knew what was happening. Two guys in the presence of a beautiful woman brought out this weird desire for acceptance and validation; that we were unique, divine-like beings worthy of her respect and interest. We performed for her attention, in a reptilian kind of way, and she reacted to this act, by saying, "You two fit right into this museum."

"I don't think she likes your boots," Hart said.

"Hey, baby, he's just playing with you," I said to her. I could tell it wasn't going well, and I wished I had some way of finding out if I knew her and then forgot her, or if I had never known her and had forgotten that as well. "Can I ask you something?"

The edges around her mouth dipped into a frown. "I guess I can't say *it's a free country and you can say whatever you want*," she said.

"Do you know how lucky you are today?" I asked her.

"To meet you two?"

"That would have been my guess," said Hart.

"Hey, man, I am serious. She's lucky. Do you know what I am saying? She's lucky. Lucky. And she has no idea how lucky she is."

"What my friend is trying to say is that, you are lucky," said Hart. "At least tell us your name."

"Sarah," she said.

She turned away, ignoring us, and resumed snapping pictures of the tattooed Chin women, showing them their image in the tiny window on the back of the camera. I wanted to tell her the story of the camera I had found and the nineteen photographs that had been taken, then lost, and the death of the photographer and the return of the camera to his family. And one of the pictures was of a total goddess. It wasn't the right moment; I knew that once I told her Kazuo's story, she would appreciate the quality of my mercy, my kindness and the depth of my creative awareness and caring, and that in the warm afterglow, any potential chance Hart had would vanish. I've always been a dreamer.

23

Hart and I had traveled across mountains, no roads, just small jungle trails, and floated down rivers, going deep inland where no foreigner had traveled for a hundred years. And after hardship and suffering—Hart nearly died—we had been rewarded with the discovery of Chin women with spidery blue tattooed faces. Sarah stepped out of a taxi in Rangoon and ran straight into four of the same women we had humped through jungles and crossed mountains to find. That was beyond good karma. She stumbled upon what were likely among the last tattooed Chin women on the face of the earth. The practice had stopped about thirty-two years ago. No young Chin women had blue tattoos on their face. Seeing one was about as rare as coming across two fucking snakes. Seeing four, that was definitely an omen.

"You know how they tattoo the face?" I asked.

"With a long, sharp instrument, one sharp jab at a time," she said.

That was a lot of jabbing and the tattoo artist didn't finish until the face was a large cobweb of blue intersecting lines. Sarah knew this. Hart liked to remind me he had been a child when the last Chin woman had had her faced tattooed. I looked at the young woman and guessed her age to be early to mid-twenties. I was about the same age, if not older, than her father, I thought. Like robots, most people in the West are programmed to compute age as one solid unbreakable inflexible linear line—son, father, grandfather, and burial dust. My grand illusion was to believe that Sarah perceived me not as a "father" but as a player.

"I've seen Chin tattooed ladies before," she said.

"Where, man? We spent four months finding them in hills so remote you had to go to the moon, take a detour right, then come back to earth."

"They aren't so remote anymore. The authorities can bus them to Rangoon," Sarah said.

"I believe you," said Hart like someone about to join a cult. The way he looked at this woman with a sense of utter sincerity. No irony, no bullshit registered in his voice. I'd known the guy for ten years and it was a revelation to learn that if Hart dug deep enough, even he could find a small pocket of sincerity to mine.

What was it about the presence of a large breasted, narrow waisted, long legged with a full-lipped smile woman traveling on her own and seemingly available that turns a friend into an instant traitor? Some circuitry malfunction, and the program which says, "Hey, my friend is under assault, defend, defend, defend" is switched off and the microchip circuit board reconfigured in a nanosecond, so that what Hart heard playing back inside his head was—"I'll do anything for a blow job, blow job, blow job. Give up a friend? Cut out his liver and stick it in a bottle in the Drug Elimination Museum? No problem."

She had moved away from both of us. I looked at Hart. He shrugged.

"She's not interested, Hart."

"The day is young."

We circulated among the Chin listening to their stories about funerals, weddings, drinking, feasts, more drinking, fishing, and hunting. Sarah moved around the Chin, photographing the tattooed women. Close up, holding her camera a foot away from the inky tattoos. I saw Hart taking it all in. "Hart, she'll never sleep with you. Give it up." This apparently didn't register. I then said to him, "Ask the Chin in their language about the giant tobacco stocks that are piled ten stories high. The tobacco the Chin are building tree houses in. Where did they harvest tons of tobacco? Or was it made out of vanilla ice cream?"

Hart said nothing. My translator wasn't listening. He had turned off and entered into another world of deception and rogue plans.

Someone in the ICU ward on a life-support system would have been more responsive.

"Are you following me?" she asked, stopping as Hart nearly bumped into her.

"Would you like to have lunch?"

Hart no longer had any interest in the Drug Elimination Museum. Aye Thit, having showed us his father's letter, looked bored trailing around after us as we trailed around with Sarah one step ahead. It was time for a drink and a fat one.

24

Lunch was at the West Point Café on Merchant Street. We sat at a table in the back. The restaurant was up the road from the American Embassy (south, east, west, north—I had no idea which direction from the Embassy). Barricades, barbwire, and security guards cut off the restaurant and embassy. If you didn't know what was going on, it would have been easy to conclude that someone on the other side of the barbwire was under house arrest. Security was security was security. The West Point Café had no security and hadn't changed since George Orwell had coughed blood into his handkerchief and called for his bill. Long wooden tables and green plastic chairs and trellises with fake creeping vines. The ambience was backpacker basic: prison gray floors and arched dirty white and green walls and quasi-communal seating. Airplane-hangar-sized ancient fans made from steel and chaotic service. Sarah said it was her favorite restaurant. She ordered rice, vegetables, and chicken off the menu. I ordered draft beer, which worked out at twenty cents a glass. For a dollar you could drink a great deal of beer.

"Hey, I like this place, baby," I said.

"I wrote my doctorate on tattooing among Burmese hill tribes," she said, handing the menu back to the waiter.

"Damn, I knew that I knew you. I just knew it."

Something in my brain clicked. I remembered her jpeg image. A profile shot. She was standing on a beach with English Bay behind her. Sarah had her own web site. She had been raised in Hawaii. Her father was an ex-Vietnam veteran and her mother, who was Thai, had been raised in Bangkok. This combination went some distance to explaining her height, bone structure and blue eyes. Sarah had been a graduate student in British Columbia and had emailed me, asking me questions about the history and social practices of the Chin. It was coming back to me. She had asked about tattoos. I had written her a couple of things about the Chin tattoo customs. I emailed her a jpeg of the tattoo instrument that was as long as a walking stick with a pointy, sharp hollowed tip. I described how the ink was poured into the top of the stick and drained to the tip. The point then punctured the skin on the face of the woman, injecting the ink point by point until an image formed. That information had been passed along to her three years ago. At first, I had no memory of our exchange. But I hadn't forgotten her picture. Like the girl in Kazuo's nineteenth photo, Sarah was someone you never forgot. Only I *had* forgotten her; she had changed her hair, and besides I had never seen her in person. Image and flesh were two different mediums. When I corresponded with her on the Internet, Sarah was finishing her doctorate at the University of British Columbia.

"I thought I knew you from some place. God, what a dummy I can be," I said.

"Don't think he's being modest," said Hart. A waiter had brought him a plate of rice heaped with vegetables.

"Listen, Hart, she emailed me about Chin tattoos. Tell him. It's true, darling. It's true." I took a long drink from the draft beer.

Sarah, her mouth ajar, leaned forward over a plate of uneaten rice, removing her glasses and staring at me, waiting until I had lowered my glass.

"You are Sloan Walcott? *The* Sloan Walcott who wrote *The Art of Chin Ways,* the book on the Chin?"

"The one and only," I cleared my throat. "Hart helped on the book."

"I supplied a few words," said Hart. "And proofreading."

He was a little despondent. She hadn't sufficiently acknowledged his presence.

"Don't be like that," I said. "Hart wrote the text. I took the photographs. It was a team effort, right Hart?"

Hart smiled and said nothing. He was the quintessential lone wolf Englishman running along the edges of the old empire, and he was someone who hated the idea of teams and teamwork. "It was a coffee table book," said Hart. "There was very little text in the book. Sloan's photographs made the book. The editor wanted photographs. He knew that the pictures would sell it. Our editor said that people wanted to *see* the Chin, the way they lived, their rituals, their living quarters, kitchens, hunting grounds, dancing, drinking, shooting—it was a coffee table book. Our editor was clear on what he liked. He didn't care too much what we had for words or writings about the Chin. He kept cutting back the text and inserting more photographs. He left just enough text so anyone buying the book wouldn't be embarrassed when a friend picked up it from the coffee table and leafed through it. Text in the book showed the owner was a *real* book person. Our book was the kind of book for people who loved books, but the pursuit of making money left no time for reading."

"Hart has an equal right to claim the book is his. I'm right. I'm right."

"It's okay," said Hart. "He always repeats himself at least twice."

"I loved the text," said Sarah.

"You read it?" asked Hart.

"How can she like the text if she hasn't read it, dummy?" I asked him.

"I found your descriptions of the mountains and rivers and jungle in the Chin state inspiring," she said.

"Hart's right. Most people who bought the book weren't book readers. You may be the first one we ever met. And certainly the only one we ever met at the anti-drug museum filled with a village load of Chin."

"Your book on the Chin changed my life," Sarah said. "I wouldn't have completed my Ph.D. I wouldn't have my university job. Everything goes back to that book. It was seminal." She sighed, looking up with doe-like eyes. "Did you ever have a book change your life?"

Seminal. All I could think about was seminal fluids.

Her intriguing question had my thinking delayed by only a slight pull in the groin. "Yeah, *Moby Dick*," I said. "I knew I hated boats. Hated the ocean. Whaling ship skipper wasn't on my list of things I wanted to do."

"I am serious," Sarah said.

"*Ulysses*," said Hart. "James Joyce's *Ulysses*."

"Man, no one reads *Ulysses* unless it is a school assignment. All people want to read is *Harry Potter.*" I saw it coming. Hart played the artist, the man of letters, a lost soul, and an ignored talent. The awful thing about such a cliché was how well Hart made it work overtime for him. He had secured Sarah's full attention. Even the way she blinked and held her hands had changed, as if her state of consciousness had been altered by the mention of that one loaded word—*Ulysses*. It had to be getting on forty years since anyone other than an English professor got laid by using James fucking Joyce as his bait in the trap. Hart had an instinct about what kind of crumb trail led to the bed.

"I've read *Ulysses*," said Sarah.

Bingo, I thought. "But, you read my, I mean our, Chin book, too," I said. Like the jockey who has just seen the mount next to him fly past, I knew I was out of the race.

For an hour I drank through two dollars worth of beer, listening as Hart and Sarah discussed the great canon of English literature. I knew Hart had won when he raised no objection to her inclusion of *Bridget Jones' Diary* in the canon. He refused all eye contact with me after that happened. He knew I was clocking him. I mouthed, "What a slut," but he refused to read my lips. Sarah had done her doctorate on "Modern Gender Politics of the Burmese Hill Tribe People as Evidenced by Body Tattoos." I had never imagined there were universities on the planet that encouraged people to devote four years of their life to researching and writing a dissertation which had several pictures attached in the appendix. She confirmed referencing our book on the Chin into a couple of footnotes in her dissertation. Probably the graphic geographic locations Hart had written that always impressed people who, like me, thought that north was exactly the direction they were walking. It also turned out that Sarah, on the strength of her graduate work, had been made an assistant professor in some cultural studies program.

"I have a friend who is a publisher in London," said Hart.

"Really, how cool," she said.

Not so cool if she had known this publisher. I had met this friend, Neil something Wormsley-Hallmark, a drunk who once got frostbite in Greenland and lost two fingers which he hammered off with the blunt end of a Swiss army knife. Neil something Wormsley-Hallmark had passed out in the Voodoo Bar. It had been his first night in Bangkok. Hart said his friend had suffered from jet lag. The ten glasses of gin probably had nothing to do with it. Neil published books—if you could call them books—pop-up books for children ages four to eight. *The Pink Cat in Paddington Station* was his all-time best seller. Neil specialized in the kind of the book that had even fewer words than appeared in our Chin book.

Sarah confessed that she had had trouble finding someone to publish her dissertation. Meaning what had earned her a doctor in front of her name was unpublished and likely unreadable. She had a stack of rejection letters in the drawer of her condo in Vancouver. One drawer, I thought. I saw a snowfall of rejection letters layering every surface of her condo. Her dissertation contained twenty pages of photographs and 350 pages of text. The title alone was guaranteed to act with the speed of a double-dose of Rohyphnol. What did she think Hart was going to do? Buy Mr. Neil something Wormsley-Hallmark a giant bottle of brand-name gin, get him to drink half of it, spring the manuscript on him? One year later, as if by alcoholic magic, a twenty-page pop-up book titled *The Blue-Faced Cats of Chinland* appears on the shelf.

"I'm looking over a novel that I am thinking of sending him," Hart said.

I spewed beer across the table, spraying Sarah's plate of rice and chicken and vegetables. "You never told me about a novel," I said.

"I think that is wonderful," said Sarah. "Absolutely cool."

"What's it about?"

"It's bad luck to talk about a work in progress."

"It never stopped Henry Miller," I said.

Back-sliding bastard, I thought. Sarah, the accidental beautiful woman, the only known groupie our Chin book had ever produced, started to treat Hart like a celebrity because he was writing a novel. I didn't believe a word of it. He had a dead ordinary life and, besides, he lacked anything approaching ambition. What he loved about himself was the lack of drive, desire or discipline to accomplish anything. The most that anyone in his old school had ever done was cut off a couple of frozen fingers in Greenland. That was culture? That was accomplishment? That was Hart. He bailed water from a rudderless boat as he drifted silently into middle age. From all indications, Hart had given up. The secret of his novel changed all of that.

"Work in progress," I said. "That usually means chapter one, page one."

Hart smiled. "The manuscript is 420 pages. I am more than half way through the polish."

"With words on every page?"

"Every page."

"Wormsley-Hallmark's four to eight year old readership will love that."

"I would love to read it," said Sarah.

"I have a copy in my room," said Hart.

"You should see my study in Vancouver. It's filled with books," she said.

"My sister lives in Vancouver. English Bay," said Hart.

He played the game well. I had to give him that. The fact he hadn't talked with his sister in ten years wouldn't stop him from using her to seduce Sarah.

"Hart flies to Vancouver—what is it?—every six months to see his sister?" I said. "They are that close." I crossed my fingers and held them up. Neither of them was paying me any attention. I'd been tuned out.

Hart and Sarah stared at each other across the table. They had gone silent. She was twenty-eight; Hart was thirty-something. I thought how much younger they suddenly looked inside the West Point Café on Merchant Street. If I could photograph a single moment of expectation with the blue flash capturing that surge of happiness, it would have been a photo of the two of them sitting at the table. Before me two people in their prime talking crazily about books, publishing, making a connection, making plans. There was definitely something heartbreaking in all of this.

This is the beginning of the story I want to tell.

LADY'S DAY

25

I sat alone in the lobby, sipping my first beer of the morning. It was just after eight and Aye Thit hadn't arrived, and Hart wasn't answering his room phone. The waitress who loves me had her day off. Another waitress brought me some notepaper and a pen. I sketched the Drug Elimination Museum and grounds and gave it to the new waitress. I had a feeling that this was going to be the big day. Saya had faith in my intuitive side, the side that came out in my dreams and my art. And I had learned to have faith in it, too. Because it was nearly always right. I took another drink and put the bottle down. Half empty, or half full? What would the Lady have said? She had lived under house arrest for nineteen months—breaking the months down into smaller pieces of time, she had been house-bound for 570 days or 13,680 hours. For 570 mornings she had opened her eyes, wondering, will 571 be the day? The day I can get into my car, drive down University Avenue and into the city? But there was much more time to sift through and account for. She'd been under house arrest for a five-year stretch as her consolation prize for winning the 1990 election. Do the math, and this comes out to another 1,825 days. Add the two periods of time together and she had done 2,395 days locked inside her house. It amounted to a lot of time alone—time to walk through all the rooms of a large house; time spent tending the garden, cooking, listening to the BBC and music, meditating, reading, thinking, dreaming and writing. House arrest must have become a way of life, of being, of seeing herself.

She had been waiting for what had to have seemed at times like a life sentence. She had waited so long that an ordinary person might have forgotten what they had been waiting for outside the house.

By the time everyone else showed up in the lobby, I had filled the notepaper with numbers of months, weeks, days and hours. Glancing at the paper, you would have thought I was a bookie.

By the time we arrived at University Avenue, it was about ten in the morning. We left Aye Thit and Zaw Min with the van, crossed the Avenue, and stationed ourselves for the second day under the lean-to, drinking beer. There was no need to order. The owner saw us approaching and handed me a bottle as I sat at the table. He winked at Hart. It was his way of acknowledging that Hart had done well—Sarah sat beside Hart at the table. Hart's blondish hair, wet from the shower, hung over his shirt collar; his blue eyes were clear, his shirt fashionably unbuttoned. He looked like an artist who pumped iron. Yesterday, Hart had played the bored artist, with a running narrative of General Custer's last stand. In twenty-four hours he had reinvented himself as an expectant artist who had cast off the dust of history and death by arrows and enjoyed the company of a beautiful woman. Yesterday was another planet, another star galaxy. Sarah had stayed up until four a.m. reading Hart's novel. I straddled a teak stool across from them. Seated at the other tables were journalists. I recognized many of the faces from the day before. All eyes were on the barricades, watching as the guards checked cars. More journalists had come than on the previous day. There was a buzz of anticipation as their conversations filled the air and merged in a greater sound carrying its own encoded message. News had traveled from table to table, room to room in the bars and restaurants and the street that this would be the day everyone had been waiting for.

The dog that had passed out under the table the day before no longer slept. He sat alert, ears erect, hopeful, as one table of journalists passed the time throwing him potato chips. The thing with a dog is it will eat whatever is thrown to it. Food is food. I watched the dog snap potato chips out of thin air. Sarah looked down University Avenue at a couple of military intelligence officers near the barricade. Hart quietly opened a paperback edition of *The Quiet American*, smoothed back the dog-eared page and read.

"She is so brave," said Sarah. "I don't think I could have done what she's doing. Her husband died of cancer. The generals refused him a visa to allow him one last visit to say goodbye. If she had gone to England for the funeral, they wouldn't have let her return. And her sons live so far away, growing older, going on with their lives without their mother. Their father dead. How can she cope with such suffering and not go insane? I'd have fallen apart."

"I wouldn't mind staying home," I said. "I never get bored. I'd paint, read, garden, and listen to music. Blow a fat one; drink a case of beer. She's had 2,395 days to think things through. At this stage she has to pretty well know what she wants and who she is."

"It is a question of choice," said Hart. "If your wife refused to let you out of the house, you would revolt."

"Think of how she's suffered," said Sarah.

I had thought about staying home.

"You get to do whatever you want inside your house and you get sympathy because you can't go out. Christ, who in their right mind wants to leave a big, grand house with a wonderful garden? What's outside waiting for her? I'll tell you who is outside her door—beggars, muggers, disease, traffic jams, polluted streets, rivers and air, wars, and ethnic conflict. Man, I say stay the fuck home," I said.

"Why did you want to come along this morning?" Hart asked me. "It has to be something more than returning Kazuo's photographs."

"That's a good question; why *are* you here?" Sarah asked. Both of them stared at me as I played with a cigarette and reached for my can of beer. Overnight, Hart had made an ally. An alliance was a powerful thing to have in Burma, I thought.

Ally or not, his line of questioning was coming from a guy whom I had begged to come with me to Burma. The trip to witness the Lady's release had been *my* idea. Hart had wanted to stay in Bangkok, keep the routine—same restaurant for lunch, same place for a drink, same short-time hotel, visit the same half-dozen hookers, play pool, work as a proofreader, and go back to the same apartment, newspapers, and friends. In some ways Hart was already older than me if age meant that you could no longer pack a case in an hour and take a taxi to the airport at a moment's notice and leave your life behind like the cheap suit that it really was. I had had to drag Hart out of Sukhumvit Road, and suddenly he had convinced himself it had been his idea all along. If he hadn't been facing the cold reality of a job looming over his life, I seriously doubted if he would have left Bangkok. He came to escape work.

"Today's my birthday," I said. "I am fifty-three."

Sarah flinched and was about to say something like, my father is fifty-three years old. I saved her the trouble. "Probably the same age as your father." Not that much younger than Kazuo's father and I couldn't imagine *him* taking a serious run at Sarah, I thought.

She looked away. There wasn't so much sadness but a desperate look of loneliness that enveloped her. I had made some kind of mistake. "He committed suicide when I was fourteen. He was forty-three when he shot himself."

Hart looked at me as if Sarah's father's death was somehow my fault. Unlike Hart, I didn't want to sleep with Sarah. I wanted her as a friend. I loved women as friends—they were the most understanding, thoughtful, and loyal friends in the world. Looking back at my life, I couldn't think of anyone but women whom I ever completely trusted with friendship. I wanted to change the subject. To get back to where we had started—my birthday and why I was in Burma—figuring that information would pull Sarah back from whatever dark void of grief she had fallen into.

"You want to know why I am here?" I asked Hart. "I want to celebrate my birthday by witnessing something memorable. When I am old and on my deathbed, buddy, I want to look back and say, hey, I was there. I was there. I was there. I saw something, man. It wasn't just another birthday. I wanted a birthday that was more than the passage of another year, one that left no trace, no meaning, and no memory. I was after a birthday that would be framed in my mind as a work of art. I trained as an artist. My idea was to create a living piece of art, something very special. I would never forget this birthday waiting for the Lady in Rangoon. It would be etched in my memory until the day I die. And I could say, I participated in this event and when the time came I gave something back that belonged to that moment. How many people can say they ever had such a chance in their life? Not many," I said, answering my own question.

"Saya doesn't mind that you're not home on your birthday?" Hart asked. Hart was the only one of my friends that Saya actually liked.

141

She thought he was sad and tormented but polite and thoughtful and harmless in an upper-middle-class English way. At the same time Hart's comment was a clever way to reinforce my marital status with Sarah. She knew that I was married. I never pretended to be single. Some women felt such information a worthy consideration before accepting an invitation for friendship. Most women loved a man who talked lovingly about his wife.

"Not after last year's birthday. Didn't I tell you about that? I am certain I told you."

I hadn't told him. "Do you want to hear about Saya?" I asked Sarah. She thought for a moment before nodding.

"Doesn't Saya mean 'teacher' in Burmese?"

This was one very clever woman. "It does," I said. "Once many years ago I was her teacher. Then one day the roles got switched."

I lit a cigarette from the fag end of the one I was just finishing. It only looked like a cigarette. Actually it was a fat one disguised to look exactly like a cigarette. It even had a cigarette filter attached. As I blew smoke from my nostrils, one of the guards at the barricade lifted the long metal arm and let a car through. A car from the other side approached, another white Toyota. Rangoon was the elephant graveyard where old Toyotas from Tokyo came to spend their retirement and, of course, what follows in short-order—for burial.

"You sure that you want to hear about my 52nd birthday?"

"Yes, tell me," Hart said.

"So do I," said Sarah.

The conspiracy between Hart and Sarah was signed, sealed and delivered. "Okay," I took a long drag from the fat one. "I had gone shopping at Villa supermarket. Hart might have told you that I do the cooking at home. My wife doesn't like to cook. And I don't like eating other people's food. It was my birthday so I planned a special menu. I brought home several bags of groceries. A half-gallon drum of pure olive oil, a case of beer, chickens, vegetables, one of those super saver thirty-six rolls of toilet paper, and fruit and ice cream. Jesus, you wouldn't believe how many plastic bags I had to carry. I get out of the taxi, sweat rolling down my neck and back, juggling all the stuff, fiddling with the house keys, dropping them. The houseboy wasn't around. Taking a deep breath, I get through the gate somehow, the dogs are barking, and I am soaked in sweat. I struggle into the house and by now I am leaving puddles of sweat on the floor, my knees are shaking from the weight of all those bags. I make straight for the kitchen. Saya comes in a moment later, and she says, 'Hey, this is Thailand. You take off your shoes at the door.' And I say, 'It's my fucking birthday. You know how heavy this shit is? Look at my clothes, do I look dry and happy?' And Saya says, 'Never mind, take off your shoes before coming into the house.' Well, I explode. I shouldn't have done it. But I kicked the fan. One of those floor fans. I kicked hard. Man, I fucking kicked it. One of the dogs, Checkers, was in the kitchen, and that fan whizzed passed Checkers' head and the dog freaked out. The dog leaped half-way up the wall and as he was jumping, he was shitting. Not some ordinary shit in the sand, but a great flying, watery shit that splattered against the wall and slowly oozed down in brown ugly streaks and gathered like the swirl of a Dairy Queen ice cream cone onto the floor.

"Saya was upset and wouldn't talk to me. It's my birthday, my one happy day a year to celebrate my coming into existence, and what happens? My wife won't talk to me. The dog has crapped on the walls. Electric blue flashes spark out of the fan. Plastic bags of food spill all over the kitchen floor. Checkers eats one of the chickens. Probably to settle his stomach. It was real ugly. I go upstairs and roll a fat one, open a beer, and try to forget what had happened downstairs. I will myself to believe that nothing this fucking weird is happening on my birthday. That night Saya slept in the guestroom. Alone in our bedroom I thought, this has to be the worst birthday of my life. All I wanted for my birthday was for the night to end. The next morning I am up early. I am hungry as hell. I haven't eaten anything solid in eighteen hours. I go into the kitchen and everything is cleaned up. I figure that Saya has resolved the madness like I did, and put it behind her. She didn't want to think about what had happened; it was better to just forget about it like some freak nightmare. I almost go back upstairs to the guestroom and kiss her, and say, 'Hey, baby, I am sorry about last night. I shouldn't have kicked the fan. I should have taken off my shoes.' Instead, I think I'll save that kiss-and-make-up speech for later, and I go downstairs and put on my shoes. Somehow the shoes don't feel the way shoes are supposed to feel. There's something soft and mushy in them. I take off the right shoe, leaning against the doorway, and have a look inside. All of Checkers' shit has been carefully, expertly, and with tender loving care stuffed inside my shoe. Now that's the reason I wanted my 53rd birthday in Rangoon waiting for the Lady."

26

No one expected Conley to appear riding in the back of an old pickup truck. He had interrogated us the day before, and his cover story was that he was a journalist. Hart didn't believe him. Neither did I. The bed of the pickup was loaded with wooden crates and empty ten-liter plastic water bottles. Conley stood in the middle of the cargo. The police at the barricades did a double-take as Conley whooped and hollered as they waved the pickup through. As the driver of the pickup slowed down, Conley, holding on to the cab with one hand, jumping up and down, his free hand raised, gave all of us the victory sign. He had an unlit cigar in the corner of his mouth. He may have thought the cigar made him look a little like Churchill—but with the red scarf tied around his throat, he looked more like Groucho Marx. The pickup stopped opposite the lean-to café and Conley hopped off the back, walked around to the driver's side and passed him some cash. Somehow Conley had found a way to get himself smuggled through the barricades and roam around inside the restricted area.

"I had a feeling that Conley was a spook," I said to Hart. "The first time he cross-examined us, I said to myself, that guy's working for the Agency."

"Or he could be just another asshole with good connections," said Hart.

Conley called, "She's out. They've let her out." The Japanese paid their bill and ran to a waiting taxi. Sprinting to the taxis, the Japanese journalists looked like they had access to serious expense accounts and good tailoring. There wasn't a drop of sweat on any of them. They reminded me of Saya. She never sweated either.

I looked down the road. There was no traffic. Conley might well have been pulling a crazy stunt. I ordered another beer from the waiter. "How do you know they've released her?" Hart asked.

"You don't believe me, General Custer?" asked Conley, giggling as he sat down at the table, stretching his hand out to Sarah. "Hi, I work for the New Times News Service in LA. And what is your name? I didn't catch your name."

She answered him as he shook her hand over the two-three-second normal handshake limit. Finally she drew her hand back. "It is wild inside. Everyone is clapping and smiling and piling into cars," said Conley.

"I don't see any cars," I said.

"Skeptic? That's good, Mr. Second in Command," Conley said.

The police lifted the barricade for the car carrying the Lady. She rode in the backseat. I glanced at my watch; it was 11.23 a.m. I thought about buying a Lotto ticket with that number. Only I wasn't sure where they were sold in Rangoon. It was a Monday. Aye Thit was sitting in the front of the van. Zaw Min saw us coming fast and switched on the engine. We climbed inside. Before I could say anything, Conley had climbed into the back of the van, pushing against Sarah. Hart sat on the other side. She was wedged between the two of them, staring straight ahead, knees locked together, with a look of terror.

"Where do you think the Lady will go?" I asked.

Aye Thit said, "I think she will go to NLD headquarters." I smacked my palm against my forehead. What a dummy. Of course she would go straight to her headquarters. It was natural for her to celebrate her release with her supporters.

Aye Thit had a brilliant instinct (though in Asia common sense was often confused with brilliance). He knew the direction the wind was blowing. Somehow he understood the basic need to go straight to the place where those who care most deeply about us would be waiting. Of course, the Lady's first order of business would be to re-establish her base with the NLD; all the people who had supported her would be waiting for her on her first day out.

We hit heavy traffic about fifty feet from NLD headquarters. Zaw Min put the van into park. Conley reached over and slid open the door. He bailed and followed after a man in a suit and tie, and was soon swallowed up in a large crowd pushing and surging towards a squat, broken-down building that housed NLD headquarters. The building was a dump. Burmese supporters jammed into the courtyard until they could no longer move. Everywhere men and women in sandals, white shirts, and *longyis* nervously waited for the Lady to arrive. They waited under a mid-day sun. More supporters stood on the flat roof of the squat building. Cars, trucks and buses slowed to a stop. Nothing moved as the snarled tangle of steel and idle engines turned into a massive traffic jam. Hart and Sarah followed a BBC camera crew through the crowd and I followed Hart. I wasn't a political scientist but this much I knew: generals, dictators, warlords, and politicians were people to be avoided in general, and specifically in Burma, where you could disappear and no one would begin to know where to look for you. The ground crawled with military intelligence officers. They stood out, dressed in dark glasses and short haircuts. In all my years in Burma, I had steered clear of politics. People had their throats slit by cops and soldiers all over the world. What was I doing here? Had I gone insane in the heat of the mid-day sun? A huge mass of people had come to show their throats to the military. I didn't want to be around when the military took out their knives. If I hadn't found Kazuo's camera, I wouldn't have gone within five miles of NLD headquarters. I might have watched it all unfold on TV. Being at ground zero, your balls toasting in the sun, in a situation that could go any way, was not my way of spending the day. I had promised Akira Takeda to deliver the photographs to the Lady and it was too late to pull out of the crowd. I filed in behind Hart, Sarah, and the BBC crew, and no one stopped us as we walked straight inside the building. No one would have stopped us if we had walked onto Little Bighorn while General Custer and his men made their stand either.

The room was small and many others packed in after us. Ten minutes after settling in, I looked around and counted about two hundred people inside the square room made for fifty people. Rows of chairs had been set up for the journalists but no one sat down. Photographers and cameramen fought each other, advancing slowly, row by row, until they stalled and couldn't advance any more. Position was everything. Officials from various embassies lined the far side of the room looking like undertakers in their dark suits and bland ties, their black laced shoes polished. Their hair and grooming looked nothing like the wig on the foreigner in the Drug Elimination Museum. Their nails were in as fine a condition as the prostitutes' in the nightclub exhibit. The Lady stood in front of a desk surrounded by her supporters, old and young men dressed in white traditional shirts and *longyis*.

Everyone in Burma, everyone in the world, had wanted to be the first to see her in those first hours. She smiled and nodded at people she recognized in the crowd of journalists and diplomats. She wore a flower in her hair. Everyone looked her over for some sign of bitterness or anger. No such emotion registered on her face. What did she feel as she looked out at us? What did it mean to her that she was free? What had been going through her head those first minutes as she drove down University Avenue and entered NLD headquarters? These were a few of the initial questions that the journalists asked.

She answered simply, directly, making direct eye contact with the cameras.

She said she felt hope. She felt ready to start again.

Journalists dripping with sweat nodded and scribbled in their notebooks. The sweat poured off their faces, splashing like fat rain-drops on their notepads and cameras and the floor. I tried wiping the sweat away from my face, but it was useless; my clothes were soaked, my hands dripped as if I had just taken a shower. My hair curled and leaked, dripping on Hart, who didn't seem to notice that my body had suddenly sprung all kinds of leaks. The still, heavy air developed an atmosphere of its own, wet and dense like the floor of a rain forest before a storm. Inside the room, the faces were pale as if in the early stages of shock after a terrible accident. The sickness of heat crept through the room, making everyone, including the undertakers on the side, irritable, pushing and shoving, trying to get a closer look at the Lady. The scramble for position was more like an English rugby scrum than an American football huddle. Bodies touching, bumping, moving sideways, then forward. The camera guys were trying as hard as they could to bring their cameras ever closer to the front. Those in front felt the attack of those behind. It was unrelenting—elbows, knees, arms, and hands flailing. Fogged-over eyeglasses and grim, determined, unsmiling faces. Everyone was on deadline and everyone wanted the best angle for the shot. It wasn't the Lady's words they were after; they wanted her, to photograph her, film her every movement. They wanted her to see them in the room. We stood three rows from her. Conley had disappeared among the diplomats, getting quotes, sharing information, confirming his connection to intelligence rather than news-gathering. Sarah stood between Hart and the BBC camera crew. NLD officials handed a microphone around the room. At one point, Sarah grabbed the microphone. She locked eyes with the Lady.

"How did you survive all that time?"

"I am a Buddhist. I meditated. I listened to the BBC World Service. And I had a chance to catch up on my reading. I looked after my garden and cooked meals. I think that was quite enough to occupy me."

Before Sarah could ask another question, a journalist asked the Lady about the role of the UN mediator in the next round of negotiations with the generals. Her face lit up and she replied how important mediation was to the process of final settlement. After what she had been through, she could put the words together not just in the right order but in the way the diplomats and statesmen understood. Hours out of house release, and she spoke firmly, with conviction and courage. Words poured out of her mouth: hope and courage. She looked tiny and fragile in front of a table thick with microphones. A small fan blew on her. She never stopped smiling, looking over the crowd inside, and acknowledging with a slight nod journalists she knew.

The world had flocked to see her headquarters. This was her moment. After eighteen months of house arrest. Forty minutes after the floor opened for questions, most of the journalists, exhausted in the heat, had lost their tongues. The heat had made their brains slow down. Or maybe after it became clear that no rant against the generals would happen, they lost interest. Evil and deep passions such as hate and revenge were what people wanted to see on TV or read in the newspapers. What they found was someone far more calm and composed and assured than they were, and it troubled them, silenced them. Whatever personal feelings she might have had, they never came to the surface. She was serene and in a state that one could only describe as a kind of bliss. Her very presence with such grace and tolerance humbled everyone in the room. She had found her weapon. Forgiveness was more damaging to the generals; they would have suffered less from the destruction of a couple divisions. If only forgiveness translated into higher ratings.

When the room was silent for a minute or two, she said, "I am going to count to three, and if I don't have another question, then the press conference will end." We had been inside over an hour. Numb and soaked with sweat, I looked around the room. Silence descended. "One," she said, and waited. "Two." Only one more to go. She surveyed the room, searching for that one person who had one last thing to ask. "After this, no one will be allowed to ask any further questions. I think that's fair," she said.

The journalists shifted from side to side like guilty schoolboys. Everyone held their breath and everyone wanted to get out of the hellhole before they shriveled like the wicked witch in the *Wizard of Oz*.

All eyes were trained on her, and secretly everyone prayed no one would ask another question. I became delirious from the heat, the cramped, sweaty bodies pushed against me. One question popped into my head; a crazy question. I had an irresistible urge to ask her, "Could you share with us what color your underwear is?" I wanted to belt out this question at the top of my voice, a question so cool that it would freeze the heat out of this room. Every TV and still camera carried like a gun would have swung around and drilled me. Hart would have dropped to his knees to get out of the shot. For approximately fifteen seconds across the airwaves of the world TV audiences would have seen me on my 53rd birthday, marking a historical moment, an unfolding of possibility in Burma, with a question about the Lady's panties. Sometimes there is an irrational moment where you feel that you are falling, out of control, driven by forces that you never knew existed. Like when Checkers, avoiding the kicked electric fan, somehow flung himself against the wall, leaving a trail of hot offerings. I could feel my face flushing red as I moved from foot to foot. I felt like Checkers. My mouth started to move. My bowels started to move. As hard as I tried to control my jaw and tongue, the words were starting to form.

"Three," she said.

The press conference was over. I slumped against Hart, my heart in my throat. I felt between my legs. I hadn't embarrassed myself. That was something. My 53rd birthday was definitely turning out better than my 52nd.

"Are you alright, old man?"

"I wanted to ask her something," I said.

"It's too late now for her to sing 'Happy Birthday'."

He gave me a gentle punch on the shoulder and a wink. A journalist rushed forward, holding a microphone and rapidly firing off more questions. "You are too late," she said. Firmness in her voice shamed him and he blushed and turned away. As I went up to her, her eyes narrowed as if she were about to scold me. "I don't want to ask you anything. I have something for you. Some photographs a Japanese journalist took of you a long time ago. His name was Kazuo Takeda. Today is my birthday and I really would like you to have the pictures."

She looked puzzled at first. I showed her the top photograph and she nodded.

"Thank you," she said, looking up from the photographs. "You must have gone to considerable trouble to bring these to me."

"It was my duty. Kazuo was killed in Japan. I promised his father I would give these photographs to you. Kazuo told his father everything about the day they attacked your car. It's in the photo. I thought you might want to have them."

"I remember that day and I remember Kazuo very well," she said, looking at the photo of the thugs at the bridge standoff with her car. "I am sad to learn of his death. Please tell his father."

Then she was gone.

"There is a story behind each of the photographs," I whispered after her.

She never heard me. There were too many people, too much pushing and confusion. It was no place to hold a conversation. As she walked away, I thought how she looked just like the photographs the dead man had taken. She hadn't changed or aged. The NLD officials closed ranks around her and ushered her out of the room.

She had glanced at the set that I had made for her and smiled and handed them to one of her lieutenants. All of this happened in about one minute. It wasn't about the amount of time; I had accomplished what I had set out to do. She was free; I was free. I could now write Akira Takeda letting him know that his son's photographs had been delivered to the Lady on the very day she had been released from house arrest and that she had looked at them and smiled. She had said she was sad about Kazuo's death and she wanted Akira Takeda to know this. I thought that would make the old man happy.

The reporters had a two p.m. deadline and she made certain they had their story in advance. And I had made my deadline—she had a full set of the photographs, minus one, the last one of the sleeping or dead girl. When I caught up with Hart and Sarah, I stretched out my arms. "She's got them. Kazuo's photographs are finally where they belong."

27

After the press conference, we returned to the hotel. I stood under the shower and let the spray hit my face. I kept thinking about the cycle of anticipation I had experienced. Like great sex, the waiting was often the sweetest part of the experience. I dried off, the fluffy towel working across my shoulders as I went out to the main room and turned on the TV. Before the Lady had been released, every hour CNN and BBC had daily news coverage speculating on the timing of the Lady's release. Speculation about her release had been the lead story day after day. The screen was filled with stock footage of her two sons and husband accepting the Nobel Prize on her behalf, of the Lady above her gate on University Avenue, addressing a large crowd gathered in the street.

This was the day of her release; she remained the lead story. That evening everything changed. The Lady's release from house arrest lost the leading position on the TV news. With the speculation over and her freedom witnessed by a room of sweating journalists, diplomats, an assistant professor at the University of British Columbia, a proofreader for *The Bangkok Post* and one birthday boy, she vanished without a trace from the news. The anticipation had been so much sweeter than the reality. Now that she was freed, she was just another third-world politician in an uphill battle with the forces of evil. And there was always another story, a better, more dramatic story. The Lady's lead story was bumped by the death of a politician in Europe.

A Dutch politician had been shot while out campaigning for a local election. The TV screen filled with long shots of the lifeless politician in a Dutch parking lot. I looked at photograph number nineteen and then back at the screen. We have seen so many images of the dead but that doesn't mean we can't still be deceived. The dead man was younger than me. He would never celebrate his 53rd birthday. He had apparently questioned immigration policies in the Netherlands. He was gay. It is the kind of world where either one of these facts was enough to get his brains blown out. Someone had put a bullet in his head. That bullet found its mark, blowing the Lady's story off the evening news. I turned off the television and stretched out on the bed, wearing a bath towel. I had been anticipating the moment when I could give those photos to the Lady. I tried to remember every detail of how she looked at them. The entire length of time couldn't have been more than a minute. Now what was there to look forward to?

Ming bowls, I thought. I was, after all, a collector: of things, people, and memories. It was time to push ahead. I phoned Hart's room. There was no answer. I phoned Sarah's room, and I could hear Hart in the background.

"I liked the question you asked the Lady," I said.

"Hart said it was your idea for me to check into the hotel," she said.

"Now that we are one big happy family, it's better you stay here. Of course, feel free to kick Hart out at any time."

She was silent. "We need to talk."

"Any time, baby."

I hung up the phone and took a long hit off a fat one.

28

Hart knocked on my door. Wrapped in my bath towel, I opened the door and let him in. "You want a hit of whisky?"

He didn't wait for an answer. I watched him fill half a glass with whisky. An un-Hart like gesture, I thought. Since discovering that he was a secret novelist, I wasn't surprised by anything he said or did.

"I am meeting Howard at Scott Market," he said.

"Another of your world-class pool player friends, or is he a fellow novelist?"

Hart drank from his glass. "He's a newspaper editor. I've known him for years. I saw him at the press conference. He might have some intel on where to locate Ming porcelain. Unless you want to hang around in your bath towel all day watching TV."

"This guy's worth a cup of coffee?"

"If nothing else, we can sober up."

"Is Sarah coming along?" I asked.

Hart shrugged and finished his whisky. "I don't think so."

"Let me phone her."

I reached for the phone but Hart stopped me. "She's busy. She's reading."

"Your secret novel," I said. It wasn't much of a guess.

"Something like that."

"Man, I can't get over that you didn't tell me about the novel."

Hart drank again from his glass. He shivered the way non-drinkers react to a hit of fine scotch, as if they had walked naked into a snowdrift.

We entered the Scott Market by walking over a small bridge rimmed with vendors. We crossed the street and sat at a table outside a coffee shop. Inside it was smart, modern and air-conditioned. In Rangoon almost no place is smart or modern or air-conditioned. We sat outside in the heat because there was a no-smoking rule inside. Elimination of drugs, cigarettes, and of course, anyone who didn't agree with the way you ran the country. Not long after the first round of drinks was delivered, Hart's friend Howard showed up. Like Hart, he was English, though about ten years older with a square jaw and blue eyes, his shirt and trousers wrinkled. The first thing out of his mouth wasn't about Ming dynasty porcelain. What he wanted an audience for was to talk about the censorship of his newspaper. Nothing was printed without prior approval. An official had to read and sign off on all the news and photos. There were general rules. No naked shoulders, bare midriff, too much leg—those photos were knocked back. "I once mentioned a 'dirt road' in a story and that had to be cut. Mentioning unpaved roads was against the security interests of the country."

"What about AIDS?" asked Hart.

"Nothing can be printed about AIDS."

"I guess that eliminates massage parlor and escort service ads," I said.

They both ignored me.

"How are you handling the press conference?" asked Hart.

Howard had finished working on the copy of the newspaper to be printed the day after the Lady's release. The censor said that they had to lead with the story of the visit by the Vietnamese President. That story of the President was going on page one. The Vietnamese President story needed background to fully explain the close relationship between Burma and Vietnam, with lots of positive reports of trade, agriculture and cultural exchanges. They were ordered to run a large picture of the President. The Lady's release story and press conference could appear on page two. But the story had to run without any photographs of the Lady or the press conference or any of the NLD leaders or any of the crowds outside the NLD headquarters.

"Why not run a picture of the Drug Elimination Museum?"

"Are you a journalist?" he asked me.

"No, but then neither are you. It sounds like you take dictation. That's secretarial work, not journalism."

Howard's lantern jaw locked and he glared at me as he drank his coffee. "If you understood Burma, then you would understand that we had a small victory. We convinced the government censor to agree to a reasonable compromise, taking the middle path, not banning the story," he said.

"You're negotiating what is news," I said.

"We are finding a way to publish news in a place where the story would otherwise have been buried."

"Are sanctions working?" asked Hart.

I rolled my eyes. I should have stayed in my room. This was a total waste of time. I was learning nothing. It was hot. Even the beggars dragged themselves along the sidewalk with more effort than usual. A mad looking Burmese man dressed up in a clown's outfit with twenty pointed wizard hats on his head came past. He was selling hats. His mouth was limned a slimy red from chewing betel nut. I took his picture and gave him some money.

"All the people who say that sanctions work don't live in Burma. If they lived here they would see that about eighty women lost their jobs because a European company shut down their Burmese plant. These women were the breadwinners for their family. Now there is no bread, no school fees, no medical, nothing. Is that the way sanctions are supposed to work?"

"Censorship of clowns," I said. "Do they censor what clowns wear or say?"

"The censor is a clown. Not that one. But a clown nonetheless. The other day, he killed a photo of a mixed marriage. He said no wedding shots, engagement photos, society photographs of any mixed marriage. That's a clown-like rule. It's a vestige of colonial times when the British took Burmese women as their minor wives. A general once bought a big ad in the newspaper raving against his son who had married a Singapore girl."

"Political correctness Burmese style," said Hart.

"As vile and repressive and virulent as anything in the West," said Howard.

I kicked Hart's shin under the table. I mouthed the word "Ming."

Hart leaned forward over the table. "You wouldn't happen to know where we might find Ming porcelain?"

Howard's eyes narrowed. No doubt he had heard this request from others passing through Rangoon. He lit a cigarette and nodded. He wrote a name and address on a piece of paper. "This man might have information."

Our Ming man was a retired doctor named Khin Aung. Half Chinese and half Mon. Burma was a country of such halves.

29

Sarah was locked in her room reading Hart's novel. I wondered how best to communicate with her. First I had put Hart on the payroll, and then it expanded to include Sarah. I footed her room bill at the hotel. If you wanted a woman's proximity, there was a price to pay. I had in my mind that she had some useful information about tattoos, and if that were the case, then the price of the room would be a bargain. I liked her from the first time we met at the museum. When it turned out that she was willing to accept my invitation to stay at our hotel across from the zoo, I took this as an omen. I instinctively knew that we would become friends. Whatever developed between Hart and her wouldn't matter. Friendship has that appealing longevity that love affairs aspire to but never attain. On the way back to the hotel, I showed her the photograph of the Burmese girl curled up on the chaise longue, her face obscured by long black hair falling over her eye and cheek. Hart had laughed and said there was likely little real mystery. It was more than likely that Kazuo had been out on a night excursion mission after finishing a hard day's work taking photographs of bullet-like holes in the rear window of the Lady's Toyota and he needed to unwind.

My questions to Sarah—"How could anyone ever know who that woman was? Can her tattoo help us find her?"

"I've heard of this tattoo. But I have never personally seen one myself," said Sarah. She was matter-of-fact and quickly handed the photograph back as if to hold it too long would contaminate her. "That tattoo is more rare than the ones on Chin women."

Hart didn't contradict her. He had his reasons. There was no percentage in a conflict over the woman in the picture.

I told Sarah my brush with disaster as I had almost begun a Tourette's rant—*fucking shit cum whore—what color are your fucking panties?*

"You're making that up," she said, laughing.

"It's true. Ask Hart. I was seized with this overwhelming urge to ask this totally insane question. I was bursting inside."

Hart said, "Foaming at the mouth. It happens often. It happened at Scott Market today."

"At the press conference, I had to cover my mouth with both hands. I was ready to blurt out *panties, tell us what you are wearing.*"

"I saw your eyes roll up. I thought it was a seizure," said Hart.

"The words were in my throat. I nearly lost it. I've never had anything that strange take hold of me, possess me like a demon. Whatever control I thought that I had, snapped. What was left was a huge sense of dread. It felt like something outside of myself had crawled inside and was using me to convey this message."

"I am glad for your sake it didn't happen."

"Think of the news value," I said.

"Gonzo value isn't news value," said Hart. "Though it might have played on Burmese TV. The generals would have liked that outburst. Just to show the kind of person that the opposition is friendly with. You would have set back the democracy movement another ten years."

A couple of hours later, I wrote a note and slipped it under Sarah's door. I wrote: "Sometimes you live a week in your life and within that week is a book. A once in a lifetime opportunity, and if you're lucky, you have that experience a couple of times in your life. In reality for most people there isn't enough in their life for a short story. If the standard were an original short story most would die with a blank page in their printer tray. I don't know the reason for sure. But I need to find the woman in that photograph. Please help me."

30

Several hours later, Sarah must have taken a break from reading Hart's novel and slipped a note under my door. She wrote:

"The KFC recipe for fried chicken was stolen from northern Burma. The Kachin state. Forget the bullshit about the secret southern recipe from Colonel Sanders. The recipe is Burmese. That's a fact.

"The girl—she's not a woman in that photograph—as I said before is not, in my humble opinion, dead. I know about death because of my father but that doesn't make me an expert.

"Hart's novel is extraordinary. Original, vital, insightful and mysterious.

"The person telling the story is a woman, an old Burmese woman who is eighty years old. At the end of her life, she tells the passionate love story of when she was a young woman. It is a war story. A story of longing, coming of age, danger and redemption.

"I've never seen a blue scorpion on a woman's thigh before. I can tell from the angle of the photograph that whoever took that picture had wanted to make certain that the scorpion was both visible and invisible at the same time. My guess is the person who made the tattoo had the same goal.

"Hart knows a Burmese we should talk to about the photograph. He's a doctor and very old. He can tell us everything we need to know about the woman in the photograph and (you will like this) he knows everything there is to know about Ming bowls."

She signed the note, "Your friend, Sarah."

This was how we started our conversation. I sat on the edge of the bed looking at the photograph, holding it close to my face. I squinted at the tattoo until it transformed itself into a birthmark. The more I looked at the mark, the more it looked like a scorpion in motion, crawling out of her body; but if you looked at anything long enough it could become whatever you imagined, a dragon, a wagon, a beer, a Ming bowl. I re-read Sarah's note a couple of times more. She had opened what was obviously an old wound: the death of her father. We continued passing notes written at odd times during the night and slipped under each other's door. It became a game to see who would fall asleep first.

A FINE LINE BETWEEN
THE LIVING
AND THE DEAD

31

Hart insisted that we visit Khin Aung and Sarah immediately agreed this was a brilliant suggestion. Before I could finish a beer, Aye Thit negotiated with a taxi driver to take us from the hotel to Khin Aung's township for about one dollar. Hart also knew how to get to the doctor's apartment and he displayed the same confidence as Hart on auto-pilot locking onto the glide path into the Floating Balls noodle stand, knowing a big bowl awaited him and that it was on credit. The three of us squeezed together in the back seat with Sarah seated between us. I rubbed against one hip and Hart took the other; if she had been milk by the end of the trip she would have turned to butter. Aye Thit sat in front with the driver who was no doubt deciding exactly how to spend his one dollar after the journey ended. Aye Thit had been to the doctor's apartment with Hart before. A small detail that Sarah had omitted from her notes to me. All of these tiny revelations started to accumulate, adding up to pathways and networks that I never knew existed. If you had asked me twenty-four hours earlier if Hart and Aye Thit—who was my man—had a secret life that excluded me, I would have said, "Man, that's impossible, Aye Thit is my man. He knows that I've looked after him and his family for ten years." The short answer, as my wife would say, was that looking after another person doesn't mean squat, because someone else comes along and promises to look after them and before you know it, you are in some kind of daisy chain of compassion, with bonds of loyalty looking like a plate of leftover pasta.

The traffic on the road was light in the early evening. With gasoline rationing, and not a lot of money, there had to be a good reason for people to venture out. We had just finished one of the most incredible days of our lives, but no one mentioned the Lady or the press conference. Like the BBC and CNN coverage, what we had observed was softly, surely rolling into the fog of the past, overtaken by new events, images, thoughts, and desires as simple as feeling Sarah's hip riding against my own in the back of a taxi in Rangoon.

I rolled down the window and hung my elbow out, bringing up my arm to take a drink of Tiger. Sarah glanced over disapprovingly. We seemed to get along better on paper.

"How do you know this doctor?" I asked Hart, leaning forward to catch his eye.

"That's a long story," he said.

"Then give me the short version."

"My grandfather met him during the war," said Hart. He sighed and looked out the window. Something was bothering him.

"Not that short a version. For example, where did they meet?"

"In Moulmein," said Hart. "Khin Aung was a youngish doctor in the district. Doctors were in short supply; even if you lacked full qualifications you were of considerable use."

"A Burmese doctor on the front lines." I nodded my head, took the last of the beer and threw the can into the street. It bounced, rolled and disappeared into the night.

"You could get arrested for littering," said Sarah.

"Darling, that's probably one of the last things they would arrest me for."

We finished the journey in silence, with me brooding over Hart's book. Only Sarah had read it. Who would be the audience for his book in Hart's dreams? Morons? Health and environmentalist crazies, people who couldn't find Burma on a map, had never heard of Tiger beer, or the Lady, or General Custer. That was the world we lived in. My art, in contrast, was superior. It wasn't dependent on words; I connected to people through images, non-verbal bursts of energy. Others took the full load straight on. My photographs were in their face. People looked and tried to understand or they turned away in horror. It didn't matter, because I got them. Images provided a clearer choice from the fuzzy-wuzzy world of words, one word after another, so carefully constructed to keep everyone happy. I broke the silence in the car with a loud belch and flicked my lighter, the flame touching the end of another cigarette. I opened another can and raised it to Sarah and Hart.

"To good old Clarke, who is circling somewhere above Burma in glider heaven," I said. In my mind's eye I saw him sitting in Lucy's Tiger Bar.

"You will like the old man, Sloan. Remember, he's eighty-two and his hearing is going," said Hart. "But his mind is sharp. He misses nothing though he complains about losing his memory, slowing down. But I don't see any lost power or memory."

"We will be gentle," said Sarah, squeezing Hart's arm. "Won't we, Sloan?"

"The idea is to find out about Ming bowls, right?"

"Khin Aung will know where to look," said Hart. "He knows everyone."

We stopped in front of a large ugly boxy apartment block. It looked like an enormous glider converted into rooms. Aye Thit, who had negotiated the fare, pulled a wad of kyat out of his blue bag and paid the driver his one dollar plus. We walked up four flights and then down a narrow corridor with an iron railing. At the far end, Khin Aung waited in the doorway. He looked much younger than a man in his eighties. His silver hair thinned in the front. He wore wire-rimmed glasses and had an easy, affable smile. He embraced Hart, pulling him close. The doctor showed genuine affection. In the way he looked at Hart, I saw something—it was as if Khin Aung were seeing someone else. Hart and his grandfather bore a striking resemblance. I had seen a photo of the grandfather at Hart's age. They could have been twins. The grandfather had been perfectly preserved in Hart. If I ever reached sixty, I hoped to look half as fit as Khin Aung. We removed our shoes before stepping through the door. In the sitting room, old original oil paintings hung on the walls. One large painting had pagodas in ruins in the foreground. I recognized the pagoda as one just outside of Pegu. Another painting featured twin *chindit* outside the entrance to a smaller pagoda that

I couldn't place. I thought of Akira Takeda asking me if I knew what a *chindit* was. When he asked the question, I knew he wasn't asking about the *chindit* in front of a pagoda but the British soldiers who fought in Burma.

"Ne Win owns three paintings by this same artist," said Khin Aung. "Ne Win's first wife loved this painter."

The paintings on the walls of his apartment immediately established a personal connection with Ne Win. Power and art. In Burma such underground cables were largely hidden, only surfacing now and again in the most unexpected places on the walls of influential people. Across from the sofa, a teakwood dining table and six teak chairs all properly lined up awaited us. There were plates with peanuts, fried peppers, and tiny deep fried chicken wings. Down the narrow hallway were two bedrooms. The apartment was clean and tidy. Carpets had been laid on the wooden floor. Looking around, it was obvious that the old doctor had gone to considerable trouble making it presentable for us.

After the introductions, Khin Aung brought out a bottle of Johnnie Walker Black. Aye Thit drank only water. From inside his blue bag, he pulled out a bottle of water and placed it carefully on a small table in front of the sofa. Hart had brought along two bottles of whisky and another bottle of rum. Khin Aung smiled broadly as Aye Thit pulled the bottles from his plastic bag.

"Hart, it has been too long since your last visit. I thought you had forgotten me. With such a beautiful woman, I can't say that I blame you." Khin Aung nodded at Sarah.

"I've been very bad, Dr. Khin Aung. Please forgive me."

The number of bottles of liquor only made sense if you understood that Hart had been taught to make amends for unbecoming behavior by delivering several bottles of expensive liquor. No offense could have survived his gift. "Have you published that book you told me about? Or is it still unfinished?"

It seemed about everyone but me knew about Hart's novel.

"A book is never finished, doctor. Until the day it is published."

"I am reading it," said Sarah. "It's unlike any novel I've ever read."

"That's quite a statement," said Khin Aung. He looked at Sarah and then over at Hart, who shrugged. "There are many fine books."

Sarah had no trouble starting the conversation. "What makes this one special is the narrator. She's a Burmese woman named Mima and as the story opens she's nearly eighty years old."

"That is ancient," said Khin Aung.

"Only she doesn't appear really old. Mima lives in a very small apartment on the outskirts of Rangoon. Her oldest son died in prison and she goes to the prison to recover his body. The prison guards search her even though she is clearly an old woman who would cause no one any harm. They aren't worried about any danger. The search is harassment, showing that the guards have power and do whatever they want. Mima submits to the search, saying nothing. She is very old and knows these men won't rape her. This all happens in the prison morgue. Her son's body is a few feet away. As they humiliate her in the presence of her dead son, a doctor comes into the room. This man is nearly as old as Mima. The guards have her dress raised up, exposing legs whittled down and creased and wrinkled with age, folds of skin hanging over the knees. On her thigh is a small blue tattoo. Seeing this tattoo, the doctor stops in his tracks. It is a perfectly shaped, small blue scorpion. The doctor orders the guards to leave the room. For a moment, it is not clear if the guards will take any notice of the old doctor. They snarl and gnash their teeth, turning and spitting as they leave, slamming the door. He whispers to Mima the word *ianfu*. His tone curls the words into a question. *Were you a comfort woman in Moulmein?* She looks deep into his eyes, trying to recall what his face might have looked like more than fifty years ago. But no name comes forth. Nothing about his presence suggests anyone she had ever laid eyes on."

"Why don't we leave it there," said Hart. "We don't want to spoil the story."

Hart had appropriated the image of the blue scorpion on the girl's thigh; he stole it from Kazuo's photograph. I was enraged at this theft. I had shown him the photograph and asked his opinion about it less than a year ago. I had no idea he was going to steal the blue scorpion. "You should have told me," I said, my voice crackling with emotion. "You should have said something. That you were going to use that photograph. It's not right. Kazuo took that picture, man. It belongs to him. What you're doing just ain't right."

Hart turned in his chair, his eyes looking directly at me. "Sloan, has it occurred to you that the book may have been written before you showed me the photograph?"

"Man, how is that possible?"

Before Hart responded, Khin Aung said, "Don't be too concerned, my friend. I've told the story about the *ianfu* to many people over the years. It is no secret that the Japanese established comfort houses in Moulmein during the war. All the girls who worked in one private house had a blue scorpion tattooed on their right thigh. The tattoo showed to whom the girl belonged. She carried that brand for the rest of her life. You may think that was cruel. At the time, it was an honor; the tattoo guaranteed the girl's quality to work at the Blue Scorpion."

Khin Aung had a distracted, dreamy look. It was as if he were about to say something and thought better of it.

Sarah sighed heavily. "What other choice did those women have?"

"What choice did any of us have?" asked Khin Aung.

"In war, men have more choice."

"That's what you believe, is it, young lady?"

He had asked about the progress of the novel as a social courtesy. He hadn't really wanted to hear about or discuss the book, or to become embroiled in a conversation about the injustice and hardship suffered by the women who worked at the Blue Scorpion. In the doctor's mind, those girls had had it good, or to put it another way, they could have had a much worse time of it. As he refilled his glass with whisky, he floated inside his memories; but this didn't last long, as his current pre-occupations were far more immediate and pressing than literary tit-for-tat or wartime brothels. Besides, given the overall state of affairs in Burma, what good or use was a single book? It meant nothing, and could do nothing to change the lives of the people. It was better, he thought, to be surrounded by art; at least to have paintings by the same painter who had been loved by Ne Win's wife. This link of images from his humble apartment to the lavish premises of Ne Win conveyed far more force than thoughts about the past.

Khin Aung rarely had guests to his apartment but when he entertained, he loved an audience, foreigners who listened to his stories. It was like being back in the classroom lecturing a fresh group of new students all filled with hope and dreams and wonder, open and ready to listen to every word. As elsewhere in Asia, no one came straight out and asked what they truly wished to have the doctor answer. We all played the game around the table, watching the old doctor dance around delicate issues of his family and money, as the two were never very far apart in his consciousness. Pride and doom flowed from both.

"I pay eight hundred kyat a month for rent," Khin Aung said, as he poured whisky from a bottle that would have cost him more than two years rent on the apartment. Sarah took out her digital camera and everyone smiled, arms around shoulders, as she took several photographs. The flash left stars in our eyes. I got up and told Sarah to sit between the doctor and Hart and took two more photographs. I took another one of Aye Thit and Khin Aung together. Aye Thit had albums of photographs I had taken of him. Sarah showed the doctor the shots of the tattooed Chin women inside the Drug Elimination Museum.

"The Shan men tattoo their bodies," said Khin Aung.

Tattoos were a way of identification of belief, of protection and honor. I took the bottle and refilled the doctor's whisky glass. He was loosening up nicely. He asked where in the world one could live in a large two bedroom apartment for seventy-five cents a month. None of us had an answer for the old doctor and this seemed to please him. What pleased him even more was that the day before his daughter, Nilar, had married. She was a plain woman with no distinguishing features. She had been lucky to find a husband, he told us. A moment later, the new husband came through the door and crossed the sitting room. He looked startled to see a table of foreigners. Young, unsure, and shy, he fled as quickly as he could after introductions were made. He disappeared down the corridor and into one of the far bedrooms. "He's a good boy," said Khin Aung. "He works as a security guard." I decided that was a good name for his son-in-law, the Security Guard. The doctor said the boy had a very good heart; he was clean and he was devoted to Nilar. This was a father's way of saying his daughter had married down. If she had at least been pretty and young, she could have chosen someone from her own class and background. But she was neither. Not long after the new bridegroom came into the apartment, Nilar arrived all smiles, carrying a fat brown bag stuffed with the kyat equivalent of two hundred dollars. In terms of sheer bulk, two hundred dollars changed into kyat made for a large bag of money, a wedding gift from relatives abroad.

Nilar couldn't stop smiling, a woman's smile of success or conquest, smug and winning at the same time. A black market Indian money trader had exchanged her dollars at the rate of 918 kyat per dollar. Examining the number was like reading a chicken's gizzard for meaning. "This number," she said, "is very good luck." By tradition, the number nine shimmered as the most auspicious number. Ne Win had romanced the number nine by changing all Burmese currency to make each number divisible by the number nine. In doing so, the old currency became worthless overnight—not particularly good luck for those holding the pre-divisible-by-nine currency. But it could have been worse, he could have changed the currency and caused all drivers to shift from the left to the right side of the road on the same day. He didn't do that. Instead, Ne Win wiped out wealth and reconfigured right-side driving on different occasions. These were little surprises to be savored. A new nine-based currency appeared like a ghost or an alien from another planet without warning and out of nowhere. A daughter rushing home with her 918 exchange rate.

Khin Aung said, "I am a rationalist. A medical man." Sipping his whisky, he had to have a rational way of seeing the world and the mumbo jumbo about lucky numbers, dates, and times was nonsense. I loved a man who drank whisky straight, held it on his tongue, shivered, swallowed, and then swore allegiance to rational thought. He admitted, nonetheless, that 918 was a very good number. Everyone agreed it was good. Nilar hovered behind him, her face glowing from her father's approval and her good fortune to be suddenly rich in kyat. Khin Aung looked over his shoulder and smiled at his daughter. Her hands rested on his shoulders, and he patted one hand. "It is a lucky number for any new bride," he said. What was left unsaid but spoke volumes was: this number supported the idea that the marriage had been the right match even though her husband was a lowly security guard. The family had been looking for a good omen and the sign had arrived in the form of a lucky exchange rate number. Nilar bent over, kissed her father's cheek, and hurried down the corridor. A door opened and closed. The night was young, and I imagined that the Security Guard curled on the bed, wondering when the strangers would leave, would learn from his new wife that the blessing of the gods on their marriage had been confirmed by an Indian black market currency trader.

"She's very much in love," said Khin Aung. "I don't really believe 918 will bring good luck any more than I believe another number will bring bad luck. But that's not what she needed to hear. Sometimes you tell your children what you know will comfort them. What is the harm in that? You see, I was very much in love with her mother."

Sarah sighed. Women love hearing an elderly man profess love for his wife; they love hearing any man shamelessly announce this matrimonial tenderness, care and affection. If you want to sleep with a woman, don't tell her that you are single; tell her that you are married and love your wife very much. That is the magic mantra that opens her legs.

"And your wife is . . ." But before Sarah could finish, the old doctor finished her sentence.

"In America. She has been there a very long time I am afraid. You know how we met? Over ice cream. I was born in Moulmein. During the war I worked as a young medical officer. I dressed smartly in a freshly laundered uniform and carried out my duties and responsibilities in the district. I have to confess that in that uniform and at that age, being a doctor, I had all the girls in the district after me. My family operated a shoe factory and a general store. One Sunday after church, a young girl came into the shop to buy ice cream. Her name was Thaw. Our eyes met the first time her tongue touched the ice cream. I saw something, I can't say exactly what, but I knew I wanted to see her again. The next Sunday she returned with her family. Again, our eyes met. That was the way we started our courtship. I treated Thaw's family to ice cream. I was the big spender in the splendid uniform. Not long afterwards, the family arrived on Saturday afternoons as well. They all sat around and ate ice cream. Now I had the Saturday as well as the Sunday ice cream bill to settle. Within a month, I had fallen in love with her. Like my daughter with her security guard, I was hopelessly in the deep end, and would have read meaning into any number or a bird perching on a railing. I asked her father, who was a Baptist preacher, for Thaw's hand. He asked if I was a Christian. I said that I was and this was to the great relief of the family. Her father, upon learning I was of the same religion, paid for *my* ice cream that Saturday. There was my omen. We had a successful ice cream courtship. Thaw's family licked their ice cream, exchanging a few words, licking more ice cream. They listened as I told them story after story of doing my rounds in the district. Because I traveled widely in the district, I was the source of gossip, news, rumors, births, illness, and death. That made me quite popular. On the way out of the general store that Saturday, Thaw's father consented to our marriage. We had never so much as held hands. Before the wedding, my wife's family sent out 120 invitations for the wedding but five hundred people showed up. People were hungry. It was wartime and there was great hardship. No one ever had enough to eat and weddings and funerals were a way to fill the belly. There might not be another chance for a free meal. Also, being a preacher, he had his church friends who prayed for free meals."

Khin Aung's life had changed by paying for a girl's family to eat Sunday ice cream, and when that generosity extended to Saturday, it was clear that this future son-in-law would be perfectly capable of understanding that a few extra mouths might need feeding. The source of unspoken disapproval of the Security Guard was clear: here was a man who couldn't feed the doctor's family; the doctor's family would have yet another cycle of mouths to feed.

"During the war," the doctor said, "few things were certain; but everyone knew there would be lots of food at a wedding. The problem was no one thought so many people would arrive. They had to divide up the food. It was like Jesus with five fish and a couple of loaves of bread."

"Your wife, she's not coming back?" asked Sarah.

He twisted a yellow gold band on his finger. The wedding ring that he had never removed. Something caught in his throat. He shook off the emotion, pointing over at one of the paintings on the wall.

"Did I tell you that that painter is my son? Several of his paintings hang in Ne Win's house."

Later Aye Thit told us that the doctor had long ago separated from his wife. His memories of the wedding had not dimmed. Khin Aung's sorrow at a failed marriage was somehow soothed by the memory of what hope everyone had held for Thaw and him. He wasn't a security guard with limited prospects. He had been a medical officer with an entire district under his authority. He had stayed the course. He had paid for everything.

Khin Aung sat at the dinner table holding his daughter's marriage certificate. He had the certificate framed. His daughter's marriage certificate had Nilar's name and the name of the Security Guard written in perfect Gothic lettering. It lay under a layer of glass as cold as ice cream and he admired the certificate as if it were a doctorate degree from Harvard. He passed the framed certificate around the table. Sarah pointed out a short notice at the bottom proclaiming that the couple had been married in a Christian wedding and that under law a fee was owed.

There was a long silence as the doctor put on his reading glasses and examined the marriage certificate. He read out every word and then lay the framed certificate down on the table. He hadn't touched the food. He looked up at Sarah, removing his reading glasses.

"I paid the fee," said the doctor. The fee was twenty kyat, about the cost of an ice cream cone.

Sarah passed the certificate to Hart. "Where will you keep it?" asked Hart.

"We will hang it here," said the doctor, pointing to the wall where the oil painting of the pagoda in Pegu was hung.

"Yesterday, we saw the Lady," said Sarah. "I know I was moved by hearing her talk. Like I have been touched deeply listening to you tonight."

Sarah glanced at Hart; he winked and flashed his perpetually passive smile. Hart had mastered the smile that Asians used whenever they had something they wished to hide, or to avoid or deny a situation. My mind was a million miles away from Ming bowls. I fingered the edge of Kazuo's photograph of the girl inside my pocket. I was ready to lay it on the table.

I want to know about the girl in the photo, I wanted to scream. *Forget about the fucking marriage to the loser in the back room, the loser, the loser. Forget the wife who will never come back, who is gone*

174

forever, forever. Fuck the Ming. The same overwhelming feeling that had hit me at the Lady's press conference, seized me, my brain ready to boil and explode. *Tell us the color of your underwear.*

"I remember her father," Khin Aung said. "General Aung San."

"You knew him?" asked Hart.

The doctor shook his head. "When I finally met him, he was dead."

"I am not following you," said Hart.

"The day General Aung San was assassinated, I was on duty at the hospital. On the day he was shot, another six men were also killed. They were holding a meeting in the conference room. The gunman burst in and shot them with a machine gun. The bodies of Aung San and his ministers were taken to my hospital. I assisted in performing the autopsy on General Aung San. He had been shot three times. Tragedy has always struck that family," he said. "A few years later, I performed an autopsy on Aung San's seven year old son. The boy had drowned in a pond. But that's another story."

"You did the autopsy on the Lady's father?" I asked.

The doctor simply smiled. There was a slight nod in my direction.

Long patches of life are like deep space, there is not much texture or density but a stillness and emptiness. Then a burst of light flashes across the darkness. So much of how life connects involves vast improbabilities. We had walked into the Lady's press conference without any right to be there, without it even being planned, and the next night, we were drinking whisky with the doctor who after reading us the complete marriage certificate of his daughter, then removed his eye-glasses and told us he had performed the autopsy on General Aung San and on the General's son. It was like falling into one of those spider holes sucking you into a parallel universe.

"I never knew about this," said Hart.

"I guess it never came up before," said Khin Aung.

"After the autopsy, General Aung San's body was displayed in Jubilee Hall. They laid him out along with his ministers inside glass coffins. People filed past the coffins every day to look at their dead leader. Later, the authorities tore down Jubilee Hall. That was a pity. It was such a beautiful structure. What replaced it was in appalling taste. But that is just the opinion of an old man wishing the past would have followed him into the present." His eyes looked down at his daughter's marriage certificate. "For many years I kept the uniform General Aung San had been wearing the day he was killed. At night, I would sometimes take out the uniform and trace the holes left by the machine-gun bullets that had ripped through his chest, piercing his heart. And I would ask myself, 'Why do such things happen? What is in our nature that makes man so violent?' And you know, I still ask myself those questions, and I still don't have any answers."

I could tell by looking in his face—his hard, unflinching eyes revealed no emotion—that he had seen a lot of dead bodies. "You must have done a lot of autopsies," I said.

Khin Aung drank from his whisky glass. "I've opened the bodies of more murder victims than I can count. Thousands upon thousands. All ages. Men and women. Children. In 1962 I examined the bodies of seventy-five students who had been shot inside the grounds of the university. Young boys with their entire life before them. All potential husbands and fathers. Darwin wouldn't have predicted the survivability of such boys. Such idealism is a genetic dead end. It rarely gets transmitted to the next generation. Each one of them had been shot in the back. The generals didn't like that I wrote in my report that the students had been shot in the back. But I refused to change reality from what it was."

You had to admire anyone who had stood up to the murderers. It was one thing to be rationalist in a medical faculty and another thing to report factually on the murder of students. "Military men tried to convince me to change the conclusions in my report," he said. "They might have been Ne Win's men. It was difficult to believe they were acting on their own, but I told them that what I wrote was the truth and once they understood I wasn't going to change white into black to suit their political purposes, they backed off. You see, the army had shot the students in the back as they ran away. They didn't want to have to admit such a slaughter had happened. That was understandable. Violence in self defense is one thing, but shooting people in the back is a different order of violence. One of the officers said that the bullet had gone through the body, so how did you know it hadn't gone into the chest and out the back? I told them that I examined each body and carefully measured the bullet wounds. What did I find? The hole that entered the back of the body and the one that exited the chest cavity were of different sizes. A doctor knows the difference between an entry and exit wound. The boys had been shot in the back. There was no medical doctor who would have said otherwise. If they didn't want my report, that was okay. They could have an officer sign another report. But my report wouldn't be changed. They knew that I'd testified in thousands of trials. And that I had educated the current generation of daughters and sons of the rich who were doctors and nurses, including Ne Win's daughter. What were they going to do? Shoot me in the back? Not likely. You see, I used to play golf with Ne Win."

"What was his handicap?" asked Hart.

"Nineteen."

Maybe you had to be English to listen to the doctor talk about facing down thugs who had massacred students and then come up with a question about the head gangster's golf handicap. I would have said something. But I didn't want to embarrass Hart. After all, the doctor was his friend, and he was doing me this big favor by bringing me to meet him. And besides, Ne Win's golf handicap just happened to be the same number as the photographs that Kazuo had taken, then dumped his camera, and a few months later got himself killed in a road accident. Showing, if anything, that the number nine wasn't always that lucky.

Hart had presented me with a golden opportunity. But before I could hand Khin Aung Kazuo's photograph of the seductive Burmese girl, Hart grabbed my hand and stopped me. "Have another whisky," he said. The doctor refilled my glass.

"You know what my pension is?" It was Khin Aung's turn to ask a question.

No one was willing to guess. "The equivalent of one dollar fifty. That is per month. Half goes for rent."

He could splurge on himself with the other seventy-five cents. That paper bag with two hundred bucks worth of kyat inside was worth ten years of pension money. At eighty-two years old, having seen as much death as Khin Aung had seen, he must have felt it was a reasonably safe bet that the witness to a half-century of violence didn't have another ten years left.

"My friend, Sloan, is interested in finding Ming porcelain. I understand there are a lot of Ming pieces in Moulmein. Since your family comes from there, you might have some advice."

Hart was slow and deliberate. One small step at a time. I had to admire that quality in him; I wanted to blurt out, *Look at the girl. Look at her, see her, see the mark.*

"I was born in Moulmein the year World War I ended. 1918. My great-grandfather traveled to Burma from China in the 1860s. He established a shoe factory. He built up his business until he had more than thirty employees. All of the employees were young women. They made very fine slippers. I lost my virginity when I was ten with one of the girls in the factory. I had come back from school and crossed the factory grounds. She was waiting for me. We went to a wooded area near the river. She was eighteen years old and I saw her cunt—black and hairy—and she undressed me. First she took off my shirt, slowly pulling it over my head, then she unbuttoned my trousers and took my penis in her hand. She looked at it very carefully, turning it over as if it were some lost treasure. I had no idea about sex. Perhaps this was it. A girl undressed you, and made a minute inspection of your organ and that was all there was to it. After she had me on the ground I found out that the organ had another purpose, another place to go. I learned from that moment never to be surprised, and never to make an assumption that can't be tested and proved."

The whisky had loosened him up but it was more than just alcohol working his tongue. He was a lonely man. Someone who had reached the top and then had grown old, slid downhill until he was forgotten. Abandoned by his wife, his daughter marrying the Security Guard, his old, cherished colonial buildings knocked down, and a buck and a half to live on each month. He was at the end of the road looking back, and he wanted us to listen to what he had witnessed on his journey. The shock disclosures mounted one upon another until it seemed there was nothing else this old doctor could reveal that would surpass his previous revelations. Nilar walked back and forth between the front room and the bedroom where her husband sat alone inside a void of silence that suggested his place—in Khin Aung's private universe—was less a husband than a long-term guest in his father-in-law's apartment. She stood behind her father, repeating her earlier gesture of putting her arms gently on his shoulders. The doctor told us that he had performed an autopsy on his own son, who died from a drug overdose. He felt nothing in doing this. Cutting the body was science, medicine—it was not related to a personality or a soul or spirit.

"My son listened to no one. He ran with a fast crowd of young men who like him had decided they had no future, wanted no future and cruised the night looking for action. They were the kind of men who died young. If there had been a war, then those restless young men would have hiked up mountains, across rivers, carrying heavy packs, their rifles at the ready. And they would have had a purpose, the killing purpose that such men thirst for in their youth. We had a long discussion and I thought we understood each other. He agreed that I would personally remove the tattoos from his body. I grafted skin from his thigh to cover them. I put him under and removed each tattoo, making his body clean and pure. I gave him what every father wishes to give a wayward son, a second chance. But after the operation, it wasn't long before it became clear that he didn't want a second chance. My efforts were pointless; only later did I realize that this task of making my son's body pure again was one that I could never win. It's an ancient fight, the one waged between father and son, and history shows that the outcome ends in grief. My son died from a drug overdose. I know this because during the autopsy, I found his new tattoo—a blue scorpion tattooed on his penis. He had done this so that I would see that I couldn't possibly win. In death, he was the victor. You see, our relationship was always combative. My son had promised never to have another tattoo. He couldn't resist breaking that promise. So he had this one last tattoo on his cock. Also he had had inserted under the skin of his cock, a small stone. The stone was suspended under the surface of the foreskin just below the tattooed blue scorpion. As much as I hate tattoos, I must say that this one was done with great elegance and style. You may wonder why he had a stone placed under the skin of his penis. I certainly had such a question. Perhaps it was to enhance the pleasure of his sexual partners. Perhaps it had some mystical connection with the blue scorpion. I never had a chance to ask him. He was nineteen years old when he died. When I performed the autopsy, I removed the small stone and put it in a jar and labeled the jar: Son's Stone."

At last when there was an opening, I asked him—"You did an autopsy on your own son?" My mouth had gone dry. There wasn't enough whisky or beer to wet down the scorched feeling in the back of my throat.

"It is my expertise. I also did the autopsy on my brother. He was killed in combat against the Karen. My brother was an officer. The being of that person, whatever they mean, is gone. I was not cutting into my son or brother, or into General Aung San or the General's son, or the students shot in the back. I worked on a body that had died. The life was gone. What was left behind meant nothing other than the burden of determining the cause of death. My duty was to establish cause even for the body of my son. I could have no special feeling for the body as I examined it. At the funeral, of course, I cried. That wasn't the medical doctor who was crying, that was the boy's father who cried."

Sarah wiped away tears. "My father and brother could never get along," she said. "There was always tension in their relationship. One rule of Father's was that we couldn't leave the house without asking him first. My brother never asked."

"Your brother died?" asked Khin Aung, who reached back with one hand and placed it on Nilar's arm.

"Yes, riding a motorcycle. When my father saw my brother's body, he said nothing to my mother or me. He disappeared into the work shed and put a bullet in his head. That's how it ended."

32

"Did your son's tattoo look anything like this?" I asked, sliding Kazuo's photograph of the girl across the table. With Nilar staring down over his shoulder, the doctor examined the photo of the girl with the blue scorpion tattoo with a detached expression. I kept thinking *this man sliced open his own son's body and looked inside. Pulled out the lungs, heart, liver, and intestines, weighed them, poked at them. Taking a knife to his son's cock and removing a stone.*

Khin Aung put the photograph down and took the cap off the Johnnie Walker Black. "This won't be a short story," he said, looking at his watch. "And, it is late. Besides, it may be that some stories are better left untold." He rolled the cap between his fingers. His eyes, glazed and half-closed, seemed to catch the glitter of light. For a moment, the old man had left us and gone somewhere deep in his memory.

"I would appreciate anything you might tell us," said Hart.

That was my man, Hart: knowing how much agony the picture had caused me, he came straight out and asked the old doctor to tell us anything he might know about the girl in Kazuo's photograph. Everyone around the table waited, as Hart's sincerity registered its magic touch on the old doctor. Khin Aung, a product of the old colonial system—Hart later said Khin Aung won fencing Blue at Cambridge (partially explaining his expertise in entry and exit wounds)—accepted the polite request from an Englishman as if it carried the full weight of authority.

"As I have already said, my great-grandfather came from China and opened a shoe factory in Moulmein."

We all nodded as he put the cap back on the whisky bottle. The bottle of Johnnie Walker had been drunk down to about one year's equivalent of rent on his apartment. "During the war, our factory had very few orders, and finally for long stretches we had no orders at all. We had friendly relations with the Japanese. We did not hate or fear them. We were not an occupied country. If anything, they represented pride in being Asian and being independent of Europe. In 1943 General Aung San went to Japan and received a medal from the Emperor himself. But he was proud of that medal. We Burmese were proud of his recognition by the Emperor. Not everything that came with the Japanese was good. Have you ever heard the Japanese word *ianjo*?"

I had a Japanese wife and a basic vocabulary in Japanese but this was a new one on me. "What's it mean?" I asked. I shook a cigarette out the pack and offered it to Khin Aung and he took it, much to my surprise. It had been decades since I had seen a doctor smoke. He leaned forward with the cigarette pursed between his lips. I lit it and he leaned back, sucking in the smoke.

"*Ianjo* means comfort house. In English we say brothel," he said, letting the smoke curl out of his nostrils. "And the Japanese word *ianfu* means comfort girl. I don't have to tell you the English word for that one. Comfort houses didn't just happen; they were opened as a policy of the Japanese military. Such things, by their nature, were done in secret, through unofficial channels, using coded messages. The Japanese had learnt a valuable lesson many years before during the Siberian campaign. This military venture started the year I was born, 1918. Over the next two years, the Imperial Army suffered battlefield dead and wounded in the low thousands. But those numbers, as terrible as they were, were small compared with the men the army lost through venereal disease. You expect bombs, grenades and machine guns to kill your soldiers. What is not expected are large casualties resulting from soldiers satisfying their animal urges with the local women. Sex killed more Japanese soldiers in the Siberian campaign than bullets and bombs. Generals worry about the needless loss of men. They also worry about public relations and their own reputation and honor. The worst was yet to come. Years later, when the Japanese soldiers launched a massive campaign of rape in Nanking, they killed and raped a large number of civilians. The rapes were reported around the world as war crimes. Japanese generals learned from these two experiences that the army could never occupy China if their men were to repeat the rape of Nanking or engage in the unrestricted, unsupervised sex of the Siberian campaign. A secret decision was made at the highest level of command to open comfort houses. You see, the idea was that with access to comfort houses, the soldiers would no longer contract diseases, and the rape of local women would stop. Regulate and control and dispense sex. Posted at each comfort house were a list of ten rules for the soldiers to read. Rule number ten was: intercourse without the use of a condom is strictly forbidden.

"After the Japanese Army arrived in Burma, *ianjo* were established in Meiktila, Mandalay, Rangoon, Toungoo, and Pyinmana. When the naval station opened in Moulmein, it was just a matter of time before the Japanese introduced the *ianjo* system. One day, an officer from the naval detachment met one of the girls working in our shoe factory. She was walking to the factory. The officer liked the look of her and struck up a conversation. As happens in these things, one thing led to another, and he slept with the girl, who returned to the factory to brag about how much money a Japanese officer had given her. We had very little money to pay our employees with. Little by little the girls started disappearing at night, slipping away with the Japanese officers, who paid them money. We lost one then two girls who moved into bungalows with naval officers. Who could blame them? They had nothing. Not even enough food to eat. The first girl to leave had a small blue scorpion tattooed on her leg. The second girl, before she left, went into town and found the man who had tattooed the first girl and had an identical one tattooed on her leg. And the third one followed suit. We were about to lose all of our girls to the Japanese. Of course we could have stood by and watched as our entire work force left to work for the Japanese. Or we could find a way to shift our business to meet the demands of the times. You might judge us as wrong. A man named Thet Way offered us a fairly large sum to let him take over a portion of the factory. We had no choice but to change the nature of the business. Over the next few weeks we still made slippers during the day, but at night the lights went out on the factory floor. We left and closed our eyes. We knew that Thet Way operated a club on the premises, but as good Christians we pretended not to know. At the club, the girls dressed in fine silk *longyis* and blouses. A few months later, they wore kimonos. Great care was taken with their appearance. They had to have a sense of style and they wore the shoes made from our factory. Thet Way called the club the Blue Scorpion. There was never a sign. It was all word of mouth. Our club inside the shoe factory was never formally on the books of the *ianjo* system.

"Officially we were a shoe factory. But in war time accommodations were made. We lived with the contradictions. Officially the *ianjo* system did not exist. Yet inside this state of non-existence were fixed rules. The Japanese soldiers and officers in the *ianjo* system were allowed only a three-minute session; what the naval officers in Moulmein wanted was companionship and sexual intercourse. Thet Way understood this desire and filled it. You must understand our position. When a family no longer has hope then nothing is left but to find a way to survive. My father understood that Thet Way would allow us to survive. Thet Way truly could read the Japanese mind. What comfort it is to have another to anticipate your most secret desires. This happened more than fifty years ago. Most of the people involved are long dead. But I don't want you to think that I am speaking ill of the dead. I am simply giving you precise facts. Our girls became identified by the blue scorpion tattoo. They were a legend among the Japanese officers. We never allowed enlisted men inside the compound, and not all the girls who worked in the factory agreed to become *ianfu*. Those who did received double the standard two-yen fee paid by the soldiers at the comfort houses that were later set up in Moulmein. My son learned of this story from my cousin in Moulmein. I had sent him to my family's house after the skin graft operation. Or should I say banished him to keep him away from a group of undesirable friends? Whether the new tattoo on his penis was done out of spite or some other motive I can't say, but he went to great trouble to have the blue scorpion tattooed on his penis. And I went to an equal amount of difficulty in removing it from his body before the funeral. Perhaps I neglected to tell you. My son was tattooed in Moulmein."

Khin Aung stubbed out the cigarette, reached across the table and shook another one out of my pack. I lit it for him. "Tell me, doctor, does the girl in this picture have the same style of tattoo as the girls during the war?"

He looked once more at the photograph.

"Identical."

"Have you ever seen such a tattoo since the war?"

"On my son's penis," he said, smiling and smoking.

"It's a mystery," said Hart.

"It is that," said Khin Aung. "The young lady here . . ."

"Sarah," said Sarah, sensing that he may have forgotten her name.

"Sarah had mentioned wanting to find Ming bowls. I think Moulmein might be the place. Four hundred years ago it was a major trading port with the Japanese. Thousands of ships passed through the port. Ming bowls were once quite common. I have a cousin who would know and I would be happy to give you his name."

As the doctor wrote out the name and address, I had a pretty good idea that this had to be the same man who had told the doctor's son the family secret about the Blue Scorpion.

THE ROAD TO MOULMEIN

33

According to Khin Aung, the rainy season was the best time to find Ming bowls in Moulmein. The rain erodes the soil. The Chinese burial sites wash into the rivers. It has happened for centuries. Traders and other scavengers wade knee deep into the rivers with sieves as if they are panning for gold only they are panning for Ming bowls from a freshly washed away Chinese grave. The Rangoon antique shops are restocked every rainy season. In the pre-war era, the lucky ones who found the loot walked or rode horse carts to the center of Rangoon where the merchants knew what was what. They bought the Ming pieces for very little money, selling them to the British. Not much has changed in all those years. The same rainy season cycle of washed-out graves, scrambling for the Ming in the rivers, journeying to Rangoon, and selling for peanuts has continued. Only there are fewer British. Sometimes one found a tiny miniature so perfect that, like the sight of a beautiful woman, it took one's breath away, or, if you passed it by, then, it broke your heart years later when the regret of losing the opportunity surfaced.

I had heard before that the best place in all of Burma for Ming porcelain was in the Mon state. The capital of the Mon state, Moulmein had been a major trading port for four hundred years. Generations of Chinese merchants sailed in and out of Moulmein on their ships. Many of them died in Moulmein and their remains were buried in that city and its surrounding villages where they kept second or third families. The motherlode of Ming. I went away from Khin Aung's apartment, believing Ming burial bowls could be found and bought for a song. And in the rainy season, the locals shops had to be bursting with Ming porcelain.

Khin Aung said he was too old to accompany us on the journey. Zaw Min begged off, saying he couldn't take us upcountry. He had a group of three women from London who had booked a tour to Arakan State. I was disappointed and tried to persuade Zaw Min to change his mind but he was firm. The English women were paying him a great deal of money. I couldn't begrudge him this good fortune, or try to match the amount of the deposit the English women had already given him. Aye Thit had trouble finding a replacement car and driver. One local thief demanded fifty thousand kyat a day and I told Aye Thit to tell the guy to go screw himself. I hated it when the locals tried to play you for a fool. I knew Burma. I had lived here. I knew the price of things, and I also knew I had a limited budget to work with. Hart had no money to kick in, and while Sarah had a little money, it wasn't enough to cover her one-third share. That didn't matter. I liked her and wanted her to come along. I told her that I would pay the freight. What was one more economic dependent on the road to all that Ming?

The next day, we hired a driver from Aye Thit's district. I guessed his age as around thirty-four years old; he had bleeding red teeth from chewing betel nut, a flinty smile and dead, damaged orange-colored skin. His threadbare clothes smelled of sweat and he hardly said a word. He squinted all the time, even with the sun to his back. I worried his eyesight was shot. Aye Thit assured me the driver had perfect vision. Hearing this, the driver squinted—you couldn't even begin to see eyes in the small slits—but he looked happy, grinning like he had figured out some riddle that tricked him into a lifetime of silence. His hands were rough, but he had long, shapely fingers like a piano player. Aye Thit had known the driver and his family for years and said that I should trust him on the decision to hire the driver.

The driver showed up at the hotel behind the wheel of a fifteen year old diesel Toyota station wagon loaded down with several ten-liter plastic jugs full of diesel fuel in the back. A rear collision and we all would end up like someone had turned a flame-thrower on us. The Toyota was a grayish color and the windows were frosted with a thick layer of dust. It looked old and used up the way a drug addict looks at the end of his life. What great glories had ever been had long passed. But this was as good as we were going to get on the budget I set for Aye Thit.

Hart and I kicked the tires as Sarah watched in the shade. She wanted to find out the source of the tattoos. Tattoos were, in a certain way, her stock-in-trade, the basis of her Ph.D., and her academic career might suddenly take off if she were to discover a tattoo art that had never been known before. She had said very little throughout the evening with Khin Aung. What she had been doing was absorbing the possibilities, drawing the connection between Hart's novel and the old doctor's stories about his father's shoe factory converted into a World War II brothel. Hart had heard these stories before. He said the doctor often told the same stories over and over again, and he was quite certain that he wasn't the first or the last person to hear them. What else could one expect from Khin Aung, sitting under his daughter's marriage certificate, waiting to die, thinking about the ten thousand bodies he'd carved up?

We walked around the car, spitting on the ground, trying to make up our minds whether this heap would make it to Moulmein. I lit a cigarette.

"What do you think?" Hart asked.

"It's okay, it's okay. Aye Thit knows the guy and says he's okay."

Hart looked over at the driver.

The driver grinned, puckering his eyes at the corners, laugh lines reeling out like an exploded supernova. I would have cast him as a hit man or a Bangkok taxi driver. Of course, it would have to have been a silent movie or an old-style Clint Eastwood film. He was someone who functioned exceptionally well without language.

Hart shrugged, and said, "Then I guess it's okay."

We hired him on the spot. We had no choice. The rains were coming every afternoon. All those three and four hundred year old dead Chinese merchants were being washed out of their graves as we spoke. At the same time, none of us wanted to come out and admit that we were all scouting for something that had nothing to do with Ming. We played out the Ming illusion much like Akira

Takeda had done with me. I should have seen it coming but I had been too single-minded—*Ming, Ming* echoed in my head like a mantra. This was what I had been led to believe was the reason for the meeting with Khin Aung. As soon as the war came up, I recalled that Kazuo's great uncle, Ichiro, had been stationed in Moulmein during the war. He was a Japanese Imperial War veteran. What if Ichiro Takeda had requested that his nephew return from Burma with a photograph of the girl with the blue scorpion? Even if that were true, it wouldn't explain Ichiro's link to the girl in the photograph, who was young and beautiful, a girl untouched by age. Either she had been a timeless Dorian Gray-like figure who had been selling herself in Rangoon, or there was a new generation of blue scorpion girls plying their trade in Burma. Kazuo may have known the answer but he was dead. Akira Takeda said I should either destroy the girl's photo or give it to him and he would see to it. Here's a man who has given me a large sum of money. He offered more money, another large sum, if I destroyed that photo and promised to forget that I had ever found his son's camera. I had refused his money. I had too many questions. Whether the lady in the photograph was still waiting for Kazuo or someone else, I wanted to know. I wanted to find out who she was. When someone said stop, that was when I wanted to go.

I kicked the tire again and smiled at Hart.

"I say we go with it."

He gave me the thumbs up.

From the shade Sarah waved. "When do we go?"

"How about now?" I said. "We got wheels, baby. We've got beer and I feel like blowing a fat one."

34

We packed our gear behind the backup ten-liter jugs of diesel fuel. The thing about a diesel car is that it doesn't hold any zero-to-sixty records. It takes time to work up to speed. We crawled through the outskirts of Rangoon. Aye Thit sat in front with the driver who held onto the wheel with both hands. His head never moved as he stared straight ahead. Sarah sat between Hart and me, and we tried to get comfortable knowing we were wedged between a betel nut chewing silent screen star and enough fuel to turn the Toyota into a crematorium and burn the five of us down to a communal lump of white ash.

Sarah said that listening to Khin Aung had been like seeing her father's ghost. Her father, like the old doctor, had been a control freak—how else do you explain all those skin transplants on the son and the removal of the blue scorpion from his penis after the boy was dead?—and it appeared that her entire family had been the target of that control. Her mother, brother and herself lived under a series of ever more repressive rules. After the war, her father and mother settled in an isolated community in Hawaii. The father had decided he never wanted to return to the American mainland. And he hated cities. The reason for his distrust turning to hatred and suspicion was the lack of rules on the mainland in general and in cities specifically. He wanted an environment where his family was secure, unified, and pacified. He had been an officer in the Vietnam war and took part in the pacification program in South Vietnam which was supposed to win the hearts and minds of the Vietnamese and turn them against the communists infiltrating from the north. Sarah's earliest memories were of her father coming back from work—he was an accountant. He loved animals and wanted his children to grow up surrounded by domesticated pets. He believed that looking after animals created character and responsibility and brought children closer to nature. The family had ten acres of land on which the father kept a collection of peacocks, llamas, turtles, swans, ostriches, rabbits, and gibbons. They lived in a three-room wooden house on the property. Her father rebuilt the house—new roof, new siding, and a large shed for his tools. All of the construction he did with his own hands. A new room was added when Sarah was about seven. He felt she should have her own room. Bunking with her brother was no longer a good idea.

Her father's goal defined itself into self-sufficiency and pacification. From the way she explained the setup, he must have thought the Viet Cong were going to slip into the compound at night and slit everyone's throat. The family grew their own food in a large garden, ate fresh eggs, chicken, fish and ostrich meat. He hired an earth-moving machine and made a pond which they could see from the kitchen window of their house. He stocked the pond with perch and catfish. These were a hardy kind of fish. And not long afterwards, they had all the fish they could eat and never had to buy from the outside. Speaking of the outside world, Sarah's father believed contact was either too dangerous or too contaminating for his wife and children. One afternoon as he labored on what would later become Sarah's new bedroom, Sarah's mother stood at the base of the ladder handing him nails and tools. The sweat dripped off his bare torso and fell on the ground like rain, her mother had said. There was a rule about how much time could pass between when he gave an order for a tool and when her mother had to put it in a bucket on the end of a rope so that he could pull it up and fish out the nails and tools. He would look at his watch as she worked below filling his request. Her English wasn't that great and sometimes she wouldn't understand the name of the tool. He would get angry with her, yell at her, storm down the ladder, walk across the field, kicking the dirt as he walked. It worked like a fast food restaurant with 150 names of hamburgers.

"Like many non-native speakers mother had gaps in specialized vocabularies. Of course she didn't know the names of many tools.

Father was demanding of her and of us. He cut out pictures of tools from a catalogue and wrote the English name for each one. This became her homework for two weeks. The rule was she had to go over the pictures and names every evening for one hour after dinner. She sat at the table as my brother and I cleared away the dishes. Then we did our homework while Father sat at the table and drilled her until she knew the English word for every possible tool ever invented. He wrote examinations for her to take. She had to pass written and oral exams. Everything was strictly timed. If she was too slow, then he failed her. If she missed more than two questions out of more than a couple of hundred, he failed her. If she failed, then she had to study an extra thirty minutes the following night, or miss dinner, or go to bed one hour earlier than the children. He always gave her the choice of her punishment.

"I remember the first night that he took my mother by the hand the way he would my brother or me and dragged her out to the shed where he kept his tools under lock and key. Two large Yale padlocks secured the door to the shed. He opened both locks and finally opened the shed door and made her stand outside as he went in and came back with a new tool. She had to name each and every one. I was eight years old and my brother was eleven. We went out the back and watched as Father held up a sledgehammer. Mother said, 'Hammer.' And Father shook his head. 'No, that is wrong. Sledgehammer. This is a hammer,' and he held up a regular hammer. But it was much more complicated than a couple of hammers. He had fifteen kinds of saws, a thirty piece wrench set, a fifty-two piece socket set, plumb bobs, long-nose pliers, lineman's pliers, groove-joint pliers, cutting pliers, long-reach pliers, and slip-joint pliers. Everything had its own specialized name. I doubt if there was a native English speaker who could name more tools than Mother.

"When it came time to build an eight-foot fence around the property, he never had to repeat his request for the right tool. He said the fence was to keep the animals from straying out and getting run over on the highway. But my mother knew the truth. He wanted to secure his family. We had lots of strict rules. At dinner the food was always given to him first. Then he passed it to my mother, who passed it to my brother and I got what was left. This was the rule, the law of the house. There was no choice but to serve food in this way. He loved us so much. Whenever he left the house, he took us along. I loved the fact that I could sit beside him in the pickup. He always felt afraid that something terrible would happen to us if he left us alone. It was as if we were going to be attacked. He said our operation rules were there for security, for our protection. After Vietnam, his distrust of the world outside his family grew larger every year. He believed that something bad would happen and he was doing everything in his power to prevent it.

"There were more rules and schedules for the animals. We had strict orders from Father to return home directly from school. Each week he posted a written list divided between my brother and me. On the list he wrote out our duties for cleaning cages, changing water, pouring out food and inspecting the animals for any possible disease or infection. Each animal was named and next to the name was either Sarah or Matthew. If we broke a rule, then he had a bamboo switch and he would make my brother drop his pants and hit his bare buttocks. He told us that in places like Singapore the rattan was dipped in horse piss before it was used to punish a prisoner. He said we were lucky to live in Hawaii. He never soaked the bamboo in horse piss. Not once did he ever hit me. That was because I never once broke a rule. I was careful. It was always between Matthew and Father. They could never work out the conflict that consumed them.

"Sometimes my brother and I traded chores. Once the fence was finished, Father bought more animals. It was like living in an exotic zoo. By the time my brother turned thirteen, he did what most boys do at that age, he rebelled. He stopped coming straight home from school. He went out to play with his friends, and I always tagged along even though I was younger. Matthew had this sixth sense about when Father would return home and we would run like hell back to our property before he arrived. Father drove an old beat-up Ford pickup. My brother could hear that pickup at least a mile away. He could be in the middle of a conversation and suddenly my brother would go still, cock his ear, and say, 'Gotta run.' And run we did, as fast as our legs would carry us, our hearts in our throats. We knew all the best shortcuts from every direction. Matthew had cut holes in the fence at two places and covered them with branches and leaves, and those openings were our secret passages back inside the property. We had to be inside before Father stopped at the front gate and unlocked the padlocks and drove inside.

"When Mathew turned fifteen, a weird competition developed between Father and my brother. Father knew that Matthew broke the basic rules of the house—that we traded chores and had our own communication system. This he turned a blind eye to. But for the overriding rule he was inflexible. That rule was: don't leave the family compound without permission. Don't go outside the fence. Come straight home from school. Do not stop for any reason. When he figured out that Matthew was violating the prime rule, Father had too much pride to confront him directly. Instead, he tried to catch Matthew in the act of rule-breaking. It became a game between them. Game is the wrong word. It was more like a challenge. Father would sometimes take off early from work, thinking that he would beat my brother home and then they could have it out once and for all. But my brother's ears and sense of timing were too good. He never fell for any of Father's traps. For more than a year, Father couldn't figure out how Matthew always won this race. Until one Friday, Matthew was running late. It was nearly dark. He borrowed a motorcycle from a friend even though he couldn't really drive. When Father came home that evening, he had the lights of the pickup switched off. Matthew, too, had turned off the headlight. He drove straight into the path of the pickup and Father must have been doing fifty, sixty miles an hour, trying to get home first. The doctor said Matthew was dead before he hit the ground. That night, Father walked around the property and found where Matthew had used the lineman's pliers to cut the fence in two places and then had disguised what he had done with some tree branches. After dinner that evening, Father went out to the shed, opened the two huge Yale locks, went inside and put a handgun inside his mouth and pulled the trigger. Pieces of skull and brains and blood splattered over the roof, walls and, of course, all of his tools. Later, I found my mother in the shed cleaning the tools, saying out loud each and every name, as if my Father was listening, and this was her final examination."

35

This was one reason why I loved women. You could put them under house arrest for years on end and when you finally released them back in the street they weren't frothing at the mouth, wielding a knife, looking to slice off the balls of the men who did that to them. A man would have turned hateful, into an enraged, mean, revengeful killing machine. Women accepted house arrest. Later they had an uncommon ability to communicate the detailed horror of their confinement as a domestic set of rules to follow. Sarah sat between the two of us and just let the story unwind in the most perfectly natural way. She wasn't asking for sympathy or comfort. She simply wanted to let us know who she was and how she got to be the way she was and how she came to find herself sitting between total strangers on the road to Moulmein. I pulled the tab off a beer and took a long drink.

"Saya was fifteen years old the first time I met her. She was an exchange student. I was a student teacher at her school in Miami. I was twenty years old and trying to earn a university degree entitling me to teach for a living. You talk about rules. Either Saya grew up without rules or, if she had rules, they never stopped her from doing whatever she wanted. The first time I saw her, she had green hair and hung out with Cubans. Long, braided green hair that hung to her waist. She was on the edge long before the whole Tokyo fashion scene moved to green hair. She was out there totally alone. She was a high school fashion leader, and that was saying something because she had the competition of all the Latino chicks. And another thing. She wore these thigh-high shit-stomping black leather boots. Her purple tinted sunglasses, which she wore inside the classroom, gave her a vaguely Yoko Ono look. She was dating a Cuban drummer who was trying to grow a goatee and sang in a local rock band. Half of the time she skipped class. She never came in with a note. Her excuse was either that she was drugged out, hung over, or dyeing her hair green. After awhile, she didn't bother making an excuse. She challenged my authority with her silence. Christ, what was I going to do? Expel her? It was one of those progressive schools and no one had ever been expelled for drugs or alcohol or not having an excuse from mom. Not that I believed in conspiracy theory, but . . . and a big but, it crossed my mind, 'Hey, this little bitch was sent to test me, to try and fuck me up so they could flunk me and send me out of the university without a degree, breaking my father's heart, my mother's heart, and generally ensuring I would end up a bum eating out of city missions, shopping at the Salvation Army.' The woman was determined to ruin my life.

"Then one day she disappeared to Japan. No formal or informal goodbye, no warning. She was gone. I didn't see her after that day. I never thought of her. To tell you the truth, I was relieved. I could graduate and get a job. I ended up doing neither one. I decided I wasn't cut out for teaching. So after five years of eating mom's cooking and shopping at the Salvation Army, I ran into her. We both were enrolled in a junior college arts course. My mom said, 'Learn a trade or get out.' That was how I found myself in Sculpture 101. There she was in class stoned out of her mind, fashioning a dildo out of a hunk of wet red clay. I knew at that moment I loved that woman. We dated for a year, and one day she called me and said, 'Sloan, I am getting deported in forty-eight hours.' And I said, 'Hey, baby, let's get married. They can't throw your ass out of the country if you are married to an American citizen.' And she said, 'I guess that's cool.' There was a long pause and I could hear her breathing on the other end of the phone. The wheels were turning in her head. *Do I let them deport me to Japan or do I marry this guy?* Finally she said, 'Okay.' I called my Mom and said, 'Hey, Mom, I finally managed to get a trade.' And mom said, 'Sloan, I am so happy, what is it?' I said, 'I am going to learn to be a husband, and I'm getting married this afternoon, why don't you and Pop come along? Sorry it's short notice. But it's an emergency.' And Mom says, 'I am going to be a grandmother.' She sounded so happy. And I said, 'Mom, no, she's not pregnant, they want to deport her because she has green hair.' Mom seemed to understand. Mom and Pop turned up and watched us get married. Pop was my best man and Mom was bridesmaid. Afterwards, I lit a big fat one and me and the bride kicked back and watched the sun set over Biscayne Bay and decided right there on the beach that just maybe the immigration people had it right after all. They instinctively understood something about the nature of life that it took drugs for us to comprehend. Some people fit right into America. Others like Saya and me, well, neither of us really belonged in America. There are too many fucking rules. *Step on a crack and break your mother's back* kind of rules. My wife said, 'We should try Asia for awhile.' And I said, 'Baby, I am willing to try anything once.'

"It was all so sweet and easy. But I am the one who should have had second thoughts. No one took me aside and said, 'You hate rules? Then I've got a news bulletin. Forget about the IRS or any other quasi-Nazi American agency, it is your wife you have to worry about.' Even if they had, I wouldn't have understood what they were talking about. Cash in and cash out rules are part of the package of being married to a Japanese woman. They know everything about all of your money. Every week she reconciles the books and if you are five dollars short you better have an explanation of how you spent that money. You have to be creative. For example, I skim my girlfriend's allowance. In between girlfriends I never say, 'girlfriend split,' I just pretend everything is cool and pocket the entire ex-girlfriend budget. It's almost as good as wild sex. When you are single you don't think about such freedom. Single guys don't have to explain why or where they spend money. They just do it. When she was a fifteen-year-old scowling in the back of my geography class and I try to think if it ever occurred to me while I was giving a lecture about mountains in Nepal that one day she would control all the money that ever came into my life. That one day this Japanese girl with green hair, black boots and huge eyes and false eyelashes would know where every baht in my wallet went. I have learned to be resourceful. It is why most men go into business—so they can find a stream of independent, unaccountable income. That's why I want the Ming bowls. I like the idea of making profits from burial bowls washed out of Chinese graves. Off the book profits are so, so sweet. And you know, there's something about the girl in Kazuo's photograph that reminds me of Saya when she was fifteen. And like Saya, I have a feeling that this girl has caused people headaches and I need to know, it has been driving me crazy since the day I first saw her photograph. Why did Kazuo take her photograph; why was it so important to his father that I destroy the photo and forget that I ever saw it? I don't like being told what to do, where to go, what to say or what to think. When that happens I think someone is hiding something, and whenever someone hides something about a woman, there has to be some deeper reason."

"Do you have kids?" asked Sarah.

About as innocent a question as *do you know there are landmines where we are walking*? I shook my head. Sarah let out a sigh.

"Mom stopped asking when we were going to have kids after our twentieth anniversary."

"You don't miss having kids?"

"My wife never wanted kids. Her mother had never wanted kids. Can you imagine your mother telling you that you were an accident? It gets worse. Her mother told her that having a kid was a horrible, destructive act. You know why she reached this conclusion? Because once you have kids you lose your freedom. You are back to making and living by rules. But the worst thing wasn't the loss of freedom—the birth of a child started a clock ticking on your own mortality. Every day you wake up and stare at your kids you are another day older, you see yourself one step closer to the grave. Suddenly time speeds up, you are living in fast-forward motion and you shrivel up like a grape into a raisin in one of those time-lapse videos. You look older than your friends who stayed childless. Over time your childless friends look as young as your own kids. Your kids hang out with your friends. They both call you 'Pop'. You cruise at the speed of light to the finish line. Kids accelerate you to time-warp speed. You look in the mirror and you're old, baby. Toasted, wasted, miserable, and those cute little faces aren't so cute any more. They grow up, and you die. And you hear in the back of your sleeping brain a little voice calling out, 'Help me. Help me.' Only no one comes to the rescue." I was thinking about Akira

Takeda and how old, sad and beaten down he looked. If we had had a boy, he might have been like Kazuo Takeda, a journalist, a traveler, a risk-taker. As I finished talking, it dawned on me what had been going on inside my head the whole time—in a strange way I didn't fully understand, I had adopted Kazuo as the son Saya and I never had.

"What Sloan means to say is they decided against children."

"That's what I said. Isn't that what I said?"

"An executive summary never hurts," said Hart.

"Aren't you going to say something about *your* family?" I asked Hart. In Bangkok I had promised not to raise his grandfather's name. This was just on the line of keeping the promise unbroken.

"When the authorities found my father's body he had been dead for a day or two. He drowned in a lake. Nothing unusual about drowning. A witchdoctor said that he could purify himself by swimming in the lake. My old man liked the idea of washing away his sins. The witchdoctor promised that the demons that possessed him could be cleansed by a swim. There was one miscalculation. The old man was a poor swimmer. When they found his body someone noticed something strange about his clothes. He was dressed in someone else's clothes. No one could explain how he came to be dressed in another man's clothes. Or even whether he had dressed himself, which seemed unlikely, as I recall he was quite fond of his clothes, or whether a native had seen his splendid but wet shirt, trousers and shoes and decided to make an exchange. After all, he was dead. It wasn't exactly going to matter what clothes he wore. Whether he was purified, dispossessed of his demons—I rather doubt that happened. But with the old man, anything was possible. Even changing clothes with a witchdoctor before making his one last swim."

"That's it? Your story?" I asked.

"I think it's a rather splendid story," said Hart.

Sarah didn't laugh, her thoughts drifting somewhere back to the naming of tools, the shed, the examinations, the rules, and she must have been working out whether her father had ever regretted having her and her brother.

Personal disclosure was a good way to begin any journey: one, possibly two, suicides, and sex with a Japanese teenager with green hair. Death and rebellion create life-long bonds among the living. And when you are seeking to put to rest the ghost of a dead man who could have been your own son, then you have an incentive to keep pushing on.

36

It would have been a gross mistake to say that the road to Moulmein was largely unchanged since World War II. It had looked much like this one or two hundred years ago. Asphalt—that great British invention—had been laid over a wagon path with no thought that it should be widened. The British had their reasons for sticking to the narrow path. Whitehall may have decided that funds appropriated for Burma were better spent on prisons, garrisons, and officers' clubs. What we had in front of us was a two hundred kilometer one-way road with the occasional two-way traffic—trucks and cars playing chicken, swerving off to the side at the last moment, then hitting the accelerator, metal to the floor, blasting like a wavy blur through one nameless, dusty thatched-roofed hamlet after another.

Vendors sold mangoes and pineapples from bamboo baskets piled on top of roadside stands. Scrawny schoolgirls passed the stands, turned and waved. We waved back, and they returned shy country smiles.

We drove for miles without ever seeing another car. When we stopped at a checkpoint, the guard seemed surprised. Our driver peeled a wadded, soiled twenty-kyat note from the stash Aye Thit handed him wrapped in brown paper. He kept the steaming, soiled package in his shirt pocket. The notes were damp and stained and smelled of mildew. After the guard lifted the metal barricade, the driver put the Toyota diesel into gear and we continued along the road. Aye Thit and I, in the old days, had been this far down the road twice before. It had been only a few months since the road was open all the way to Moulmein. Excluding foreigners, like house arrest, or variations on those themes, was a way of life. In our prior trips, once we had crossed the Sittang Bridge, the road was blocked by the army; venturing beyond their checkpoint was not just off-limits, it would have been suicide. Any time the Burmese army said access was denied, you took them at their word; the road wasn't a computer game to be hacked. We had turned around and gone back. The total resolve of the Burmese army reminded me of my wife.

An early afternoon sun shimmered on the river by the time we first saw the outline of the hugely imposing iron girders of the Sittang Bridge. British iron. The large bolts lined up in perfect rows holding the girders in place, each the size of a fist. Running far beneath was a swirl of brownish waters. The Bilow River, at the widest point, measured one mile. Being stranded on the other side, it made for a very long swim for the British forces, especially with the Japanese on the banks with their machine guns.

"Look at the iron. That iron was brought here from England," I said, sounding as proud as any Englishman about the fact that so much iron could have been smelted in Birmingham and transported to make a bridge in Burma. At least I think it was Birmingham. "The British bombed the bridge in 1942. They blew it up so the Japanese couldn't use it to march on Rangoon. General Smyth gave the order. After they took out the bridge, the good general found out that he had left men on the wrong side of the bridge. The Japanese side of the fucking bridge. The general's plan didn't factor in time for the men to cross before the strike. Once the bridge was bombed, these men were stranded in the wrong place at the wrong time. You know what they did? They built rafts from bamboo doors and floated across the mile-wide river. If God serves you lemons then you make rafts."

"Those blokes were very resourceful," said Hart. "But, then, they had to be, didn't they?"

"The British bombed this bridge by moonlight."

"First we built it, then we blew it up," said Hart. "That kept the steel mills in the Midlands in business. They built the planes that bombed the bridges, then supplied the iron to rebuild what had been destroyed. It was a perfect circle of destruction and reconstruction. The entire lesson of capitalism could be taught from the history of this bridge."

Sarah glimpsed a golden pagoda on the opposite side of the Bilow River. "It's beautiful," said Sarah.

"Bombers flew in at three hundred feet. This was at night and they were doing 280 miles an hour. One of the pilots circled in low over the bridge and dropped his bomb, then pulled up too slow. He saw that pagoda straight ahead. He banked sharp to the right. He nearly cleared it. Near isn't the same as clear. The pilot shaved four feet off the left wing."

"He hit the pagoda?" asked Hart.

"He fucking hit the top of *that* pagoda. What kind of cosmic good luck is it to fly into a pagoda and live? He limped back to base on one and a half wings. You have to believe that Buddha didn't think he had done wrong bombing the bridge. Look at the river. Visualize the water churning with hundreds of lifeless bodies. Under the bridge, the river was clogged with bodies. The bones of long dead Chinese sloping into the river, along with their Ming bowls and miniatures, wrapped in their grave clothing. The Bilow River ran blood red. Think of that wide river churning with corpses. And not just Japanese and long dead Chinese, but British soldiers trying to swim or raft across this river. If you listen long enough you can hear the echo of death rattles, the gurgling of the drowning, the machine guns, the bombs falling."

"You have an active sense of imagination," said Hart.

"I bet you a bottle of whisky that you didn't know that the Yorkshire Light Infantry fought at Sittang Bridge."

Hart smiled. "Sloan, I double the bet."

"Name it."

"Did you know that in 1775 Cornwallis led the Yorkshire Light Infantry into battle against the Yanks at Guilford Court House in North Carolina?"

"We won that one, Hart."

"Actually, if my schoolboy history serves me, you actually lost that battle. Cornwallis' troops kicked the ass of a Yankee army twice its size."

"When you win a battle but lose a war all you have left to talk about are the battles you won."

"Like the Americans with Vietnam."

"I think it's a beautiful day and I love the river," said Sarah.

What followed was a long silence as we thought about her father building the perimeter fence around the family house and teaching Sarah's mother the names of tools. She didn't take sides in our squabble over ancient battles but listened and smiled, taking it all in and giving no hint of her feelings or opinion. It must have been one of the rules of her household. *Don't show your feelings.* Whatever shaped her attitude prepared her to become a perfect poker player. If she played bridge, she would have made a fortune. These were games with complicated, fixed rules. I could see her sitting passively at the table as her father flashed pictures of various tools, taking it all in, watching in an attentive way, wondering what new kind of tool would next confound her poor mother.

She slumped back in her seat. "In Saigon, during the war, my father had a tattoo put on his arm. The image he chose was a green dragon breathing red flames. When he worked with his shirt off, I used to watch the dragon move as he flexed his muscles, hammering or sawing. I dreamed of that dragon flying over our heads, flapping giant bat-like wings and circling the animals we kept. In my dream it lived inside Father's shed."

And I thought to myself, this woman had one weird, deranged childhood. But, then, among the people who lived our kind of lives, a strange family seemed to be a prerequisite for admission to leading a happy life trekking muddy third-world roads and believing that such a life was superior to one entombed inside a tinted SUV racing along an expressway. Hart's father was the opposite of Sarah's. There were no rules in Hart's childhood. As a child, Hart was always treated as an adult. He slept when he was tired. Woke when he was rested. Went to school when he felt like it—which wasn't often. At eleven years old, Hart was totally illiterate. After an oral interview, the headmaster concluded that Hart was advanced for his age—his social graces from being in the company of adults his entire life gave him a highly polished and elegant manner—and recommended that Hart be put ahead several forms. After a couple of weeks, the teachers discovered that Hart couldn't read. He could write his name but nothing else. He had all the graces of a duke and the literacy to match—the perfect background for a future proofreader on *The Bangkok Post*. But his conversational skills had a perfectly tuned quality. In his mid-teens, his father's mistress encouraged Hart to read. Soon he found himself drawn into the world of books and decided that he wanted to be a writer. About the same time, his father was appointed the ambassador of a small African country—he was fleeing the mistress—a country that had been in the pocket of the communists during the Cold War. The only economy was agriculture and mining and witchcraft. Warlords ran the gambling dens. Thugs robbed merchants in broad daylight. Life expectancy was thirty-six years. Africans hunched over in dusty fields under a boiling sun armed with wooden sticks, digging in the hopelessly infertile ground and planting seeds that never grew. Those were Hart's memories. I wouldn't have been surprised if Hart had his own share of flying dragon dreams in his childhood.

Not long after we entered into the Mon state, the Toyota was coated in a thick layer of red dust. Our driver never moved behind the wheel. You would have to be dead to have any less motion. He kept the windows rolled down and clouds of dust blew off the fields. Red Mon clay settled on the driver's hair, coating his crown with layers of dust. He looked like a terracotta warrior dug out of the ground by the Chinese. Silent, frozen in an eternal position at the frontline, waiting for the attack. A crown on his head. If we didn't find any Ming bowls, the backup plan would be to sell the driver as an ancient warrior-king.

The Terracotta Warrior—with a capital "T and "W", as we started to refer to him—was dying to take a leak. He pulled the car onto the side of the road. Saying something in Burmese to Aye Thit, he got out, walked five paces through the tall grass, squatted down until he almost disappeared, hiked up his *longyi*, stared the way a dog stares—half embarrassment, half necessity—and did his business. I lit a fat one, took a long drag, offered it to Sarah. She shook her head, and I then passed it to Hart, who never passed on anything. The proofreader instinct caused him to examine the hand-rolled object of beauty, looking for a flaw, and, finding none, he took a hit, and passed it back.

"I have an allergy to smoke," she said.

She sniffled, a plain, long-suffering expression crossed her face, and she coughed as I rolled down the window. "Sorry, darling. This should help."

I turned to flash my winning smile. Her mouth dropped open. Not a good sign. In her dreams she had witnessed flying dragons. What I saw in her eyes I could not quite find the right word to describe: horror, terror, fear, or fucking disbelief. Then I saw she wasn't looking *at* me but *over* me. I slowly turned and looked over my shoulder. Outside the window, a cobra reared up as if suspended in space, its hood fanned out the size of a basketball. I had the fat one between my lips and was looking straight into the eyes of a cobra. Fully extended, the cobra was close to ten feet in length. The girth of its trunk was about the size of my leg. I tried to say something but nothing came out. The cobra's head and my face were separated by a few inches. No one moved or said anything. Hart slowly opened his door and inched his way out, pulling Sarah with him. I heard him open the door. But there was no way I could turn and follow after Sarah. I was the offering to the cobra. I was going to die on the road to Moulmein. I was on the wrong side of the Sittang Bridge like the men General Smyth had left behind in order to bomb it.

"Hart, tell Saya that I loved her right to the end. Right up to the moment when this giant motherfucker of a cobra sunk its fangs into my face."

"Stay calm," he said. "You're not going to die."

"Easy for you to say," I said.

"Father kept snakes. But I never remember seeing one that big," said Sarah.

"They hate smoke," said Hart.

"You think I should offer him a hit? Or just let him bite the shit out of me and have done with it?"

With almost no movement, I slowly inhaled on the fat one until my lungs were about to burst. At the same time, the Terracotta Warrior, in a bat-like motion, raised himself up out of the tall grass and, standing upright, fiddled with his *longyi*, going through the ritual of unwrapping it, airing it, and wrapping the *longyi* tightly around his body. He stomped through the grass, his red mouth framed against the blue sky, walking towards the car. Either his footfalls or my sudden exhale of two lungfuls of smoke spooked the snake. The cobra dropped like it had been cut in half and slithered away into the grass. Stoned or scared, it fled into the grass. Sweat poured off my face, splashing onto my pants. I let out a long breath, shuddered, opened the whisky and took a long drink. I handed the bottle to Hart, and he took a swig.

"That didn't happen," I said, rolling up the window.

I crawled over the seat and out of the car, standing in the road with my entire body shaking. A kid on a bicycle rode past, clocking me with awe and sympathy as if I had just come out of a major seizure. All I could think about was how big that fucking cobra's hood was and how close it had been to my face. I should have been dead. Either the fat one or the Terracotta Warrior had saved my life.

"That absolutely did not happen," I said.

Hart offered his hand. "Shake on it."

After we climbed back into the car, I opened a fresh bottle of Laphroaig, raised it to my lips and drank straight from the bottle. My throat had gone dry. I lowered the bottle, wiped my mouth with the back of my shaking hand and handed the bottle over to Hart. He drank and passed it back to me.

"When bad things happen you learn to deal with them," Sarah said.

I slowly lowered the bottle for the second time and put back the stopper.

"Sure thing," I said. "It didn't happen."

"I saw the snake."

"You have one vote. Hart and me have two votes."

"You haven't asked Aye Thit or the Terracotta Warrior."

"This is a backseat democracy," I said. "The front seat has no vote. They are hired hands working for a wage."

"It doesn't seem fair," she said.

"Think of it as a voting rule for the car. At least women can vote."

"I should have stayed home," she said.

"You see that river?" I asked. "That's where many men would have agreed with you about staying home."

She looked out the window on the right-hand side. Another narrow river snaked along the road. Infantry died crossing that river, I thought. Nineteen forty-four was a brutal year in the Burma campaign. War acted as a good diversion, banishing images of killer snakes and unequal voting rights. A war fought many years before Sarah had been born helped; all the horror drained away, poured into words and old photographs, allowing her to walk the dried riverbeds of history, never getting wet. The Bilow River melted away as a thin strip of silver along the edge of the horizon, a glowing late afternoon amber sun in our faces; vast, empty sugarcane fields stretched towards the distant mountains.

We passed a sign that announced our entry into the Mon state. The road circled through rubber plantations, pineapple fields and rice paddies gleaming under the monsoon clouds covering a range of mountains marking the no-man's land with the Karen. The land was never far from water in any direction. Rice paddies, rivers, canals, and creeks ran under and alongside the road. The road was surrounded on both sides by water, rising above waterways, twisting around a bend, crossing canals and streams. The village houses were built from bamboo and wood beams. By late afternoon, the village schools disgorged students onto the road. Scores of munchkins dressed in white shirts and green shorts skipped and ran under bright umbrellas along the side of the road. None of them seemed more than six years old or taller than three feet. Like hundreds of Hobbits skipping, dancing, running and playing along the way to a fair, dressed in their finest, sticking close together in groups, laughing and chattering. Fifteen minutes after the rain stopped, the red dust rose up in the air behind them as they ran along. The mountains on our left rose to three thousand feet. Gray wisps of clouds lay flat like a blanket against the green underbelly of the valley. The rain returned an hour later, and the color of the road turned black as the rain fell.

We stopped for another toll booth. The Terracotta Warrior paid from his wad of notes and we passed through as the barricade lifted, and soon we were crossing one bridge after another every kilometer as if surrounded by a sea, our car floating on a magical carpet. The marshy green landscape receded as the land opened up to fields dotted with cashew trees and wild mushrooms. Aye Thit said there was a lot of money to be made in cashews. Picking wild mushrooms was a better business than smuggling car batteries and shirts. He wailed about his sister's misery and his brother-in-law with the pickup truck embargoed across the border in China. The family misfortune made him sulk and the rain and the vast spaces of Mon country added to his misery. He suddenly had an urge to pick a bag of wild mushrooms. The Terracotta Warrior pulled the Toyota over to the shoulder of the road and Aye Thit climbed out and picked mushrooms. The sun poked through the clouds. I saw him along the side, bent over, his bamboo hat keeping his head protected from the late afternoon sun. Mon women wearing Vietnamese-styled conical bamboo hats walked along the edge of a rubber plantation, the light rain slanting off their hats. They watched Aye Thit picking mushrooms. He smiled and forgot for a moment the brother-in-law who seemed forever imprisoned across the border in China. I thought of how proud he had been in the Drug Elimination Museum when we read the article written by his father. His life had been difficult, full of tragedy and pain; we were all happy to watch the delight on his face as he held up a large mushroom for us to see and smiled before dropping it into his bag. For a moment, his mind was no longer on the pickup and brother-in-law in China.

37

One thing I notice in a strange place is what has gone missing or is absent or silent. For instance, we never saw or heard a plane, train, or bus. After hours on the road, a couple of cars and trucks had approached from the opposite direction; otherwise we had the road to ourselves. No vehicle ever came up behind us. We were alone in a maze of waterways. Dirt poor villages made of bamboo and leaves suddenly appeared only to be swallowed up a few moments later by sugarcane fields. When a large truck approached, it seemed like a major intrusion; our car and the truck were squeezed as close together as I had been with the huge cobra. The wheels of the Toyota slid off the road as the Terracotta Warrior drove inches away from the water. In the villages, we never saw an adult walking along the road, perched on a porch, or working in the fields. The population appeared to be composed exclusively of snotty-nosed children walking under umbrellas, hand-crafted bags slung over their narrow shoulders, their oversized heads bobbing as they drifted along the road. Older boys played football in an open field. Each time we saw a river, I raised the question, "Hey, anyone see any Chinese bones or Ming vases tumbling into the river? Should we stop and have a look? Pan for Ming?"

We never stopped. We were like an army patrol on a mission and there was no time for personal diversions. Our goal was to reach Moulmein before nightfall. After the rice fields came more sugarcane fields, and after the sugarcane fields, the landscape opened up to miles and miles of rubber plantations. Rows of rubber trees with the uniformity of Chinese soldiers on a parade ground ran along both sides of the narrow road, creating a tunnel of trees. Carved between the rows of rubber trees, a soft, quiet green velvet carpet of grass covered the ground. It was impossible to look down the gaps between the rows as mist rolled in, blurring trees and grass into a uniform, dense grayish background. There was the hint of a lost world with no clue of how it was connected to the outside modern world. No billboards, motorcycles or used car lots, no television, canned food, microwave ovens, convenience stores, shopping malls, restaurants. Globalization had stopped at the Sittang Bridge. A soft rain washed over the miles of rubber trees and road, soaking the bamboo houses in the occasional villages, and abruptly the landscape shifted, opening up, treeless, water and sky, as the rice fields ran ten kilometers to the edge of the sky. We passed a pagoda and not long afterwards the road wound through a village of the Pa-o tribe. The Pa-o didn't eat beef, and wore orange turbans and black blouses. They looked good in the annual ethnic parade. In the distance, young boys in T-shirts and sandals tended a herd of water buffalo. Unlike Bangkok with its motorcycles racing over every sidewalk and road, going in any direction like rat packs instinctively scrambling down every drainpipe-like shortcut, we saw only one or two motorcycles. Instead of motorcycles, peasants pushed Chinese-made bicycles up steep hills, and lazily rode on the flat roads around the rice fields. Aye Thit spotted one of the Chinese bikes and started yammering about his brother-in-law holed up without any hope across the border. He shook his head and looked sad, telling us once again how his sister couldn't go outside the house because everywhere she looked she saw goods made in China and this made her cry. Staying indoors hadn't helped. Fruit and vegetables smuggled in from China showed up on the dinner table. Since it was impossible not to have contact with goods smuggled from China, she cried most of the day and night. It was so unfair. These smugglers had made a profit. They had come home to their wives and children. We had no answer for Aye Thit, and he had no hope.

Tanton was the first real town after the Sittang Bridge, if "town" is the right word for a place with several muddy roads and bamboo houses with rusty tin roofs. The months from September to February were the harvest season and the rubber plantation workers carried their buckets down the rows of rubber trees, draining the white liquid so that Chinese bicycles would have tires. Many of the workers lived in Tanton and the surrounding small villages. In the middle of Tanton, three or four large pigs grazed and grunted along railway tracks, stuffing themselves with overgrown weeds. From the ramshackle look of the railway tracks, it looked like it had been a long time since the last train had passed. Mothers scrubbed soap on to their naked children at a concrete public well next to a signpost at the junction in the road. Lathered up giggling children's voices filtered through the car as I rolled down the window to toss out an empty can of Tiger.

Another missing item: Burmese flags. In Rangoon, red flags hung lifelessly from every balcony of derelict colonial buildings, offices, shops and schools. Aye Thit said the authorities said that if you didn't fly the flag, then you got no cooking oil. That was the rule. Flying the flags showed how much you loved Burma and the government and you got your cooking oil. Rangoon was awash in red flags. Streets were lined with red flags in Rangoon. Rangoon reminded me of America post-9/11. But in the Mon state, not a single red Burmese flag appeared on a house, government building or in the road. The Mon must have had independent access to cooking oil. Maybe they found an alternative to cooking oil.

After leaving Tanton, the Terracotta Warrior had his work cut out for him, as the road was overrun with large numbers of chickens, ducks, pigs, dogs, and goats. He honked, slowing down for animals every time we approached a village. This was the same road that Kipling had used when he traveled to Moulmein. Kipling didn't write about the domestic livestock on the road. But he did write about Moulmein as the city that lay on the other side of the Bay and how, in the rain and fog, the dull gold spire of the Moulmein pagoda poked out from the mist. Kipling had actually been to Moulmein; it showed in his writing. He had also written about Mandalay, about the Bay—except there was no Bay in Mandalay—and the flying fish—there were no flying fish in Mandalay either. Authors often corrupt reality with fits of imagination; but it is another thing to completely falsify the reality of a real place because those who know the truth of that place scream louder than a couple peaking together in a perfect orgasm. My father was no writer, but he knew the difference between saying that flying fish hovered above the Orange Bowl football games and the creative flair in making you think twice about words and everyday things. Father used to say, "You remove the 'gas' from orgasm and the balloon of desire collapses." He was a little vague on what that gas was. He also said "Bread is the delivery system for peanut butter," every time mom pulled a loaf of bread out of a bag after coming home from the supermarket. He didn't think much of Kipling.

Some say paradise was a crafted illusion destroyed by science which sanctioned dropping the full load of cause and effect on such illusion causing collateral damage to myths and sacred beliefs. It is better to keep things basic. People living in the countryside understood that you planted rice seedlings and you harvested rice. You stuck a small rubber tree into the ground and few years later you were selling raw rubber to Goodyear. In ancient times, you buried a Chinese corpse in the ground, and you could be certain that you would reap a basketful of white and blue ceramics. You took a photograph of a girl showing leg with a blue scorpion tattoo on her thigh, then left your camera behind, and you were guaranteed that someone, one day, would find that camera, develop the film, and chase down that image. Was she an illusion of paradise? Was she another prostitute made up to look like an angel? The nature of our mission had changed since the night we sat around the table listening to the old doctor's stories. I suspected, though, for Hart, that he had known exactly what he had wanted from the beginning, and had done nothing to unravel my belief that I was doing myself a big favor paying his passage out of money embezzled from the girlfriend's allowance. The joke was on me. I understood his point of view: if a Nubian sun god worshipper demanded to pay you for showing him the sun, take his money, smile and then run.

This didn't make me angry with Hart. We shared a common purpose—digging up the past, searching for artifacts of value, classifying them for beauty and meaning and profit. Blue tattoos and blue ceramics. Red clouds of dust blowing off the fields. Unearthing the leavings of the Chinese and Japanese who had gone to the Mon state and then vanished, not without a trace, but with slivers of their desires and pleasures salted away waiting for rediscovery. Four hundred years ago, Moulmein had been an important port city, a trading port, and given the geography and time, sailing ships with their cargo and traders would have been common. Plenty of Chinese ship owners, merchants, and dealers came equipped with their own plates and bowls. During the war, Japanese naval personnel and army detachments headquartered in Moulmein but they came without any fine china.

The Terracotta Warrior dropped us off at the foot of the passenger ferry terminal in Martaban. Aye Thit had discovered that the last car ferry for the day had already departed. But we had the option of sailing on a passenger ferry. Looking around at the shacks on the muddy lane, damp and dark in the rain, everyone voted to take the passenger ferry. The plan was that the Terracotta Warrior would bring the car over on the first ferry in the morning. After the Toyota pulled away, we walked over to a small street market. Two vendors sat perched behind a makeshift stand of old boxes and sold durian. Hart studied the durian before selecting one. One of the women wielded a large knife and sliced open the prickly greenish outer shell. I sat at a table with Sarah and Aye Thit and watched Hart returning across the dirt road with the lobes of durian laid out on newspaper like the results of an autopsy on a Martian brain. I drank a Tiger beer and tried to breathe through my mouth.

"Don't get that stuff near me," I said, as Hart pulled up a stool. "Unless you want me to power-vomit all over your shoes."

He was too happy with his prized durian to notice. "It seems we are always waiting," he said. "First for the Lady to be released, then for a car and driver, and now for a ferry."

"Learning patience is learning the true nature of life," said Sarah. "My mother used to say that."

Hart used his fingers to pull apart one of the lobes of durian. The yellowish flesh looked smooth and firm, but turned to a sticky goo the color of a tobacco-stained cigarette filter. It looked like a special effect out of a horror movie seeping into his fingernails and covering the creases of his knuckles, making his hands look like they were melting. Hart stared at the substance that had disintegrated into a lush, yellowish slime.

"If your condition doesn't clear up in a day, see a doctor," I said.

216

"It's a bit overripe," he said, sliding a small wedge of yellow goo into his mouth.

Sarah found a packet of tissues and offered them to Hart. His hands dripped the soft runny durian like wet house paint. She pulled out one, then a second and started cleaning his hands like a mother would a child. He said nothing as she worked one hand and then another.

"Aye Thit, have some durian," Hart said.

The little smile on Aye Thit matched the small movement as he moved his head from side to side.

"Eat that yellow slush and hug a squat toilet for the rest of the night," I said.

I paid for my beer and the bottles of water Sarah and Aye Thit ordered. Then we walked across the road to buy our tickets on the ferry, which was docking. Hart walked alongside. "Don't touch me," I said.

"I saved your life," he said. "That cobra would have fanged your face if it wasn't for my quick action."

I didn't remember any quick-witted action by Hart that saved my life. The Terracotta Warrior rattling the last dewdrop off his Fred was what had likely saved my life. It wasn't the right time to cure Hart of his illusions as he dripped and smelled of rancid durian.

"Hart, for the sake of argument, let's say that I owe you my life. But that doesn't entitle you to breathe durian on me."

"I wonder how you two ever became friends," said Sarah. "But then I often wondered how my father and mother ever married."

The ticket attendant sitting behind the window looked Sarah up and down, and, after concluding that she wasn't Burmese, demanded that we all pay the foreigner premium to go on the ferry. That amounted to one dollar each. Mr. Banker removed three one-dollar bills and spread them on the counter. A cigarette was wedged in the corner of my mouth, smoke curling up, as I took the tickets from the attendant. By then the ferry was tied up and we walked straight on board. It had an old, well-worn deck with a number of low-slung wooden benches with slatted seats. You had to be no more than five feet tall to sit on one of the benches without your knees pushing through your chin.

"In late January 1942 as the Japanese 55th Division drove the British out of Moulmein," I said to Sarah, "they crossed from Moulmein to Martaban by ferry. They had to run the ferry themselves. The local Mon and Karen captains and crews had fled the scene, seeing that there was no percentage in working for the losing side."

"You know a lot about history," she said.

"You can't go to someplace and not ask who was there before you."

"I do it all the time," said Hart. "It's liberating."

While the ferry was still docked, the rain blew through the passengers huddled on the deck. At first it was a thin rinse, more of a mist than rain. But a few minutes after departure, the mist turned to rain. The first mate appeared out of nowhere, tugged on my arm, and gestured for us to follow him. It didn't seem possible that we would be sinking already. But it was that kind of day. The ferry listed slightly on the starboard side, knocking some of the passengers off balance. Howls and screams. The first mate led us up the stairs and into the stateroom which was painted Greyhound bus depot green; the kind of green you want to be looking at when a heavy swell hits. Having paid the foreigner premium, we found that it entitled us to the comfort of special quarters. Let them shout and holler and cry on the deck below—we were destined for better things. The windows fit in wooden frames and rattled in the wind and rain. The windows slid into side notches so they could be lowered or raised. The first mate closed two of the open windows. That helped some, but it didn't stop the rain gushing through the cracks in the floorboards or falling from the ceiling.

"Has anyone ever drowned in a stateroom?" I asked.

"That's the kind of question my father would have asked," said Hart.

"I am sorry. I didn't mean. I . . ."

"It doesn't matter."

"Over here," said Sarah.

She had discovered the one dry place. We huddled together. It was like being back in the car again. Through a slit in the wooden frames, the Gulf of Martaban appeared in a grayish mist. We talked about Kipling's fraud on Mandalay. Why, exactly, had he gone to Moulmein? To frequent a brothel or to find antiques and other

218

treasures? Or was he simply curious about how far the white man's burden stretched through the Burmese countryside? With Orwell, it was easier. He had gone to Moulmein as a colonial official and supervised hangings.

"Orwell's complicity in hanging the locals had a profoundly disturbing effect on him," said Hart. "I am certain they fully deserved it. The men he hanged."

"From an English point of view," I said.

"I am against capital punishment," said Sarah. "It is wicked and primitive."

"I agree," I said.

"Some men should be hanged. Just be done with it," said Hart.

"The Burmese should have hanged Kipling for lying about Mandalay," I said. "His proofreader could have been his second."

"You don't have seconds at hangings. That's dueling."

"I am a little bored with being a second," said Sarah.

The ferry crew had done its best to ensure our comfort on that wreck of a ship. After the first mate left, three crew members arrived in the stateroom carrying our bags, their hair and faces dripping wet from the rain, and stored the bags in a small storage cupboard off the main stateroom. This room was intended for dignitaries, meaning anyone who could afford to pay a dollar for the pleasure of taking the boat to Moulmein. The British officers fleeing the Japanese must have used it. That meant the room was for foreigners with money or guns or both. The distinction between the occupation and liberation of a place was all in the eye of the beholder. The line shifted, blurred, and twisted depending on the point of view of the soldier, the girl, the locals and those who invited themselves into the city. Some would navigate the boat for anybody; others took to their heels and fled to the hills.

There was no doubt in my mind that like Kipling, Orwell or Kazuo's uncle, we had arrived in Moulmein following a long tradition of outsiders marching from the jetty down the Strand Road, looking to discover loot, men to hang, and buildings to occupy. Mainly they had arrived like the three of us, looking for an answer to blue-scorpion-like riddles that we believed might shed a beacon of light on ourselves.

38

Think of the worst day of your life, and then imagine yourself changing places with a coolie working the jetty at Moulmein. Work that job for an afternoon and, at the end, ask if what you had recalled as your worst day still holds open. Imagine a long line of young men, their faces, necks, legs and hands coal black; their blue shirts and shorts oily with sweat and grime, spidery legs bowed; their backs hunched under the weight of huge bags of dried fish and fruit. None of the boys looked normal. Harelipped, strange depressions in the side of their skulls, sunken, dark-rimmed eyes, rickety legs and swollen knees—young men physically scarred with medieval-like horrors from birth defects, disease and other unknown causes of deformity. No wonder Orwell felt immense guilt hanging such people.

"They ain't humping Ming bowls in those bags," I said.

Sarah gasped. Three coolies broke free of the throng on the pier and grabbed her luggage, then Hart's and finally mine, and disappeared into the crowd with the speed of muggers. We tried to follow them down the narrow gangway. They were swallowed in a sea of unwashed faces.

Sarah shouted after them, "Come back."

She was convinced they had stolen her bags and struggled against the tide of the crowd to follow them.

"Chill. They are just doing their job," I said.

"Sloan's right," said Hart.

"Promise?"

"Hey, baby, have I ever lied to you?" I asked.

"I bet you say that to your wife."

She was right. I did say that to Saya.

A few minutes later, we emerged onto the street, and the coolies worked to stack our cases onto a trishaw. Sarah was immediately relieved. She touched her cases, checked the locks, and finding that everything was in order, turned and said, "You were right." I beamed.

"Yeah, baby, you gotta have some faith when you travel," I said.

Aye Thit ran ahead to bargain for a good price with the coolies and the trishaw drivers. He overpaid the jetty coolies, giving them a couple hundred kyat. Even Aye Thit, as squalid as his life was, felt a twinge of pity for them. The thin trishaw drivers with flat bellies, sinews and veins breaking the surface of their hard calves and thighs, watched the money being handed over and smiled. They could see Aye Thit was a soft touch. They stood on their trishaws dressed in ragged shorts and sandals, sniffing the sea air, and thinking that at last a good payday had arrived.

Our bags had been perfectly balanced in two large piles divided between the two seats of the three-wheel bicycles. In the gentle rain, dozens of trishaws lined the street outside the jetty entrance. The trishaws, designed for underfed, small locals, presented a problem to foreigners whose diet allowed them to grow much larger asses. Each trike held two passengers who sat back-to-back. We were large, big people, and I was more bottom-heavy than either Sarah or Hart. The passenger seats looked about the same size as a carry-on luggage measuring box used in the departure areas of airports. If your bag didn't fit into what someone decided was the exact dimension of an overhead storage bin, then, hey, buddy, you had to check it in. If your ass didn't fit in the trishaw, the only choice, at the jetty, was to walk a couple of miles in the rain to the hotel. No doubt the Japanese Imperial Army marched down the Strand in the rain; the Chindits surely crouched from door-to-door, shooting and chasing out the Japanese, but I was *riding* to the hotel. I struggled to fit into the seat. I wiggled until my body was wedged into the narrow metal frame intended for people who never grew larger than 110 pounds. I was a six-pack of beers away from a long, wet march. If a tire had blown out there would have been no way to jump free as the trishaw spun out of control. Once in the trishaw, I had no idea how I was going to get out. I could be stuck in a trishaw for days, begging people to show me their Ming.

Hart and Sarah climbed into a second trishaw and Aye Thit climbed into the seat opposite to me. I was so firmly stuck that I couldn't pivot around and see Aye Thit. He tapped me on the shoulder. "It's okay. I'll get you out," he said. I didn't have to look to know that he was grinning.

They had all slid into the seats without any problem. Young people, I thought. Wait until middle age pounced and deposited its payload of blubber on their buttocks one fine morning. The drivers stood straight as they pedaled, trying to get as much traction as they could for the size of their load. We slowly drove down the Strand with the river on our right. A couple of minutes into the ride, a smart-assed driver on a horse cart came up alongside, reining in his horse. The horse had an underfed, dogged appearance; its ribcage pressed hard against its hide, outlining every bone. The driver and his passengers laughed, thinking it was funny that our trishaw drivers had earned such bad karma. Our drivers labored hard, sweat mixing with the rain, as they pedaled their heavy load of large foreigners. There was no apparent malice in the laughter. Instead the reaction was more a mixture of surprise and delight at such an unexpected sight; an opportunity to feel good about themselves coupled with an innocent, genuine curiosity about foreigners.

The horse cart contained a family; the father sat in front beside the driver and the mother and two daughters sat in Sunday dresses in the back. The whole family and the driver had to weigh less than Hart and me. The horse cart driver decided to make a game of racing the foreigners in the trishaws. His strategy was to allow our drivers a head start before he cracked his whip against the bony ribs of his broken down horse. The beaten animal shook its head, did one of those floppy, wet mouth splutters before breaking into a full trot. The two young daughters giggled, covering their faces, spying us through splayed fingers. The horse easily passed our trishaws as our drivers pumped the pedals, veins in their necks the size of ropes. Their best efforts were doomed, defeated by the superior energy and strength of a half-starved horse. The horse cart stopped about fifty feet ahead and the driver held the reins, smirking as he waited for us to catch up.

"Man, they beat us and now they want to taunt us. Humiliate our drivers. That's ugly," I said.

"The horse is ill," Hart said.

As we came closer, the old horse's tail flew up and it took a massive dump in the middle of Strand Road. One of those messy, green runny bowel shots that makes one holler to the heavens, "Thank you God, for not letting me become a vet." In sheer volume, what the horse's bowels produced made Checkers' shot across the kitchen wall a thin wiggle of fecal hieroglyphics. It made my back ache just to look at it. That horse was the driver's meal ticket and from the look of its shit, his meal ticket wasn't long for this world. Self-interest doesn't always prevail when it comes to winning a race. Competition is the way animals, people, and things are weighed, judged, used up and thrown away.

Turning around, Sarah asked, *"Ianfu?"* She was trying to make herself heard against the heavy breathing of the driver. Hart had confused her by asking whether she remembered the scene in the manuscript where the action had been set in a comfort house situated along the Strand Road. He didn't say comfort house, though. He used the Japanese word, *ianfu*. She remembered Khin Aung had used the word to mean comfort women. I was confused, too, looking around for any sign of a brothel, but saw nothing, no building or sign that looked remotely like one.

"I thought you said this was the road where there are comfort women," said Sarah, as her trishaw with Hart in the back pulled up alongside mine.

"It's in the novel," he said. "Comfort house on the Strand Road."

She hadn't caught his words and responded, "We are going so fast, all the buildings are a blur."

"I have no idea if there are working girls on the Strand Road, Sarah," said Hart.

"I think the horse cart wants a re-match," I said.

Our drivers pedaled past the horse cart and the family waved and laughed. The horse cart driver let us get about fifty yards ahead before cracking his whip. A couple of minutes later the horse ran past us again.

"If he stops again, shoot the horse, Aye Thit."

"I don't have a gun."

"I'll pay for the gun. Just do it." It was in our bones that losing was never a good thing. This time the horse and cart kept going. We turned into the Ngwe Moe Hotel which looked across the Moutama River at Blue Island, a rim of land against the horizon as neatly manicured as a Patpong whore's eyebrows.

I tossed an empty beer can and it tumbled along the Strand, and then I wadded up an empty cigarette packet and tossed it.

"You are littering," said Sarah. "First it was cigarette butts, then food cartons, beer cans, and newspapers. Is your mission to throw junk on every road in Burma?"

I hadn't thought of it that way. I just chucked useless stuff out the window. "Hey, Aye Thit, did you bring my coffee?"

He said he had some finely ground Dutch coffee—actually it was from Indonesia, as the Dutch couldn't grow coffee in the Netherlands—and he reached into his magic bag and produced the jar. He smiled as he showed it to me. I twisted a little in my seat and caught a glimpse of the coffee. Aye Thit had unscrewed the lid so that I could whiff the coffee.

"That's real good. Aye Thit, I need a massage. My back is killing me." I arched forward, feeling the bones crack.

"Littering isn't a substitute for exercise. But it is a novel idea," said Hart.

"Nagging is far worse than littering. You can hire people to pick up trash," I said.

They were beating up on me. A wolf pack tearing off my flesh.

"You don't look well," said Hart.

"Ever since the boat accident in the Chin Hills, I've had a bad back," I said. I was the last one out of the trishaw. Aye Thit on one side and Hart on the other, they counted to three and then slowly pulled me out like a cranky, rotten wisdom tooth.

39

It drizzled as the trishaw boys unloaded our bags and hauled them into the hotel lobby. In the failing light they looked far more fragile, small, and hungry than when they mingled with dozens in the same condition at the jetty. Racing with the horse cart had taken away their strength and spirit. They must have known the race was lost before they started, but that knowledge hadn't stopped them from trying the impossible. They were no different from the farm boy soldiers in World War I who, hearing an officer blow a whistle, climbed out of their trench and charged German machine guns. Perhaps Sarah's father might have revealed the source of this impulse to attack against nearly zero odds of success but he had killed himself—and there was an answer in his rebellious final act. I stood looking at the island on the river across from the Ngwe Moe Hotel. The others had gone in with the trishaw boys. I finished a cigarette, dropped it on the wet road, and caught up with Sarah and Hart at the front desk. Their heads bowed as they filled out the ledger. A letter was waiting for us; Khin Aung's cousin had delivered the white envelope. Inside was a handwritten note: we had been invited for dinner unless, of course, we were too tired by our journey. I reread that line again, thinking how English it sounded and how no one in Thailand ever wrote anything remotely like this to a total stranger. Reading on, the letter gave a phone number and said we should have the receptionist phone, and a motorcar would be sent around for us. I looked at the word "motorcar" again. What other kind of car was there? I thought of the Terracotta Warrior and wondered if he would sleep in the back of the Toyota, coiled up next to the plastic jugs of diesel fuel. Aye Thit had advanced him money for a room and food. I had this gut feeling the Terracotta Warrior was a soul brother; he would pocket the hotel money in the same way that I embezzled girlfriend money. Not more than an hour after we checked into three separate rooms—Sarah and Hart maintained the appearance they were not sleeping together—the cousin's car and driver arrived. It was an old Honda. At least it *might* have been a Honda. The car was ancient, manufactured in a time when people called cars motorcars; this car could have been a prototype test-driven by officers of the Japanese Imperial Army on the back roads of Moulmein. Keeping a car next to water had a corrosive effect on paint and metal: paint peeled like sunburnt skin from the front fender, duct tape covered a long scar of a crack on a window—there was a bulge under the tape that looked like a bullet hole—and rust holes ate through the wheel wells, letting the rain accumulate and slosh in mini-waves as the car moved. The tires were perfectly smooth like a bar *ying*'s ass—the treads worn away.

On the other hand, staying at the Ngwe Moe Hotel wasn't exactly staying at the Ritz or the Oriental Hotel. Car and hotel were approximately matched in status. The driver got out and opened the back door. We piled in. It smelled like the thick humid air of the stateroom in the ferry. Aye Thit rode shotgun. Half-way down Strand Road, a horse cart and driver appeared ahead; as we approached, it looked like the same horse and driver that had defeated us in the race.

"Is that the same guy?" I asked, rolling down my window and looking out, rain hitting my face.

"That's him," said Hart, who was leaning out the other side.

Sarah sat in the middle with her arms folded. Women had their own sense of revenge but it rarely played out against the winner of a horse cart race. Hart's remembrance of things not too past was as fresh as mine. I couldn't get a good look at the driver or the horse and was convinced that even if I had, I wouldn't have been able to swear an oath they were the same as the driver and horse who whipped our ass and drained the morale from our trishaw boys. Hart rolled down the window—he harbored no such doubts—and gave the driver the finger as we sped past. It was dark and raining and I doubted that the horse cart driver saw Hart's gesture. The whole thing was over as fast as a bullfight featuring a blind matador, as my father used to say. But whether the driver saw it or not didn't much matter. As he pulled himself back into the car, I could see that Hart felt a lot better.

"Are you okay?" asked Sarah.

His right arm was wet and rain had splattered one side of his hair and face. Otherwise he looked okay. "That was the bloke who raced us earlier."

"I didn't see his face," said Sarah.

"Believe me." Hart locked eyes with her as if her belief in the identity of the horse and driver was the defining moment of their short relationship.

"I believe you."

What else could she possibly say? Hart never bothered to ask me. He knew better. After all, he had kept his novel a state secret. And we had done one book together. Hart must have understood that the trust we had established during our adventures in the Chin state and the writing of the book could no longer be drawn on. The trust account had been overdrawn. When a relationship goes into the red, even the identity of strangers can't be conceded.

40

Obviously Hart's undisclosed manuscript bothered me. For whatever reason he had decided not to show it to me. Fine, I accepted that. But we had lunch once a week and he never once *mentioned* that he was working on a book. All I knew was that once a very long time ago he had written the text for *The Art of Chin Ways*, and over the next ten years he had treaded water hanging out and playing pool. It was only recently that he had acquired a position as a proofreader at *The Bangkok Post*. Less than twenty-four hours after meeting Sarah, he had given her the manuscript. I was left to pass notes back and forth with her. She read the manuscript on *her* bed that first night in Rangoon. Her only outside communication to the world was with me. How twisted was that—a friend had remained silent about a literary project, and not only did he exclude me, his best friend, but within the space of less than twenty-four hours Sarah had the manuscript. And what did I have? Notes penned by Sarah slipped under my hotel room door. There were "rules." I couldn't go to her room; I couldn't phone her room; nor was I allowed to ambush her as she slipped a note underneath the door. She had been raised in a rule-obsessed household. Her father a paranoid compulsive-obsessive. That kind of thing could be genetic. My dad and mom raised me in a household with few rules but lots of slogans and useful bits of everyday information: faith healers wipe their ass like everyone else. Use salt water to remove caramel candy stuck in your teeth. Dad invented this slogan after consuming a bottle of wine one Christmas Eve—Never cut the lawn in suede shoes.

Hart had managed to get *The Art of Chin Ways* published. What mattered, he said, was not just finishing a book; it didn't exist unless others could read it. After our book came out, Hart said it was out of his head and he could get on with his life, and that his fondest hope was never to wake up with another book cooking inside his bean.

One night, camping in the Chin state, the two of us, after dinner and local whisky, went around and around about the nature of books, war and killing. In Chin culture there was a rule that *no act of a man was a crime when he was drunk*. That led to the inevitable disagreements over whether any man could kill and wage war in a sober state. Knifing a man's guts onto the ground, dashing the brains out of his skull, burning, smashing, dismembering, exploding, drowning—the mutilation of bodies was better done after consuming lots of beer. Being English, Hart argued that violence by drunks was a product of weakness of character by inferior men who lacked fundamental courage. Such men weren't warriors; gutter brawlers, yes, but men with no stomach for the real sustained brutality of lethal conflict. They were three-minute men in the sack and two-minute in a fight. And "fight" was the right word. Always proceed with care when using the word "war." Since the time of hunter-gatherers throughout Burma the history was one of raiding parties, ambushes, skirmishes, plundering, attacks organized by tribes, clans, and villages, and blood feuds. The cauldron always frothed and bubbled. In World War II, it boiled over into larger battles, more soldiers, more foreigners, more makeshift graveyards, but basically they were the same tribal ingredients that Africa and Afghanistan stewed in as they slaughtered each other endlessly in the name of the principle, one big chief, many tribes kissing his fat ass. One step removed from Somalia where the cauldron never cooled. Flip a coin. Heads or tails, it didn't matter, someone's throat got slit. Same, same for the history of the Mon state. Memories of old feuds, grievances, greed, and jealousy told you there would always be bands of armed men setting up ambushes in the mountains.

There was almost no electricity in the countryside at night. Except for oil lanterns and candles, the fields along the side of the road lay in virtual darkness. Moonlight illuminated the watery surface in the distance. The headlamps of the Honda on high beam followed the contour of the road, never shining more than twenty feet ahead. It was a solitary journey on a dark night. A cold chill blew through the window that Aye Thit had opened in front.

Hart shivered, hugging closer to Sarah. "When I was seven my father was driving on a country road in the East Midlands. I remember feeling very cold. I curled up and looked out the window. I saw phantom horses and seventeenth-century bearded soldiers in armor with swords and spears. I thought our car would crash into them but we sailed through like a hot knife through butter. I asked my father if he had seen the figures galloping across the road. And he said, 'Mounted horsemen riding through the fog on their way to battle?' This caught me by surprise, I raised my head to find him smiling at me. 'With beards and swords and spears?' I asked him. And Father said, 'Only special people see these men on their way to battle in the Civil War, the War of the Roses. It is a special gift.'"

Sarah touched his forehead with her fingers. "That's what makes you a novelist."

I looked at the road, thinking I would vomit. Aye Thit rolled up the window. Something in the air hinted of a whiff of cordite; it stung the inside of my nose. I rolled down my window in time to hear the screams of the dying. All of this, even I knew, was coming from inside my head.

"Do you hear them?" I asked.

Neither Hart nor Sarah replied. She was nursing him and he had surrendered to her care. I heard the moans and cries and screams. Where did the voices come from? Perhaps the war dead from books I'd read, from Hart's stories about his grandfather gathering intelligence for the Chindits prior to a battle. Stories and tales recorded in books, pamphlets, and web sites, buried in archives where the dead mostly lived after everyone else had forgotten them. Clarke spinning yarns about flying gliders in Burma. Looking in the darkness, I saw Clarke's face flying across the window. In another twenty, thirty years, not a living person on the planet would remember men like Clarke, or that they had ever existed, or that they had died in Southeast Asia. That was the way the world spun. Get used to it—no one survives for long, entire tribes and civilizations disappear, and only a handful of names remain lodged in the collective memory, living on in the minds of those who never knew them. That was why we had had a duty to publish *The Art of Chin Ways*. I'd secretly hoped Hart would write other books, and that I would feature in all of them. As a friend, he was required to do his part not to let time swallow me up, not let me disappear forever. When my time came, I planned to be cremated and have my ashes spread in the Chin Hills. I told myself people would read about me in Hart's books, and they would walk those hills with my name on their lips. Sarah had read our book; it had changed her life.

"I am so happy that you read *The Art of Chin Ways*," I said.

"It is a wonderful book," she said.

"Once we found a bookstore on a side street in Rangoon that had copies of our book," said Hart. "Two original copies from the publisher and a half-dozen photocopied and bound copies. Sloan asked to see the owner. A little old man wearing a soiled singlet and boxer shorts shuffled out of the back room. Sloan said, 'Hey, baby, my friend and me wrote this book.' He held up one of the original copies. 'And if you like we will autograph them for you. Even the pirated copies. No problem.' And do you know what the owner said?"

I hated this story. Sarah said, "He wanted a dedication or something?"

"No, he didn't want us to sign the books. That would make them second-hand, and he would have trouble selling them. And Sloan tried to explain, 'That makes them more valuable.' The old Chinese man shrugged his shoulders and helped himself to one of Sloan's cigarettes. 'In Rangoon, less valuable. I sell books in Rangoon. I know value.'"

"That old man took one look at Hart and thought we were con artists. He didn't know about autographed copies."

"He didn't want to know," said Hart. "He had a passion for selling rather than a passion for books. You rarely find a bookseller who has both."

That was true.

Sarah's hand-written notes had hinted that Hart's passion had gone into the novel, but as far as I could tell, I was nowhere to be found in that novel. It is one thing to feel excluded by a friend, but when a friend fails to preserve your identity, then you vanish, and for all practical purposes you never existed. Other than me, who now remembers Clarke? I could be his last living link.

Since I was a kid in Florida, I had wanted to make a living from my dreams. The ultimate job was to have people pay for the products of my imagination, buying my photographs, sculptures, and paintings. I created each for a reason—an invitation for another person to lock in, dream that dream to the end of the line, wherever that takes them, climb down onto the platform and find themselves at the destination they want to be. That was what an artist did. And what the artist found was that most of the people at the other end were like the bookseller in Rangoon. Forget about creating objects of beauty or flights of imagination—in our neighborhood the motto was "show me the money."

Poor Hart, he had all but given up on himself by settling for a proofreading job and Sugarcane and Shrimp. I hadn't dragged Hart to Burma; he had planned to return. Something had compelled him to journey to Moulmein. He had smiled when I told him about Akira Takeda's wish that I destroy the photograph of the girl.

"He's a single-minded man," said Hart.

"I didn't know you knew Akira Takeda?"

"That's strange. I met him in Bangkok. I thought you knew."

"Knew what?"

"That Saya told him how I found our publisher," said Hart. "You must have told her that story a hundred times."

And so I had. She must have told Akira Takeda in Japanese right in front of me. I wouldn't have known.

"She was trying to help," Hart added, seeing how deflated I was.

Help me. Help me. I taught my birds these words. I could hear their voices inside my head. In between my meetings with Akira Takeda, Hart had been meeting him and more than likely with Saya acting as his translator. I stared at Hart but heard voices as I saw his lips moving. I felt myself falling, confused, angry, and betrayed, and I felt the cocoon weaken, then break and looking down, I saw nothing to break the free-fall state into which I had entered.

41

When people are nervous about the unknown, they fall back on what is comforting. In Sarah's case that was tattoos. She talked about them in the car.

"It is the collective belief in ritual and superstition that people cling to for meaning. Tattoos, like the cross, are products of faith and belief. They have nothing to do with any rational explanation or proof." This sounded vaguely like a lecture that she had given a number of times before.

Hart, who was almost twelve years old before he learned to read, let his eyes glaze over, his mind somewhere else. He watched the moonlight playing on the fields.

"When you were a little girl, did you ever dream about your father's tattoo?" I asked. "His tattoo. The one on his arm. Your father's tattoo."

Hart swallowed a giggle. It was his way of telling me that I was repeating myself. I knew. I knew. I knew. These lapses, the slight repetitions, gave him cause for joy. The way you smile when you see a hairless dog or featherless bird; its mere existence was funny, weird, and a little sad.

"Did that fire-breathing dragon fly through your dreams, swoop down like a giant bat, follow you around, asking you to recite rule after rule?" I said.

Personalizing the lecture was one way to put some blood into the veins.

She nodded. "It's true. How did you know?"

"I used to dream of my father's amusement park burning down. I was always on the Ferris wheel and stranded at the top, the flames licking at me and my father could hear my screams."

"In boarding school I dreamt of Africans fornicating in a huge vat of cottage cheese and slowly turning themselves into white schoolmasters," said Hart.

"I don't believe you," I said in the darkness of the backseat.

"It might have been plain yogurt," said Hart.

Dreams, rituals and tattoos were the opposite of science and the world of experiments. Unless a theory could be verified by others it wasn't science; it was religion or belief or mysticism. Bullshit on toilet walls. But without any strand of sacred belief left at the bottom of the cup, what magic remained? Sarah occupied a world of tattoos. Filaments of magic and ritual surrounded the Shan's tattoos. The Shan and Chin adorned their body with their mythical images and writing, used precise rules for the artist applying the tattoo. Rules, safety, and tattoos co-existed as protection against the evils and dangers of the world. Struggle free of the safety net, and you were lost. Abandon worship and devotion because there is no evidence and you were condemned. Accept that nothing was made to last and you found despair. Fight against the conclusion that after you scratched your way up the diamond walls, when you peered over the top, what you saw wasn't paradise but another wall. Acknowledge that it didn't always work but keep trying to beat the horse and cart driver. Anxiety and distress waited at the finish line. Had Sarah's father believed in the power of the tattooed dragon? Or was it done when he was weak and drunk; done outside the normal rules or done because it fitted a rule? It hadn't mattered; the dragon tattoo hadn't stopped Sarah's father from blowing his brains out.

"After we go back to Rangoon, I want to take you to the zoo," I said to Sarah.

"That might be fun."

"It is the only zoo with a chicken in a cage," said Hart.

"Is that true?"

I nodded. It was true. "There's a sign on the cage, and it reads, 'Chicken.' And inside is one of the worst beat-up chickens you've ever seen."

"In a zoo?"

"Across from the snake house," I said. "On the opposite side are deer. But there was no controlled breeding program. Deer breed like rabbits. It looks like a concentration camp for deer. No third world prison ever looked that bad."

"There are no coincidences," said Hart.

"Everything converges," I said. "Like meeting Sarah at the Drug Elimination Museum with the Chin. Like you meeting Akira Takeda and neither my wife nor you mentioning this to me."

"You're repeating yourself."

"You think those were all coincidences?" I asked. "That zoo's been there for a hundred years. You have to go to the Amazon rain forest to find older trees. If you go to the zoo and the Drug Elimination Museum then you will see all you ever need to see to understand Burma. Baby hippos live in a pit, mouths wide open, and tourists drop bunches of bamboo leaves in their mouths. All day long they see a tourist, they charge, stand with their mouths open and wait for food to be thrown in. Exhausted tigers and lions stretch out sleeping. Crocs eyeball-to-eyeball with the deer in the next cage. They're not thinking about mating; they want food. Deer on the hoof. Natural born killers. Squalor. Neglect. Overcrowding. Boredom. Cruelty. None of the animals live free. They all die in their cages. You see the Burmese staring at the big-game animals—elephants, giraffes, lions—and they are entertained. They see that chicken in a cage, that one, solitary bird, and they don't look so happy because they are looking in the mirror."

"You are rather gloomy, old boy," said Hart.

I snapped open another Tiger beer and drank.

We continued the journey in moody silence, the car awash with images of dragons, chickens and snakes. My eyes closed, head rested back, I thought of Kazuo's photographs bursting into flame. It was all that he had left. Nineteen images and I was his guardian. I wasn't going to let him disappear.

THE BLUE SCORPION

42

As it turned out, Khin Aung's cousin didn't live in Moulmein but in a village north of the city. It had to be north as that was the direction the car was heading. The arc of headlamps swiped across a large, rambling teak house. A large coach bus was parked outside, dark and vacant, no evidence of a driver or passengers. The intersection ahead was silent and motionless as death. Crossing the windshield, the wipers groaned and whined like an injured animal. The driver, who had driven essentially blind, squinted through the opaque windshield. He parked the car beside the coach, cut the engine and switched off the headlamps. The windows fogged over and it was pitch dark as I opened the door on my side and stepped out. I heard Hart slurping, moving drool around with his tongue. It was too dark to see whether his tongue was connected with Sarah's. I visualized Zaw Min with his pants around his ankles on the balcony with Twe Twe pretending she was bobbing for apples, her glasses fogged over as she bore down, holding her breath in the dark, forgetting everything—that must have made a slurpy, whiny moan like the one coming out of Hart's mouth. We sat in the dark for a minute until the sound stopped. The driver opened the door.

The house also served as a bus station. A schedule was posted on a corkboard hooked on a large nail pounded into the side of a huge teak beam. Inside a Chinese man in a white singlet and copper-colored *longyi*, his thick glasses on the end of his nose, hunched over an account ledger. Light from an oil lantern streaked over his face, leaving dark shadows on his forehead and down his neck. He looked up as we filed inside the room. It was difficult to determine his age. His hair was thick and black and cut short along the sides. Late fifties or early sixties would have been a wild guess. A nonsensical expression lingered on his thin lips as he looked over each one of us with the same concentration he devoted to the numbers in the ledger book. I could see him in the pit, nudging against the concrete barrier, mouth open, waiting for someone to throw in a handful of bamboo shoots. The driver slipped over to the desk, leaned down and whispered in his ear. The man never broke eye contact with us. He nodded and closed the ledger book, slipped it into the top drawer of his wooden desk and inserted a key, locking the drawer. Then the driver disappeared up a flight of stairs.

"Khin Aung told us that you were cousins," I said.

Aye Thit translated and the Chinese man nodded. For the first time he smiled and his sharp yellow teeth showed between his lips. "And that his son had stayed with you."

The statement of fact managed to quickly erase a flicker of a smile. He ignored the reference to Khin Aung and his dead son, and instead told us through Aye Thit that the teak house with the eighteen-foot ceilings had been in the family for five generations. The family operated the local bus station. He gestured to the far end of the room where a dozen old Chinese bicycles were parked. "Vocational school students park their bicycles here. There is a school nearby," Aye Thit translated. "There are always bicycles left over at the end of the day. Upstairs there is a sewing factory and the living quarters."

"Thank him for sending the car and driver. And then ask him if Khin Aung explained why we have come to Moulmein." I said to Aye Thit. But as I watched the man at the desk I had a feeling he understood everything I had just spoken.

"You are looking for the past," he said in English.

"That sounds like a warning," said Hart.

He shrugged his shoulders. "My name is Thwin. I am afraid my English is poor. I prefer to speak Burmese."

"Your English is just fine," said Sarah. She offered her hand. He blinked and then shook it with one of those limp-wrist attempts at a handshake.

Sarah scoured his arms for tattoos. He had none showing. The Chinese—unless they were Triad—rarely offered their flesh for tattooed images. Horned dragons with flapping wings lowered their status and unlike the Shan they didn't believe in the magical powers a tattoo conferred. Ground-up rhino horn to make old Fred stand up straight and proud, that was a different story. Thwin had been puzzled by Khin Aung's request for Ming pieces; he had said to Khin Aung on the telephone that he had no idea if there were any Ming pieces in his village. But he knew the local Chinese and if anyone knew whether any Ming could be found, then his brother would know. The brother collected antiques.

"Can we meet your brother?"

"That is possible. Meanwhile, if you could wait a little bit."

Since he had sent a car to our hotel and had us driven here in the dead of night, I assumed it would be possible. Waiting, that was all we had been doing since we arrived in Burma. It was the default option to which the entire country was set. I looked for a place to sit down.

On the flagstone floor was an old table honeycombed with tiny termite holes that had rat teeth gnaw marks on the legs. It looked like zoo furniture. No way I was going to settle my ass in that spider nest. Behind the table, shoved against the wall, three ancient-looking four-poster teak beds were lined up like in a rundown furniture showroom in some swampy county in the deep South where incest wasn't a taboo. Made from the same print, each bed had a thick wooden indestructible frame and hand-carved legs. They smelled of rat urine and oil lantern fumes. The beds were enormous and together they covered an entire wall. Sarah went over and sat on the edge of one. Hart sat on the one next to hers, and I sat back on the last bed.

"A family of six could sleep in this bed," I said.

"I've had smaller rooms," said Hart.

"I think they are elegant. I'd love to own such a bed," said Sarah.

That shut us up. The beds were extravagant, absurd relics; stored between a bus station depot and a bicycle car park, they provided a weird waiting room, and added a sense of mystery. Nothing had been stacked on the beds—no mattresses, pillows or bedding. From the accumulated dust, it must have been years since those beds had last been in service. Thwin half-turned, looking at Sarah.

"They are very old," he said in English.

Beds brought out the English language in upcountry Chinese.

Hart sneezed, once, then again. "We're talking heavy dust."

"Scientists say allergies are inherited," I said.

"That's true," said Sarah.

Bingo.

"Have you ever seen a hippo sneeze?" I asked.

"From dust?" asked Sarah.

"No, from Tiger beer. It happened at the zoo in Rangoon. I aimed for the baby hippo's mouth, but missed and hit its nostrils. Or it could have moved its head. Do you remember that, Aye Thit? You caught the full blast."

"I remember," he said from the opposite side, where he was sitting on the old table.

On a large supporting beam near the beds, a calendar had been nailed. It was the kind of calendar where the months were torn off but the one image stayed the same for twelve months. You had to make the judgement that you wanted to stare at a woman for twelve months. The woman on the calendar was fully clothed. Most of her neck was covered. She couldn't have had more clothes on her body if she were boarding a charter flight from Miami to Havana. I looked at my watch.

"You think that your brother will be long?" I asked.

Another taller, slightly older man—early seventies—suddenly appeared with ghost-like silence at the bottom of the stairs. No one had heard or seen him until he had walked past the bicycle stand. He smoked a cigarette and on his left hand wore a ruby ring on his pinky that forced you to notice his long, tapered fingers like a concert pianist's. His eyes fell on Sarah and he stared at her for a full minute before continuing his walk across the long room.

"This is my brother Hwae," said Thwin.

"I see you've found the beds. They are old like everyone in this house," Hwae said.

"But we survive," said Thwin.

"Yes, we have a knack for staying together."

Skin the color of whalebone, a square, solid jaw, Hwae stood beside the oil lantern so that we could all have a good look at him. His bearing was proud, dignified, secure in the knowledge that everyone but the Chinese people were barbarians who lived on the opposite side of a great wall. And there we were, sitting on his Chinese beds. He nodded at Sarah. "You must be tired from your journey, and then I brought you all the way here before you've had your dinner. I must apologize." Like his younger brother pouring over the ledger book, Hwae had a precise, careful, cautious manner. He invited us upstairs. He told us that his family had lived in that house for five generations. This was the second time we had heard this story. Hwae said that his younger brother, who ran the coach bus business, had work to finish so unfortunately he wouldn't be joining us. He was sorry about the inconvenient time and the sudden invitation.

"I would have waited until you were settled, but I am leaving for a trip to Tokyo in the morning and this is our only chance to meet."

"It is an honor, sir," said Hart, extending his hand.

Everyone in the household had been anticipating our arrival since Khin Aung had phoned from Rangoon with the news that three foreigners required his assistance. He hoped that the journey had not been too stressful as people are often afraid of traveling at night in Burma. The army had been known to abduct recruits to hump supplies and ammo inside the Shan states war zones, plucking them off the streets and highways and bundling them into the back of trucks and vans. If looking for night adventure was the goal, the army guaranteed that they were more than happy to help you find it. I liked Hwae's sense of grace and humor. It made me like him and encouraged me to trust him.

"We came to Burma to see the Lady," I said after a lull in the conversation.

Hwae smiled. "I hope Aung San Suu Kyi can restore electricity so that at night I can read and feel the breeze from a fan." Waiting for electricity in Burma was like waiting for Godot.

While the rest of the world had waited for the Lady's release, Hwae continued waiting for electricity. None of the toys of the modern world worked without electricity. We followed Hwae into the upstairs which opened up into a vast, open teak room with unexpected angles, warps, bends, and doors. The floor—smooth and polished—sloped towards one end. The room looked like a nineteenth century factory where the money had run out halfway through the loft conversion. On one wall framed photographs of ancestors stared out from behind dusty glass. Hwae pointed at a stern blurry man with a weak chin and half-lidded eyes; he was the first generation, the start of the dynasty. The last photograph was Hwae's father, who had a toothy smile and rimless lips like his sons—and who turned out to be Khin Aung's uncle.

"It's like a Cook's tour of a stately home in England," Hart whispered.

I lit a cigarette. "If I had relatives that looked like that, I'd keep the photographs under the beds downstairs," I whispered back.

"I believe continuity is important," said Sarah, loud enough for Hwae to hear.

Unless you live in a zoo.

As Hwae wound up the potted history of his family, I thought for a minute of the official at the Drug Elimination Museum where we ran into Sarah and a large number of Chin villagers examining jars filled with dead babies.

"No deformed fetuses," I whispered to Hart.

"The family doesn't look like they are into drugs," whispered Hart.

"Could you repeat that Hwae? I am afraid my friends were talking and I couldn't clearly hear what you said about your great-grandfather's award."

Both Hart and I stared at the floor. I smoked and listened to Hwae repeat his speech about some act of bravery and heroism, wondering if it had been the Chinese who sold the mannequins bent over in the downhill-ski position to the Drug Elimination Museum. That would have been a brave thing to do.

In the far back of the room—actually on the other side of the house—several women worked under oil lamps, working the pedals of old sewing machines with their bare feet. Once or twice they stole a glance at the foreigners looking up at the old framed photographs on the wall. Finally the lecture was over. A table had been set and Hwae invited us to sit down. He walked across the room and opened the drawer in an old wardrobe with large claw feet and spires and wreathes and fruit carved along the sides and top.

"I want to show you something," said Hwae.

He removed a long ceremonial sword in a silver case. He carried it to the table laid out in his open hands and sat at the head of the table. "The British awarded my great-grandfather this sword. He was rewarded for helping the British wage a campaign against the *dacoit*." Hwae handed the sword to Hart to examine.

"Skirmish is a Germanic word. It means to fight with a sword. My grandfather taught me that. Also, nowhere except Burma or India does one ever hear the word *dacoit* used for local bandits," said Hart.

"It is a colonial word," said Hwae. "Inscribed on a colonial-era sword."

One man's *dacoit* was another man's freedom fighter. If you were the Sheriff of Nottingham, Robin Hood would have been a *dacoit*. Bandit or patriot—or warlord or general, murderer or soldier, terrorist or martyr—depended on your point of view. It had been enough to drive George Orwell out of the business of hanging *dacoit*.

Hart pulled the sword from the scabbard. On the silver blade was the inscription that Hwae had memorized and a date: 1895. The blade was engraved with swirls of lotus blossoms. One could imagine that with two hands on the hilt, using the sword baseball slugger style, the head of the *dacoit* would fly off his body as easy as hitting a homerun over the right-field fence.

"My cousin said you were English," said Hwae.

"I am English," said Hart.

"He was born in Africa," I said.

"It seemed like a convenient place for my mother to give birth," said Hart, handing me the sword.

I touched the tip of the blade. It was surprisingly sharp.

"I am American," said Sarah. "But my mother is Thai."

"There were Americans here during the war," Hwae said, watching me run my finger down the length of his great- grandfather's sword.

"My father was in the Vietnam War," said Sarah.

"I meant World War II. Americans and British fought the Japanese in Burma long before you were born. Before your father was born."

He was what my father used to call a time jumper. Like a hummingbird, he hovered around 1895 before diving headfirst into 1942 and sucking out the nectar. What he failed to mention was that conflict had been a feature of life long before 1895 and nothing had changed to the moment we sat in his teak house fortress. A bus depot with scary old Chinese beds and oil lanterns, crammed into a colonial period teak house with a wall of dead relatives stretching back more than a hundred years. No wonder Sarah was confused.

"Oh," she said, blushing. "I didn't know you meant *that* war."

He patted her hand, comforting, as if to say, I'll slow down the pace of changes between the last hundred or so years. Hold on for the ride.

"My great-grandfather built this house and once we had many beautiful objects that he collected. Things are not so good in Burma for a very long time. We lost many things. Only a few items we have never parted with."

It was time to cut the crap and find out some hard facts. "Khin Aung said you had information about Ming bowls and cups and saucers," I said.

"Wait here," he said, before disappearing around a corner.

"He may have gone to load the ceremonial gun," said Hart.

Hwae reappeared carrying three bowls. He carefully placed them on the table in front of Sarah. This gave him a chance to brush up close to her. After they were lined up in a row, he stood back.

"This, I am afraid, is all that is left," he said.

I looked at each one before handing it for examination to Hart and Aye Thit. The light was dim and it was difficult to make out exactly the period of each piece. But this much was for certain: none of the bowls dated from the Ming dynasty. Hwae said they had been in his family for a hundred years. That definitely wasn't Ming. One had a hair-line crack running from the lip to the base, a second piece had a small chip off the lip. Only one had somehow survived unscathed. The three bowls had arrived in the household around the same time as the silver sword.

It was impossible to know what Hwae intended by the display of the sword and the old, useless, china pieces. He was working up to something. Some men cultivated ambiguity with the skill of peasants working a rice paddy. Was he trying to sell us the bowls? Or was he trying to display what meager spoils had, at the end of day, found their way into the hands of the fifth generation? He could see the look of disappointment on my face. I snuffed out my cigarette in an ashtray, blew out a cloud of smoke and shook my head. "Man, we were really hoping to find something from the Ming dynasty. I mean, this is nice and it has been an honor to see what your great-grandfather collected, but it's not Ming."

The three bowls were once again lined up on the table. Hwae leaned over and picked up one of the bowls with a chip or crack and offered it to Sarah.

"I want to give this to you. Please take it."

"It should stay in your family, for the sixth generation," she protested. He persisted. She didn't know whether she should take such a valuable heirloom. Hwae insisted again. After looking at Hart, who nodded, and at me blowing smoke, Sarah relented and accepted the bowl. For five generations the bowl had been waiting for Sarah's arrival. Tomorrow Hwae would be in Japan and we would have returned to Moulmein where Khin Aung had said with confidence we would discover a motherlode of freshly unearthed Mings. We had gone all the way from Rangoon to find the cache of Ming vases and bowls washed out of the Chinese burial sites and all we had found was an old sword and some ordinary hundred year old blue and white porcelain bowls that someone's great-grandfather had eaten rice out of before accepting a ceremonial sword from the British for turning in his enemies and competitors as *dacoit*.

I felt discouraged and started to rise from the table. As far as I could tell, I was hungry, having missed dinner, needed a drink and wanted to light a fat one—and to get on the road to Moulmein.

Sarah reached over and took the photograph of the reclining girl out of my shirt pocket. She passed it to Hwae. He put on a pair of reading glasses then carefully examined the photo. He turned it over as if some writing like that on his great-grandfather's sword might reveal information. "Sloan is trying to find out information about this woman," said Sarah. "She has a blue scorpion tattoo on her thigh. If you look closely you will see it." The oil lantern provided a yellowish light that washed out much of the picture. Even at my angle, I could still make out the dark outline of the tattoo against the light-colored flesh. Hwae looked up from the photograph and called a name into the other side of the room.

Shortly afterwards, an old Burmese woman emerged out of the darkness from the direction of the sewing machines. The sound of the soft rhythm of the pedal-powered sewing machines followed her. She walked straight to the table and looked over Hwae's shoulder at the photograph. She wore no makeup and her wrinkled face was creased with a spider web of lines coiling out from the eyes and mouth; loose flesh hung down in folds from her neck. Dignity showed through the worn-out face, and her eyes sparkled as she looked at the photograph.

"Would you mind if I had a closer look?" she asked.

I nodded, "Do you know anything about this girl?"

"My eyes are tired and old and I don't see as well as I used to," she said in perfect English. After my experiences in Thailand, it remained a shock to have an old Asian woman speaking the kind of English that had died out with Hart's grandfather's generation.

"Let me introduce you to my sister," said Hwae.

She turned to her brother. "They came for something other than old bowls and pots. They came looking for someone," she said. Khin Aung no doubt had told her about the conversation we had had about the comfort houses in Moulmein during the war, and how we knew that the family slipper factory had been, in part, converted into a private club catering to the Japanese naval detachment that had moved into the city.

"I want to know all that you can tell me about the blue scorpion tattoo," said Sarah. She was earnest and endearing and this made the old lady smile.

"Of course you do, my dear," she said. "And I have been waiting a lifetime for someone to ask."

Her hand, withered with age, reached out for Sarah, who took her hand. We followed them back to where the sewing machines worked by lantern light.

43

The house had the feeling of a run-down museum. It could have used some exhibits. Mannequins of British officials hanging *dacoit* would have been good. Instead, there were lots of old, cramped, cluttered bookcases and chairs and tables. Cushions with hand-sewn mountains and valleys and rubber plantations were scattered here and there; but they were in some kind of order, like a fold-out book, a kind of map of the world. Victorian pieces the size of dinosaurs gathered dust. The ancient Chinese beds were being stored in the bus depot because there was no room left upstairs. Burma was a series of historical breaks, ruptures and discontinuities. Punctuated equilibrium. Men like Hwae proudly showing his great-grandfather's ceremonial sword as if it had been awarded yesterday. Women sewing by lantern light. And, the big prize, the girl in the photograph, with a blue scorpion tattoo, a talisman from a half-century before. The people living in this house didn't seem like the type who would have allowed the history of that image to disappear. The old woman stared at the tattoo as if it were a clue to a fossil record; after a long gap, suddenly another species of blue scorpion had appeared looking exactly like the blue scorpion that everyone has assumed had long ago become extinct. Kazuo captured on film what no longer existed, then lost in his camera, recalled the girl and the tattoo in long conversations with his father. I had a copy of the photograph. The old woman had seen something in that photo that made her smile. It was the first time anyone in that old teak house had smiled.

She sat heavily with her arms folded in her lap on an oversized rocking chair decorated with cushions, white with blue mountains, deer, and forests. A small oil lamp and smoking paraphernalia at her elbow; she casually reached over to the table and found her pipe. She packed it with tobacco pinched from a small canister. Her fingers nimbly felt across the table until she found the matches. She lit the pipe and leaned back, letting the smoke rise. I knew that feeling of the hit scoring the right neurons inside the brain. She smiled, sucking on the pipe, as if she had found an opening in the fabric of time, a small tear, just big enough for us to crowd through along with her. She motioned for Sarah to come closer and to sit on a chair near her. After Sarah sat down, the old woman took her hand and squinted through her glasses at Sarah's palm by lamplight.

"You have very fine hands," she said. "There was misfortune in your family. But things are much better now. You like certainty, knowing what you can and can't do. You will one day find your soul mate, the man you've been waiting for, and when you find him, it won't be easy but you will know him." She carefully closed Sarah's hand. "But you didn't come here to learn your fortune or to make your fortune in Ming. Khin Aung said you asked about the *ianfu*. Comfort girls from the war. That was such a long, long time ago, but in my mind—inside here," she tapped the stem of her pipe against her hair. "I can remember what happened fifty years ago better than what I had for breakfast today. The girls who worked in comfort houses were not only Burmese. They came from Japan, Korea, and China. The Japanese ran the *ianjo* system. They used outside traders who sold girls to the military for a thousand yen each. Like selling cattle or logs," she paused looking at me, "or Ming plates. Once they were sold, an *ianfu* cost a soldier two yen. Once a woman had slept with five hundred soldiers, she had worked off her selling price. She was free to return home. Most didn't return; they stayed. There were practical considerations. How were they going to safely return to Japan or Korea or China in the middle of a war? You couldn't walk. There were no commercial boats. They were stuck. You must have seen how isolated we are. Add to that isolation the uncertainty of war. Better to stay where there is a roof over your head and you have friends. So they stayed after five hundred, after a thousand men, after they could no longer remember how many men they had slept with. Safe, that's what they thought. Even though morning and night bombers dropped their bombs.

Fighting could be heard from the mountains and fields. Flashes from explosions lit up the sky at night.

"The Japanese left nothing to chance. In front of the wooden shacks where the girls worked, the men waited. They smoked cigarettes. They had time to read the sign posted in Japanese, which laid out rules like strict military orders they had to follow."

"Rules, what kind of rules?" asked Sarah, her head tilted to the side.

"Military life means following the commands of superiors. Discipline and rules were the backbone."

"I know exactly how rules work," said Sarah.

"These rules were very different from any you would have experienced," said the old woman.

She had her point of view: an *ianjo* was an adjunct of the battlefield. Rules were rules of the military. Above all, they did everything to control sex. While no firm rules told you how to ambush the enemy—you played that one by ear—sex with an *ianfu* was regulated by strict, unbendable rules. Confusing killing with fucking usually caused serious derangement. It simply was better operational policy not to kill what you fucked, or fuck what you killed.

"Did the women understand the rules?" asked Sarah. "Was it explained to them what they could and couldn't do? If not, they would get into trouble."

Don't leave the house. The prime rule of her father spun around in her head.

"Most of the working girls couldn't read the sign with the rules," said the old woman. "Most couldn't understand Japanese. They were hardly aware how they had been dragged into the *ianjo* system, knowing only that money had passed hands and they had been sold and until the debt had been paid, they were no longer free.

"I remember one Japanese soldier, he was just a boy, who had learned Burmese, standing in front of the sign, translating it for a young girl dressed in a kimono. She was giggling the way school girls do as he stumbled in Burmese, making all kinds of unintended mistakes."

She reached behind her back and produced one of the cushions and handed it to Sarah. "Read it," she said. "The original rules were in Japanese. But I translated them into English."

Sarah moved closer to the lantern and read the rules stitched into the cushions in fine lettering. And I was thinking, Christ, why didn't I get a grandmother who stitched whorehouse rules on cushions and passed them around to guests in lowly lit rooms. And Hart was probably thinking, how many of those cushions could be stuffed into a nine liter salmanazar?

1. *Only authorized personnel are permitted on the premises.*
2. *Show the attendant your pass before entering.*
3. *Pay two yen to the attendant in advance and present your receipt for one condom.*
4. *Pass expires after twenty-four hours and no refund is permitted.*
5. *Enter room shown on your receipt.*
6. *Hand your receipt to the attendant before entering the room.*
7. *No alcohol in the room. Having alcohol is an offence and will be punished.*
8. *Apply a solution provided to you after intercourse. Leave the room at once.*
9. *Anyone in breach of military orders must leave the room at once.*
10. *Never have intercourse without using a condom.*

Sarah looked up from the pillow. In one day, she had gone from living in a house divided fifty-fifty between men and women, governed by a pillow full of rules, to one that was 100 percent female, with the rule-maker's brains splattered on the ceiling of his work shed and the brother dead.

"Those were the rules. Now you have an idea about comfort houses. Now you can understand what it meant for the Blue Scorpion to exist outside the *ianjo* system. No formal rules were posted. It was a secret, private club for officers. The soldiers who visited an *ianfu* were given three minutes to do their business before the attendant banged on the door. 'Hurry up, others are waiting, get going,' the shouting echoed down the row of shacks. It takes little imagination to see how nothing erotic or pleasant took place inside these roughly built shacks. The girls had no privacy and they had to service many, many men each day. The Japanese naval officers wanted girls, but girls who worked outside of this system. My cousin, Khin Aung, may have told you about the day an officer found a girl who worked in the family shoe factory. Her name was Saw and she was a sweet girl who had been born in Moulmein. Her family had suffered greatly in the war and the money the Japanese officer offered was irresistible. Khin Aung's father was a religious man. He disapproved of Saw going with the Japanese officer and fired her. That caused a near-rebellion among the other thirty girls, who felt that Saw had done the only thing possible given the circumstances. They refused to work until Saw was offered her job back. This caused a serious disruption. A compromise was reached when an unused part of the factory was leased to a half-Chinese ship chandler named Thet Way. He had bought a consignment of Chinese beds for next to nothing. They were very beautiful and ancient beds. Perhaps you may have seen three of the beds downstairs? They were once part of the Blue Scorpion.

"Thet Way was a clever and resourceful man. He hired someone who had lived in Tokyo to decorate his corner of the factory. He knew his market. One day six tables appeared. Tablecloths and fine china plates. Then a piano arrived. He found someone to play the piano. A small kitchen was built, and upstairs partitions separated the space into rooms, each with a Chinese four-poster bed. For its time, and, in the middle of a war, a grand place. No one knows how much Thet Way paid to have the authorities look the other way, but no one doubted that large sums passed between hands. In the war, you would think there was very little money. The officers drew a small monthly salary, and after 1944 the Japanese army was virtually cut off, without money. Despite all of these difficulties, Thet Way attracted Japanese men who had put their hands on money—and there will always be such men—men willing to spend it on women. Within a few months, the money Thet Way collected each week far exceeded the revenues from the shoe factory. Thet Way acquired more space and more girls. He hired a seamstress to make kimonos for the girls. He had illustrated magazines of such Japanese fashions. Being a chandler helped. He never had trouble finding material at a knockdown price. The Blue Scorpion girls didn't look like *ianfu*.

They were a class apart. Thet Way hired a Japanese sailor to give them Japanese lessons. At this point, he paid compensation to Khin Aung's father, as the girls no longer had time to work in the shoe factory. As the factory had almost no business, the money Thet Way paid allowed for it to appear as if the factory was productive. What of course *was* productive were the girls.

"Thet Way wormed his way in with a senior naval officer, then a second officer and so on until he had more officers under his control than the commander. Going from ship chandler to supplier of girls—a pimp I believe is what you call it—seemed a natural extension of his business. By supplying quality girls, he was able to control the supply for Japanese naval ships. And there was a handsome profit in such a monopoly in war. The girls working for Thet Way were treated as hostesses. Once they began learning a few words of Japanese their attraction and value increased.

"The sex business is not as simple as supplying goods to ships anchored in the harbor. Sometimes girls would fall in love with a customer. Or more often, a customer would fall in love with one of the girls—sometimes with more than one girl at a time. This caused problems. It wasn't uncommon for two officers to fight over the same girl. For all of its cold, calculated rules, the *ianjo* system had one good result: it guaranteed that the men never formed an emotional attachment with any of the comfort girls. It would have been impossible to do so. How could any man, even a soldier who is lonely and frightened and far away from home, fall in love with a strange girl whose language he doesn't know, when after three minutes of laying eyes on her, someone is banging on the door telling him to finish his business? He couldn't. And he didn't. That meant the system worked. The Japanese soldiers were near the frontlines. The *ianjo* were part of the logistical support and supply run by the military. Get the soldier bullets, clothes, water, food and sex and brainwash him that the highest glory was to die in battle for the Emperor. And, at least in our region, the Japanese military comfort houses kept their troops fit for combat. It was rare to hear of a Burmese girl being raped by a Japanese soldier.

"What Thet Way did was subversive. The atmosphere inside the Blue Scorpion was relaxed, and men became attached to the girls, and girls to the men. The military created killing machines but couldn't ever totally destroy the possibility of romance. Sex and romance is like a gin and tonic. The mixing of the two creates a cocktail that is sublime in the pleasure it brings. Thet Way's genius was supplying the right mix of music, makeup and dresses, and food so that the romance had a chance to take root. And I can tell you, yes, that is exactly what happened.

"Thet Way said, 'Money and war share a basic quality. There are two sides to each. If you have a note face up it has the same value as when you receive it face down.'

"I kept the books for Thet Way. That was my job. I recorded the daily take for drinks and food, for sitting with the girls, for going to the back room with a girl. A mistake would have meant I was dismissed. I made no mistakes. The accounts always reconciled. I was quite good at math. Thet Way had slowly trusted me and so I received more responsibility for other parts of business. This, I know, is how he came to open and furnish the club. A bookkeeper knows all the secrets simply by looking at the money coming in and going out. He had his fingers into every pot. He found out that men who sailed on ships wanted tattoos. Thet Way learned the art of tattooing. When he delivered goods, he would often tattoo several sailors. Considerable art was involved. The right instruments and the right inks were essential. Such items were in short supply during the war. This meant he could charge a premium price and the sailors, having seen his art, were happy to pay his fee. He had the good fortune of finding an Indian trader in distress, and part of the goods he bought was a pot of blue ink. I know that he paid a small amount for these goods and that he hoarded them underneath a secret trapdoor covered by a Persian carpet in his private quarters. His great fear was losing the girls—having them snatched, kidnapped, or stolen—from the slipper factory. If a Japanese soldier held a Burmese woman, how could Thet Way prove that the person held worked for him? If one of the girls had been injured or indeed killed, the problem of identification would have been a serious test. One day Thet Way burst into my office. 'I am such a fool,' he said, slapping his forehead. 'It is so very simple. I tattoo the girls. Identical tattoos. Each time someone sees that tattoo, they know it is Thet Way's merchandise. Leave her be. Bring her back. They will know what to do. And I have indigo ink and that is perfect. But for the life of me, I am unsure what this tattoo should be. A dragon? No, too Chinese. An anchor? After all most of our customers are navy officers. A flower, say a lotus or a rose? But I hate tattooed flowers. Perhaps a swan? But not all men like birds. What can I do?'

"And I said, 'Why not a scorpion? That way the girls will feel a kind of power, and the men may feel it, too. The sting in the tail will make them careful to be nice to the girls.'

"Thet Way was not the kind of man to ever acknowledge the contribution of another human being. I could see the wheels turning in his skull. His eyes grew large and he showed his teeth, stained with tobacco, in a lurid grin. 'Thank you for reminding me of my favorite tattoo. I've perfected the scorpion. No one could ever do a more beautiful scorpion than me.'

"'That's why I suggested it, Thet Way. Your skill is legendary.'

"A week later he gave me a small raise. Enough time had passed that he trusted that I wouldn't associate the increased salary with my modest suggestion of a scorpion for his tattoo project. During that week, he lined up each of the girls, and with a degree of grace, frenzy and elegance, he tattooed an identical blue scorpion on the right thigh of each girl. More than one of the girls cried out, biting her lip, from the pain. Thet Way wrote in a ledger book who cried and who fought back the tears. 'Pain is the evil twin of sex,' Thet Way said. Their knees buckled and several girls passed out. He wrote this in the ledger. How they fell. How long they needed to recover consciousness. Thet Way kept working with the tattoo needle. Some girls opened their eyes and seeing him hovering above, lapsed back into a state of unconsciousness. Those girls were returned to the factory. Other girls turned white and trembled as the needle touched their skin. I recall only one of the girls who showed no expression as the needle pierced her skin, pushing the ink under the skin. She had found a way to take herself outside her body. She showed no evidence of pain. Thet Way liked this girl and the blue scorpion on her thigh was a tiny bit larger and fiercer than those on the other girls. One had to look very closely to see the difference. But it was a difference that mattered.

"After the last day of tattooing, with the weakest girls culled and returned to the factory floor, Thet Way announced that from then on everyone was to tell customers that the name of the club was the Blue Scorpion. No sign hung on the door. Word spread fast enough. The Japanese liked the name. And Thet Way bragged that the tattoo was the girl's protection, her passport, her way of ensuring that wherever she went, no one would ever mistake where she belonged or to whom she belonged. Not long after the reputation grew and the money poured in, some pirate saw a chance to trade on the Blue Scorpion's success. Other women who were not employees of the slipper factory (meaning the Blue Scorpion) started turning up in Moulmein with scorpion tattoos. This act of piracy made Thet Way furious. He felt robbed and cheated. It was a declaration of war. After some detective work—one of the imposters had been located and tortured into fingering the pirate—Thet Way discovered that his foe was a Chinese doctor in another part of town. The same doctor who examined the Blue Scorpion girls every week for signs of disease and gave Thet Way a report of any cases (and he provided the reports to a navy doctor). Thet Way swore an oath in my presence that he would revenge this betrayal. He bought a pig and kept it behind the factory. Early each morning, while the girls slept, Thet Way practised various scripts of the Chinese word "death" on the pig. The skin of a pig is very much like that of a human. The pig was tied down and squirmed and cried as Thet Way pierced the skin with the tattoo needle. After a week, there were dozens of tattoos on the pig. After he was satisfied that he had discovered a pirate-proof design, he had the pig killed and the meat found its way into the club. One morning Thet Way arrived at the factory early. The Blue Scorpion girls were still sleeping in their Chinese beds. He had his tattoo gear and his pot of indigo blue ink. The sleepy girls, rubbing their eyes and squinting at the morning sun, lined up and heard Thet Way give a little speech that the Japanese had ordered a minor modification to the tattoo. There was nothing he could do, he said, but comply. The girls understood compliance. That was their job. And he promised the procedure would be less painful than the first time; it would be over before they knew it and they could climb back into bed and sleep. Each girl sat in a chair, half turned away from the needle, and uncovered her right thigh, looking up and then away from Thet Way as he worked the tattoo needle. It wasn't the thigh he intended to mark; he chose the area near the vagina and tattooed a small Chinese inscription. He tattooed in neat Chinese script the number 44 that when spoken sounded the same as the Chinese word for death. After that, we had no problem with others trying to use the tattoo for favor or privilege. The doctor inspected the girls for disease and saw the message Thet Way had left for him. Two weeks later, the Chinese doctor was found in an alley with a sharp instrument stuck in his back. No one could ever say who had killed the doctor. All one could say was that the weapon was a long tattoo instrument with a needle at the sharp end. Whether it was the unlucky number or the rumor that Thet Way was powerful enough to get away with murder, I am not certain.

"He had gained respect from the Japanese officers, who were tough men. But even these hard men respected the fact that these girls were in a class of their own. The Japanese came to the club and they bought drinks for the girls and paid to take them to the big Chinese beds, but none of them ever mistreated them. The horror of war was ugly enough and what Thet Way had provided was a sanctuary where for a few hours a man could forget that the next day he could be killed. The Blue Scorpion girls weren't *ianfu*. They weren't treated as prostitutes. As far away as Toungoo and Pyinmana our girls' reputation spread and we would have stragglers from other units coming into the club to see for themselves. But as with all good things, it came to an end.

"I remember the day that Moulmein fell to the British. Not as a result of victory after a long battle. Nothing as grand as a house-to-house battle campaign. The end came without the bang and with only a mild whimper. That morning, the 18th of August, I was at my desk. Suddenly the fighting stopped. The explosions stopped. The machine guns you sometimes heard from the distance had gone silent. It was a terrible silence. I went out into the street and followed a crowd down to the pier. I arrived in time to see General Kimura meet General Sakurai. They wore their uniforms. They saluted each other, bowed, then embraced. It was true, then, and not British propaganda—the war had actually ended on the 15th of August. The Emperor had announced that the war was over and the Japanese had to 'endure the unendurable.' Only later did I learn that the month before, after Rangoon fell, Aung San no longer wore

257

his Japanese general's uniform. He had changed into a *longyi*. He knew the war was over. But we felt a genuine sadness. It wasn't just the Japanese who had to bear unbearable feelings and endure the unendurable. It was all of us. Shattered glass could be swept up, blown-up buildings rebuilt, streets repaired, the dead cremated and boxed for shipment back to Japan. But there were things we could not forget. Boys crying for their mothers, missing arms, and legs, tangles of flesh that didn't look human, bubbles of blood flowing out of necks and mouths. Young men liquefied by a direct hit. By early that evening, the Blue Scorpion had opened for business and the first of several British officers arrived, looked around, and called for drinks. The sake bottles were destroyed and the whisky bottles opened. The war was over. It was as if the Japanese had never existed. With the British in the city, it was business as usual."

44

The number 44 tattooed on whores. If I were as smart as Hart, too clever by half, then I would have written an entire book with forty-three chapters with the sole intention of slamming in a chapter 44. It would be the shortest, most carefully crafted, factual and objective chapter, a monument to death. If you were Chinese, you knew that 44 was the number of death. The Chinese avoided the number 44 like Americans skated around the number thirteen. 44 was unlucky for them. But it is a fact that if you count up the dead in Burma from World War II, this is how the two sides stack up: 71,244 British were killed and 106,144 Japanese. The Chinese would have instantly perceived the balance of 44s was death's signature. Let's assume that in the near future, there is a UN resolution to disarm Iraq from smallpox bombs and anthrax missiles. It will use the number 44. Count on it. And when it happens, you think that will be a coincidence? I don't think so. The Americans know a resolution incorporating 44 would lock in the Chinese vote on the Security Council. Smallpox, anthrax, and 44—they will get the picture. On the other hand, unless you're Chinese that's a load of crap.

In America, most people didn't take chances crossing swords with the number 13. Elevators in America have buttons for the twelfth floor and 12A and one for the fourteenth floor. Our superstitious numbers produce fear; others people's numbers making them crazy are funny or stupid.

The number 4 四 in the Chinese language sounds the same as the Chinese word for *death*. It's not something embroidered on cushions in Beijing. If one 4 was death, then double 4 had to be doubling up death.

No Chinese happily accepts a hotel room with number 44 on the door. If I built hotels in China, I'd number the rooms 43 and 43a and 45. But what I'd be worried about—after running the probability of the last two numbers in the casualty count being exactly the same for Japanese and British in Burma from World War II—is strange for an American. It isn't 13 or the devil's 666 you have to be worried about but being pierced, impaled, skewered on the pointy horns of the twin 44s.

The old woman talked about death and how a crooked Chinese doctor had tried to cheat Thet Way and had been killed. Thet Way was a brave man who had personally added the Chinese script "44" to the thigh of local girls greedy for the safety they had enjoyed as slipper factory girls. I thought to myself, listening to this old woman, what a coincidence that this alignment of numbers arose at this point in her story. We hit the number 44 head on like a car crashing into a wall. Or to put it another way, sitting in the burnished oil lamp light as the old woman spun her tales, who would have predicted that she would pull the Chinese death number out of the hat?

She jumped from 44 to Ichiro in the blink of an eye.

45

The first time she mentioned Ichiro's name I jumped from my chair. I asked her if his family name was Takeda, and she smiled and sucked on her pipe. Ichiro was Akira Takeda's uncle, Kazuo's great uncle, and now, for the first time, his name floated across the teak house like a ghost.

"I *know* Akira Takeda. That's Ichiro's nephew. You know what I am saying?"

She nodded.

"I know many things about Ichiro. But I am certain you are tired and wish to return to Moulmein."

"I've never been less tired in my life. Please, keep talking," I said.

She puffed on her pipe. "The first time I saw him, Ichiro appeared in the club one evening with two friends. He was a tall, slender boy of no more than twenty-three or four. He was fresh and handsome and all the girls tried to get his attention. They wanted him to invite them to his table. They were all dying to be chosen. I worked the bar that evening—Thet Way had fired the bartender for stealing and he asked me to fill in. He was my boss. What could I say?"

She seemed to lose the thread of the story. "Okay, so you were working that night," I said. "What did Ichiro do? What did he say? Did you talk to him?"

"I saw how each girl tried to seduce him—with a song, a smile, a touch along the back of the neck, a cool towel applied to the forehead. All the time he talked to his friends as if the girls didn't exist. His actions, his youth, his freshness made them wild in their competition. It was only when he caught the eye of Min that he stopped talking to his friends. She was a Shan girl with a heart-shaped face, white skin, and very small feet. She had enormous brown eyes. Min was the girl who had showed absolutely no pain when Thet Way tattooed the blue scorpion on her thigh. The first evening they met, Min wore a beautiful geisha dress and white socks, her hair bundled up on her head. She had an exotic look, a lovely girl with a swan-like neck, her lips full and inviting desire. Ichiro saw her out of the corner of his eye. He watched her the way a cat watches a mouse. She pretended not to notice. He liked her attitude. This girl was different from the others. After a couple of drinks, he called Min over to the table. Her job was to go when beckoned, to entertain customers and make them happy to spend their money. Before she walked to Ichiro, she lingered. Not long but long enough for him to see that this was a girl with her own mind, a live, free spirit that was unbroken. After she joined Ichiro, he and his friends drank sake but she left her glass untouched. She refilled their glasses as they reached the halfway mark as she had been taught by Thet Way. Otherwise, she carried out her duties by sitting close to Ichiro, nodding and smiling, showing no emotion, her hands folded on her lap.

"Most men desire what is just out of reach. If there is no resistance, no competition, the fun of the chase is destroyed. Min instinctively understood this need of men and she used a detached, politely distanced approach with all customers. Ichiro could not take his eyes off her and finally his friends started teasing him. He leaned over and whispered to Min. She slightly turned and looked into his eyes and nodded. A moment later, she led Ichiro to the back room as his friends clapped and yelled after him. Then, as now, in this room, the light came from oil lamps. You see how little has changed for us? Unless we look in the mirror we have no way of knowing that we have aged. It was in that light that Ichiro first saw Min undress beside the Chinese bed. She didn't know that night, but Ichiro had never made love before. His friends had been bragging about the number of women they had slept with and Ichiro had laughed and said nothing. He had been ashamed of being a virgin.

"Min saw his shyness and understood immediately what it meant. It was rare for any of the girls to have a virgin. Like a man taking a virgin, a woman like Min understood this man would always remember this first time. No matter how many other women came into his life, it would be this room, this light, her body that his memory would always return to in idle moments, when in the arms of other women, and alone, in the midst of daydreams. She wasn't going to waste this opportunity. She gently helped him out of his clothes. They kissed in the innocent way that children kiss. She stroked his chest and listened to him talk about his family and home and his dreams. Though she spoke very little Japanese she could pick out key words and that was enough to understand how lonely this boy was and how much he simply wanted someone to listen to him. She massaged him until he was erect, and then she carefully climbed on top of him, easing him inside. She was lighter than air. He hardly knew she was there. His hands glided over her breasts and stomach and came to rest on her legs. In the lamplight, he had his first glimpse of her blue scorpion tattoo. He touched it first with his finger, tracing the line to the tip of the tail. Then he brought her forward until she straddled his face; he ran his tongue over the scorpion. They rolled over on the bed, and she guided his erection back inside. He groaned. His eyes were half-closed as she rose up from under him, squeezing his hips, his hands pressed against her breasts. She did everything she had learned that pleased a man so that this one man would never forget her. They didn't need language that night or the nights that followed when they retreated to the same room. Not long after the second time with Ichiro, Min refused to go with the other men who came to the club. Thet Way threatened to send her back to the slipper factory. But she stood her ground. She knew that the drinks customers bought simply by having her in their company made Thet Way's threat hollow. He was after all a businessman and he remembered her capacity to endure pain.

"Remember Min was only slightly younger than Ichiro. Being about the same age added an element of familiarity, romance and security to their relationship. Yes, they had met in a club where the women were prostitutes, selling themselves every night to whatever stranger would pay the price. The girls understood the need for men to believe the illusion that something more than a transaction was taking place. Men were the true romantics, and like fools, easily parted from their money. It was easy with some sake, a delightful group of friends, relaxed surroundings, and the appearance of an angel-like girl with white skin and tiny feet. As tough as Min was in the face of physical pain, as much as she understood the dream-machine she participated in, she fell in love with Ichiro. Are you surprised? You shouldn't be. The Japanese sailors and soldiers were boys, most just out of their teens. They had just started their life when they found themselves in a war and were told to fight and die. Only a couple of months after they arrived, the men changed; they started to go mad from the hardship of jungle fighting and the disease and lack of food and sleep, and the bombs and the rattle of machine guns that cut down their friends. Abandoned and forgotten, those boys died in the tens of thousands. Every girl knew of men that had slept with her who had been killed. Sometimes they cried. When you are young it is hard to accept another young person's death. We weren't at war with Japan. The Japanese were more like us. It was easier for us to help them than the British.

"In April, as the Japanese prepared to abandon Rangoon, we learned they were moving headquarters to Moulmein. Ichiro's ship was ordered on a supply mission. He told Min that it was a routine mission and that she shouldn't worry herself. They were already lovers and had secretly planned ways of escape together. The night before he left, Min cried. This was the girl who thought nothing of Thet Way's torture with the tattoo needle. This was the girl who had never chased after a customer, who could withstand any amount of pain. Her heart-shaped face composed like a painting showed a brilliant cold beauty that could freeze a man. We had news of other towns falling. The girls in one *ianjo* had taken cyanide along with the Japanese soldiers rather than surrender. Min shared the fear of every lover in war: that her man would be sent away never to return. Every day she sat at the table where she had first seen Ichiro with his friends. She waited and waited for him to return. After the war, the club was no more. Thet Way was rich enough to move to Rangoon, where stories of his business ventures returned over the bamboo telegraph. But he was the exception. The rest of us were plunged into chaos and poverty. We didn't know what would happen to us. How we would feed ourselves. After time, the slipper factory started up again. But communication with Japan was next to impossible.

The Americans occupied Tokyo and the countryside in Japan. So many Japanese soldiers were missing or in camps or prisons. Min, however, never gave up hope, day after day, until it broke all of our hearts. She carried his child. And when that baby was born, he became the center of her life. A baby boy who had his mother's fine beauty and his father's height. He grew into a man, and that man married and he, too, had children. He was killed in the 1970s. And Min, well, she looked after her grandchildren until she died in 1996. Cancer killed her. When the doctor came he asked her, 'Do you have pain?' And Min, her eyes glossy and yellow, shook her head. 'No, I am fine,' she said. She had one wish before she died. She prayed to see Ichiro for one last time. She worked her needle into a cushion, praying as she sewed patterns and words. If there is a God, he turned away from Min. She never had a chance to say goodbye, because, you see, he had promised his mission was routine and he would quickly be back in her arms."

The old woman got up from the rocking chair and walked to the end of the room where several girls worked at the foot-pedaled sewing machines. She stood behind one of the young women and put her hands on her shoulders, leaned down and looked at us as she whispered to the girl. The girl looked startled as if awakened from a dream. She slipped her legs out from the sewing machine, stood up and took the hand of the old woman. Together they crossed the long room. The girl knelt beside the rocking chair, and the old woman sat down heavily, putting an arm around her shoulder. Leaning over, she kissed the top of the girl's head and undid her hair. An avalanche of long black hair rained down, touching the floor where she knelt. "Mya, I want you to say hello to our guests," she said.

I inched forward for a better look. Mya was the girl in the photograph. "It's her. The girl in Kazuo's photograph," I said.

Sarah wept softly, her head resting against Hart's arm.

Mya's grandmother had been Min. The old woman had made it doubly clear that Min hadn't been an *ianfu*—a comfort girl. Had Kazuo any idea that this girl was his own relation? "Okay, I have a few questions, let's say about a million questions. First, why would this girl pose for Kazuo?"

The old woman looked at me, her eyes narrowed. "One thing that Min regretted was that Ichiro had never had a single photo of her.

Remember her striking beauty? What woman wouldn't be excused from some vanity when blessed by such beauty? About the time she found out that she was ill and would die, she came across a way to contact Ichiro. The last thing that she wanted was for his memory to be disturbed by her wasting body. That wasn't the woman he had fallen in love with almost fifty years before. For months and months she passed her time while dying by embroidering cushions. The cushions are everywhere in this house. Hundreds of them. They are the history of her time. My time."

She wrapped an arm around the Mya's waist and brushed her hair. "Many people said her granddaughter bore a striking resemblance to Min. Hwae found someone in the next village to tattoo a small scorpion on her thigh. An arrangement was made that someone would be sent to our village and a photograph could be taken. No more than one photograph. Kazuo arrived in 1996 and he took that photograph. That had to be one of the happiest days of Min's life. She felt that she could die. There was only one problem: the camera was lost and with it that one photograph and the memory of a woman and her love."

I pulled the photograph from my pocket, leaned forward and put it on the old woman's lap. "Is that the photograph?"

She lifted it between her fingers and with Mya looked at the photo. She handed the photograph to Mya. A brief smile crossed his lips as she looked at it with obvious pride. "That's me."

"Then you remember Kazuo?" I asked her.

She nodded. "Very well. He said that we were related. And that meant that I was his cousin. He asked me to dress as a geisha so he could take my picture. But he was only allowed one picture. That was okay because he only wanted just one. Kazuo asked me so many questions and talked to me for such a long time."

Then she paused, looked at the photograph and sighed before handing it to the old woman.

"What else did he say?"

"That he was sorry. Sorry that his father's uncle never came back for my grandmother. But none of that mattered any longer, he said. Despite whatever had happened during or after the war, nothing could change the fact that we were family. He said that he would put our family back together. And I believed him. I was a foolish girl. My grandfather lied to my grandmother, and Kazuo lied to me."

"He tried to do the right thing," I said. "But it didn't work out."

"Is that why you came to our village?" she asked. "Kazuo sent you? He should have come himself. He promised he would. And he broke his promise. Just like my Japanese grandfather. I waited just like my grandmother waited."

"Kazuo's dead. He died in Japan."

Mya leaned forward, her eyes wide, nostrils flared, shaking her head. "Kazuo's dead?"

"He died in Japan," I said. "He had planned to return to Burma. Then the accident happened. Or they said it was an accident."

Hart leaned forward, his head close to Mya. "My friend is telling you the truth. Kazuo didn't lie to you. He was a man of his word," he whispered.

"A man is only as good as his word," said Sarah, staring at Hart.

46

No one spoke for a long time. The mechanical sound of the sewing machines at the opposite end of the room filled the void.

Sarah reached forward; her fingers touched Mya's hand. "Please tell me your grandmother's story. My father said the rule was that the person who knows best what happened was the person to tell the story."

"Why do you want to know?" asked Mya.

"What happened here has finished. We are part of it now. And we need to know what tools we can use to repair things. Sometimes evenly badly damaged things can be fixed if you have the right tools. It is hard to let anyone into your heart when it has been broken."

Mya looked at the old woman.

"Your grandmother told the story many times. Why not tell it again? What is the harm?" the old woman asked.

"Please tell us," said Sarah. "Tell us and we might be able to help you. I can't promise I can do anything. That wouldn't be fair. But I will do whatever I can and so will my friends. That's why we are here. To help if we can."

Min had pieced together information from overheard conversations, gossip from the girls, customers and Thet Way. Over the years, her memory and dreams forged images and scenes that no one person including herself could have witnessed in their entirety. Those memories and dreams had been handed down to Mya. When Kazuo had arrived in the village with his camera, in exchange for permission to take a single photograph of Mya, she confided that he had provided her additional information. She was convinced that she knew Lieutenant Ichiro Takeda's full story. She said that Kazuo had believed her version and had taken many pages of notes as she had discussed the personalities and the events. Her story began on the morning of April 21, 1945. Lieutenant Ichiro Takeda was called into Captain Kikan's cabin. The captain was his commanding officer. The young officer saluted Captain Kikan, who looked extremely distressed. The Allied Land Forces Southeast Asia planned to retake Rangoon. What the allies didn't know was that General Kimura planned not to fight to the last man in Rangoon but to move his headquarters to Moulmein. From his new base he had enough divisions to prevent an allied invasion of Siam. Of course, it was not easy to just walk away from a city like Rangoon. At headquarters, there were hundreds of decisions that had to be made quickly and men with the right expertise had to be assigned. Orders were made listing what was to be destroyed. Another list detailed what was to be to transported overland and by boat to Moulmein. The objects on the two lists which General Kimura kept on his person at all times shifted, changed; items added, removed, scratched out, once, twice, three times, and then re-written in again. Bridges, electrical works, heavy guns, tanks, trucks, ammunition, replacement parts, horses, mules, boxes of cigarettes, food supplies, documents, prisoners of war, children, women, and bank vaults filled with Japanese occupation rupee notes. All of these things and people had to be organized, priorities made, orders issued, and supervised.

Ichiro's uncle (his mother's brother), Colonel Aoki Shoji, was stationed at headquarters in Rangoon. He was close to General Kimura and had seen the great worry over how best to evacuate the city before the allies swept in with thousands of troops. One matter that troubled General Kimura was the contents faithfully stored in a warehouse on the edge of the city. He had ordered Colonel Aoki Shoji to personally secure the warehouse and to ensure that the boxes inside were safely transported to Moulmein. Inside the warehouses were tens of thousands of boxes that had been carefully kept in large chests. The boxes contained, according to the warehouse manifest, the ashes of 38,973 Japanese who had died in Burma. It was a priority for the morale of the men that it be known that the ashes of their fallen comrades would be shipped to Tokyo and interned in the Yasukuni Shrine. Colonel Aoki Shoji was given a free hand to make whatever arrangements were needed to remove the chests and ensure that no damage or loss occurred to this cargo. He knew one person that he could rely upon to undertake this mission. A man just out of boyhood but nonetheless a competent, dedicated sailor who was stationed in Moulmein. This was Ichiro Takeda, the son of his younger sister, who had the command of a small boat, a boat just the right size for the chests. He knew that by choosing Ichiro, if he succeeded, no matter the outcome of the war, one member of their family would be honored to the end of time for courage, selflessness, and dedication to the Emperor and the Japanese people.

If Captain Kikan harbored any envy for not being given the assignment, he showed no outward signs of it. The order was clear: this young officer had been given an urgent mission of utmost importance; he should depart immediately. The nature of the mission was secret. Nowhere in the order was it written what Lieutenant Ichiro Takeda was to do other than to report upon arrival to Colonel Aoki Shoji for further orders. The order he had received had been countersigned by General Kimura himself. The Captain stared at this order for the longest time before handing it to Lieutenant Takeda, who for the first time read the order and looked up, puzzled.

"You must mention these orders to no one. They are secret. Do you understand?"

Lieutenant Takeda said that he fully understood.

"Please leave now. Outside you will sail with the six men I've assigned as your crew."

Lieutenant Takeda felt numb as he left Captain Kikan's cabin. His mind raced as he thought of going ashore to tell Min that he had orders to sail. And he also knew that this wasn't possible. The moment he left the dock, he would have been followed and likely arrested for insubordination. His only comfort was that the order had been co-signed by his uncle, a distant, stern man for whom he never had felt any true affection. But he knew that, as his mother's brother, his uncle would have chosen him to honor her.

When Lieutenant Takeda arrived in Rangoon on the morning of the 23rd of April, the air-raid sirens were sounding. Allied bombers flew overhead and their bombs found targets with deadly accuracy. Lieutenant Takeda dived for cover along with his six men. Not more than twenty meters down the street, bombs killed a three-member gunnery crew, showering arms and legs and blood in the air, and that red rain of flesh fell down on Lieutenant Takeda and his men. He rose to his feet and picked his way through the rubble, around a corner and inside a colonial building with the front windows shattered and caved in. He found a soldier hiding inside and demanded that the soldier take them to headquarters. The young soldier shook from fear, his mouth dry. No sound came out. Lieutenant Takeda pushed the soldier into the street and told him to lead them or he would kill him on the spot. He had drawn his service revolver and pointed it at the soldier. He had never killed a man at close quarters. Finally the soldier, seeing the determination in this young officer, led him down a side street, as the bombs continued to fall. By the time they reached the headquarters, they had climbed over dozens of dead men. A bomb had hit two horses and the raw, red flesh splattered across the road, leaving a huge tongue of gore and tangled meat that stopped only a foot away from the entrance. Inside officers, men, and civilian staff were running and shouting and cursing. No one seemed to be in control of the situation. He walked down the corridor and stopped an officer, asking where Colonel Aoki Shoji could be found. The officer said the colonel's office was on the second floor; turn right, and it was the second office on the left. Lieutenant Takeda led his men up the stairs. They didn't walk, they ran. Debris from the ceiling fell in a fine, feathery dust so by the time they entered Colonel Aoki Shoji's office, they looked like ghosts. Lieutenant Takeda tried to remember the last time he had seen his uncle. The year was 1934 and his uncle, who was then a major, had orders to ship out to Manchuria. The memory came back: it had been at the 60th birthday of his grandfather, Colonel Shoji's father, his mother's father. Ichiro Takeda had been thirteen years old on that happy family occasion. This seemed like a lifetime ago. His voice had not quite settled in a firm tone; he remained in the soft light that blurred childhood from adulthood. His hands were too big, and he felt awkward and shy as if everyone was staring at him, thinking him ugly and stupid. He was, of course, neither, but a fine, strong, good-looking boy even then. Even as he walked into that office, his heart jumped in his throat. To see a man he hadn't seen since he was a boy, a man who had been a hero to him, caused more anxiety than the bombs.

As he entered the colonel's office, he saluted a small man with short gray hair, who was on a phone that had gone dead. Colonel Aoki Shoji slowly dropped the phone and looked at his nephew. The colonel recognized his sister's chin and eyes in his nephew as he returned the salute. The young Lieutenant couldn't help being startled by how his uncle had aged. "You are slow in arriving," Colonel Aoki Shoji said.

"The crossing was difficult. But that is, I am aware, no excuse. I ask your forgiveness." Lieutenant Takeda bowed his head.

The men selected by Captain Kikan didn't know this man was a blood relative. Lieutenant Takeda was grateful to the captain for not revealing this relationship. His uncle said and did nothing that would have indicated that the lieutenant was not just another young naval officer about to receive orders.

Colonel Aoki Shoji pulled two fat envelopes from his desk. "You protect these envelopes at all cost. Do you understand, all costs?"

"Yes sir, I do. It means all of my men and I must die rather than allow anything to happen to them."

"There are six other boats requisitioned for your mission. You will need all of these boats if you are to succeed." He looked over the men that filled his office, assessing their height, strength, their condition. In a separate order to Captain Kikan he had been specific as to the qualities of the men who were to be assigned to accompany Lieutenant Takeda. The captain had done well. Other men would be needed to help, he thought. Everyone was in a panic, struggling to keep alive, waiting for orders to leave the city, and carrying out their duties prior to evacuation. "If you need other men, then you must enlist their help on the spot." He handed Lieutenant Takeda a small envelope. "Inside is an order authorizing you to requisition all personnel you deem fit. It is signed by me. If any man refuses, you shoot him. Is that understood? And if there are no soldiers, then use civilians. Use whomever you must. But you are not allowed to fail. Is that understood?"

Lieutenant Takeda said that he understood. It was one of those moments when a man has a sudden clarity about events and his destiny. The only thing that he didn't understand was the mission to be accomplished with these boats and men. "Inside the envelopes are the names, rank, birthdays and dates of death of Japanese soldiers. There are 38,973 names in those envelopes and orders from General Kimura as to your duty to transport these dead men to Moulmein and then to Yasukuni Shrine in Tokyo."

Lieutenant Takeda was somewhat relieved as six boats and six men should have been more than adequate to take such a cargo to Moulmein.

"The ashes are stored in a warehouse. My driver is downstairs. His truck has the number 2,791 on the back. He will take you and your men to the warehouse now. Dismissed."

Not one word of familiarity had passed between Lieutenant Takeda and his uncle. The bombers had left by the time they reached the street and a crew was cleaning up the remains of the horses. They found the truck a few yards away. It had suffered a direct hit. The body of the driver was a piece of flesh the size of a large sake bottle. Nothing had ever appeared less human looking. There was no point going back upstairs. He had his orders: do whatever was necessary to secure the cargo. Another truck came down the street. Two other trucks followed in a convoy. Lieutenant Takeda stood in the middle of the road, waving his hands. The driver stopped and stuck his head out the window. "Get out of the way, I have orders to leave the city. Everyone must leave now."

The young lieutenant pulled the driver out of the truck and kicked him hard in the ribs. The driver howled in pain and rolled in the road, his uniform soaking up horse blood, the blood of men, the rain of raw flesh. Lieutenant Takeda climbed into the driver's seat and ordered his men to climb into the back of the other two trucks. He had secured his convoy. He had one problem—he didn't know where he was supposed to go. He drove on for about a mile, trying to figure out how he was to reach his destination with the driver assigned dead. He tore open the smaller envelope; inside was the command authorizing him to requisition personnel to accompany him to the warehouse. There was a map showing the location. He put the truck back into gear and waved at the men behind him to continue to follow. An hour later, he pulled in front of the warehouse and cut the engine. He climbed out of the truck as his men arrived in the two following trucks. The man in the second truck got out and walked over.

"Sir, do you know what these trucks are carrying?"

It had never occurred to Lieutenant Takeda to consider what cargo he had hijacked for this mission. "Whatever it is, get rid of it. We have our orders."

By then two of his other men had arrived, and one of them said, "Sir, with respect, we have all the personnel we need to carry out our mission, sir."

Lieutenant Takeda followed his men to the back of the truck and pulled back the tarpaulin. Inside were about twenty young, very frightened girls in geisha costumes, sitting on crates of Japanese occupation rupee notes. His mouth dropped as he turned and looked at his men, who stared down at their feet. "And the other two trucks?"

"The same cargo, sir."

One of the men cleared his throat. "Sir, they can help us load the trucks."

And so it was to be. For the next three hours, Lieutenant Takeda, his six men, and about sixty comfort women helped load the boxes containing the ashes of 38,973 dead. Sweat stained the shirts of the men. The geisha dresses, soiled and wrinkled and torn, no longer looked like the finery they had first appeared when Lieutenant Takeda had pulled back the tarpaulin to look inside. On the way to the boats, the sailor who had come up with the brilliant idea of enlisting the women to load the trucks had a second brainstorm. "Sir, these women had only one chance to save themselves. We followed our orders. That can't be denied. But I don't think our orders would be compromised if we took them with us to Moulmein, sir."

Lieutenant Takeda did the math in his head. Ten women to a boat supplied by his uncle along with one each of his men. And he had his own boat from Moulmein. The women could help on the journey and besides, his man had a point, they were very young girls, and their innocent faces made him feel the pain of leaving Moulmein without saying goodbye to Min. If it had been Moulmein that was being evacuated he surely would have wanted someone to see her to safety. As Rangoon was collapsing around his ears, it crossed his mind that the Japanese soldiers might have the same wish about these women.

"They must help on the boats."

"That goes without saying, sir. We will see they do their share of work."

Lieutenant Takeda left with the ashes of nearly forty thousand dead Japanese soldiers and sixty comfort girls as their escort. Days after Lieutenant Takeda reached Moulmein, Rangoon fell and the headquarters of the Japanese army established itself in Moulmein. Upon mooring his boats, Lieutenant Takeda was met by Captain Kikan and a small band of officers. The boats and the cargo were quarantined. The *ianfu* were set free in Moulmein. They were free to go home—an impossibility—or to present themselves at the local *ianjos* and ask to be taken in. Lieutenant Takeda had a new set of orders. The ashes were to be removed to Siam. This would be far away from fighting, as everyone expected the allies to advance on Moulmein. Colonel Aoki Shoji wanted to take no chance that the ashes would fall into the hands of the allies. Arrangements had been made with Imperial General Staff in Bangkok. Lieutenant Takeda would personally accompany the remains.

Mya—exhausted from the heat and recounting of old memories—clutched one of her grandmother's cushions to her breasts and rocked back and forth. She fell into silence.

"Thank you," said Sarah, giving Mya's hand a squeeze.

I had pieced together the rest from what Akira Takeda had told me in Bangkok.

"I know the rest," I said to Sarah. I picked up where Mya left off.

The mission made Lieutenant Ichiro Takeda a national hero in Japan after the war when the sorrow was unbearable and the thought of this young, handsome officer risking all to honor the fallen touched the hearts of millions. He was the caretaker of that grief. The role of the other men and the sixty *ianfu* were airbrushed from the picture. When all had been lost, he had been anointed as the one at the darkest hour to single-handedly return the souls of so many dead soldiers to their homeland. In choosing Ichiro Takeda, his uncle had guaranteed his nephew an important role in post-war Japan. While Ichiro never aspired to a political career, he acted as a king maker. As the years advanced and the war slipped into memory for a generation that never knew war, those around him did all in their power to ensure that the knowledge never reached his ears that all those years before, the young lieutenant had fallen in love with a Shan girl and fathered a child in Moulmein. Min had been the first girl he had ever made love to.

Ichiro Takeda's life wasn't easy; in a manner of speaking, he lived in the clutches of certain right-wing factions who used whatever means were necessary to stop Ichiro from ever learning these facts. It was only when Min lay dying of cancer that a message found its way to him through the old Chinese merchant, Thet Way. Thet Way might have been the only man alive that Ichiro would have believed. Those around Ichiro reminded him that Thet Way was a pimp, brothel owner, trader of flesh and secrets and his testimony was totally unreliable. Thet Way told Ichiro that his granddaughter Mya was the very image of her grandmother. That was all it took to seal his decision; Ichiro had been carrying around an image of Min all of those years and the chance to possess such an image became an obsession. Thet Way was paid a sum of money and sent away. Ichiro then did what his uncle had done all those years before—he enlisted the help of his nephew, a young, handsome photojournalist who had an assignment in Rangoon to cover the Lady. Kazuo's luck, unfortunately, was not as deep or wide as his uncle's had been. The dark forces surrounding Ichiro got wind of Kazuo's mission. Along with their contacts in Burmese military intelligence, they had Kazuo followed. They reported back that Ichiro the great hero had indeed fathered a son, who had been killed in 1979 fighting the communists. This son had sired a daughter named Mya, and Kazuo had photographed that daughter under the watchful eye of her grandmother. When the report came to her of her son's death, had she felt pain? Min again shook her head. Pain was in a universe she had yet to visit.

An attempt to steal Kazuo's camera had failed. Kazuo knew he was being watched—he thought it was by the Burmese security forces—and as he was about to be searched at the airport before departure, he hid the camera. His plan was to return to Rangoon to retrieve it. He waited for months but each time he applied for a visa, it was denied. Frustrated, Kazuo started talking about the photograph to his father. Word of these discussions drifted to the ears deployed to listen to Kazuo's plans and dreams. He had been warned to forget about Burma, the girl, the camera. But he couldn't get this out of his mind. He had failed his uncle, a great Japanese hero, and he worked day and night to return to Burma. The man who was driving the truck that killed Kazuo on the highway was said to have a connection with a right-wing group. Nothing firm could ever be established and no case was ever brought.

And then Sarah leaned forward and touched my hand. "I know this exact story." She turned and smiled at Hart. "It's the story of Hart's novel."

"There are certain women that a man would do anything for," said Hart.

"And there are certain things a man promises that he never lives up to," Sarah said, her voice low and firm.

I didn't say anything. "Now you understand why I was asked to destroy the photograph and forget that I ever saw it. Those around Ichiro have a long reach. They can grab anyone, anywhere, anytime. They can take you. Like that," I said, snapping my fingers.

Gaps remained in Akira Takeda's story about his family background. Akira had told me what he thought I needed to know. Just enough information to keep me from becoming too interested in Kazuo's final photograph. I wondered how Akira would take it once he learned that I, like his son, Kazuo, had gone to the source where the true nature of things might be explained. In a way, I understood why Akira had found it impossible to tell me more than he did. It had always been up to me to uncover the real story. But I had no idea I would track down an old woman and one of his blood relatives in a teak house in the Mon state. Was the blue scorpion story now complete? I looked at the faces around the room and understood that this was one of those stories that could never be complete.

Sarah said something I tried to digest. She said the story I had told was the story told in Hart's novel. It was like the hundreds of cushions with too many images, too many words, filled with too much pain for me to comprehend at once. I needed some time.

THE FLY IN AMBER

47

The next morning in Moulmein, I sat in the dining room of the Ngwe Moe Hotel drinking a cold Tiger and asked Aye Thit if he had any idea how many cushions were in the teak house. He shrugged. "About two hundred," he finally said.

I nodded. That was a fair ball-park number. "You think Hwae will take the girl to Tokyo?"

"He said that was his plan."

Noncommittal replies such as this one were why the Burmese security police wired gonads to hand-cranked generators and held cushions over faces in displays of mock suffocation. "He said something to you in Burmese as we were leaving and I heard the word Tokyo. I thought he might have changed his mind."

"Of course he is scared. But what can he do?"

Aye Thit was saved as the Terracotta Warrior, with his drooling smile, strolled into the room. The Toyota was parked outside the window of the dining room. Aye Thit led him over to the table and a waitress brought a pot of hot coffee and filled his cup. Despite the goofy grin, the Terracotta Warrior didn't appear to have had a great night. His eyes were as red as his mouth. A fresh load of betel nut had been loaded into his mouth sometime during the ferry crossing to Moulmein. He looked happy to see Aye Thit, but he would have looked happy to see the coffee arrive or the falling of a leaf. An indiscriminate happiness; it wouldn't have mattered if we had been working for Japanese or Chindits or men from the moon. Whatever the active ingredient of betel nut was, it took the

Terracotta Warrior to some state of consciousness beyond the frontier of pain and boredom.

I hadn't slept well the previous night, dreaming weird dreams of being lost inside a vault containing the ashes of dead Japanese. Young girls danced around half-naked in geisha outfits, showing their bellies—I said it was weird—and out of the middle of the tangled bodies was Mya from the teak house, the girl in Kazuo's photograph. But she wasn't dancing. She was on a small ridge, looking into the distance. I heard an explosion and out of the dust and debris, Sarah appeared, carrying a Shan tattoo book, kneeling beside the girl, touching the blue scorpion on her thigh. After I woke up in a start, I couldn't go back to sleep. I tossed and turned before rolling out of bed and switching on the light. I lit a fat one. Next door I heard the murmur of voices, ones that I recognized. Sarah and Hart were talking but I couldn't make out what they were saying. Sarah's voice was raised in a shrill tone. I heard her say, "Why? Why? Why?" And thought she was starting to sound like me. Her voice trailed off and I couldn't hear what she said after that.

Then the voices on the other side of the wall fell into silence and I thought, what a night. As far as I could tell, this was the first night they had shared the same room, and they ended up in shouting as if they were already married. Welcome to the institution of marriage, buddy, I thought to myself. Checkers letting fly against the kitchen wall. I kept on listening, thinking the fighting had fallen into a lull and one or the other would find the energy to launch a new attack. But I heard nothing. No voices, no shifting mattress springs doing an accordion number. They must have fallen asleep. I lay back on my pillow. I envied them their peace and the release brought by sleep. I could never sleep after a fight with Saya. She slept like a baby. I would brood and wonder if the damage of a quarrel could ever be repaired.

The fat one didn't improve my mood and I thought, *Yeah, she's right. Kazuo's dead.* And we had hit a brick wall. I wondered if they were really taking Mya to Japan. I hoped not. I sat brooding about what hadn't been accomplished in our journey to Moulmein. Not a single piece of Ming china. As we left the ancient teak house, Hwae said, "There's not been any Ming in Moulmein for years. When a piece does surface, the Indian traders find out and get their hands on it fast." Khin Aung's boast that Moulmein was filled with Ming period porcelain was just that—a boast—and I was sucker-punched by self-interest that knocked me into the open sewer of greed. Greed was something one wallowed in like a pig. Like a pig with the word death tattooed in Chinese all over its body the day before it is clubbed to death.

Sarah walked away with one piece of Chinese porcelain, a simple blue and white bowl, which she clutched tightly. It couldn't have been worth more than twenty dollars. But I had managed to find the girl in the picture. Better yet, I had met her. It was no longer of any importance to me whether Kazuo's photograph of her ever found its way to Ichiro. That was not my business. It seemed right that Mya should have it. Let her and the old woman and Hwae decide what to do. Destroy it, keep it, blow it up to billboard size, I no longer cared. What did concern me was whether Ichiro would accept her as his granddaughter, and by doing so, acknowledge that he had chosen a duty of honor to his country as a higher duty than his duty of honor to the woman he loved. Or would those surrounding him commit whatever act was necessary to protect the legend of the great caretaker of souls? History had a strange way of stretching and breaking lives. Sometimes a single photograph changed history. Like the photograph of the little girl running naked down a dirt road in Vietnam with a mushroom cloud of napalm behind her, her skin on fire.

Akira Takeda had made a special trip to Bangkok not to thank me so much as to warn me. I was the guy who was all puffed up, thinking, *hey, I am a hero, I am doing a good deed by tracing the camera and photos back to the holder.* Wasn't that the right thing to do? And the other shots were of the Lady under attack in Rangoon. Kazuo had been in the teak house. He had seen the pillows, heard the stories, and photographed the girl. The only photograph that Akira Takeda had been interested in was the one I had not sent him. The image of a beautiful semi-nude that he could describe from memory; a photograph that his son had taken and that might have been connected with his death.

As the well-known photographer of a standard work on the Chin, I understood better than most that a photo is worth ten thousand words. What I came to understand was that Mya's photograph represented the entire story of the life of a young and beautiful woman who had fallen in love with a young Japanese officer and bore him a son who in turn fathered the girl in the picture. That was one serious photograph and that was obvious from the way the old woman had clutched it like a small bird in her chicken-feet-like hands, careful not to ruffle a feather or leave a mark. I had no idea after what I told the people in that room whether they would go through with the journey to Tokyo. But as far as I could see, that was not my problem.

I was determined to find out how my good friend, Hart, whose trip to Burma by the way, I was financing, had come to write a novel—and from what Sarah had told me—a partial story, one that contained essential details described by the old woman. He had never met her before. The main characters in the novel were comfort women working in Moulmein. They worked in a club called the Blue Scorpion. From everything I had gathered from Sarah's account, the novel's central character bore a close resemblance to the old woman in the village. Inside the dimly lit teak house, Hart said almost nothing. He couldn't take his eyes off the old woman. By the end of her story, a sense of defeat had fallen upon him. I had no idea where this sense of defeat came from. The same probably could have been said of the Japanese. One moment, it was *banzai*, fight to the death, never surrender, and in the next breath, it was enduring the unendurable from which death was no release.

When Hart sat down at the table, his eyes were red and he hadn't shaved.

"I say we throw in Moulmein. Cut our losses. Get the hell out of here," I said. "There ain't no Ming bowls, plates, saucers, burial urns in Moulmein and haven't been for thirty years. So what's keeping us?"

"It's okay by me," he said, buttering a cold piece of toasted white bread.

I drank from the bottle of Tiger.

"If we start out after breakfast, we can make Pegu by night-fall."

He shrugged, using his knife to spread another layer of butter.

Sarah came in and sat down next to me. She looked in slightly better condition. Her hair was tied back with a blue ribbon and she wore a T-shirt with the Thai alphabet on the front and blue jeans. The chair next to Hart looked very empty. Why had she sat next to me? They must have had some fight last night.

"Sloan wants to go back to Pegu," Hart said.

"But we just got here last night," she said.

"There's no reason to stay," said Hart.

"To tell you the truth, Moulmein bums me out," I said.

Hart bit into his toast, made a face, then dropped it on his plate and tried the coffee. The coffee jolted him back to life. He looked alert for the first time since sitting down. "That was quite a night," Hart said.

Sarah blushed and looked inside her coffee cup.

I couldn't figure out exactly what they had been fighting about. Money and sex fights always came way down the road. They had just started the journey, and if there was a fight at the start, some kind of madness had to be at work.

48

The sky to the far horizon was blanketed gray with blotches of blue peeking through, the clouds forming and splitting as if a falcon's talons had ripped them to shreds. There was the smell of rain in the air; and like the smell of sex, the scent of rain was unforgettable in what it conjured, what it promised. Not long after the car ferry left the pier, we walked up the steel staircase to the bridge and looked at the sky and the distant bank. The captain, dressed in a ragged T-shirt, sat behind the controls smoking a cigarette. He smiled at Sarah and sat more erect, the way a predator does when it sniffs the wind blowing through the grass of a savanna, and spots a deer grazing. An old Burmese man in a gray hat, three-day beard, his *longyi* hiked up so that the cloth bunched up between his legs, slept on a cot in the corner. His mouth was wide open and along one side of his mouth were rows of silver and gold teeth. In World War II after a battle, the Burmese picked their way through the dead using large stones to knock out the teeth of dead soldiers. Not all of the soldiers were quite dead. The stones bashed out teeth, fragmented jaws, splattered brains. When you were starving, waiting a few minutes for someone to decide to die was a long time.

From our vantage on the bridge we looked down on the half a dozen trucks parked on the main deck. Hart and Sarah squatted down along one side. Neither one of them had said a great deal since we finished breakfast. An awkward, polite silence fell between them. I left them to their thoughts. My attention turned to a Burmese boy whose ribs showed through his skin. He jabbered away with Aye Thit. The boy looked about eleven or twelve years old and had weird tattoos. Shirtless, his only article of clothing was a ragged pair of shorts that hung low on his emaciated waist. He had the gaunt look of a street urchin, a stowaway; a kid like this didn't just stumble onto the ferry by mistake. He had been staring at me from the moment we arrived on the bridge. The kid couldn't take his eyes off me and it was making me a little crazy.

"How old is that kid?" I asked and Aye Thit translated.

"Fifteen," Aye Thit said, after conferring with the kid.

"No fucking way," I said.

"He says he recognizes you from the movie," Aye Thit said.

I'd been in only one movie. A couple of years ago, I was in Rangoon and a local production company was shooting a thriller. They needed a foreigner to play the role of a foreign jewel thief. Someone—actually it was Aye Thit—suggested to the director that I might be right for the part. I thought it was a long shot. Have you ever heard of anyone being in a Burmese movie? I can't imagine anyone but a few Burmese have ever seen a Burmese movie. I showed up, thinking they would want me to read for them or at least do some kind of a screen test. No reading was required. My part called for no dialogue. But, then, I spoke no Burmese, and I don't think the director wanted the foreigner speaking Burmese *or* English. "Screen test?" They thought I was joking. They were ready to shoot right then and there. I was hired on the spot.

Out of nowhere, I got to play the part of the jewel thief opposite one of Burma's leading actresses. She didn't understand a fucking word of English. We sat at a table on a side street in Rangoon, and the director told me to talk to the movie star as if she was a client and I was trying to sell her some hot gems. I started talking to her but she wasn't taking in anything I said.

"Hey, let's go back to my place and you can get down on all fours and examine Mr. Fred, see him salute," I said.

She smiled and nodded. This was kind of fun. I could talk dirty on film and no one seemed to mind. I drank from a bottle and leaned across the table, "Hey, baby, anyone ever tell you that you've got fabulous tits?"

She furrowed her brow and I thought, what if she really does understand what I am saying and is just faking a lack of English skill for nationalistic reasons?

286

"What about we get naked? You and me, baby. And I bring along a big black dildo and we *both* get on all fours, smear honey on our bodies, and bark like dogs. Are you into that kind of drama?" But this time I got a full-mouth, big smile. The director said something in Burmese and the star's smile vanished. She stood up from the table, offered her hand. I shook her hand but she had a weak handshake. She pulled her hand free and disappeared. I never heard her speak a single word. It might have been a silent movie to save expense on sound.

I turned and said to Aye Thit, "Was I just fired?"

"No, the scene's over. They're done. We can go now."

"Impossible," I said. "He only took one take."

"They only have money for one take."

"What if it is terrible?"

"No one will know."

This was a case of destiny. How else can you explain how a kid who hadn't eaten in a week standing on the bridge of a ferry sailing from Moulmein remembered me from that one-take scene? I played a jewel thief and talked dirty to a beautiful actress who never once lost her smile. Aye Thit cross-examined the kid to make certain he wasn't confusing me with someone else or another movie which featured a foreigner who happened to look like me. Aye Thit made the kid describe every detail of that scene. There was no question about it. The kid had seen *my* Burmese movie. But he hadn't remembered Aye Thit, who was also in the same scene, sitting at the same table. I had carried off a memorable performance.

"Were you really in a movie?" asked Sarah.

"Aye Thit, tell her, was I in a movie?"

"He played a part in a movie. It is true."

That was Aye Thit in English; simple, short, straight to the point.

"You didn't know I was famous," I said, sneaking a look at Hart.

"An Oscar-winning performance, I am certain," said Hart.

"Man, when you get your novel published, what prize will you win?"

Hart had the expression that I imagined that Thet Way had seen in the tormented eyes of the pig as he worked the tattoo instrument under the skin.

Not everyone possessed a streak of genius. My small claim was an ability to find convergences of unrelated information and unrelated people, making sense out of what everyone else had overlooked. How the Chinese words for the number four and death sounded the same, like pair and pear, or bear and bare. And seeing the number forty-four in both the British and Japanese casualty rates in Burma during World War II. No one had made that particular connection. It had been lying dormant for almost sixty years, waiting for this to happen, and then I drew the dots together. Perhaps that convergence—not yet complete though hinted at—had explained why General Stilwell had such a difficult time using the Chinese troops against the Japanese in Burma. They had procrastinated in joining the battle. The Chinese had promised the moon in terms of combat troops and delivered a detachment the size of a Girl Scout's troupe spreading across a wide terrain to sell cookies.

In every direction from the bridge, the sky was limned with large, gray clouds. A light rain fell on the distant shore. The weather moved out to sea and towards us. I turned back to the boy. He wore blue sandals and smoked a cigarette. Sarah knelt beside him examining the tattoos on his arms. He looked like a beat-up eleven-year-old. Red juice bled through his teeth, draining down his gums, making him a teenaged version of the Terracotta Warrior. He had either been eating Mon dirt on some back road or chewing betel nut. He squatted down, eyes puffy, staring at me. He stood up, turned and spit over the railing. I handed him my private bottle of whisky and told him to take a drink. He didn't understand.

Sarah shot a look of disapproval. "He's too young, Sloan."

"Bullshit, at fifteen, he's already middle-aged. In this part of the world, you have to speed up learning."

"Don't," she said to the boy. She pointed at the bottle that I held out.

He ignored her or maybe he didn't understand her concern.

Then I told Aye Thit to tell the kid in Burmese to take a drink. He put his lips to the bottle and took a long gulp. The bottle came away from his mouth and his eyes were boiling with puffball flesh underneath; the smile suddenly vanished from his face. He turned, hung forward from the waist over the railing, and power-vomited the whisky in a long brownish arc that held suspended in the air before it rained on the deck below. Whatever had been inside his stomach hadn't mixed well with the whisky. Vomit splattered the cargo of a large Nissan truck stacked with green barrels. The drivers sat under the shade of a walkway on the opposite side, talking and smoking. They jabbered away with each other unaware that a fifteen year old film fan had spewed his guts all over their sugarcane and bananas. The boy wiped tears from his eyes as he raised himself off the railing. He had a crooked smile.

"Not bad," I said. "You want another drink?"

The kid stared at the bottle and slowly shook his head.

"You see, I've cured him. He'll never drink again."

The captain on the bridge called out for a drink. I ignored him. No way I was going to give him a drop. The kid was more willing to talk after his stomach settled. Aye Thit wormed out of the kid that he had been the first mate on another ferry. But his ferry had been out of action for weeks and he had no idea if it would ever be repaired. They were waiting for a spare part to arrive. He had time to kill until the ferry was back in service. He decided to hang out on the ferry that was still in service, going back and forth as if the daily crossings were some sub-college Ferry Navigation and Operation Course 101.

Not long after the young boy vomited his guts out, a skinny Indian showed up on the bridge. About the same size as my stunted fan, the Indian wore a red baseball hat with the words "No Fear" sewed in blue letters on the front. He was barefoot and wore a faded light green *longyi*. His face was long and thin and bat-like ears rose above the baseball hat, giving him an alien appearance. A two-day stubble of beard was flecked white; his weak chin, hollow cheeks, and rat-like yellowish teeth made him look sad, suspicious, and hungry. The Indian's large brown eyes fell onto the boy, who after looking at the Indian, leaned back over the railing retching again. From his thread-worn shirt, he removed a plastic pen and made a note on a piece of paper, folded the paper, and put it in his pocket. He looked like a clerk. An umbrella was strapped to his back. But he wasn't a clerk; he sold curry puffs with smashed up grayish green vegetables spooned inside. He looked like someone who prepared himself for the worst and he told us in Burmese (Aye Thit translating) that he wasn't someone to be toyed with.

He stepped away from the railing and demonstrated a couple of karate moves. His knuckles facing up, he jabbed hard, his arms punching the head of an imaginary assailant. It made no sense why anyone would attack a skinny barefoot Indian vendor on the bridge of a broken-down ferry from Moulmein. Unless it was to steal his food tray, and from the look of the food, that seemed a remote possibility.

"He says he has a brown belt," Aye Thit said.

"Ask him the name of his school of karate," I said.

Before the Indian replied he dropped down onto the floor of the bridge and did a push-up on his thumbs. "Man, one fucking push-up. That is no recognizable school. I used to do thirty thumb-ups. Tell him that."

Aye Thit translated, as the Indian did a number of squats using the railing the way a ballet dancer warms up. Then he performed a couple of more kicks, arching his bare feet, and honored us with another demonstration of his hands swiping through the air. I grabbed one of his hands mid-air and examined it. The hand was too smooth on the side where it should have been rough, callused.

"How old are you?" I asked the Indian.

"Forty," he said.

"Man, you can't be forty. You look sixty. I am fifty-three and you could be my father. You, my man, are the most fucking beat-up forty-year-old in the world. Translate that for me, Aye Thit."

I could tell that Aye Thit made no effort at a literal translation.

"The reason he looks so young is that he never eats meat. He never drinks, and he never smokes."

No question in my mind that whatever Aye Thit had translated left out my verdict about the Indian's age. "I didn't say he looked young. I said he looks fucking ancient. A bit of booze and meat might make him look younger."

"He says that he weighs forty kilo."

"He weighs his age."

Aye Thit grinned. The Indian's pin-sized head had a narrow, long face with huge eyes and a large, hooked nose. Sarah took a camera out of her bag and photographed the green cobras tattooed on both the Indian's arms. The right arm had a cobra with the hood expanded. I considered telling the Indian about the ten-foot cobra that had tried to come through a backseat car window and stick fangs into my brain but I decided Aye Thit was having one of those *I am not going to translate what you really said* kind of days. When you're exiled in another culture, your life becomes a series of long bad translation days. The translator decides what is passed on. So what happens? Meaning, always in transition, gets bogged down between two languages, entangled, familiar and foreign, and what I understood about this Indian was only some vague approximation of what Aye Thit wanted me to understand.

Everyone stared at the Indian's tattoos and the boy's tattoos.

"You could do a second doctorate on the tattooed ferry people from Moulmein," I said. "Or invite him to your university on a scholarship. He might want to learn karate."

The Indian pressed his tattooed cobras flesh against the strange lines on the boy's arms. Was this child abuse or some kind of ritual that tattooed people did to each other as a kind of fraternal greeting? The kid wasn't too upset by the Indian rubbing his tattoo against him. The Indian bounced back from the kid and performed another series of quick chops at some invisible snake or tiger. The funny thing was that the kid and Aye Thit and the captain and first mate accepted the Indian's conduct as normal behavior. Maybe in the Mon state this was what people did. Brushed their tattoos together then shadow boxed against devils only they could see.

I grabbed the boy's arm and studied his tattoos.

"Hey, you're an expert on tattoos, what do these mean?" I asked.

Sarah shrugged. She didn't know.

The boy had tattoos that had no apparent meaning, as if some alien in a baseball cap with bat-like ears had taken him aboard a space ship and branded him with strange geometric patterns like those that appear in English fields. Aye Thit finally managed to get a story out of him about the tattoos. When he was eleven his mother and sister had dragged him to a man who was reputed to have a fine touch with tattoos. They lived in Mandalay. The needle had been a searing pain that shot through his entire body. He screamed, pissed himself, and passed out by the time the man had started to work on his left arm. I liked the kid. I wadded up the empty pack of cigarettes and handed it to him. He did the right thing. He tossed the garbage off the bridge. Sarah made a face. "You aren't exactly a great role model." She was right. I wasn't any role model but I liked the kid and he liked me. I was the only movie star he had ever met. That's what Aye Thit told me.

But the Indian karate expert by then had already co-opted Aye Thit as an ally. Once your translator turns his loyalties, you can be sure the communication is tainted. He bent Aye Thit's ear non-stop, whispering and waving his arms around. He pulled a slingshot from his shoulder bag. The forked part of the slingshot had an etched-in image of a cobra. The Indian was into snakes in a major way. He took a totally smooth ball from the same bag. "Dried clay," said Aye Thit as the Indian loaded it into the slingshot. He half-turned, assumed the firing position, pulled back on the slingshot and fired. The weapon was the Indian's failsafe protection system in that rare incidence that he confronted someone who actually knew the difference between various karate schools, and had actually gone to such a school, and started to kick him all the way back to Bombay. His slingshot made me think of the thugs who had attacked the Lady's car, and Kazuo's photographs of the damage to the rear window.

The Indian's parents had immigrated to Burma from Bombay in the 1940s. He took another ball out of his shoulder bag and shot it at some imaginary target on the horizon. He knocked out the taillight on a truck below. He blew the fucker to smithereens, showering red glass across the deck. "Direct hit, daddy-oh," I said. "You aced that fucker. Now try for the other light. Then go down on the main deck and tell those truckers what school of karate you belong to." The Indian wasn't buying my attempt to egg him on—you can't buy what you don't understand. He wasn't a great karate expert and he couldn't speak more than a couple of words of English, but he wasn't stupid. He immediately gave the slingshot to Hart and his hand conjured up a couple of mud balls. Hart looked at the slingshot and smiled. The Indian blinked, waiting to see if Hart would take the slingshot.

"You're getting set up, Hart," I said. "Those truckers will rip you a new asshole. He broke a taillight. They ain't gonna be happy."

Hart loaded a ball and fired over the deck and at the water. If you squinted you could see a little white fizz from where the mud ball hit the surface.

"He keeps the slingshot in case he's attacked," said Aye Thit. As if we hadn't figured that out.

Who was going to attack the Indian? He was barefoot, dressed in a crumpled *longyi* that had been washed against rocks in some polluted river and an old shirt. He kept wrapping and unwrapping his *longyi*, each time staring down at his dick as if to confirm it was still attached; the gesture was surely the indication, at the very least, of some nervous affliction. But it was more than that. The Indian gave every sign of paranoia. It was displayed in every twitch in his face. The push-up on his thumbs and high kicks and karate moves were posturing to release stress, show skill and agility, and scare away possible attackers. Or he might just have been showing off for Sarah. How many times do you get a captive audience on the deck of a ferry from Moulmein? How many women like Sarah had he persuaded to touch his cobra as he unwrapped his *longyi*, checking out his personal equipment inside. He might just have been a pervert.

"Ask him how much he wants for the whole tray of samosas?"

Aye Thit pointed at the puff pastries that oozed grease. "Two dollars for all of them."

"Man, that is 1,800 kyat. He's never had 1,800 kyat in his pocket once in his life. They are butt ugly. Tell him that. Those samosas are health hazard pieces of shit, and I am not buying them to eat. I am buying them as ammo. Hart's gonna shoot every one of those suckers into the river. You want pollution? I'll give you fucking pollution."

I bought the lot for one dollar. A massive rip-off but when you are on a ferry in the middle of a river the size of the Pacific and out of ammo, you have to compromise. I gave the Indian a dollar and gestured for the boy to give the tray to Hart.

"Don't do it, Hart," said Sarah. "It will humiliate that poor man."

He had got to her. First he had turned Aye Thit, then Sarah.

"Poor? He's got a dollar. He can buy shoes."

Hart looked at the Indian, who smiled, folding the dollar and slipping it into his shirt pocket behind his plastic pen. The Indian didn't give a rat's ass what we did with the samosas. He was glad to be rid of the stinking greasy mess festering in the heat. He knew the shit was lethal garbage. He was probably going to throw them away. I picked one off the tray and handed it to Hart. "Shoot this fucker as far away from this ferry as you can. Five dollars says you can't hit the barrel on that truck. See the one sticking out from the blue tarp?"

This was a test of Hart's loyalty. Would he side with the Indian and refuse?

With money involved, Hart loaded the pastry and fired. It disintegrated in mid-air and a million crumbs exploded over the deck. "Man that was ugly."

Sarah turned away from the bridge, folded her arms, and shook her head. This was the old cold-shoulder. If she could have, she would have been over the side doing the breaststroke to the mainland. Hart fired several more. The last one must have had a rock in it because it remained intact as one hard encased projectile that tore through the tarp on one side and made a deep bong-like sound as if someone had rung a temple bell. "You owe me five dollars," said Hart.

I fished a wad out of my pocket and peeled off a five-dollar bill. The Indian's eyes grew as big as saucers. He'd sold the whole lot—there were only a half-dozen left—for a dollar. And Hart made five times that amount for a direct hit using a malignant object that the Indian passed off as food. After I flashed the money, he huddled with Aye Thit. A few minutes later, Aye Thit, looking as sheepish as hell, told us the Indian had another job. It turned out the Indian was a sergeant in the Moulmein district fire brigade. There were six men in his unit. He made Aye Thit promise that as soon as we returned to Rangoon we would immediately go to the Ministry of the Interior and file a petition for four uniforms, three pairs of boots, and a small monthly stipend. He wrote these items on a slip of paper and gave it to Aye Thit. As Aye Thit read the list of requests from the shopping list—he had sworn as the Indian's blood brother to deliver it—the Indian jabbed the air with his hands, kicked, did a couple of push-ups, and never broke into a sweat.

I watched Hart pocket the five-dollar bill and something fell into place.

"One thing I've been meaning to ask you, Hart. Other than Sarah, have you shown your book to anyone?"

I knew he had told Sarah she was the only person who had read it. I also had a gut feeling that Hart had lied to her. "I sent it to a friend," he said.

"In London?" I asked.

"How did you know?"

"Lucky, I guess. Like the Indian hitting the taillight of the truck," I said, looking down at the truck. Slowly the threads were coming together. How many cushions had Min embroidered before something clicked in her mind? She wasn't ever going to see the love of her life again. She could sew and sew and wait but nothing would fill the gap that had been created when Ichiro returned to Japan as the custodian of the ashes.

49

On the road to Pegu, Sarah sat near the door, hands curled around the blue and white bowl given to her by Hwae. She mindlessly ran her finger around the rim, looking contented. Have you ever seen the face of a contented woman, two or three levels away, lost in her own world? It is one of the most beautiful sights in the world. The new seating arrangement put me in the middle. It was like being back on the trishaw from the jetty to the hotel only this time the ride was a couple hundred kilometers. Neither one of them wanted to talk about it. I got to play interpreter the way a child carries messages during factional infighting in a family. "Are you hot?" Hart asked. I turned around and looked at Sarah. "Are you hot, baby?" And she answered, "Have I complained about the heat?" And I turned and said to Hart, "She's cool, dad." I was content in my role as translator, though, and watching Sarah play with the bowl. It was nothing special, an ordinary piece of china. But I kept that thought to myself.

The Terracotta Warrior slowed as a herd of goats strayed into the road. "Those are wild goats," said Hart.

I did a double-take, leaning down and over Hart's shoulder, trying to see the goats. Three of them appeared along the road. Hart's promise of "wild" goats had me going for a brief moment. I spotted a bell hanging from a leather collar around the neck of one of the goats. "That goat has a bell around its neck."

"Evolutionary adaptation," Hart said, winking at Sarah.

He was fucking with me. Okay, he wanted to play that game. I had no problem with his invitation to dance. Ever since the ferry, I had been waiting for the right moment.

"You don't know anything about fucking goats," I said.

"Ask me."

"What shape are a goat's eyes?"

Hart wrinkled up his nose and looked to Sarah for moral support. She ignored him, looking out her side of the window. "Ah, no fair asking Dr. Sarah. What shape is the iris of a goat's eye?"

I had him stumped. An opening emerged in the herd and the Terracotta Warrior drove on.

I bent low to look out the window as we passed more goats. The Terracotta Warrior was driving too fast to get a look at a goat's iris. "The iris is square. That's a fact. The only creature on the planet that has a square iris is a goat. That's why Christians associate the goat with Satan, the devil. Pagans worshipped the goat. Devil worshippers used the goat as a central motif. Those who exist on the dark side know exactly about a goat's eye."

"Okay, a goat has a square iris." A tired insincerity colored his voice.

"Aye Thit, tell the driver to stop the car the next time we see a goat. I want to show Hart a goat's eye."

"Aye Thit, tell the driver to step on it. I believe, you, Sloan."

"Fuck that, we are stopping the car."

"I just conceded the point."

"But you don't really believe it."

"Then why would I concede it?"

"Because you aren't curious about the eye. You've never once looked at a goat's eye. All those years in the field, on mountains, going along rivers and rough roads, you've probably seen ten thousand goats but you never once stopped and said, *hey, man what shape is a goat's eye?* You get a visit from some heavy Japanese people who have a bag of money and those people, I can assure you, know the shape of a goat's eye. You really should know who you are dealing with."

"I don't know what you are talking about," said Hart.

He stonewalled. Not that I expected him to spill his guts about playing the Judas goat. "Read the Bible, Hart. Judas had a goat's eyes."

He shrugged. "What you're saying—the Bible teaches that if you look a goat in the eye, that's fifteen years bad luck," said Hart.

"That's not in the Bible."

Just then I saw three or four goats ahead grazing in tall grass just off the edge of the road.

"Stop the car."

Aye Thit passed along the order and the Terracotta Warrior braked, and pulled onto the verge. I reached over Sarah and opened the door. She climbed out. I followed her, turned and leaned my head back in.

"Come on, Hart, I want you to look hard into the eye of a goat."

"I am happy to stay here, thank you very much."

"We ain't leaving until you look at the eye."

He sat with his arms folded. I lit a fat one and leaned against the car and waited. A moment later, Hart opened the car door and got out. We stood on opposite sides of the car and looked at each other over the roof.

"What's this about, Sloan?"

"The shape of a goat's eye. And the things a friend takes money for. They're connected."

"You're fucking mad. Barking dog mad."

The smoke curled out of my nose. "I don't think so. You know exactly what I am talking about. So, why don't we go check it out?"

Sarah got out of the car and walked to the edge of the verge, one hand on her hip, the other clutching the bowl. She stared at the goats.

"What are you trying to prove, Sloan?" Hart asked.

"Prove? I don't have anything to prove to Dr. Sarah. The case has already been made. The jury's in, the verdict's handed down. The sentence is about to be delivered." Smoke curled out of my nose. They both looked at me like *I* was the devil.

Hart rolled his eyes. "I hate it when you get like this."

Aye Thit had walked ahead and waded through ankle high grass, sneaking up on the goats. I grabbed Sarah's hand. She didn't resist as I led her down a small gully.

"They don't look so wild close up," I said.

"I was making a joke," said Hart, who followed behind.

"Square eyes is no joke."

We were within a couple of feet of the goats. One of the goats turned around, chewing its cud, grass sticking out of the sides of its mouth, and stared at us. "See the eye, Hart. Did you see it? I mean really look at it?" I turned and looked at him. He stared down at his feet. "You haven't looked, have you?" His head came slowly up but the goat had turned around by this time. "That's okay, we can wait until the goat looks back again. We can wait for as long as it takes. This is important, Hart. It's important. Real important."

"I want to get back to Pegu. It's getting dark. The driver won't put on his lights. We are all going to die."

"There. Look. What shape are the eyes?" The goat had shifted around, its head rising up above the grass. Its large eyes were a milky soft brown.

"Square," said Hart.

"Are you sure?"

"The fucking eyes are square like blocks."

"Was I right?"

"You are right."

"You sold your soul to Akira Takeda. I almost sold mine for ten grand. But I refused to destroy the photograph of a blue scorpion girl. What did you do? You stole the story from his son. Let me guess the title of your novel?" I said, touching my forehead, my eyes closed. "Blue Scorpion."

Hart clenched his fist. I waited for him to take a swing. His set up was even more pathetic than the Indian fireman on the ferry.

"It isn't my novel, I never said it was. Everyone assumed it was my novel," he said. "When did I say, *I wrote this book? I am the author? I am the big-cheese novelist?* Never. Not once. Not ever."

"You're repeating yourself," I said with some pleasure.

He exchanged a glance with Sarah who was only a couple of feet away. She heard everything. Her hands cupped around the bowl, her eyes staring at Hart.

"What do you mean?" I asked.

"He means the Japanese photographer who lost the camera wrote it," said Sarah.

I slumped down in the grass. No more than two feet away the sound of bells came as the goats fed, looking back, watching us.

Aye Thit had gone back to the car and brought me a beer. Foam poured down the side of the can as I took a drink.

"Kazuo wrote the book. But it is in English," I said.

"He wrote it in English because no one in his family could read English," said Hart.

"I should have figured that out."

Hart nodded. He knelt down in front of me. "His old man gave me the manuscript. He knew I was a writer. You are the one who told him that I was a writer. You also told him that we worked together on a book. And how my grandfather had been in Burma during the war. He came to me with a request. Help him find a publisher for Kazuo's book. He was clueless about how to go about it. The book had been written in English. He couldn't understand most of it. All he knew was that his son had written it and the book was set in World War II Burma. It was a love story from the Japanese point of view. I told him I had no idea if anyone in England would be interested in such a book. He persisted. I said I would do my best. I said it would probably need editing. Not that Kazuo wasn't a star pupil in English, but it might be worth having a native speaker have a look. He offered me money. I didn't take his money."

"You turned down money? You were going to work for free? Sugarcane and Shrimp would turn a trick for free first."

Hart stepped forward and threw a punch. I stepped to the side and slammed a hard, right hook to his nose, and followed up with an elbow just below his throat, knocking the wind out of him. He collapsed into the grass. Sarah ran over and knelt down, putting her arms around him.

"You hit him," she screamed.

"He tried to hit me," I said. "What was I supposed to do? Kiss him?"

Hart coughed until he was blue in the face. When he finally stopped, I knelt beside him. We were all in the grass. Goats eyed us as they grazed. Aye Thit and the Terracotta Warrior leaned against the car and whispered in Burmese. Hart staggered to his feet and tried to ram me with a head-butt. His right shoulder glanced off Sarah's side and the blue and white bowl flew into the air. The bowl hung in the air long enough for the Indian with his slingshot to have hit it with a dried-up samosa. The Terracotta Warrior leaped headfirst and caught the bowl. No one could believe it. Here was a guy who sat for hours and never moved an inch, and he had to possess one of the fastest reaction times on the planet. He walked over with his red-mouth grin and handed her the bowl. I had been thinking, Hwae should have given her one of those pillows. She sobbed and put her arms around him, giving him a hug. From the way things were going she would be riding shotgun next to our hero and Aye Thit would be demoted to sitting with the other two goats in the back.

"Hart, why don't you stop fucking around? You can't box. You can't even fight dirty. Your only visible skill is attempted plagiarism."

"What do you want from me?"

"You didn't tell me," I said. "Why didn't you tell me?"

"I brought the manuscript along to edit," he said, still catching his breath.

"You used Kazuo's novel to seduce Sarah," I said.

"He never said he wrote it. I just assumed," said Sarah. She continued standing next to the Terracotta Warrior. A goat strolled up to within a foot, raised its head and looked at us.

"Man, Hart, you are such an evil fuck. Look at that goat's eye. Look at it closely. That is the shape of evil."

"Have you told me everything about your deal with Akira Takeda?"

"I told you about the photo, buddy. I told you I met him. I did say, hey, look at these photos I took. What do you think?" I couldn't look at him straight without wanting to punch him.

"Did it ever occur to either of you that maybe, just maybe, Akira Takeda set up both of you?" said Sarah.

All the time I was thinking that Hart was right: you looked in a goat's eye and you earned yourself a fifteen-year streak of bad luck. And from all I could see, we had already started with a load of bad luck even before we started tracking down goats.

The nearest goat was a foot away from Hart. Hart turned over in the grass, resting flat on his stomach. Sarah walked over and squatted beside him in the grass. Hart pushed his face as close to a goat's head as you could ever want to do. He stared long and hard at the shape of the goat's cornea.

"You are right, Sloan. The eyes are square."

"What did I tell you?" I said.

"What I did was unforgivable. I know it was wrong. Dump me on the road. I'll walk back."

We all kept staring at the goat. A poor stupid creature eating along a road in the middle of nowhere. "Thet Way's tattooed pig must have been something," I said. "Death tattooed a hundred times."

Hart laughed. "Pigs don't have square eyes," he said.

"A pig's eyes are like a human's eyes. Same, same with their skin."

Hart extended his hand. I shook it.

"We can go now," I said. "We came together, we go back together."

"That was one of my father's rules," said Sarah.

"Kazuo wrote the book to honor his great-uncle," said Hart. "But honor depends on your point of view. I have a feeling others didn't want the book published."

"You think some right-winger found out about the book and had him killed?" I asked.

"I don't know," said Hart. "Was he killed because of his photo of Mya? Or because he wrote the book? Or it might have been just an accident."

"Akira wanted to find a way to have Kazuo's book published," Sarah said. "Because he is an honorable man."

"The tragic part is Ichiro lived a life to honor the dead; but he gave up on living his own life once he left Burma. Just like Min finally gave up," said Hart.

We returned to the car. I brushed the grass off my trousers and watched as Sarah walked ahead, then Hart, in a kind of single-file column, like a platoon following a jungle trail. By the time you reach fifty-three years and find yourself standing on the back roads of Burma, having stared at the square eye of a goat, you start to appreciate certain realities. Much of the human condition is wasted on secrets and lies and waiting to discover that most truths are too fearful to admit. Much of life is like reading a bad translation of a great work of literature. We can never know the original.

50

After the ferry docked, and we climbed into the car, I ended up in the middle with Sarah on my left and Hart on my right. I rode the hump. After checking out the goats, Sarah was back in the middle and I was back against the window where a cobra could bounce through and fang my frontal cortex. Whatever had gone on between them at the hotel in Moulmein had spilled over and was on its way to being cleaned up. She had fallen in love with the author of the book. Listening to the love story about Ichiro and Min, and how that love had been forever destroyed by the events of war, they had been hugging each other. A strong feeling had been ignited. It was the kind of emotion that one either acted upon or it was lost. She had gone to his room. That had been her commitment. Hart had confessed about the true authorship of the book. She felt betrayed. The best thing that had happened to him was when I punched him in the nose. Blood gushed out and ran down his chin, dripping on his shirt and pants. He looked like the mannequin in the bar exhibit at the Drug Elimination Museum. New sign posted on the wall: *Doing drugs makes you bleed*. She fell on her knees, took his head in her hands, and cleaned him up with a towel that Aye Thit got from the car. She asked him in a tender, motherly tone if he were all right. Hart would always be all right. He smiled and kept on bleeding; it was the best thing that he could have done. My knuckles had been hammered, but did I receive any sympathy? Not a word of inquiry from the fair Doctor of Letters. Even Aye Thit looked at me as if I was a criminal.

By the time we were twenty kilometers from Pegu, the sun was swallowed up in the trees beyond a distant field. The Terracotta Warrior slammed his foot to the floorboard. A diesel took some time getting to speed but, like an old milk horse, once it smelled the barn, there was power and energy one wouldn't have expected. For some reason, on the highways in Burma no one switched on lights until after the road disappeared into dead darkness. There were no streetlights. The moon, hidden by the clouds, leaked no light into the night. It was as dark as it can ever get. Only a bat-like radar prevented head-on collisions. On the narrow road, there was almost no warning from the large trucks that came straight at us like silent trains out of control. The driver barreled straight toward our car as if to avenge that broken taillight the Indian had shot out with his slingshot on the ferry out of Moulmein.

"Why did you have it in for the Indian on the ferry?" Sarah asked.

"Not that he was creepy looking. He could have used a face transplant. But I don't care about that. He was a complete phony. I hate phony-baloney people."

"So do I," she said.

Hart stayed silent. It occurred to me. I was the only one in the backseat whose father was still alive. My father hadn't shot himself or drowned himself. He had stuck out the disappointments, the failures, and heartaches that accumulated until they spilled over into despair. But he had moved ahead of the onslaught because he knew at the end of the day what he was and that was enough for him. He didn't try to be more or less than that. My hatred of phony people came from him. Hart was a lot of things, but I never thought of him as a phony. It took the love for a woman to flip him into such a state of desperation.

I couldn't see the faces of anyone in the car except for the brief moment when a truck two feet away turned them on for an instant.

"He didn't have to tell you," I said to Sarah.

She didn't say anything.

"What I am saying is that he tried to do the right thing."

"He should have told me before," she said. "Like the first day when he gave me the manuscript to read."

"I had made a promise to Kazuo's father that I wouldn't tell anyone about it. He made me pledge as a point of personal honor. I swore on the memory of my father."

"Is that true?" she asked.

"Akira Takeda made me promise not to disclose the photos. So, yeah, it fits."

"I try to keep my promises," said Hart. He looked at me, the smile coming off his face. "He was scared of what might happen if anyone knew what he was doing in Bangkok."

That was the patch that fixed the gaping hole in the tire. Sarah and Hart were back on the road. I started to feel guilty for slugging him. Akira Takeda received the pledge for a number of good reasons, the prime reason being that Hart's life might be at risk if word of the manuscript and his role leaked back to Japan.

Rolling into Pegu, the city was shrouded in darkness. Power outages often left the streets pitch-black. Aye Thit told the driver to stop the car and he asked some men standing in the shadows where we could find the best hotel in Pegu. I had told Aye Thit we wanted the very best hotel and we didn't care how much it cost.

"I am going to be honest with you, Sarah."

"I appreciate that," she said.

"I want to take a girl tonight. I am telling you now. So you don't get offended or find out from someone else. Not that I need to explain myself. Or ask for your approval. I don't. It's that, with all the things we haven't been saying to each other, I didn't want this to be another one of those things."

She sighed. "Do what you have to do."

I didn't have to explain to Aye Thit what condition applied in arranging a hotel: the management could have no objection if I brought back a girl. Pegu wasn't Bangkok. And Pegu hotel owners mostly had objections because the police would crack their heads if they found out a foreigner was taking a prostitute to his room.

The first hotel Aye Thit's informants in the shadows whispered about was on the main street. We hiked up two granite staircases to reach the lobby level. Aye Thit spoke with the clerk behind the counter, a grim-faced little man with a large cheroot stuck between his teeth. He sucked on the cheroot as Aye Thit confirmed the good news: the rooms were five dollars and I could take back a girl. "Why don't I check it out?" I said to Hart and Sarah. "I am certain you two have things you want to talk about."

Aye Thit, the clerk and me climbed another two flights of stairs and followed the clerk down a narrow dirty corridor; he stopped and unlocked a door, reached inside and flicked on a light. The room was a wreck as if every truck we had passed on the road in had crashed through it. Have you ever wanted to know where the queen mother nest of all mosquito-nesting places was located? The nest was inside this room. Stephen King could have written a bestseller that was set in that room. No problem taking a hooker to this room, only within ten minutes all of the blood would have been sucked out of her. Five bucks was all it cost to spend a night inside a room infested with mosquitoes. This wasn't a hotel; this was a time-warp biological experiment left over from the war. I was bitten half a dozen times in the thirty seconds I spent inside the room. I stubbed out a cigarette against the wall in protest. Given the state of the room, the clerk didn't even notice.

"How was it?" asked Hart.

They were standing close, shoulders brushing. I figured some reconciliation was in progress. "In the morning, forget about break-fast—you'd need a full-body blood transfusion."

"Mosquitoes," said Hart.

The thing about traveling with someone you know, they know without a lot of explanation what lies behind the irony of a phrase. People get married because the sex feels so good; they stayed married because they can speak in short-hand.

Aye Thit knew that I was steamed about the lies he had accepted as truths about the room. Outside the hotel, we had managed to pick up a new member of our party. A young pimp promised us that he not only knew where the best girls might be found, he also knew exactly the right hotel for us. He was about fourteen years old, shifting from one foot to the other, hands in his pockets, looking like he hadn't eaten in a couple of days. There was nothing like missing a couple of meals to motivate a boy to find a moneymaking opportunity, and that was exactly what I was.

"He doesn't seem to recognize you," said Hart, needling me about my bit-part in the Burmese movie.

"It's pretty dark outside," I said.

"Or he doesn't go to the movies," said Sarah.

The team spirit was slowly gathering force. We climbed into the car, and the Terracotta Warrior followed the kid's directions to the hotel. We pulled into what looked like an abandoned logging road, and then bounced around for five minutes until our fucking nightmare was realized. The hotel used in Hitchcock's *Psycho* would have been the Oriental Hotel compared with this dump. The clerk at the front desk demanded thirty-two dollars for a room. I wouldn't have given him thirty-four dollars for the whole fucking hotel. The power was out and there was a fat yellow candle on the front desk casting deep shadows on his ugly pock-marked face. He looked like he'd been tortured, fried like squid on some electrical grid, nursed back to life, and stuck behind the desk of this dung-heap of a hotel. After I pounded on the counter, he relented and said he had a room for twenty-two dollars. He followed my eye line to a sign behind the counter with the room rates posted. He looked back at the sign. Twenty-four dollars was possible but only the basic room. Basic room? The hotel could have been a cave dug into the side of a dunghill. Aye Thit said we should at least have a look at a room. Mr. Pock-marked Face led the way carrying an oil lantern. We looked like villagers climbing a switchback road on a mountain on our way to kill Dr. Frankenstein's monster. We went outside the main entrance and walked along a stone path and then back into a building and down a hallway while the front desk clerk rattled a fistful of keys. He opened the door to the room and I swear to God, a bat shot out. Then two more bats burst out of the door. Just like those truck drivers on the road from Moulmein, the bats managed to fly within inches of our heads without hitting us.

"Basic room," he said. I wanted to smack him along the side of the head. I wanted to burn down the fucking place. Set it on fire and roast wieners over his burning head.

"Let's get out of here. Twenty-four dollars for this place? Who is the last lucky person who stayed in this room with Mr. Bat? Robin? Get me out of this place before I kill this fucker." I pulled the kid by the ears. "And you, you recommended this shit hole. I am giving you one more chance to produce a room and if you don't, man, I'm volunteering you for porter duty with the Burmese Army on the frontlines right in the fucking heart of the Shan state. You understand what I am saying? Humping sixty-pound packs through minefields. I've had a long day and I need a room and I need a woman. Aye Thit, do we have any cold beer left? But it's gotta be cold. I mean cold, cold until it bruises your fingers just holding the can. Bats, fucking bats."

The kid got my point. He seemed a little rattled. Humping ammo in the hills during the rainy season was no good. He could end up cobra meat. He understood that I was kidding because Aye Thit told him I liked to kid around. But the kid was smart enough to know that Aye Thit wasn't in control of the situation. That you should never trust translations. We returned to the front desk and I put out my cigarette in the fuck-head's candle. The whole place went dark. "I hope the bats come and eat your eyes out, then your tongue and finally your fucking heart. Don't ever try and rent a room here for more than two dollars and then only to war criminals or terrorists. You got that?"

The next hotel seemed half the way to Rangoon. We finally turned off the road onto a surface that one day might actually become a road. It was rocks and valleys and eroded red mud. Our Terracotta Warrior stared straight ahead and drove like he was behind the wheel of an armored personnel carrier delivering troops to the front. At the top of the ridge was a sign: Five Star Hotel. It was more of a motel than a hotel, with small rooms off a central walkway. The Chinese owner had electricity and the smug smile that comes from possessing light when everyone else is living in darkness. The dining room was across from the front desk, and the dining room French doors, with gauze-like curtains over the glass, had been left wide open. Inside the room hundreds of carved teak *ngats*—mystical fairy-like beings with pointy hats and shoes with the toes curled up—were stacked on shelves. I had a good feeling about the place. A boy with a handful of keys led us to the rooms and we were all smiles. No problem taking back girls. Our pimp was relieved—no hard marching through the jungles of the Shan state with sixty-pound packs of ammo. After we checked in and washed up, we went for dinner. Aye Thit let our pimp pick the restaurant. The outside seating area was a slab of concrete with a few tables and chairs; it was dark and full of mosquitoes. The owner, who seem to recognize our pimp, brought out coils, lit them, and shoved them under the table. Mountains of seafood came: fresh fish and prawns the size of a man's forearm and plates of vegetables and rice. The pimp ate like he had never eaten before. As he dived into the food, the Terracotta Warrior showed some mobility of upper body movement for the first time since he rescued Sarah's bowl. The bill came and cost three times more than it should have cost. I figured the pimp got not only a doggy bag for his family—who was his uncle—his parents were both dead—but a kickback for bringing us to the restaurant. It didn't matter. We had a room. We were fed.

Hart and Sarah went back to the hotel and the pimp and Aye Thit set out to find a girl. I sat in the dark slapping mosquitoes and drinking beer, interrogating the owner about local antique shops. With my white face, there was no way I could show up at a brothel. The cops would go crazy. It was okay to send in a raiding party. Aye Thit knew my taste in women. I trusted him. They must have gone to four or five places before they found a girl who would go sight-unseen to service a white man. The problem was most of them had no papers. They were scared to go into the street. If they got stopped, their asses were thrown into jail. This was no sweet, smiling *mai pen rai* culture; in Pegu, like the rest of the country, there were hard, evil, unbending men who would happily eat you alive if given half the chance. They didn't care if you wrote letters to the newspaper and told all of your friends to boycott Burma; it was boycotted, there was nothing else anyone could do to deter them.

I made a note of the name of an antique shop from the restaurant owner. Likely this was a relative, and I made another note to throw the first note away. I returned to the hotel and waited. A half an hour later, there was a knock on my door. I opened it expecting Aye Thit and the girl. Sure enough they were standing in the doorway smiling. And right behind them was Sarah.

"Hey, baby, I am happy to see you. But could you come back say about nine hours from now? I've got some business to take care of," I said.

She walked straight past me and into the room, sitting down on the bed. Aye Thit looked at the girl and said something to her in Burmese. She looked confused. I looked confused. "Aye Thit, go and get me a cold Tiger."

He pulled a can from his blue bag and pulled back the tab and handed it to me.

"Aye Thit, tell the girl to come in. And you come in as well," Sarah said.

My main man, my loyal friend for a decade, did exactly what Sarah asked, and told the girl in Burmese to come into the room. She shyly walked over to Sarah, who patted her hand on the edge of the bed. The girl sat down.

"This wasn't intended as a conference call," I said.

"Sloan, shut up and listen."

"Is that a rule?"

"It's a rule."

I turned around a wooden chair and sat on it so as to rest my arms holding the beer on the back. "Sarah, I love you, baby. But you are stepping way over the line here."

"Was last night a hundred years ago? The old woman talked about what life was like for the women in Burma during the war. Has anything changed? The Japanese left their dead for Ichiro to haul back to Japan. The British buried their dead. Those who were survivors left. Didn't you listen to anything she said about what life had been for those girls?" She put her arm around the prostitute on the bed. "Is this the way you want to go? I can understand that if last night had never happened, you could pretend that this is some kind of fun and games, and everyone can pretend to have a great time. When you saw the girl in the photo Kazuo had taken, what did you feel? Once she wasn't just that girl. But had a name. Mya. Or did you feel nothing? Do you believe that what you are doing is right? I say, it's up to you."

"Christ, Sarah, I only know that I need a woman. That's natural. In fact, sex is the basis of human nature. Who says a politically correct attitude about what you can do and what you can't do is a rule? That I have to accept such a rule? Why do you think I don't live in America? I am going to give the girl enough money to feed her family for the next month. There's nothing personal on either side. It's a transaction. What's so wrong about that? Does that give me square goat eyes because I want to pay for sex?"

"Then pay me," she said.

I took a long drink. "Pay you for what?"

"Sex. Isn't that what you are buying? Pay me the same that you would pay her."

"Go back to Vancouver and your university and teach students about the meaning of tattoos. But don't come into my life and tell me who I can fuck and on what basis. It ain't right. Let me ask you something," I said.

"Ask away."

"Do you love Hart? Or was it the book you loved?"

That stopped her cold for a moment. She squeezed the girl's shoulder.

"I understand now why he didn't want to tell me."

"But the fact remains he didn't tell you at the time. So do you love him or not?"

She drew in a long breath. "Yes, I love him."

I slowly stood up from the chair. "Then marry him."

"She plans to," said Hart, standing in the door.

"Then congratulations. Now can everyone please clear the fuck out of my room?"

"You still don't get it," Sarah said. "This girl has no more choice than the girls who worked in Japanese comfort houses. Nothing has changed. Not in this country, and not inside the head of the foreign men who invade this country and I can't understand why of all people, you, Sloan, still don't get it."

"What don't I get?"

"She has dreams. They may not be your dreams or dreams that mean anything to you. And you might laugh at them because they are so small and simple. But for her those dreams are her hopes, her universe, her everything, and when someone like you comes along with money, wanting a fuck, she goes dead to herself, and you help kill off a part of herself, who she is, and what she dreams. Until one day, she is old and used up and she only faintly remembers whatever dreams she had. All she remembers is being used for the dreams of others and thrown away to embroider pillows. That's always been the basis of empire and conquest. From the Romans to the Americans. The soldiers grow old and look back misty-eyed at the best years of their life—like my father—but what you saw in that old woman in the village was what you should see in this girl tonight, submission to a nightmare that will never end unless you help end it. Hart said that you came to wait for the Lady's release. And when she was allowed to leave her house, we were all there together. I saw how that moment touched you. You saw how the people everywhere celebrated her release as their best chance to break the cycle of terror. Look at this girl—who is waiting for her release? Who will give her a chance to live free? Will that person be you, Sloan?"

I said nothing.

After a long moment of silence, all eyes on me, I walked the girl out of the room, handed her too much money and she left, going down the walkway past the door with all those creepy wooden *ngats* stacked up like dead bodies on tables and shelves.

The next morning we met into the dining room and for the first time we saw the dining room in daylight. Conversation was kept to a minimum. The room dwarfed us; it was the size of a basketball stadium. Three separate sinks and towel racks lined one wall spaced about ten feet apart. An arrangement of sinks and racks used in a hospital or prison. Cobwebs covered half of the *ngats*; spiders were using the *ngats* as a walkways for webs and food storage.

"I am glad you did the right thing last night," said Sarah.

"Now be a good girl, and eat your eggs. I bet that was one of your father's rules."

"I sometimes broke a rule."

"Good idea," I said.

"But I never broke the important ones," she said, smiling, pushing the plate away.

"My rule is I need to buy something. I want a bargain. You understand that Aye Thit. I am not going home without an antique."

"He needs to make a killing," said Hart.

My first decision was to buy two of the pointy-hatted *ngats* from the Chinese owner. Bookends for the girlfriend's room, well, what had been girlfriend's room, which was my room, and would be used for a future girlfriend?

"I always wondered who bought that kind of stuff," said Sarah as the Chinese owner wrapped them in newspaper.

51

After my binge on *ngats*, my next target of lust was a thousand year old necklace. I had seen the piece in a shop on our outward-bound trip to Mon country. I kicked myself for not buying it on the spot. The necklace was in Maung Gyi's antique shop near Shwemawdaw Pagoda in Pegu. In his early thirties, Maung Gyi had enough money to splurge on expensive haircuts, good clothes and shoes, and designer sunglasses. He had artistic hands, an actor's nose and chin and jaw, and the hard, black eyes of a soldier. I had bought stuff from him before. He was one of Aye Thit's contacts and if he passed the bullshit test with Aye Thit, then that was good enough for me. During our brief stop in Pegu before setting out for Moulmein, we had driven to Maung Gyi's shop. I looked him up and down, figuring something about the way he was dressed or stood or talked was out of place. Then I saw it. He had his shirt buttoned to his throat. I knew he was hiding something.

I said, "Maung Gyi, what the fuck's inside your shirt? You bastard, you are holding out on me. Unbutton or I'll tear it off." He struggled. I nearly ripped off his shirt to find it. "Look, look, look. Very beautiful and you hide. Why are you hiding this from your friend? How old is this?" I turned the finely etched gold globes the size of a baby's fingernail over and over. There were dozens of these globes getting smaller and smaller, with old beads, blue and red and gray, strung between the globes.

"How much?"

"Four hundred dollars. But I have a man who wants it. He comes from Singapore next week. Can not sell to you, Sloan. Must keep."

Yeah, sure. I figured he was conning me. He made me stop and think, *Do I really want this piece? What is he really trying to do by holding it back?* I needed time to sort through these questions. Four hundred dollars was a lot of money. I didn't want to be left short for all of those rare Ming burial bowls washing up in river banks in Mon country. Besides, we weren't going to Mon country for weeks. I had plenty of time to beat the guy from Singapore. All the time on the road I was thinking what a big mistake. We were going to look for Ming and there was this incredibly valuable necklace that I couldn't make up my mind to buy. I never seem to learn the basic lesson of the road. You see something like a perfect necklace and you don't think about it. You buy it. Then and there. Take out the cash and put it on the table of a greedy merchant like Maung Gyi and watch him strike like a cobra. If you don't act on impulse, later on you suffer, brood about not having that necklace and wondering if some rat-bag from Singapore had shown up early because he smelled someone else was closing in for the kill.

The Terracotta Warrior, who was once again on auto-pilot, skidded to a stop, one tire of the Toyota going over the curb as he parked in front of a row of antique shops. You could throw a Ming bowl and hit the central pagoda in Pegu across the intersection. "Good location," said Hart. Sarah and Hart were holding hands.

Every time Sarah looked at me, she smiled. I returned the smile. I was happy to no longer ride the hump in between the two of them with my nose stuck in the left ear of the Terracotta Warrior.

The tourists passed the shops on their way to the pagoda. I stood in front of the metal gate to Maung Gyi's antique shop; it was rolled down and padlocked with a big bronze Yale padlock. Our man wasn't anywhere around. We tried some of the other shops. No one knew where the owner was. We asked around for Ming bowls and antiques and everyone pointed at the locked shop. None of these vendors had any money. You needed money to pay for diggers to go and dig up the Chinese burial sites. You needed money to go into the villages and find the stuff already dug up and snap up the shit before some barefoot Indian or Chinese asshole beat you to the looted bowl. We walked around the outside of the other shops. The others sold handicraft pieces made of wood, paper, string, bronze. Kitsch *ngats* (mine were infinitely better) and Buddha images and necklaces and bracelets. Kites and wind chimes. The kind of stuff the first settlers used to buy Manhattan from the Indians. There were no customers. The shop owners looked wretched in the misery of days passing with only flies and mosquitoes to swat and kids to feed.

Aye Thit phoned to Maung Gyi's house and his wife said he was on his way back from Rangoon. We drove to his house to wait for his return. The house was in a small bamboo hut village with muddy roads and half-naked children playing in brown puddles. Maung Gyi also owned a pool hall with a corrugated roof and a small restaurant next door. On the ground floor of his house, a goldsmith shop was set in the back. There was a bench with tools where Maung Gyi made bracelets and necklaces, which he sold to tourists. I am an expert on jewelry. He knew that I knew my gems and settings. Some old witch with snarly hair and red teeth showed us inside the house while Maung Gyi's wife ran around holding a snot-nosed baby balanced on her hip, throwing things in drawers. Gold pieces and beads and tools. She had the paranoid look of the Indian on the ferry. Most people in Burma were stretched emotionally, on the breaking point, living through smuggling, manufacturing fake antiques, recycling old cars, sewing machines, typewriters, lamps, and motorcycles, clothes, glass, and paper. They had nothing else. When something was thrown away you could be certain there was no possible other use; it was exhausted, spent, dead, beyond redemption. When Maung Gyi finally arrived thirty minutes later, he walked in the door all smiles. Aye Thit had phoned him while we were still in Moulmein to tell him to expect us. And to ask him if he still had the necklace. He told Aye Thit it was still around his neck. Wrapped inside Maung Gyi's smile was a nervous edgy twitch as if someone from the government had arrived and asked him to produce the books for his pool hall and restaurant.

"Where's the necklace?"

"In Rangoon. I have buyer from Singapore come tomorrow."

"Bullshit, it's mine. I am buying it."

"It's karma," said Sarah. "Let it go, Sloan."

"Look, I let the girl go last night. Am I right? Am I right?"

"Tell him he's right so he will stop asking," said Hart.

"We were very proud of you."

"I want that fucking necklace. I ain't letting that go."

On the drive back to the shop, I convinced Maung Gyi to go back to Rangoon with us to get the necklace. I decided I would put him up front with Aye Thit and he would ride the stick shift all the way to Rangoon. He had left the necklace—or so he told me—at one of the antique shops owned by a friend inside the Shewagon Pagoda. By the time we arrived in Maung Gyi's shop in Pegu, all I could think about was getting my hands on that fucking necklace in Rangoon. I had to have it. Sarah picked up teacups and saucers in a display case—she saw fifty variations of the bowl Hwae had given her and her heart sank a little—and Hart looked around at rows of old clay pots on a shelf. Just above where Hart stood, I spotted a piece of amber on a dusty shelf. I picked it up, examined it, and did a double take: inside was a fly. A small bubble angled above the fly's head. The bubble, I figured, was the fly's last gasp before being suffocated 250 million years ago. If this were real, it would be the find of a lifetime. God knows how much it was worth. I took Hart aside. "Look at this. It's fucking amber. You see that fly? It's 250 million years old. I am going to be a millionaire. This is my reward for my good deed last night. I let the girl go and I get the fly in amber."

Hart turned the piece of smooth honey-colored amber the size of a tiny American football over in the palm of his hand, looking at the fly from every angle. He handed it back. "I don't know anything about amber."

Sarah walked over and looked at the object.

"I know amber. This is amber. Tree sap that turned hard as rock millions of years ago," I said.

"That's amber?" she asked.

"Not so loud. Of course, it's amber."

I collared Maung Gyi, "How much is this?"

"Fifty dollars," he said.

"Too much."

"Then don't buy it," he said from behind his designer sunglasses.

"I know you already have a buyer from Singapore."

"That's for the necklace," Maung Gyi said.

"Thirty dollars. And you are going to sell it to me. You fucking owe me. I told you not to sell the necklace. I told you I'd be back for it. And what do you do? You go to Rangoon and try to sell it. Where's your loyalty, man?"

I shoved thirty dollars into his hand and put the amber piece in my shirt pocket. In the car I showed the amber to Aye Thit. "You think it's old?"

Aye Thit nodded. "Could be old."

I showed it to Sarah. "It looks like a housefly, Sloan," she said. "I don't think there were houseflies millions of years ago. I mean, there weren't houses a million years ago so how could there be flies?"

I didn't like her attitude. Just because there weren't any houses 250 million years ago doesn't mean there weren't flies. Houses didn't evolve flies. She might have been an expert on Shan tattoos but she obviously knew nothing about evolution or amber. And Hart piped in saying, "Perhaps flies were hanging around waiting for us to evolve and build houses and give them a name."

I had sunk thirty bucks into the amber with the fly inside. "Sour grapes," I said. "I found it. Maung Gyi didn't try to sell it to me. I had to twist his arm to get it from him."

When we finally returned to Rangoon and met downstairs in the hotel lobby, I waited for the waitress to deliver a double scotch. After she set the drink down, I showed her the prize purchase of the day. "Aye Thit, ask her how old she thinks the fly is?"

I handed her the amber and she studied it for a couple of minutes before handing it back. "Maybe three years old," said Aye Thit. He was laughing as he spoke. "But it could be younger, she told me. It could be three weeks."

Hart sprayed beer out of his nose as he watched my reaction to Aye Thit's translation of her verdict into English. I had serious questions whether this girl was really a possible source of affection or just another vulture looking to climb onto my bandwagon and apply for girlfriend's allowance. "Tell her it is old," I said. That only made it worse.

Aye Thit was so goddamn loyal that he tried really hard to look at me with a straight face as I ordered him around. "She says doesn't know much about flies. If you say it's old, then it is probably really old."

"Aye Thit, level with me, how old do you think this fly is?"

"Two, three years old."

"It can't be," I said. "When I get back to Bangkok I am having it tested. If Maung Gyi cheated me, I am going to show him the lab report and get my money back. Do you think he cheated me?"

Aye Thit shrugged. "I don't know. Better to get it tested."

I put the amber piece with the fly suspended inside in my pocket and concentrated on getting the necklace. We had gone with Maung Gyi to the antique shop inside the Shewagon Pagoda. The shop attendant said the boy with the necklace had left. Why wasn't he at the shop waiting? Maung Gyi didn't know and smiled one of those defenseless, stupid smiles that explained nothing but a passive, stubborn resistance to any further questioning about the mission of the boy. When was the boy coming back? No one seemed to know. I strong-armed Maung Gyi into making a couple of phone calls and said, "Five o'clock." We dropped Maung Gyi at the antique shop and drove back to the hotel. I needed a drink. Back at the lobby bar, Sarah and Hart sat in the overstuffed chairs, waiting for me.

"Sloan, if the amber is fake, what about the necklace?" asked Hart.

I pulled the amber piece from my pocket. I had been studying it for hours. I sat down directly opposite Sarah. The waitress brought my double Scotch without waiting for my order. I put the amber piece on the table. Everyone stared at it. "I just got off the phone with my wife. She phoned Akira Takeda in Tokyo and filled him in on a few details."

That had their attention. "Ichiro is coming to Rangoon next week. An unofficial reunion of Japanese military has been organized. They are getting together for old time's sake. He wants to meet his grand-daughter. It is safer if he meets Mya in Burma. Aye Thit passed the word to Khin Aung, who will phone Hwae and set it up."

"The reunion is a cover story," said Sarah.

"Saya told Akira Takeda about the pillows."

"Did she mention Kazuo's novel?" asked Hart.

I reached over for my drink and took a long sip, smiled at Sarah, and then raised my glass to Hart. He nodded as he leaned over and slipped his hand around Sarah's.

"Saya told him that I figured out about the novel on my own. She said he sounded relieved, and was sorry he hadn't trusted me with the information. I said that we would both help see that a publisher was found."

Kazuo's book was like a fly trapped in amber. The real thing was invaluable. But the fake was worth nothing. It depended on Kazuo's interpretation of what had happened all those years ago. There are so many ways to tell a clever story, but it is difficult to find the true narrative, one that is faithful to the lives of characters. Whatever souls had been trapped and preserved in Kazuo's book—Ichiro, Thet Way, and the young bookkeeper, and the blue scorpion girl who felt no pain and waited and waited for the love of her life to return, writing her life story on pillows—one thing was evident: there was no sure way for Akira Takeda to test the amber of his son's story. He would simply have to wait. And keep on waiting and accepting the possibility that he might never know if the truth would ever reveal itself.

LaVergne, TN USA
11 December 2010

208370LV00005B/77/P